KAREN CHARLTON

THE SCULTHORPE MURDER

THE DETECTIVE LAVENDER MYSTERIES

THOMAS & MERCER

Text copyright © 2016 by Karen Charlton

Published by Thomas & Mercer, Seattle

www.apub.com

ISBN-13: 9781503938243
ISBN-10: 1503938247

Cover design by Lisa Horton

Printed in the United States of America

For my father,

Tony James

With all my love – and thank you for your help with Chapter Thirty-One.

Love you, Dad.

xxx

Chapter One

Tuesday 20th February, 1810
Middleton, Northamptonshire

The storm woke Billy Sculthorpe.

His slanting eyes flew open in horror when the first flash of lightning rent the air. For a split second, he saw the unnatural glow of his dark furniture and sensed it straining towards him. He held his breath. The thunder exploded directly overhead. Billy clutched his ears and wailed in terror. Rain lashed against the window like the stones hurled by the bully boys, torrential and unforgiving.

Billy cried out and swung his stunted legs over the side of the bed, determined to race to his mother and the safety of her warm arms. But he stopped dead when his feet hit the cold floorboards.

Ma had gone. His pa had taken her away for burial.

A fresh wave of grief flooded through his quivering body. The wind moaned down the chimney and rattled and grated the loose roof tiles above his head. He sank down in the voluminous pool of his nightgown with his stubby hands slapped over his ears. Desperately, he tried to remember his mammy's voice and words.

'Ah sure, there's nottin' to be afeard of, Billy-Boy,' she would soothe. 'Tis just water from the Well at the World's End pourin' over Middleton tonight. 'Tis a watery veil, like a lady's veil. It keeps out the Dark Elves of Elphame and protects us from their evil.'

Another jagged bolt of white hot lightning split the sky outside.

'Mammy!' He clutched his shoulders and rocked on his bare heels, braced against the next clap of thunder. He longed to be back in her arms and hear her whisper soft prayers of protection into his ears. But Pa had planted her in the ground like an apple seed.

'You be brave now, my Billy-Boy,' she'd said as she died. 'Yer no child no more. Be brave . . .'

A strangled sob escaped his throat. He held his breath and waited for more thunder. It never came. Was the storm moving away? His ears strained against the howling wind and the rain hammering down on the tiles, demanding entrance like the little folk. No, he had it wrong. Ma always said the rain kept the faeries away. They curled up inside the leathery leaves of evergreen bushes during a storm.

The wind still bent the boughs of the trees and rattled the panes in the window but the thunder had gone. He released his breath in a noisy gasp of relief and felt a surge of pride in his own bravery. Mammy would be pleased.

Suddenly, the old oak at the end of their yard groaned with the weight of the wind and Billy's innards lurched. The hair stood up on the back of his neck as the ancient tree shifted and creaked again.

It was Black Agnes. She was rattling the branches with her iron claws. Soon she would reach inside the cottages of the village to snatch the children with her metal talons and drag them back to her cave. She would skin them alive, devour their raw flesh and then tan their hides to wear as an apron around her waist.

Black Agnes rattled the oak tree again and he knew she was here for him. Fear bubbled up inside his gut. Black Agnes wanted his hide for a trophy.

Another fork of brilliant light shot down like a serpent to bite the earth. *She will see me!*

Biting back his scream of fear, he staggered to his feet and lurched towards the door.

'Ma!' He threw up the latch and burst out onto the landing. 'Mammy!' he screamed.

He stopped short and blinked at the strange sight before him. The door to his mother's bedchamber stood open. Three silent, dark-faced creatures watched him from inside the room. A pocket lantern on the floor cast their demon-shadows onto the crumbling plaster walls behind them. The whites of their eyes glowed unnaturally bright against the blackened skin of their faces. One of them held his ma's chair in his hands.

Billy knew them in an instant. The water from the Well at the World's End had failed to protect him. The liquid veil of safety had been ripped apart and the Dark Elves of Elphame had streamed through the rent from their world into his. They were in his home, seeking out his father's gold and stealing his mother's furniture. There was a witch at his back and now the Dark Elves stood before him, their faces as black as pitch.

Billy sobbed, sank down onto his haunches and clutched his face in terror.

''Tis the cretin,' growled a voice.

Suddenly, one of the elves gave a blood-curdling yell and leapt forward with a cudgel grasped in his claw. Warm urine poured down Billy's frozen leg and splattered over his bare foot.

His short arms flailed helplessly in defence. It was no good. The blow fell and the cudgel crashed into the side of his head.

Searing pain. A blinding flash of light . . . then nothing.

Chapter Two

Thursday 1st March, 1810
Market Harborough, Leicestershire

The Leicester-bound stagecoach swerved off the road and plunged into the shallow ford on the outskirts of Market Harborough.

Detective Stephen Lavender braced himself for the impact as the lumbering vehicle hit the river, slowed and lurched over the rocks on the river bed. For a brief moment, the ceaseless rumble of the carriage wheels that had reverberated in their ears since they left Northampton was silenced and replaced with the hiss of splashing water and the grating of churning pebbles. The coach lurched up the opposite bank of the Welland and rejoined the road. The clatter of hooves and the incessant racket started again.

'I'm so sorry, treacle.' Across the aisle, Constable Woods apologised profusely to the pink-cheeked and startled young girl into whom he had pitched when the carriage left the road. The collision had knocked her reticule out of her hands. Still apologising, Woods bent down to retrieve it from the floor.

Woods' embarrassment was short-lived. With a blast of his horn, the guard heralded their arrival into the town. The coach swerved into Lubenham Lane and swept under the carriage arch-way of The Bell Inn. The exhausted drivers reined in the horses and the ostlers leapt across the stable yard to meet them. In a few moments, the steaming animals were unbuckled and led away while other men attached the harnesses to fresh horses that stamped and snorted impatiently.

Lavender stood up stiffly, opened the carriage door and climbed down into the yard. A welcome blast of cold evening air stung his face and he relished its freshness after two days spent in the stuffy atmosphere inside the coach. It was nearly six o'clock but the nights drew in early at this time of year. Lanterns glowed around the walls of the yard, illuminating the frantic activity around him. Servants and porters bustled around the coach, loading and unloading trunks and valises for the next leg of the journey. Out of the corner of his eye he watched Woods retrieve their luggage.

The landlord, a small, sharp-faced man with huge sideburns, appeared. 'Welcome! Welcome! Frederick Newby at your service, gentlemen,' he boomed in a surprisingly large voice for someone of his diminutive stature. 'We have good beds, commodious rooms, hot meals, a well-supplied larder and the best of liquors for those who wish to avail themselves of our hospitality.'

Lavender glanced across at the inn and tried to assess the qual-ity of the place. Brightly lit inside, the mullioned windows glowed attractively against the stuccoed walls of the timber-framed tavern, casting pools of warm yellow light onto the gleaming cobbles of the yard. This inn was probably as comfortable as any in the town, he decided. He was hungry and thirsty and his body ached from the bone-rattling journey. But his business was urgent and Captain Rushperry wouldn't wait for them all night.

Woods joined him on one side and the landlord on the other. The tavern owner's eyes darted over Lavender's tall frame and assessed the smart cut of his dark coat and spotless white cravat.

'You look like a man who appreciates the finer things in life, sir,' he said. 'Would you care to partake of a glass of one of our fine wines?'

'You have a room for the night?'

'Yes, sir. A most commodious room for you and your man – and an excellent supper.'

The guard of the coach blew an ear-piercing blast from his coiled horn, while the driver thrashed at the reins and yelled out a warning. Lavender, Woods and the innkeeper hastily stepped back against the wall as the vehicle jolted forward. It swung around and rumbled smoothly out of the narrow arched exit of the courtyard, its lantern swaying behind it.

'We will lodge here tonight,' Lavender said, 'but we have business to attend to first with Captain Rushperry at the Town Hall. Kindly have our bags taken to the room and point us in the direction of the Town Hall.'

'Why, Captain Rushperry himself regularly frequents my establishment!' the excited man exclaimed. 'And the Town Hall, 'tis only a step away! Go back to the sheep market in the Square and follow the buildings up towards the church. The Town Hall stands directly behind it. I'll have a good supper waitin' for you, on your return. I hear from your accents you're strangers to the town. 'Tis far better you return here tonight to our comfort than end up in that filthy den of sin, The Angel.'

Both police officers glanced up curiously. 'What's wrong with The Angel?' Woods asked.

Their host shook his head sadly and dropped his voice to emphasise the seriousness of his next comments. 'The landlord encourages the rabble from the new canal,' he said, 'the wharf hands and those dirty bargees. There's heavy drinkin' and fights there every night. 'Tis not the place for a discernin' traveller like you, sir.'

Lavender bit back his smile. The nature of his job meant he was regularly immersed in the seedier side of the crime-ridden capital.

He had broken up more brawls between the drunken hell-cats of Covent Garden than he cared to remember and he often rubbed shoulders with the ragtag and scum of the Seven Dials. But this man wasn't to know about that.

They set off to follow the coach back to the main road. 'There'll be a glass of my best brandy waiting for you!' the landlord called after them.

'Fine wines? Brandy?' Woods said. 'I think the fellah thinks you're a bit of a tosspot, sir.'

Lavender smiled. He'd sensed Woods' disappointment when he'd turned down the offer of immediate refreshment from the landlord. But even a rumbling belly never dampened his constable's good humour. 'He's certainly keen to gain custom for his inn,' Lavender replied.

They turned the corner into the broad market square and the medieval spire of St Dionysius' Church immediately drew their eyes as it rose up into the evening gloom of the sky. A few people scurried past them but the square was deserted apart from the lamplighter busy at his work on the far side.

Criss-crossed with empty animal pens, the square was also dotted with cast-iron tethering posts. The stench of the animals and their excrement still hung in the air. It overpowered the smell of roasting meat and coal fires that drifted from the chimneys of the tall houses lining the square. Despite the best efforts of the lamplighter, many of the buildings had fallen into shadow. They picked their way carefully round the stagnant puddles and indiscernible piles of refuse littering the street. Wisps of straw rustled across the cobbles in the light breeze.

The town suddenly felt eerie and hostile to Lavender and he had a surge of homesickness for his warm and spacious home back in Marylebone, followed by an intense pang of longing for the dark-eyed woman who waited for him there. He shook his head and expelled a loud breath in frustration. *Concentrate on your job*, he told himself. *The sooner the case is solved, the sooner you'll get home to Magdalena.*

The Town Hall was a three-storey rectangular building of red brick, with stone dressings around the Venetian windows in the upper levels. The ground floor consisted of a row of open vaulted bays for the use of the town's butchers which stank of blood. The assembly rooms and the courtroom upstairs were reached via a stone staircase on the outside of the building.

Captain Rushperry waited for them in a small office adjacent to the main courtroom. His desk dominated most of the room and the large magistrate himself seemed to dominate the rest. Lavender knew Rushperry had a distinguished military record but the man had obviously grown fat through inactivity since he had retired his commission. Unsmiling, Rushperry eased his bulk out of his chair and extended a podgy hand across the desk towards the two policemen. 'Thank goodness you're here!' he said.

Lavender and Woods pulled up a pair of hard-backed wooden chairs and sat side by side, squashed between the desk and the glowing fireplace.

Rushperry's greying eyebrows knitted together as the policemen removed their hats and gloves. Deep lines stretched across his broad forehead beneath his wig. 'I'll be honest with you, Lavender – we're beleaguered with crime up here in Leicestershire and Northamptonshire,' he said. 'I'm grateful to Bow Street for lending us your assistance. Do you have the invoice?' Rushperry's eyes were deep-set in his fleshy face but they shone with concern and were swollen with lack of sleep.

Intrigued, Lavender bit back his questions and pulled out a sheaf of documents from his pocket. To hand the magistrate a bill for the services they were about to render seemed almost churlish after such an enthusiastic welcome but Bow Street Police Office only parted with its detectives for a fee. Lavender hoped Rushperry would still be as enthusiastic about paying for their assistance at the end of the case.

Rushperry pulled his oil lamp closer. He rubbed his forehead and examined the invoice with tired eyes. 'Everything seems to be in order,' he said at last. 'The Dowager Countess Fitzwilliam of Rockingham Castle commissioned your help with this murder investigation. I understand that Mr Sculthorpe used to serve her in some capacity. She is very distressed and is following the case with interest. I will send the invoice to the estate steward.'

Lavender's eyebrows rose in surprise. He'd assumed that the Magistracy had requested help from Bow Street Police Office. The involvement of Lady Fitzwilliam was a new development. He racked his memory for information about the Fitzwilliams of Rockingham Castle. If he remembered rightly, the elderly dowager countess had an impeccable pedigree. She was the daughter of the Marquis of Rockingham and the sister of an ex-British prime minister.

'I'm glad you have brought your constable with you,' Rushperry said. 'You'll need him.'

'What has happened?' Lavender asked. 'In your letter you asked for our help following a brutal attack on an elderly man in his own home by unknown assailants. Is this a murder investigation now?'

Rushperry drew in a deep breath and sat back. 'Yes, the situation has changed. When I penned that letter to Magistrate Read, I believed we were dealing with robbery and assault.' He paused. 'Unfortunately, we now need your help to solve a murder.'

'The victim has died?'

Rushperry nodded. 'William Sculthorpe passed away two days after the attack. He never regained consciousness sufficiently to tell us about his assailants. Due to the viciousness of the assault on such an old man, the coroner has ruled out manslaughter and decided this is cold-blooded murder.'

'Poor old beggar,' said Woods. 'The shock of the attack probably did for him, as well.'

'Quite,' said Rushperry. 'I see you're a compassionate man, Constable Woods.'

'Well, we've all had parents, haven't we?' Woods said. 'How old were the poor fellah?'

'Mr Sculthorpe was eighty-six years of age.'

A spontaneous growl escaped Woods' lips and his fists clenched in his lap.

'That's a remarkable age for anyone to achieve,' Lavender acknowledged. 'And it's even more surprising Mr Sculthorpe survived the initial attack.'

Rushperry shook his head and his jowls quivered. 'By all accounts, Sculthorpe was a quiet man, in very good health and with no known enemies. Since his wife's death last August, he had lived peacefully in his cottage and scarcely allowed himself the common necessities for existence.'

'If he were poor, what did the robbers hope to gain?' Woods asked.

In the distance, the church clock chimed. Rushperry pulled out a silver pocket watch and snapped open the cover. He frowned and sighed when he saw the time. 'There's a rumour in the parish that William Sculthorpe was worth several thousand pounds,' he said. 'The rumour also suggests his meagre lifestyle was self-inflicted and a result of his penurious disposition rather than an indication of real poverty.'

Lavender frowned. 'So what is the truth? Was Mr Sculthorpe a wealthy man who preferred to live frugally? How much money did they steal from the property on the night of the robbery?'

'I can't answer any of those questions,' Rushperry admitted. 'We have no idea what he had in the house at the time of the robbery but we have found correspondence from a London bank, Messrs Down, Thornton and Gill. I have written to them, informing them of Sculthorpe's death and asking for clarification of his financial affairs, but as yet I have had no reply. Gentlemen, I'm afraid I shall have to leave in a few minutes. I have another meeting at seven o'clock in Foxton. Unfortunately, I can't defer my departure for more than another five minutes.'

'Of course,' Lavender said. 'We won't detain you much longer.'

Rushperry pulled a ledger from beneath a pile of papers and handed them across to Lavender. 'We held an inquest at The Bell Inn here in Market Harborough, two days after Sculthorpe died. The coroner's report is contained in this ledger along with statements from the doctor and a witness.'

'There was a witness?' Lavender asked. 'This should be helpful.'

'There were two witnesses but their accounts differ in content: one man claims there were five murderers, the other said three. However, this second witness is unreliable.'

'How so?'

But Rushperry just shook his head and waved a dismissive hand in the air. 'I have to confess, Lavender, I find the whole affair very perplexing.'

Lavender felt a twinge of excitement rise within him. He lived for the challenge of a difficult case.

'The reliable witness is the constable for Middleton and Cottingham, a sound chap by the name of Jed Sawyer,' Rushperry continued. 'He came across the gang in the street as they ran away from the scene of the crime and they attacked him too. They beat him badly and he is unable to return to duty at present.'

'So you're a constable short?' Woods asked.

'Not now you're here, Constable Woods,' Rushperry replied with an attempt at jocularity. But the smile died quickly from his lips. A new wave of exhaustion swept over his fleshy features. 'To be honest, gentlemen, the constabularies of Northamptonshire and Leicestershire are stretched beyond belief at the moment. We have had a sharp rise in crime, which spills over our borders, and we're struggling to cope. But I have arranged for one of Market Harborough's own constables, young Sam Clancy, to accompany you to Middleton at half past eight in the morning. He's a good lad – keen. You can meet him here tomorrow.'

'Thank you,' Lavender said. 'Under the circumstances, that's generous of you. What are these other crimes you're dealing with?'

The magistrate raised his left hand in a gesture of helplessness. 'We have the Luddites in the north breaking the machinery in the mills and now we face a rise in petty theft and drunkenness since the canal wound its way through the two counties.'

'I've heard the canals can bring great prosperity to an area,' Woods said.

'Yes, you're right, Constable – the price of our coal has halved since the canal reached Market Harborough last year. But canals also bring troublemakers in their wake. On top of this, we have just had a nasty murder to deal with down in Wellingborough – and if that wasn't enough, there is another gang of thugs robbing and terrorising the area south of Market Harborough.'

Lavender sat up straighter.

'Two weeks ago,' Captain Rushperry continued, his voice rising in indignation, 'these villains entered the house of my fellow magistrate, Robert Marriot. They aimed a pistol at his wife Elizabeth, and robbed them.'

'Were they hurt?' Lavender asked.

'No, but they put them both in fear of their lives. Fortunately, these criminals are known to us – and to the rest of the county. The local news-sheet, the *Northampton Mercury* . . .' – and here his scowl revealed just what he thought of the *Northampton Mercury* – '. . . has dubbed this gang "The Panthers" and has sensationalised their crimes.'

Woods' eyebrows rose and a smile twitched at the corners of his mouth. 'The Panthers, eh?'

'Yes, they're named after one of their leaders, Benjamin Panther. They are notorious. Robert Marriot recognised them when they broke into his home in Preston Deanery. They're armed and dangerous. Every available constable we have in Northamptonshire is trying to find these devils. We just don't have the men to deal with yet another murderous gang up here on the Leicestershire border and I'm grateful to get your assistance.'

'Is it the same gang who attacked Mr Sculthorpe?' Lavender asked sharply.

Rushperry threw up his arms in another gesture of despair. 'That, Detective, is one of the things I hope you will find out. The Panther Gang usually threaten their victims with pistols, and poor William Sculthorpe was beaten to death. I can't help but mark the difference.'

Lavender nodded, rose to his feet and put on his gloves. Woods stood up beside him. 'We won't detain you any longer tonight, Captain Rushperry,' he said. 'We have plenty to think over and I'm sure Constable Clancy will be a great help tomorrow.' He tucked the ledger Rushperry had given him into the inside pocket of his coat.

'I will be back here next Tuesday,' Rushperry said. 'We always hold a petty session of the magistrate's court here on a Tuesday. If you need me I can be reached at home: The Elms on the Leicester Road. Oh, and by the way, Lavender, can you call on Lady Anne Fitzwilliam at Rockingham Castle at ten on Saturday morning? It's just a courtesy visit, you know how these things work, but it shouldn't take long.'

Lavender nodded.

'And one last thing before you both go . . .' Rushperry broke off and slid open a drawer of his desk. 'The day after the attack, Constable Clancy found this in the gutter further down the street. It may or may not be relevant – but it's certainly intriguing.' He handed a small, muddy cloth bag to Lavender and fished in his coat pockets for something else. 'This may have been used to carry away some of the stolen money from Sculthorpe's cottage.'

Lavender took off his right glove, inserted his hand into the opening of the bag and examined the limp rag in his hands. *A nondescript item probably used for carrying coins*, he decided. It could have belonged to any shopkeeper or household in Middleton.

Rushperry finally found what he sought. He pulled a crumpled note out of his inside coat pocket and passed it across the desk. 'This paper was screwed up in the bottom corner of the bag. As I said, we have no idea if it's connected with the crime or not – and I never mentioned it at the inquest. But if it's relevant, it makes for interesting reading. It's another mystery for you to solve, Detective.'

Lavender unfurled the scrap of paper, smoothed out the creases and stared hard at the spidery handwriting in the dim light. He could just make out the words:

'This is the last payment you old bastard. Leave me alone. J.W.'

Chapter Three

Night had already wrapped its dark and starless cloak around the chilly streets of the town as they climbed down the stone staircase of the Town Hall. A noisy altercation taking place outside The Angel Inn caught their attention. Against the bright backdrop of the well-lit tavern, two shadowy figures squared up to each other, shouting. Their clenched fists were raised, ready to strike. Lavender and Woods paused to watch. Suddenly, a third shadow appeared in the doorway of the inn and blocked out the light. This giant man cursed and added his booming voice to the argument, threatening both of the men with a good hiding if they didn't clear off. The two assailants stepped back, turned and staggered away in opposite directions. The colossus who had broken up the fight waited until they had disappeared before returning inside the tavern.

'I've a fancy to visit that place,' Woods said. 'I'd like to see these boatmen the townsfolk keep moanin' about. Besides which, I've a thirst for a tankard of ale right now.'

The coroner's report burned against Lavender's chest in the

inside pocket of his coat. He longed to return to their room in The Bell Inn to read it but he'd deprived his good-natured constable of sustenance for long enough. 'Very well,' he said. The two men fell into step as they walked the short distance to The Angel.

'What did you think of Captain Rushperry?' Woods asked.

'I think he is a careworn man besieged by a tidal wave of crime,' Lavender replied grimly.

Woods nodded. 'It sounds like there is a lot of trouble in this county.'

'And troubled men can make mistakes.'

They approached the pair of slim stone columns that supported the crumbling portico above the tavern doorway. Wall lanterns on either side of the entrance cast pools of light on the short flight of steps up to the door, above which a plaque bore the words: 'Albert Kilby – Licensed to sell beers and strong liquors'.

Woods stopped in his tracks and pointed up to the sign. 'Me ma were a Kilby before she married me da,' he said. 'Her family worked the northern rivers and cuts on barges but she were in service for a while before she wed.'

'I didn't know that.' Lavender knew Tilda Woods for many years before her death. A tiny, sweet-natured old woman, Tilda had been devoted to her burly son and her grandchildren. Lavender had always assumed she was a Londoner like the rest of them. 'What's a "cut"?' he asked.

'The canal.'

They entered the tavern and paused for a moment to let their eyes adjust to the light and the fug of tobacco smoke. The plain exterior of the building belied its brightly lit and gleaming interior. Lavender had the sensation they had entered a different world. Dozens of polished copper and brass plates and ornaments stood on the high shelf over the dark wood panelling of the tavern's walls. They were also arranged along the shelves behind the bar, interspersed with pottery ornaments and painted Toby jugs. A line of lace-edged painted china plates and several mounted horsetails also decorated the walls.

'This looks pleasant enough,' Woods observed. They sat down at a table and hailed a barmaid. Parched with thirst, they downed their first mug of ale quickly and ordered another. To Woods' delight, the tavern also sold pies and gravy. He promptly ordered a double helping for himself and a portion for Lavender.

'Our host at The Bell Inn will be disappointed if we don't eat there tonight,' Lavender warned.

'Oh, I don't think I'll disappoint him with me appetite,' Woods said with a wink.

Lavender glanced around and took in the rest of the clientele. A dozen working men, uniformly dressed in collarless shirts, dirty jackets and fall-fronted corduroy trousers held up with wide belts, sat slumped around the low tables. Lavender recognised the significance of those wide belts. Favoured by the dock workers down in London, they provided valuable extra support for the stomach muscles of men who spent their days lifting heavy weights and heaving on ropes.

A couple of the men had glanced up when they first entered the tavern but they had quickly lost interest in the newcomers and returned to their pipes and conversations. A hum of low voices, heavily accented and with the occasional snatch of dialect, filled the air. One group of men was laughing at the story of how a mule had 'taken a look' at the cut. Lavender worked out that the animal had fallen in the canal. Another group played a noisy game of dice at their table in the corner.

'It's not a "den of sin", is it, sir?' Woods sounded disappointed.

'No,' Lavender agreed. The boat men were a swarthy race, he decided, but placid. The flagging conversations around him suggested that most of them were tired out after a hard day's labour at the wharf. Like other men who worked outside every day of the year, they had been weathered like a piece of old leather by the elements. Several had coal dust ingrained into the lines of their faces and they sported an interesting array of scars, missing fingers and tattoos. One man had an eye-patch.

'Mind you,' Woods added, 'I wouldn't like to meet Landlord Kilby down a dark alleyway.' Lavender followed Woods' gaze over to the bar and nodded in agreement. The white-haired giant who had broken up the earlier fight now stood wiping a glass behind the bar with his apron. Lavender suspected that the apron had been made out of a bed sheet. A curly mat of white hair protruded from the open neck of Kilby's collarless shirt and more hair formed a soft, white down on his thick forearms and the back of his huge hands. Lavender had no doubt that this hairy brute was Albert Kilby. Probably in his mid-fifties, there wasn't an ounce of fat on the tavern landlord. He would be a formidable opponent in a fight; the man was pure brawn.

Beside him, a tall and unsmiling woman poured ale into two tankards. Tendrils of lank, dark hair had escaped from her hair pins and hung limply around her heavily lined and sallow face. Her shoulders were rigid as if she was compensating for the pain caused by an injury in another part of her body.

Kilby glanced up, catching Lavender's eye. A friendly smile lit up his large, round face.

Their hot pies arrived and they devoured them quickly. While Woods tucked into his second portion, Lavender ordered a brandy, sat back against the settle and let his mind drift back to their new case and the added complication of the armed band of desperadoes who were terrorising the south of the county. '*Every available constable we have in Northamptonshire is trying to find these devils,*' Rushperry had said.

Lavender's lips twitched in distaste. The 'devils' who scared a fellow magistrate and his wife near to death in Preston Deanery had provoked a full-scale manhunt but when an ordinary old man was brutally slain, the judiciary could barely spare a constable to investigate. This shouldn't have come as a surprise, he realised. After all, he had twelve years of experience of working within this system and he knew British law was designed to protect the law-making classes. He sighed and shook his head to chase such cynical thoughts out of his mind. It was his job now to get justice for William Sculthorpe. And he would.

Woods glanced up, his mouth full of unchewed pie. 'So what do you think?' he mumbled. 'About this murder?'

'I don't know.' Lavender suddenly felt exhausted. It had been a long day. 'I need to read the coroner's report and get a good night's sleep. I suspect we will have a tough time putting the pieces of this puzzle together. We've got an elderly man, who may – or may not – be quite wealthy, who was robbed and murdered by five – possibly three – men.'

'And meanwhile, there's that gang, the Panthers, lurkin' around the county,' added Woods. Lavender heard the excitement in his constable's voice. The nickname given to the Preston Deanery thieves by the local news-sheet had clearly fired Woods' imagination. 'And there's that strange note found in the bag,' Woods added. 'What did you make of that? Was Sculthorpe a moneylender, do you think?'

Lavender shrugged. 'Let's not make assumptions,' he warned. 'Perhaps it's simply a note passed on to a shopkeeper in Middleton by a customer who was paying off the last of a debt. Maybe the shopkeeper had been haranguing him for the money. You can take the cloth bag around the shops when we get to Middleton and see if anyone recognises it. But we'll keep the contents of the note to ourselves for a while and make discreet inquiries about who owns the initials *J.W.*'

The giant shadow of the landlord fell across their table. 'Ar do, gentlemen,' said the colossus. 'Alby Kilby, landlord. Is everythin' to yer satisfaction?'

'The pie was excellent,' Lavender said.

'And the gravy,' Woods added, wiping the last of it off his chin with his sleeve. 'This is a pleasant place you have here, sir. I like them brass and copper plates.'

The landlord beamed at the praise. 'That were moy Rosie's doin',' he said, pointing to the thin, sullen woman behind the bar. 'She's done this place up real nice.'

'I think my wife Betsy would like one of them pretty plates with ribbon,' Woods continued. 'Do you sell them?'

Despite his weariness, the edges of Lavender's mouth twitched into a smile as his indefatigable constable drew the burly landlord into conversation. Woods had the 'common touch' with folks, a quality he knew he lacked.

'I'll ask moy Rosie if she has one to spare,' Kilby said.

'Have you ever worked on the cut yourself?' Woods asked.

The landlord threw back his great head and laughed. His mop of white curls quivered and the candlelight shone through his bushy whiskers. 'As man and boy,' he said gruffly. 'My first barge on the H'Oxford were a leaky old tub called the *Greyhound*. I went from one end of this country to another, humpin' coal, grain and pottery on and orf that ruddy boat. A've even bin down your way – to Lunnen – with an 'orse called Silver.'

Kilby pointed to a mangy, grey horsetail pinned to the wall beside the bar. 'There's Silver's tail. Yer keeps yer luck in the tails of yer horses,' he said. 'Yer should never throw them away. T'Oxford's bin troublesome fer years at the London end, mind,' he added. 'What with the tides and the flash locks. The Grand Junction Canal'll be a far better road for the narrowboats when they've finished buildin' it.' Lavender smiled at the idea of the boatmen calling the canals 'roads'.

'What brought you bankside?' Woods asked.

Again the landlord pointed to his wife. 'Moy Rosie inherited a tidy sum from her uncle – and a bankside tavern to boot. We ran The Fox up at Braunston fer years afore we came down here.'

'Do you still have family on the canals?'

Kilby nodded. 'Two of our lads is still workin' the narrowboats up on T'Oxford. Our eldest be a number one, a marster boatman,' he said proudly. 'He has his own boat, the *Adelaide*.'

An argument had broken out at the dice table. Kilby half-turned towards the players. The man with the black eye-patch was red-faced and on his feet. Kilby's shaggy eyebrows met across his wrinkled forehead as the player banged his fist down on the table.

'My old ma always said she had family on the Oxford canal,' Woods informed him. 'She moved down to London. They were Kilbys too. Do you think we're related?'

The landlord shrugged, his eyes still riveted on the arguing dice-players. 'Mebbe. There be half a dozen or more Kilby families workin' the cut out of Coventry. What were her name?'

'Tilda. Matilda Mary Kilby.'

The huge man suddenly tensed and his broad shoulders jerked. 'A've never heard of her.' Abruptly, Kilby turned away and went to warn the dice-players to behave.

'Shame that,' Woods said and resumed his assault on his second pie.

They finished their drinks, pulled down their hats and returned through the chilly marketplace to the empty taproom at The Bell Inn. Their zealous host was at their side within seconds of their return. 'Gentlemen! Good to see you back from your business. I have taken your luggage up to your room and a fire has been lit. Now what can I get you? We have a lovely mutton stew and dumplin's or there's lamb cutlets.'

Woods grinned. 'I feel partial to a bowl of mutton stew.'

'I'm afraid I seem to have lost my appetite,' Lavender murmured. He smiled and shook his head. 'Perhaps just a glass of brandy for me?' He had known Woods for twelve years but he still found himself in awe of his constable's gargantuan appetite.

Lavender took a guttering candle from one of the windowsills and removed himself to a table in the quietest corner of the tavern. Unbuttoning his coat, he pulled the coroner's report out of his pocket and spread the loose papers out on the table before him. His tired eyes had trouble deciphering some of the handwriting in the poor light but he wanted to start on the case.

Woods chatted awhile with their host, then sat down opposite Lavender to eat his third supper of the evening.

'I don't know where you put it all,' Lavender said. 'I'd have had indigestion after the second pie.'

Woods belched, grinned happily and slapped his thigh. 'Hollow legs,' he said. 'Anyway, what's in those there papers?'

Lavender pushed back a lock of dark hair with a weary hand. 'I've only read the result of the autopsy on William Sculthorpe, so far,' he admitted. 'The old man's heart gave out two days after the attack; this was the cause of death. The doctor who carried out the autopsy said Sculthorpe took a severe blow to the face and had deep lacerations on the back of his head as well. The laceration and swelling down the right-hand side of his face made the old man unrecognisable.'

Woods' spoon of stew hovered momentarily in midair before continuing its steady rhythm towards his mouth. Lavender noted his constable's hesitation and the corners of his mouth twitched with humour. 'The bleeding had been severe,' he added wickedly. 'Sculthorpe was slumped in a large pool of blood when they found him.'

Woods' spoon paused again and he grimaced. 'The right-hand side of his face?' he asked. 'Was the assailant caudge-pawed, do you think?'

'Left-handed? That's a good observation,' Lavender said thoughtfully. 'But it depends on the angle of the attack. The only other thing of note in this report is that Sculthorpe's fingers were black – presumably with ink.'

'Perhaps he were writin' something the day he died?'

Lavender shrugged, laid the paper on the table and pulled out another sheet. 'This is a statement from Doctor Wallace, the physician who attended the dying man.'

'Is he one of them who saw the murderers?'

'No. Despite his own injuries, Constable Jed Sawyer raised the alarm and after his neighbours discovered Sculthorpe unconscious and bleeding in his home, they fetched Doctor Wallace. At first, everyone feared the old gentleman was dead. But Doctor Wallace discovered Sculthorpe's insensibility arose from the wound he had received to his head and face and the large quantity of clotted blood which had settled in his mouth.'

Once again the spoon hovered in midair, then Woods dropped it back into the bowl with a clatter. 'I think I'll leave the rest,' he said.

Lavender hid his smile. 'With proper assistance, Sculthorpe recovered slightly, although he never regained his wits. Doctor Wallace describes similar injuries to those mentioned in the autopsy but he adds that Sculthorpe was half conscious, covered in blood and appeared to be having palpitations. The doctor was alarmed at the bright redness of the old man's complexion – oh, and Sculthorpe lay in a pool of his own vomit.'

Woods shoved the bowl firmly away from him across the table. 'I'm surprised he could see Sculthorpe's face beneath all the blood,' he said.

Lavender didn't respond. His eyes focused on the last paragraph of Doctor Wallace's report and he frowned.

'What's the matter?' Woods asked.

'It looks like Captain Rushperry forgot to tell us something important.'

'What?'

'After Doctor Wallace had done what he could for the old man, he went upstairs and attended to Sculthorpe's injured son.'

'Son? What son? Rushperry never mentioned a son.'

'No, he didn't,' Lavender agreed, 'which is rather strange. Sculthorpe's son is known as Billy Sculthorpe. He was also viciously attacked by the villains.'

Woods frowned. 'Were he badly hurt?'

Lavender nodded. 'He'd been knocked unconscious by a blow to the head.'

'Heaven and hell! So there's three of them injured by these thugs: the two Sculthorpes – and Constable Sawyer.'

'Yes.' Lavender shifted through the papers on the table looking for something. 'Most strange. And there's no witness statement in this report from Billy Sculthorpe, either. The only other thing is a statement from Constable Sawyer.'

'Perhaps Billy Sculthorpe were too badly beaten to give one?' Woods suggested.

Lavender gathered up the pile of papers and replaced them in his inside coat pocket. 'That's enough for tonight, Ned,' he said firmly. 'I'll read Constable Sawyer's account of events tomorrow and we'll learn more when we arrive in Middleton. We shall seek out Billy Sculthorpe and gain a first-hand witness account from him ourselves.'

Chapter Four

Friday 2nd March, 1810
Market Harborough, Leicestershire

They had shared a room on many occasions before while out of London on a case and Lavender was accustomed to sleeping through his constable's heavy snoring. But neither man slept well that night. Woods was restless, very restless. He tossed and turned in his creaking bed. He murmured and called out in his sleep. At one point, Lavender heard him calling out for his mother.

At the first sign of dawn, Lavender gave up trying to sleep and sat up on the edge of his bed. He sighed wearily and pushed back a lock of stray hair. He might need to find a barber while in town, he realised. He'd needed a haircut for a while now and there had been no time back in London. Magistrate Read had sent them straight out to Leicestershire the moment they had solved their last case. On top of this, his last few days in London had been frantic. He had organised the banns for his forthcoming nuptials and taken a whirlwind tour of the shops with Magdalena to purchase furniture for their new home in Marylebone. They hoped to marry at Easter.

His hair had a tendency to curl if he let it grow out which he didn't like, although Magdalena had once hinted she found it attractive. The thought of Magdalena made him feel better and he imagined her in their new bed with her black hair strewn across the pillow and her long, dark eyelashes resting gently on the flawless golden skin of her cheeks.

He walked across to the window and pulled back the thin drapes. The red fingers of dawn reached across the overcast sky above the smoking chimneys of the houses on the other side of the street. Roof tiles gleamed with moisture from last night's rain. A few night lanterns still glimmered on the dripping walls of the houses but an occasional warm pool of light from an uncurtained window spilled down onto the cobbled road below. Market Harborough was rousing itself for the day.

He washed himself, pulled on his breeches and shirt against the cold and set up his shaving mirror on the washstand. A pair of inscrutable, hooded brown eyes stared back at him in the mirror. He ran his hand over the stubble on his jaw and picked up his shaving cup to lather the soap. Woods suddenly let out a bellowing roar, sat bolt upright in the bed and began to fight with his blankets. He lunged too far – and promptly fell out of bed.

Lavender burst out laughing. Woods scrambled to his feet, clenched his fists and glared at him across the room, his eyes still glazed with sleep and confusion.

'What the hell are you dreaming about now, Ned?' Lavender asked. 'You've been thrashing about all night.'

Still dazed and muddled, Woods sat down on the edge of the bed and put his head in his hands. ''Twere one of those bodies we dragged out of the Thames,' he mumbled from between his fingers. 'They'd accused me of the murder and chased me across Westminster Bridge.'

'It serves you right for eating three suppers,' Lavender said, as he lathered his chin. 'How you manage to sleep with all that food swirling around in your belly is beyond me.'

Thick, fair hair framed the boyish face of Constable Sam Clancy. A wide grin spread across his features when Lavender and Woods approached and he extended his hand towards them. 'Sam Clancy, sir,' he said. 'Captain Rushperry has asked me to accompany you today. Can I say what an honour it is to be workin' with a Bow Street detective, sir?' He had the bluest eyes Lavender had seen for some time and they shone with excitement.

'You may say that,' Lavender said. 'This is Constable Ned Woods, a horse patrol officer, also with Bow Street.' The cuffs of Clancy's dark coat reached well over the hand that shook Lavender's but despite being too big for him, the coat was well-brushed and his shirt and plain waistcoat were also clean.

'Horse patrol officer?' Clancy's eyes widened. 'It's an honour, sir, an honour. I've taken the liberty to organise three horses for our trip to Middleton today. We breed the best horseflesh in the country in these here parts. I hope they'll meet yer approval.'

'I hope they will too,' Woods growled. 'We ain't used to riding queer prancers.' Despite his gruffness, Lavender knew the young man's excitement had amused Woods. They'd had to deal with a large amount of resentment and jealousy from provincial constables in the past and Clancy's enthusiasm was a welcome change.

At the stables, Woods made a great show of inspecting the horses Clancy had picked out for them. He ran his hands over their flanks and fetlocks and lifted up their hooves to inspect the shoes. For a moment Lavender thought he would force open their mouths and inspect their teeth too. Finally, Woods stood back and announced that they were a decent set of gallopers.

Young Clancy, who had been hovering behind him, bristled with pride. 'You'll have to come back for the horse fair at Northampton,

Constable Woods,' he said. 'You can buy some real beauties there for yer horse patrol.'

They mounted the horses and clattered out of the stable yard. Clancy led them down the high street, chattering over his shoulder as he went. The streets were busier now with wagons and people.

'We'll take the Rockingham Road to Middleton,' Clancy said. 'It's about seven miles to the village.'

'Rockingham?' Lavender suddenly remembered Lady Anne Fitzwilliam's interest in the case and his summons to the Castle. 'Isn't this one of the seats of Earl Fitzwilliam, the Whig politician?'

'Yes,' Clancy replied. 'Most of the villagers in Middleton and Cottingham work on his estate.'

'Is that what William Sculthorpe did in his youth? Was he a farm labourer?'

Clancy glanced back at Lavender, a troubled expression on his face. 'I can't rightly say,' he said. 'Sculthorpe and his family didn't move into the village until three years ago. They came here from Brighton. I don't know anythin' about his work or trade.'

Lavender nodded. This made sense. Common labourers didn't amass large fortunes – or usually attract the interest and concern of dowager countesses. Sculthorpe probably wasn't a common labourer.

'To tell the truth,' the lad continued, 'it's been difficult to find out much about him. Mr Sculthorpe and his wife lived quietly and didn't mix much with the rest of the village. They didn't even go to church on a Sunday.'

He broke off to point out the ancient stocks and the whipping post in the Church Square but Lavender had stopped listening.

Alby Kilby stood at the side of the road in a greatcoat, hunched up against the cold and glaring at them. He had pulled his hat down over his face but there was no mistaking his huge frame. Had Kilby already learnt who they were? Policemen weren't popular and many people distrusted him and Woods once they knew of their occupation. The contrast between the genial host of the previous night and this rigid, scowling man couldn't have been greater. But something else niggled at the back of Lavender's mind. The way Kilby crossed his arms across his broad chest, clamped his jaw and held his head reminded Lavender of someone, although he was damned if he could remember who. With an inexplicable sense of unease, Lavender searched through his memory, trying to place the landlord's face. He failed. They'd never met before, he was sure of that. He'd never forget a fellow as physically distinctive as Alby Kilby.

Clancy led them down a narrow street to the east of the town and on to a meandering country lane. 'The River Welland is the border between the two counties,' Clancy said, pointing to the bridge ahead. 'Once we cross the river we'll be in Northamptonshire.'

'Tell us about them Panthers,' Woods said.

'Constable Sawyer is convinced it were them who attacked him and the Sculthorpes.' Clancy's voice rose in excitement.

'Is he now?' Lavender said. But his sarcasm blew away in the breeze and didn't register with the enthusiastic young man.

'Oh, yes. He's quite convinced it's them. They roam the two counties attackin' innocent folks in their own homes.'

'We've heard about the robbery and assault at Preston Deanery,' Woods said. 'What else do you know about them?'

'Four of them met up in Northamptonshire County Gaol last year,' Clancy explained. 'David George and Bill Minards were old mates, and a nasty pair of criminals. But they weren't successful. They'd been arrested for burglaries and robberies and sent to the county gaol to await trial. In gaol they formed an association with Ben Panther and John Taffs, who were also awaitin' trial, havin' been arrested for theft at Rothwell.'

'Wait a minute,' Woods said. 'Are you tellin' us you already had these villains locked up last year?'

Embarrassment flitted across the young constable's face. 'Yes. Four of them appeared at the Summer Assizes. George and Minards were both found guilty and sentenced to transportation. But Ben Panther and Taffs were released because of lack of evidence.'

'So Panther and Taffs were on the outside, and George and Minards were on the inside of the county gaol?' Woods asked. 'What happened next?'

Clancy shuffled uncomfortably in his saddle. 'Ben Panther and Taffs brought along one of Panther's mates, Ted Porter, and the three of them sprung George and Minards from prison by forcin' open their cell window.'

'Ha!' Woods' snort of disapproval startled a rabbit in the undergrowth at the base of the hedge. It disappeared in a flash of white cottontail.

'They've been on the run ever since,' Clancy added miserably.

'Ruddy useless provincial gaols,' Woods chuckled. 'I'd have liked to see them try to break out of Newgate in London! What a farce!'

Crestfallen at the criticism of his constabulary and judiciary, young Clancy fell silent.

The road stretched out for miles before them, lined with a high hedgerow of hawthorn and hazel, entwined with the fresh green shoots of honeysuckle. On the other side of the hedge, a vast expanse of flat, brown, furrowed fields stretched away for miles beneath the overcast sky. Even the sheep were mere dots in the distance. Far away in the north, mist shrouded a long ridge of dark forest. A stone church tower peeked out from the treetops, suggesting a hidden village at its base.

Occasionally, Lavender caught sight of farmers toiling behind their ploughs, but for the most part the landscape lay empty of people. Shy creatures scurried into hiding in the hedgerow beside the road as they passed. Vivid yellow primroses at the base of the hedge broke up the monotony of the different shades of green and brown. The silence was deafening. Even the birdsong was distant and muted.

Lavender shuffled restlessly in his own saddle. 'Let's quicken our pace,' he said to the others. Clancy rose in his stirrups, leant forward and urged his horse into a gallop. Lavender and Woods followed.

A rush of cold wind lashed against Lavender's face. This, and the exertion needed to keep his seat on the powerful animal, revived him. It shook out the tiredness from his mind and body and sharpened his senses.

They slowed their pace as the lane climbed up the side of a wooded ridge. At the summit of the hill, they reined in their tired horses and took in the magnificent view below them. Weak sunlight forced its way through the clouds overhead and Lavender appreciated the quiet beauty of the green- and gold-tinged rolling landscape before them.

As they descended down the steep hillside into the village, they passed a stinking lime kiln. Dust-covered men turned their heads to watch them pass. A group of young boys outside a redbrick school also watched their progression with interest.

The main part of the village of Middleton, a long, single street of stone cottages and farms, lay at the bottom of the hill. Halfway down the street stood the blacksmith's forge, opposite a water trough and a black, iron-handled pump. Woods filled up the trough and they let their sweating horses drink while they swigged from their own hip flasks.

A creaking wooden sign further down the street indicated the location of a solitary shop and the delicious aroma of freshly baked bread suggested a bakehouse nearby. The main road through the village was a rutted mud-track where chickens picked their way delicately between piles of animal dung. A group of women stood talking further down the street while small children played at their feet in the dirt. This was the last place in England where Lavender would have expected to investigate a brutal murder.

'I imagine you'll want to speak to Constable Sawyer first,' Clancy said.

'No, let's start with the scene of the crime,' Lavender replied.

They left the horses with the blacksmith, then Clancy led them down a short alleyway to two humble stone cottages set back from the road and facing each other. He stopped in front of the most dilapidated of the cottages. Paint peeled away from the low, rectangular window frames and wooden door, and weeds sprouted up around the step. 'We've left it alone for you,' he said. 'Captain Rushperry were most particular about that.'

Lavender glanced at the cottage directly opposite Sculthorpe's home. A curtain twitched in an upstairs window and he glimpsed a pale face.

'Wait' he said, as Clancy reached for the door handle. 'Did anyone ever ask these neighbours if they saw or heard anything on the night of the attack?'

'Yes, I did,' Clancy said, bristling with pride. 'There's only Miss Bennett in the house opposite. She looks after her bedridden mother. She said she didn't see or hear anythin' out of the ordinary. There were a terrible storm ragin' that night,' he added. 'Most folks never heard anythin' over the noise of the thunder.'

'Maybe that's why the thieves picked that night to carry out the robbery,' Woods said.

The young constable pushed open the creaking oak door and they stepped inside the musty gloom of a cramped hallway.

'Why isn't the door locked?' Woods asked.

'Folks tend not to bother lockin' their doors in this part of the world. They don't expect any trouble. I searched for a key but never found one.'

'Well, there's no doubt how Sculthorpe's attackers entered the property,' Lavender said wryly.

They turned to a room on the left first. 'This was the old man's bedchamber,' Clancy said.

A single bed stood against the far wall of the room. Lavender pulled back the thin drapes across the window to let in more light. The bed sheets and blankets were rumpled and trailed over the edge onto the wooden floor as if the sleeper had been roused suddenly and left the bed quickly. Across an old hard-backed chair lay a fraying white shirt, a pair of darned woollen trousers and an old black coat with tarnished buttons. Everything was folded neatly and on top of the clothing sat a battered black Bible.

'It doesn't look like the intruders came in here,' Lavender said. He picked up the white shirt from the pile of clothes. 'Was Sculthorpe found dead in his nightshirt?'

Clancy nodded.

'So, the thieves – or perhaps the storm – wake up the old man,' Lavender said, 'and a few moments later he stumbles across the intruders in his kitchen.'

Apart from the washstand and a battered trunk on the floor, the only other furniture in the room was a tall cupboard in the corner. A large wooden cross over the mahogany bedhead broke up the monotony of the crumbling plaster walls. Candle stubs sat in stands on the floor and a razor and shaving cup rested on the washstand. The spartan nature of the room reminded Lavender of a monk's cell.

Woods lifted up the lid of the trunk and rifled through the contents. 'Old clothes,' he said, 'and these.' He pulled out a pair of creased and battered working boots from the bottom of the chest. Despite their obvious age, they had a strange sheen and gleamed like satin. Woods peered closer and laughed. 'Heaven and hell!' he said softly. 'He's varnished them with wood varnish, tryin' to make them look like new. This old man weren't payin' out for a new pair of boots!'

Lavender moved across to the tall, narrow cupboard in the corner of the room. 'So if the clothes are in the chest, what's in here?' He tugged at the handles of the two doors and frowned when they refused to yield.

'I can't find the key to that either,' Clancy confessed.

Lavender pulled his pocketknife and a length of thin wire from his coat pocket. 'Well, luckily for you, Clancy,' he said, 'Constable Woods and I have spent a lot of time with some of the best picklocks, thieves and coves in the capital.' He inserted a blade into the tiny lock and twisted. Still the door refused to budge. Abandoning the knife, he tried a folded loop of the wire. Clancy moved closer and watched. The door swung open with a quiet click. Lavender reached up for the inside catch of the second door, released it and pulled it back.

The men stared in silence at the glittering, silver-gilt and enamelled artefact that stood before them on the shelf in the cupboard.

'Now we know why Sculthorpe and his wife didn't go to the village church,' Lavender said.

'What is it, sir?' Woods asked.

'It's a Catholic reliquary,' Lavender said. 'Judging by the candle stumps set around it, Sculthorpe used it as a shrine for worship.'

A beautiful gilt carving of the Madonna and child stood on the lid of the box surrounded by two angels. Above their heads rose three pointed arches, which culminated in elaborate silver finials. Although the artefact was only some ten inches high, the arches and finials emphasised each apex and gave the impression the figures were seated in a cathedral of immense proportion and wealth. Translucent blue enamel was used as a background for the main carving and also on the fragile and decorative side panels.

Lavender pointed to the intricate paintings on the side panels.

'These are scenes from the life of the Virgin and the Infancy of Christ.' The translucency of the enamel reminded him of the stained-glass windows in Westminster Cathedral.

'Sculthorpe were a Catholic?' Clancy's face registered shock.

'It would appear so,' Lavender said.

'Do you think there's money in the bottom?' Woods asked.

'I doubt it,' Lavender replied. 'You're more likely to find the mummified finger bone of a saint in there.'

Clancy shuddered.

'That's the purpose of a reliquary,' Lavender told them, 'to keep ancient religious artefacts safe.'

Carefully, Woods supported the statue and lifted the lid of the box. 'Eugh.' His face crumpled in disgust and he lowered the lid far more quickly than he had raised it. 'It looks like hair and a bit of scalp. It's not Sculthorpe's missin' fortune, that's for sure.'

Clancy sighed and shook his head. 'I can't believe he were a Catholic. Everyone said he were a decent old man.'

The corners of Lavender's mouth twitched. 'Not all Catholics have three heads and horns,' he said.

'Is this valuable?' Woods pointed to the reliquary.

Lavender frowned and tried to assess the value of the glittering object. To his untrained eye it looked more elaborate and antique than the family reliquary owned by Magdalena. Silver-gilt and enamel weren't particularly expensive but the skill of the craftsmen who had made it was exquisite and he had no idea about the antiquity of the piece.

'I don't know. It needs to go to an expert for valuation,' he said. 'In the meantime, I recommend we take it back to Market Harborough with us for safekeeping tonight. Let's examine the rest of the cottage.'

They crossed the hallway into the kitchen and paused in the doorway, shocked at the carnage that lay before them. The wooden chairs in the room had been upended and smashed and someone had yanked out the drawers from the wooden dresser and tipped their contents onto the floor. A stained and sagging fireside arm-chair had been ripped to shreds. The stuffing from the cushions had been kicked around the room. The mantelpiece above the fireplace had been swept clean of its objects, the clock and the ornaments. These now lay shattered on the floor among the broken crockery, strewn papers and kitchen utensils.

Clancy pointed to the gap between the dresser and the corner of the room. A large bloodstain covered the flaking plaster on the wall.

'The neighbours found Mr Sculthorpe down here,' he said. 'He'd been knocked backwards and had slumped down into this corner against the wall.'

They opened a window to let out the unpleasant smell of rotting vegetation that permeated the room, then meticulously examined the debris of William Sculthorpe's life. Broken pieces of pot crunched beneath Lavender's boots as he scooped up the papers lying on the floor.

'Receipts,' he said, disappointed. 'Receipts for everything – food, coal, socks and tobacco.' He had hoped to find more detailed accounts or correspondence among the scattered papers.

He moved over to the fireplace and examined the inside of the chimney for secret ledges and alcoves. His glance rested on the greasy pan and the cracked and dirty food plates thrown on the floor by the hearth. He picked up the iron pan and sniffed it.

'Fried ham,' he said. 'Sculthorpe had fried ham for his last supper.' A black residue on the bottom of the pan attracted his attention. He poked it, drew back his blackened finger and sniffed. Frowning, he put down the pan and moved into the scullery at the back of the kitchen. The food shelves were bare apart from a half-empty basket of rotting mushrooms. He carried it back into the kitchen and moved over to the light by the window. 'Here's the source of the smell,' he said.

'What is it, sir?' Woods asked.

Lavender poked the congealed mass at the bottom of the basket again and lifted his inky hands to show the other two men who had gathered round. '*Coprinopsis atramentaria*,' he said. 'Ink cap mushrooms. No wonder Doctor Wallace said Sculthorpe's fingers were black when they found him.'

Clancy frowned. 'Aren't they poisonous?'

'Not usually,' Lavender replied. 'Only if ingested with alcohol. Did Sculthorpe drink spirits or ale?'

'Yes, I think so,' Clancy replied. He moved across to the other side of the room and pulled out a bottle from under the table. 'It's half-full,' he said, 'and it's brandy.'

Lavender took the bottle from him and raised his eyebrows at the label. 'It's expensive brandy, as well. It looks like our victim wasn't quite so miserly when it came to treating himself to some of the finer things in life. Is there any evidence he had been drinking this on the night of his death?'

They glanced around the debris. Woods bent down and picked up the shattered remains of a glass. Carefully, he ran his finger along the residue on the bottom and licked it. 'Brandy,' he confirmed.

'But what does this mean?' Clancy asked.

'It means,' Lavender said, 'we now know why William Sculthorpe had palpitations, vomited and was red in the face when Doctor Wallace went to assist him. The man had poisoned himself with ink cap mushrooms and brandy. When the thieves attacked Sculthorpe, he was already a dying man.'

Chapter Five

'Does this mean we're no longer lookin' at a murder charge?' Clancy asked.

'That will depend on the coroner,' Lavender said calmly. 'He will make a decision when he's apprised of all the facts. It is obvious to me that both Doctor Wallace and the coroner failed to recognise that Sculthorpe's symptoms suggested he'd been poisoned. They were distracted by the injuries he received during the attack.'

Woods' mouth had been hanging open in surprise. He closed it and shook his head. 'I'm not surprised about that. Who would have thought the poor old fellah had poisoned himself on the day he was attacked?'

'We're still looking at a vicious robbery where three people were badly injured,' Lavender said. 'We need to catch those villains and bring them to justice, whether they were ultimately responsible for Sculthorpe's death or not.'

'I wouldn't want to be in that coroner's shoes and have to sort out this pickle,' Woods said.

Lavender turned to Clancy. 'Where did the neighbours and Doctor Wallace find Sculthorpe's son?'

Clancy led the way up the narrow wooden stairs and paused on the landing between the two bedrooms next to an ominous dark stain on the wooden floorboards. 'The neighbours found Billy Sculthorpe here,' he said. 'He'd been hit on the head and was slumped on the floor, unconscious and bleedin' badly. He were terrified when he came round. The thieves had scared him out of his wits.'

'Where is he now?' Woods asked.

'Mrs Tilley at Willow Cottage has taken him in until he recovers. She has rooms to let. Captain Rushperry has agreed to pay for it until Sculthorpe's financial affairs are settled. Doctor and Mrs Wallace have accommodation there too. I think the doctor wanted to keep an eye on him and make sure he recovered.'

'Who were these neighbours who found the Sculthorpes, raised the alarm and fetched Doctor Wallace?' Lavender asked.

''Twere Frank Bunnin', the landlord of The Woolpack, his nephew, Isaac, and one of their customers, Harry Goode. Constable Sawyer staggered into The Woolpack to raise the alarm after he was attacked. He knew there'd be someone still there.'

'That were good thinkin',' said Woods.

Young Clancy beamed. 'Yes, Jed Sawyer is a real hero. Anyway, the Bunnin's and Harry Goode came straight here. Frank Bunnin' sent his nephew to rouse Doctor Wallace when he saw the terrible state of the Sculthorpes. They thought the old man were already dead.'

'Yes,' said Lavender. 'I've read about his injuries in the coroner's report. What time did this attack take place?'

'Frank Bunnin' said it were just before ten o'clock. He were about to call time in the tavern and shut up for the night when Jed Sawyer staggered through the door with his face smashed up and a broken arm.'

'So how is Mr Billy Sculthorpe now?' Lavender asked. 'Has he recovered enough for us to interview him about the attack? Or is he still out of his wits with fear?'

Clancy shuffled his feet and dropped his eyes down onto the bloodstain on the floor. 'I can't rightly say,' he said. 'Captain Rushperry told me to leave him alone. He weren't to be interviewed.'

'Why is that?' Lavender snapped.

'Billy Sculthorpe's a bit simple-minded.' Clancy glanced up, embarrassed. 'He's an imbecile.'

'An imbecile?'

'Yes.' Clancy fixed Lavender with his troubled blue eyes. 'You know, one of those simpletons who never go out. Sculthorpe and his wife kept him shut up in the house. The villagers knew he lived here, of course, but no one ever saw him.'

'His evidence will still be valuable,' Lavender said.

Clancy shook his fair head. 'He said three dark spirits attacked him that night – but Constable Sawyer said there were five villains.'

'Dark spirits?'

'Yes, elves or sommat.' Clancy tapped his head. 'He's touched, feeble-minded.'

Lavender sighed. He now understood what Captain Rushperry meant when he said one of the witnesses was unreliable.

Lavender remembered a similar situation up in Northumberland the previous year. On this occasion, he'd overlooked the mute, childlike brother of the missing heiress Helen Carnaby during his investigation. This had been a terrible mistake – and an innocent young woman had paid with her life. 'We still need to speak to Billy Sculthorpe at some point,' he said firmly. 'Let's examine these rooms while we're here.'

The first bedchamber they entered was Billy Sculthorpe's. Lavender and Woods stopped in surprise at the entrance.

'Gawd's teeth!' Woods exclaimed. Lavender felt the hairs stand up on the back of his neck.

Sheets of paper were stuck all over the rough stone walls of the room, covered with pencil drawings of fantastical and sinister mythical creatures. Slavering, red-eyed wolves glared out at them, disturbed from their feast of maggot-ridden carrion. Venomous serpents curled around the pages, crushing their prey to death in their coils. Scowling Valkyries hovered in the corners like angels of death.

Billy Sculthorpe obviously had a fevered imagination. Lavender pulled a drawing from the wall and examined it. Despite the untrained hand of the artist and some awkwardness of proportion, Billy Sculthorpe had talent. There was dexterity and skill in the shading and smudging of the figures and their features.

'How old is Billy Sculthorpe?' Lavender asked.

Clancy shook his head and shrugged.

Woods stood immobile and tense in the doorway. 'What is all this?' he growled.

'The life's work of Billy Sculthorpe,' Lavender replied, simply. He walked across the room to the corner where pencils, paper and crayons were scattered across the floor and piled haphazardly on an old chest, along with some ragged and well-thumbed books. The books were a collection of illustrated children's fables and Celtic fairytales but Lavender wasn't surprised to also find a book of Norse folklore and an illustrated copy of Dante's *Inferno* among them. Billy Sculthorpe had copied out several illustrations from these books onto paper.

Lavender glanced around the rest of the simply furnished room and wondered how Billy's mother could have afforded all this stationery and the books. Books were not common among working people, but then again, he reasoned, most of them didn't have a jewelled reliquary in the closet either.

'It looks like the thieves didn't venture inside here, either,' he said. The thin blankets on the bed were rumpled but there was no sign of disturbance anywhere in the room.

'They were probably too spooked by these damn pictures to step over the threshold,' Woods said with a scowl.

Lavender smiled. 'What's the other room across the landing?'

'It's the bedchamber of the late Mrs Sculthorpe,' Clancy said.

'How do you know this?' Woods asked.

'Their neighbour Miss Bennett told me.' Clancy led the way into the final room in the house. 'Miss Bennett came in here to help Mr Sculthorpe clear out his wife's things after her death last August.'

This bedchamber had been ransacked by the thieves. Chairs were piled on a chest in one corner and the rug in the opposite corner had been pulled back, exposing the floorboards. Several of the boards had been prised up. Lavender and Woods walked across to the gaping chasm they had left exposed.

'We've no idea what was in there,' Clancy said. 'Captain Rushperry thinks this is where Sculthorpe kept his money hidden.'

Woods dropped to the floor and shoved his hand into the hole beneath the floor. He drew it out empty. 'Nothin'.'

'Sculthorpe must have told the thieves about this hiding place before they knocked him senseless to the ground,' Lavender said.

'You think so?' Clancy asked.

'I know so,' Lavender replied. 'Why else come upstairs to this exact spot? Why else leave the rest of the house undisturbed?'

'It makes sense, sir,' Woods said. 'If Sculthorpe hadn't told them about this place, they'd have soon turned over the other rooms in the house. They'd have forced open the cupboard in his bedchamber for a start and soon discovered that reliquary thing.'

Lavender nodded, dropped down onto his haunches beside Woods and stared into the chasm as if searching for inspiration. He tapped on the floor with his fingers as his mind whirled.

'They must have disturbed Billy Sculthorpe with the noise they made prising up the floorboards,' he said. 'Billy will have come out of his room onto the landing to investigate and they attacked him there.'

He stood up. 'I think we have seen everything there is to see here. I'm disappointed we haven't found any accounts ledgers. They might have told us how much money Sculthorpe kept in the house and how much was stolen.'

Clancy looked impressed. 'Do you want to meet Constable Sawyer now?' he asked.

'No.' Lavender glanced out of the window at the cottage opposite. 'I want to meet the neighbour, Miss Bennett.'

Clancy's eyes widened. 'But she said she didn't see anything!'

'It can't but help to ask her again, son,' Woods said.

Clancy's mouth dropped open slightly, then he clamped his lips together. Silently, he led them back down the stairs and out of the cottage.

Lavender rapped on the door. It opened immediately and the pinched face of a middle-aged woman peered out at them. She had a mop of frizzy grey hair beneath her white cap and a pair of spectacles balanced on her thin nose that magnified the size of her troubled brown eyes.

'Miss Bennett? I'm Detective Stephen Lavender from Bow Street Police Office in London. This is Constable Edward Woods.'

'Good mornin', Miss Bennett,' Woods said.

'And I understand you already know Constable Clancy?'

She nodded and pulled her woollen shawl tighter around her shoulders. She swallowed hard and a muscle fluttered in the sagging skin of her neck.

'May we come in?' Lavender continued. 'I would like to ask you some questions about the Sculthorpes and the night Mr Sculthorpe was attacked and murdered.'

She stood back and let them squeeze into the cottage. It was half the size of the Sculthorpes' home and had only one tiny downstairs room. Two faded armchairs stood in front of the hearth and a table with more chairs was pushed up against the opposite wall. A steep wooden staircase climbed up the third wall to the bedroom upstairs. The table was piled high with clothes and a sewing box full of needles and thread stood open next to them. Miss Bennett must take in mending to survive.

Yet despite the overcrowding, the room had a homely feel to it that Sculthorpe's cottage lacked. The mantelpiece and windowsill were cluttered with china knick-knacks. Clean lace curtains hung at the window and quilted cushions added a bit of comfort to the sagging chairs by the fireplace.

'I don't know how you think I can help you.' Miss Bennett sounded strained. 'I've already told you everythin' I know.'

'I'm sure you've done your best, Miss Bennett,' said Woods gently, 'but we know from experience, sometimes folks are so shocked after a terrible event like this that some details go right out of their minds. 'Tis only natural. Have you remembered anythin' since?'

She sank into one of the chairs by the fire and fiddled with the fringe of her shawl. 'No. I didn't see or hear anythin' apart from thunder and lightnin'.'

Woods sat down, unbidden, in the chair opposite, with concern and sympathy etched across his face. Clancy stayed by the door and watched quietly. 'Did you know the family well?' Woods asked. 'Were it a dreadful shock for you?'

She nodded. 'I've done my best to help out Mr Sculthorpe since his Bridget died. It's not been easy with havin' to care for Mother too, but I've tried to be a good neighbour.'

'I'm sure you have,' Woods said. 'What were the family like?'

'He were very private,' she replied. 'He'd nod and say "hello" but Bridget were the friendlier one. She didn't mingle with many folks in the village but we spent a bit of time together. She were quite ill when they moved here from Brighton and I were sorry when she died. She were Irish, you know?'

'Irish?' Lavender said, surprised. 'Was Mr Sculthorpe Irish too?'

'No, they'd met and married down in London and young Billy were born there. He were a Londoner like you. Mrs Sculthorpe were many years younger than him though. About thirty years, I think. She were only in her fifties when she died. I were very frightened when I heard what the Panther Gang did to the Sculthorpes. I lock my own door every night now – and never go out after dusk.'

Suddenly, there was a sharp knock above their heads. Miss Bennett glanced up at the wooden beams of the low ceiling. 'It's Mother,' she said. 'She's awake. I must go up to her soon. She's been bedridden since her last seizure and sleeps most of the time.'

'Dorothy!' The voice drifting down from upstairs was frail but insistent.

'You must be a great comfort to your ma,' Woods said. Miss Bennett nodded again. 'I don't suppose your ma saw anythin' on the night of the attack, but did she hear anythin' in the alleyway outside? May we go upstairs and ask her?'

'Dorothy! Dorothy? Who are those men?' Miss Bennett glanced uneasily at the staircase.

There was nothing wrong with the old woman's hearing; their voices must have carried upstairs.

'Would you mind if we questioned your mother ourselves?' Woods asked.

Miss Bennett stood up. She looked like she was about to refuse.

'It's important to our investigation,' Woods said quickly. He also rose to his feet. 'We'd be grateful for your help.'

'Very well,' she said with a sigh. 'But you mustn't stay long or you will tire her. Please give me a moment to make sure she's respectable before you go up.'

*

The elderly Mrs Bennett wore a fraying bed cap over her white hair and a shawl over her bony shoulders. The hand that clutched the quilt up to her neck was like a bird's claw. She reminded Lavender of a little sparrow, sharp and alert.

Woods introduced everyone and asked the questions.

'Yes, I heard them scoundrels,' the old woman said immediately.

'You never said so before!' her daughter exclaimed.

'Well, no one asked me, did they?'

Ignoring her daughter, the old woman turned her head back to Woods. 'The storm had both of us awake – and she got up to use the pot.'

'Mother!' Mortified, Miss Bennett sat down on the second bed in the room. Her face crumpled with distress and she wrung her hands in her lap. The three men stared at her.

'I heard them – and so did she,' the relentless old woman continued, 'but she didn't know I were awake.'

Woods turned back to the old woman in the bed. 'It would be a great help, Mrs Bennett,' he said, 'if you could tell us exactly what you heard.'

'Voices,' she replied immediately. 'They were excited voices. I heard them voices drift down the street when they left the house.'

'How many voices did you hear?' Lavender asked.

'I think it were three, yes, definitely three.'

'Do you know what time this was?'

A bony finger pointed to the scratched wooden clock on her bedside table. 'It were half past ten,' she said. 'I saw the hands of the clock when the lightnin' flashed.'

Lavender took out his own pocket watch and flicked it open.

'I thought it were strange for the old man to have company so late at night,' Mrs Bennett continued. 'He normally went to bed by nine. Ask her.' She pointed at her daughter. 'She'll tell you the same.'

Silence fell in the room. Lavender turned back to Miss Bennett, who sat hunched forward on the bed, her head lowered.

'It were like Mother said.' Her voice crackled with emotion. 'When I rose . . . when I rose . . . I looked out of the window and I saw three men leavin' the Sculthorpes. They were laughin' and went up onto the high street.'

'Where a few moments later they bumped into Constable Sawyer,' Lavender said.

'Thank you, ladies,' Woods said. 'This has been very helpful.'

'I'm sorry I didn't say somethin' before.' Miss Bennett turned her face towards the policemen. Her large eyes were wet with tears behind their spectacles. 'But I were so frightened by what had happened. I thought if I spoke out, those Panthers would come back to hurt us.'

'Silly goose,' said her mother.

Chapter Six

'Well, I'll be damned,' said Clancy as they walked back into the village high street. 'I never thought for a minute Miss Bennett were withholdin' information from me when I questioned her.'

'Sometimes a bit of persistence is needed, lad,' Woods said kindly.

Lavender halted in his tracks and glanced around the quiet road with its terraces of light-stone cottages. The smell of fresh baking still permeated the air and his stomach rumbled. It was a long time since breakfast and the long horse ride had sharpened his appetite. 'Is there a bakehouse in the village?' he asked.

'Yes,' Clancy replied. 'Mrs Tilley at Willow Cottage – her who lets out the rooms – she also runs the bakehouse.'

'Take us there,' Lavender said. Woods' eyes lit up at the mention of food.

'It still doesn't make sense, though,' Clancy said. He led them across the road and back down the street in the direction from which they had first arrived in the village. 'There were five men who attacked Constable Sawyer, and this was before the tavern shut at ten o'clock. So how did two women see and hear three men leave Sculthorpe's cottage at half past ten?'

'They didn't,' Lavender said. 'Their bedroom clock is fifteen minutes fast; I checked it against my own pocket watch. They saw the thieves leave Sculthorpe's house at a quarter past ten.'

'My goodness!' Clancy glanced at Lavender with fresh respect. 'I'm learnin' a lot today.'

They approached an L-shaped stone building set back from the road. A weather-beaten sign reading 'Willow Cottage Rooms to Let' swung in the breeze above their heads. A pretty garden bordered the short path to the front door, full of yellow primroses and tall, large-leaved lemon and pale lilac hellebores.

'Oh, we haven't started yet,' Woods reassured Clancy. 'Stay by our side, lad, and you'll be amazed.'

When Lavender pushed open the low door a tiny bell jangled to announce their arrival. They ducked below the lintel and entered. The bakehouse was the converted kitchen of the cottage. A large black range and several bread ovens filled most of the rear wall. In the middle of the warm room stood a long, well-scrubbed oak table, covered with loaves, pies and tarts of every size, shape and description. Behind the table stood a neat, brown-haired and heavily freckled woman in a frilled white cap, a striped dimity dress and a large white apron. Her sleeves were rolled up and her forearms were speckled with flour and freckles. 'Good day, Constable Clancy,' she said, smiling. 'Hungry again, are you?'

Clancy grinned.

'Who's yer friends?'

'Mrs Tilley?' Lavender asked. She nodded. 'I'm Detective Stephen Lavender from Bow Street in London and this is Constable Woods.'

She bobbed a curtsey. 'Pleased to meet you, sir. You've come to

49

catch the gang who murdered poor Mr Sculthorpe, I suppose? How can I help?'

'Is Doctor Wallace at home?' Lavender asked. 'I understand he lodges here. I would like to have a word with him, if possible.'

She shook her head. 'I'm afraid Doctor Wallace is out at his surgery in Market Harborough. There's only Mrs Wallace here at the moment.'

Lavender bit back his disappointment. 'The doctor practises medicine in Market Harborough?'

'That's right. They're just lodgin' here for a few months while their new house is made ready in the town. They've recently moved down here from Glasgow with their son, Jack. I'm afraid Doctor Wallace doesn't return home until about seven in the evenin'.'

'I'll call on him tonight,' Lavender said. 'In the meantime, Mrs Tilley, I understand Billy Sculthorpe is recovering from his injuries here in your care.'

'Yes. Captain Rushperry is payin' for his lodgings until they sort out his father's affairs. The poor soul has had a terrible ordeal.'

'Would it be possible for us to speak to him?'

She narrowed her eyes and scrutinised him coldly. 'I don't think all of you should go up to him – you'll scare him witless if you all troop into his room.'

'I understand,' Lavender said, nodding. 'Constable Clancy can remain downstairs but we'll eat first.'

'Can I interest you in a pigeon pie, perhaps?' Her face brightened. 'They're fresh out of the oven and still hot.'

The men nodded, handed over their coins and gratefully took hold of the warm pies. Unwilling to go back out into the cold street, they moved to a corner of the shop and enjoyed their meal. The pies were crammed full of thick gravy and tender chunks of pigeon breast with its distinctive livery taste. The warm, flaky pastry melted in their mouths.

'That were very tasty,' Woods said. Mrs Tilley beamed.

The doorbell tinkled again and two women with wicker baskets entered the bakehouse. They cast curious glances at the three men in the corner as they chatted with Mrs Tilley. When they had gone, Mrs Tilley wiped her floury hands on her apron and led Lavender and Woods through the rear door of the kitchen out into the cool hallway of the main house. They climbed the staircase and stopped outside a room on the first floor.

Mrs Tilley knocked tentatively on the door. 'Billy?' she called. 'Billy, there's some gentlemen to see you. Can they come in?' There was no reply. Lavender heard something shuffle across the floor.

Mrs Tilley sighed. 'He's not used to company,' she said. 'They kept him hidden at home and he never went out. He stays in this room all the time and draws things, horrible things.' She shuddered. 'He's used every piece of paper I have in the house.' She knocked again, sharper this time. 'Billy, we're comin' in now.'

The drapes were drawn across the window but a fire crackled in the grate of the darkened room and gave off a warm glow. In the gloom they saw a small, chubby figure in a voluminous nightgown seated on the floor surrounded by crayons and paper. Although he was seated, Lavender could tell Billy Sculthorpe was probably less than four foot tall. Billy glanced up towards them and Lavender heard Woods take a sharp intake of breath.

'Now, Billy! What have I told you about closing the drapes?'

'It will damage my eyes if I draw in the dark,' Billy replied in a flat, monotone mumble.

'That's right,' Mrs Tilley said. 'And you won't be able to draw if you damage your eyes.' She marched across to the windows and pulled back the drapes. Light flooded into the room and Billy blinked rapidly. A podgy hand shot up to protect his upward slanting eyes from the glare.

Mrs Tilley walked back to him and ruffled the thin, fair hair poking up out of the bandage encircling his flat forehead. 'Now you be a good lad and answer this gentleman's questions.' She walked towards the door. 'I'll be downstairs in the bakehouse if you need me, Detective,' she said.

For a moment Woods and Lavender just stared at Billy Sculthorpe. Apart from the bandage on his head wound, the man before them still had a mass of yellow bruises across his flattened face from the attack of the previous week. Unabashed, Billy stared back at them through his strange eyes. His mouth drooped and his jaw was slack. His thick tongue, the cause of his strange speech, protruded slightly from his mouth.

Billy Sculthorpe had some form of cretinism. Lavender had seen several of these disfigured and stunted creatures before, but he had never known one to survive into adulthood. Most cretins died in infancy or ended up hidden in asylums by their families. Worse still, some were smothered at birth by their parents. He had pulled the body of one out of the Thames last year. That baby girl had looked only a few hours old.

'My mammy says it's rude to stare,' Billy said suddenly. 'She calls me Billy-Boy.' He had a slight Irish lilt to his flat tone.

'Yes, she's right about the starin',' Woods said. He didn't correct Billy's use of the present tense when he talked about his mother. 'I'm called Ned. Can I talk to you for a moment?'

'I'm a cretin,' Billy said. 'But you're fat.'

Woods laughed and moved across the room. 'You may be right there, young man,' he replied. 'I eat too many pies. Do you like pies?' Woods sat down on the bed and leant a bit closer to the man on the floor. Billy twitched and shuffled back a fraction. Lavender caught a glimpse of his bare foot as he moved. There was a large separation between the young man's big toe and his second toe, another symptom of his condition. 'Ah sure, I like pies,' Billy said warily.

'Mrs Tilley bakes good pies,' Woods said. 'I've just had one. It were oozin' with thick gravy. Do you like Mrs Tilley's pies?'

Billy nodded and stared at Woods curiously. Lavender stood still and let Woods take the lead in the conversation. Woods, the family man. Woods, the loving father of four children – four beautiful, perfectly healthy and normal children.

Woods pointed down to the half-finished sketch of a large dog on the paper in front of Billy. The vicious-looking creature had malevolent eyes. 'What you got there, Billy-Boy?' he asked. 'What's that?'

'It's Black Shuck,' Billy said. He poked at the drawing with his pencil. 'He likes the water. He only comes out at night when it rains. He rolls in puddles and wades through streams swollen by the rainfall.'

'Sounds like a nice doggie,' Woods said.

'Ah no,' Billy corrected him. His face was deadly serious. 'His howl can make your blood run cold. You don't want to meet him in the dark.' His tongue poked out at the corner of his mouth again.

'I'll remember him,' Woods said. 'Was Black Shuck out and about in Middleton durin' the night of the storm – the night when those men broke into your home and attacked you and your da?'

Billy's puffy eyes narrowed and his flat forehead creased up in a frown. 'No,' he said and shook his head. 'I didn't see Black Shuck but he may have been outside howlin'. I wouldn't have heard him over the thunder. Black Agnes was abroad though,' he added. 'She tried to steal the children.'

'That were cruel of her,' Woods said sympathetically. 'Who else did you see that night?'

Billy flinched and his eyes dropped down to the floor. 'No one believes me, for sure,' he said sulkily.

'I will,' Woods promised.

Billy lifted his head and stared straight at him. 'The Dark Elves were there. The water from the Well at the World's End had poured out and they got through the breach.'

'How did you know they were the Dark Elves?'

'Because of their black faces, silly.'

Woods hesitated, lost for words.

'See, I knew you wouldn't believe me.' Billy lowered his head.

'Oh, I believe you, lad,' Woods said quickly. 'I'm just a bit shocked, that's all. It's grim news about them elves. I'll wager they were up to no good.'

'They were stealin' Mammy's furniture. I saw them takin' it.'

'How many of them were there, these elves?' Woods asked.

'There were three.'

'Did they take anything else?' Lavender asked suddenly.

Billy glanced across at him. 'Who are you?' he asked, his voice heavy with suspicion.

'I'm Stephen,' he said. 'I'm a friend of Ned's.'

'I don't have any friends,' Billy said. 'No one likes me.'

'Now, now, son,' Woods said gently. 'I think Mrs Tilley likes you. She seemed right fond of you to me.'

'Ah sure, Mrs Tilley likes me,' Billy brightened, 'and Doctor Wallace. But the bully boys don't.'

'How old are you, Billy?' Lavender asked.

'Mammy says I'm twenty-four years old. My birthday is the Feast of St Mary Magdalene. Mammy will bake me an almond pastry on the day.'

His eyes shone at the thought and his slack mouth curled up into a huge smile. *He looks quite nice when he smiles*, Lavender thought.

'St Mary Magdalene is the sweetest and strongest of the saints because her love was so great. Did you know this, Stephen?'

Lavender smiled back. 'No, I didn't,' he confessed. 'Thank you for telling me. I have a lady friend called Magdalena.'

'Oooh!' Billy laughed and his smile lit up his chubby face. Lavender and Woods found themselves smiling too. 'A laaady. She will be sweet and strong, for sure.'

Strong, maybe. Lavender smiled. 'Sweet' wasn't an adjective he would normally apply to Magdalena – she had too much spirit to be sweet.

Billy picked up his pencil and turned back to his paper. 'I will draw her for you. You must come back tomorrow.'

Lavender took a step forward and leant down towards the young man. 'Thank you, Billy,' he said. 'I will look forward to it. We'll come back tomorrow. But before we go, please tell me, did you see those bad elves take any of your father's money?'

Billy glanced up at him and frowned as if Lavender had asked him a stupid question. 'Of course not,' he said. 'They'd got it wrong.'

Lavender opened his mouth to question him further but closed it again. Billy had turned his back on them and bent over his paper again. They had been dismissed. Lavender caught Woods' eye and jerked his own head in the direction of the door. Woods nodded and stood up. 'We'll leave you for now, Billy-Boy,' he said.

But Billy Sculthorpe was too engrossed in his work to reply. The figure of a woman with flowing hair and a swirling gown appeared on the paper beside the evil hound, Black Shuck.

Chapter Seven

They closed the door gently behind them and paused on the chilly landing.

'What now?' Woods asked.

'This case gets more complicated by the minute,' Lavender said grimly. 'I need some time to think. We also need to send Clancy back to Market Harborough with Sculthorpe's reliquary as soon as he has introduced us to Constable Sawyer – and we need to find a place to stay in this village tonight.'

Woods smiled. 'Well, I reckon we should visit The Woolpack. You can do your thinkin' over a tankard of ale and we can ask about a room for the night while we're there. That pie were very tasty but I need something to wash it down.'

Lavender nodded. The salt in the gravy had left him with a thirst.

They collected Clancy and walked the short distance to the tavern at the end of the village high street. This double-fronted house had low rectangular windows on either side of the door and a wooden sign above it that read 'Francis Bunning: Cobbler'. A large assortment of men's working boots stood in rows in the low windows.

'This is an inn?' Woods asked, surprised.

'Yes, Bunnin' has turned his parlour into a taproom for the local farmers,' Clancy explained. 'It gets quite busy at night. By day he works as a cobbler in the outhouse at the back. A lot of the folks in the village have two occupations.'

'Very enterprising,' Woods said.

Bunning's deserted parlour-cum-tavern was a cold, plain, drab room with scuffed and muddied floorboards and a few low tables and stools. An ancient longcase clock in the corner of the room broke up the monotony of the furnishings. Badly scratched and battered, it was missing the glass cover that should have protected the white face with its twelve Roman numerals. Yet despite this, the exposed hands of the clock still continued their juddering, stilted journey around the dial accompanied by a sonorous ticking. Instinctively, Lavender pulled out his pocket watch and checked the time.

Clancy leant closer and peered over his shoulder. 'Well, this clock is set at the right time anyway,' he said.

Lavender snapped shut the casing and returned his watch to his pocket. 'You're a quick learner, Constable Clancy,' he said.

A young woman with long unkempt hair sidled into the room draped in an old gown that was several sizes too large for her. Her shoulders slouched forward as she walked and the dirty hem of the gown trailed behind her on the floor. She carried three tankards and a jug of ale in her hands. 'You be wantin' ale?' she asked. A sensual smile spread across her face.

'If you don't mind so early in the day, Susie,' Clancy said pleasantly. 'How are you keepin', by the way?' He sat down at one of the low tables. Lavender and Woods followed his lead.

The young woman placed the pewter tankards in front of them and pushed her body next to Clancy's shoulder. 'Oh, I be keepin' fine,' she drawled in Clancy's ear. 'All the better fer seein' you, my bonny lad.' She leant forward to pour out the ale and her gown fell away to reveal her deep cleavage and the curvaceous mounds of her flesh. Her breasts strained to be released from her bodice. Clancy blushed but his eyes couldn't help themselves. 'That's grand, Susie,' he said lamely.

'Thank you for the ale,' Lavender said as he picked up his drink. His tone cut through the atmosphere of enforced intimacy like ice. 'Can we speak to Mr Bunning?'

'Which one?' The girl glanced up at him and smiled. She twirled a loose strand of greasy hair around her dirty finger. 'There's two of 'em Bunnin's at work in the back.'

'Mr Frank Bunning,' Lavender said. The woman made no attempt to leave. She eyed Lavender up and down. The tip of her tongue flicked out and licked her smiling lips. 'Yer an 'andsome swell,' she drawled. 'Do yer have a sweetheart?'

'I do,' Lavender said. 'We're to be married soon. Leave the jug on the table before you go.' The girl scowled at the abrupt dismissal and sidled back out of the room.

'That's Susie Dicken, Bunnin''s housekeeper,' Clancy said. 'He took her out of the poorhouse to work here.'

Woods drained the last of his ale from his tankard, gave an appreciative belch and reached for the jug. 'Looks to me like she's the kind of gal who keeps more than the kitchen range stoked on a night,' he said with a wink.

Clancy smiled. 'Bunnin''s smitten with her,' he whispered. 'There's rumours he plans to marry her.'

'Good luck to the man,' Woods said as he refilled his tankard. 'Those gals from the poorhouse can be jiltish ladybirds.'

A bald, plain-looking man in his mid-forties appeared, wiping his hands on a soiled cloth. Shoemakers' tools, pliers and a hammer poked out of the pocket of his grey apron. Frank Bunning had an unhealthy complexion and small, nervous eyes. Despite the chill of the room, he also had beads of sweat across his pale forehead.

Lavender introduced himself and Woods.

'I've already told Constable Clancy everythin' there is to be said about that dreadful night,' Bunning said, frowning. 'I don't think there is much I can add.'

'Tell me again,' Lavender said.

Bunning shrugged. ''Twere a bad night,' he said. 'That storm brewed for hours. Some of my regulars came in early and disappeared back to their homes before the rain came. By the time the storm broke, I only had a couple of customers still in here.'

'Can you remember who they were?' Lavender asked.

Bunning's large, white forehead creased into a frown. 'Old Pete Jarman were one of them. He never misses a night, does Old Pete. He spends hours sat by my fire with a single tankard of ale.'

'Anyone else?'

Bunning shook his head. 'I can't remember,' he said, 'but I remember the shock when Jed Sawyer staggered through the door and told us he'd been pounced upon by a gang of villains.'

'What time was this?' Lavender asked.

Bunning pointed to the old clock in the corner. ''Twere just afore ten o'clock. A quarter off the hour. I'd just checked the time and were thinkin' about shuttin' up for the night. There didn't seem to be much profit in stayin' open for longer.'

'What kind of state were he in?' Woods asked. 'Sawyer, I mean.'

'A bad one,' Bunning replied. 'His face were bloodied and the bastards had nearly broken his arm. He'd had to run fer his life.'

'What happened next?' Lavender asked. He wanted to ask what a 'nearly broken' arm was but decided to stick to his main line of questioning for the moment.

'Well, me and my nephew – and Harry Goode, he were still here – we raced down to Sculthorpe's cottage as fast as we could. I thought the old fellah had already gone but when Doctor Wallace arrived, he said Sculthorpe were still breathin'.'

'Did you see or hear anyone in the street when you left here?'

'No, the streets were deserted. Sawyer said the gang had run off in the opposite direction. The whole village were shut indoors, waitin' out the damned storm.'

'This Harry Goode,' Lavender asked. 'Who is he?'

'He's a labourer up at the Home Farm. Why?'

'I wondered if he'd been in the tavern all night.'

Bunning frowned as he struggled to remember. 'Yes – no. No. He'd come in a few minutes earlier. He said the storm had woken him up and he might as well sit in here with a brandy as at home.'

'And he arrived before Constable Sawyer came through the door?'

'That's right.'

'You've been very helpful, Mr Bunning,' Lavender said. 'Just one final question: did William Sculthorpe ever drink in here?'

Bunning nodded. 'Yes, he were partial to a glass of brandy,' he said. 'He once let it slip that Lady Anne from Rockingham gave him a bottle or two now and then. When it ran out, he'd come in here.'

Lavender frowned. 'Lady Anne Fitzwilliam sent William Sculthorpe brandy?'

Bunning nodded. 'It's about the only thing I know about him. Quiet, broodin' old fellah, he was. When he came here, he'd buy a glass and sit with Old Pete by the fire. A right pair of miserable bookends they were.'

'This is helpful,' Lavender reiterated.

'Well, I does what I can.' Bunning seemed embarrassed by the compliment. 'What happened that night were shockin'. Sculthorpe were a miserly old beggar but he didn't deserve to die like that.'

Lavender asked him about a room for the night, and the landlord confirmed he had an empty bedchamber upstairs.

Suddenly, they heard the outer door open and felt a draught of cold air swirl through the room. In the hallway outside a man laughed. 'Afternoon, Susie,' said a loud voice. 'My, you look like a rum duchess today.'

'It's Constable Sawyer,' Clancy said, rising to his feet.

A stocky man in an old black coat with tarnished silver buttons entered the room. A dirty sling held his right arm against his chest. Susie Dicken sidled in behind him, grinning.

Clancy greeted Jed Sawyer warmly and introduced Lavender and Woods. Sawyer grasped Lavender's hand like a vice and shook it firmly.

'Jedediah Sawyer, sir. At your service.' Sawyer was about fifty years old. A shaggy, unkempt mane of grey hair fell down to his shoulders from beneath his hat.

Sawyer turned and gave Clancy a friendly slap on the back. The younger man staggered beneath the force of the blow. 'Is he doin' well, assistin' you in your inquiries?' Sawyer asked. 'He's a good lad is Sam. Known him ever since he joined us as a Johnny Newcombe. Taught him everythin' I know, I did.'

'It didn't take him long to do that,' Clancy quipped. Sawyer threw back his head and burst into laughter. His teeth were black with rot and several of them were missing.

'Constable Clancy's help has been invaluable,' Lavender said, smiling.

Sawyer carried another stool over to their table and joined them. 'I heard you'd arrived. I've been lookin' for you all over the damned village,' he said. 'I might have known young Clancy here would be in a tavern. He likes a knock-me-down, does our Sam.' He winked at the younger man, who flushed. 'I'll take a bumper tankard of ale with these gentlemen, Susie, my love.'

The woman disappeared out of the room, quickly followed by Frank Bunning. Lavender sensed the landlord's relief that his own interrogation was now over.

'So how are your inquiries proceedin', sir?' Sawyer rubbed his bushy sideburns with his hand. 'Have you made any arrests yet?' His bright eyes beneath his thick, greying eyebrows flicked curiously between Lavender and Woods.

'I'm glad you've found us, Constable Sawyer,' Lavender said. 'I wanted to ask you in person about the events of the night of the attack.'

Susie returned with her jug of ale and a fresh pewter tankard for Sawyer. 'Give us a kiss, wench,' Sawyer said with a grin as she poured his drink.

'Eugh, yer need a shave,' she complained.

Sawyer raised his bandaged elbow. 'You try shavin' with one good arm, gal,' he said. 'Mind you, the other rammer still works fine,' he added with a grin. To prove his point, he grabbed the woman around her waist and pulled her down into his lap.

She squealed and scrambled to her feet, laughing. Ale slopped over the edge of her jug onto the stone floor. 'Gerroff! You old goat!'

Lavender sat back and quietly watched their horseplay. Sawyer's injuries didn't seem to have damaged his high spirits, he noted. The woman eventually escaped Sawyer's clutches. He deftly tossed her a coin for the ale and she sidled out of the room.

'Rammer?' Woods said. 'I haven't heard that expression for a while. It's army slang, isn't it? Musket-ramming arm. Were you in the army?'

'Aye, thirty years ago.' Sawyer grimaced at the memory. 'I were a swaddy with Lord Cornwallis and the 33rd in the Americas when those bastards kicked us out of the colony. Took part in the Siege of Charleston, I did – and the Battle of Yorktown, where the buggers finally beat us.'

'Those must have been hard times,' Woods said sympathetically.

'Yes,' Sawyer said. 'I were injured, worn out.' His face brightened and he pointed to his bandaged arm. 'A bit like now. I'm a bad bargain now as a constable.'

'Oh, I'm sure you'll still be able to help us with our inquiries,' Lavender said. 'I read the statement you wrote for the coroner's inquest. In it, you said you were doing your evening patrol through the two villages when you saw the villains.'

Sawyer took a deep gulp of his ale, then wiped away the moisture from his mouth with the back of his sleeve. 'Yes, that's right. I were just walkin' down the high street. I saw several men comin' out of the alleyway where Sculthorpe lived –'

'When was this?'

'Just after half past nine.'

'How many men?' Lavender asked.

'There were three at that point. They had blackened their faces with sommat. I took out my cudgel, yelled at them and moved closer. I saw the whites of their eyes in those heathen-black faces beneath their hats.'

'What happened next?'

'I looked down the alley and saw two more villains leaving Sculthorpe's front door. Then the bastards set about me. It happened so fast I didn't have time to run. One of them swiped me with a cudgel of his own and another smashed me in the face.' His hand went instinctively to the cuts and bruises across his cheek and nose. 'I thought the sods had broken me nose, I did.'

'So there were five men in total?'

'Yes, there were five. Definitely five. I hit out with my own stick and I reckon I hit home – one of those bastards will have had a sore head the next day. But there were too many of them for me and my rammer were killin' me with the pain of it. I managed to get past them and belted hell for leather down here. I knew I'd get help from the Bunnin's.'

'It were courageous to try and tackle them villains on your own,' Woods said.

Sawyer gave a short laugh. 'Or bloody foolish,' he said. He took another swig of his drink. 'But we law men have to do what we can, don't we?'

'Yes, we do,' Lavender agreed. 'When did you and the others return to Sculthorpe's house?'

Sawyer shrugged. 'A couple of minutes later.'

'Was there any sign of your attackers?'

'None. Isaac Bunnin' and Harry Goode raced down the street after them, while Frank and I went into the house to check on old Sculthorpe and his son. We found them in a bad way. When Isaac and Harry came back, they said they'd seen no one. The bastards had disappeared. Isaac went to get Doctor Wallace.'

'What was the weather like?' Lavender asked.

'Still pourin' with rain. It were a devil of a night.'

Lavender turned to Clancy. 'Are there any stables in the village other than at the forge? They might have escaped on horseback.'

Clancy shook his head. 'I asked at the forge the next day,' he said, 'and at the hostelry in Cottingham. Nobody left any unattended horses in either village on the night of the murder.'

'So, unless they abandoned their animals at some remote spot outside the village, they must have travelled on foot,' Lavender said thoughtfully.

'The thunder would have scared the horses to death,' Woods added. 'They'd have tried to bolt – especially if they were left out in the open.'

'So the attackers disappeared into thin air somewhere along the road to Cottingham or Rockingham,' Lavender said.

'It seems so,' Sawyer said. 'Which makes me suspect it were that Panther Gang. They're notorious for just disappearin' after a robbery.'

'Possibly,' Lavender said. 'Do you have any other suspects?'

Sawyer laughed. 'Half the village has come forward with suggestions,' he said. 'There's a few folks around here who want to pay off old scores by pointin' the finger at their feudin' neighbours.'

'Are any of these leads promising?' Lavender asked.

'Old Sculthorpe had been seen arguin' in the street with a local farmer the week before the attack,' Clancy said, 'but I interviewed him and he has an alibi. He claims he were tucked up in bed with his wife.'

'Who is he?' Lavender's eyebrows rose along with his hopes.

'Caleb Liquorish,' Clancy replied. 'He's the churchwarden at St Mary Magdalene's in Cottingham.'

Lavender frowned and his hopes sank again. He and Woods paid little attention to alibis provided by wives, but Liquorish's respectability made him an unlikely suspect. However, it was still worth following up.

Sawyer shook his shaggy head as if he could read Lavender's thoughts. 'You'll waste your time investigatin' Caleb Liquorish, sir,' he said. 'He's a rich man. Old Sculthorpe's money wouldn't interest the likes of him.' He jabbed his finger on the table to emphasise the next point. 'It were the Panther Gang who did this,' he said. 'You mark my words.'

'I understand there are rumours in the village that William Sculthorpe was a rich man. Who started these tales?' Lavender asked. Clancy and Sawyer glanced at each other, shrugged and shook their heads.

Lavender turned to Jed Sawyer. 'Did you, or anyone else in the village, know the Sculthorpe family were Catholics?'

Sawyer's eyes lit up. 'I knew his missus were originally from Bog Land,' Sawyer said, 'but I didn't know they were papists.'

'Is that why they murdered him, do you think?' Clancy asked. 'Because he were a Catholic?'

Woods shrugged. 'We still have trouble sometimes down in London,' he said. 'There's still arson attacks on property and businesses owned by Catholics – but no murders.'

Lavender turned back to Clancy. 'How far have you travelled with your inquiries?' he asked. 'Have you asked the property owners along the road to Rockingham if they saw or heard anything unusual?'

Clancy looked embarrassed. 'There hasn't been time to spread out so far,' he said. 'I only had one day here – and in Cottingham – after the attack. Captain Rushperry said there were no point once he knew you two were comin'.'

Lavender nodded. 'This will be a line of inquiry we can pursue,' he said to Woods. 'We'll spread out along the roads into and out of the village and ask those who live by their side if they remember a gang of strangers that night.'

'And what about the money bag I found the day after the attack?' Clancy asked. 'The one with the strange note screwed up in the bottom? I handed it straight to Captain Rushperry.'

'Yes, what about it?' Sawyer asked.

Both constables watched Lavender curiously. He shrugged. 'I suspect it's nothing,' he said. 'An angry note from a customer pursued by a shopkeeper for a debt.' He rose to his feet. Woods and Clancy followed his lead. 'You have been very helpful, Constable Sawyer,' he said. 'We'll leave you in peace now to enjoy your ale. Take care of your bad arm.'

'Any time, Detective,' Sawyer said. He tapped the sling. 'This is healin' nicely and I'm no slacker. I should be able to return to work soon and help you catch these blackguards.'

Chapter Eight

They returned to Sculthorpe's cottage and collected the silver reliquary for Clancy to take back to Captain Rushperry in Market Harborough.

Lavender breathed a sigh of relief as he watched the young constable canter away down the high street with the precious object carefully wrapped in sackcloth in his saddlebag.

'Why are you so keen to get rid of him?' Woods asked. 'You've been frosty with both young Clancy and Sawyer all day.'

'It's your imagination, Ned,' Lavender said. 'Let's take a walk. I need to clear my head.' Woods shrugged and fell into step beside him. They walked in the direction of Cottingham, striding in companionable silence.

The rows of light-stone cottages ended abruptly and the road took them into an area of common land that had been cleared and divided into strips for the villagers to grow vegetables and herbs. To their left the meadow sloped downhill into the Welland valley. In the centre of the meadow a rush-fringed duck pond glimmered in the weak sunshine. Sheep, lambs and geese grazed on the lush grass.

Ahead of them, the road veered up to the right and entered Cottingham, Middleton's neighbouring village. The two communities were less than half a mile apart. Stone cottages with slate roofs and smoking chimneys lay dotted up the wooded hillside. At the summit of the ridge, the towering medieval steeple of the Church of St Mary Magdalene, with its arched belfry windows, finials and stone tracery, rose majestically above the tree tops. Lavender had made enquiries about the church before they left the tavern. Frank Bunning had informed him that St Mary Magdalene served the parishioners of both Cottingham and Middleton. Magdalene. Magdalena. Lavender smiled and remembered Billy Sculthorpe's words earlier. His beloved was haunting this investigation – he felt her presence with him at every turn.

He stopped beside a drystone wall and leant on it, arms folded in front of him. His eyes followed the contours of the gently rolling valley before settling on the duck pond. Pairs of mallards and a solitary swan scavenged for titbits among the reeds. Woods stood beside him at the wall.

'So what do we think about this murder then?' Woods asked.

Lavender smiled. 'One of these days, Ned, I shall ask you the same question and I'll expect you to have the answers.'

'Well, that'll be a short conversation,' Woods replied, smiling. 'Solvin' these mysteries is your job – I'm just here to provide the backup. It would addle my old brain to have to think so much.'

Lavender smiled again. He always welcomed the opportunity to talk through a case with Woods. 'To be honest, Ned, my own brain is addled at the moment. I can't work out why these witness accounts are so different. Five men attacked Jed Sawyer –'

'It were brave of him to confront them,' Woods said. 'The man's a hero.'

'Yes, quite. And we have three other witnesses,' Lavender continued, 'who tell us there were three people in the Sculthorpes' house on the night of the attack.'

'Yes, but they're two scared old ladies and a simpleton.'

Lavender paused for a moment. 'I think Billy Sculthorpe is a strange creature but I didn't find him simple-minded. He might not be able to dress himself but I think he knows what he saw.'

'Perhaps three of them were in the house while the others stood guard outside?' Woods suggested.

Lavender nodded. 'Yes, that would make sense. And perhaps the three men Miss Bennett saw leaving the house after ten o'clock were Sawyer and the other men he had recruited to help Sculthorpe. Maybe she didn't see the robbers, maybe she saw the rescuers. But what is the motive for this crime, Ned?'

'Theft, surely?'

'If so, why lash out at the old man and cause fatal injuries after he had already told the thieves where he hoarded his money? Why hurt him when they had already got what they wanted? In my experience this is more akin to an act of vengeance or hatred. It's also at odds with the *modus operandi* of those devils, the Panthers.'

'The what, sir?'

'Their *modus operandi*, or their method of working. Rushperry told us the Panthers are armed. I assume they jam a pistol barrel into the temple of their victims and make them hand over their money and jewels. As far as we have heard, the Panthers have never beaten anyone senseless during a robbery.'

Woods eyes widened beneath his shaggy grey eyebrows. 'So you don't think it were them?'

'Not at the moment,' Lavender said. 'And then there is the location and the weather to consider. Look around you, Ned.' He swept his arm around over the wall and pointed at the rolling fields, the secluded woods and the quiet villages on either side. A flock of crows rose cawing from the treetops in the copse below. The men stood in silence and watched the noisy birds as they wheeled and circled in the sky.

'What am I lookin' at, sir?' Woods asked eventually.

'The isolation, Ned. Sculthorpe was reputed to be a rich man – although we have found no evidence of this yet. But who knew about his alleged wealth? Rumours started in Middleton would barely have spread beyond Rockingham. So how did a gang who operate in the south of the county hear about the thousands of pounds William Sculthorpe allegedly kept in his house?'

'I see what you're gettin' at,' Woods said. 'But how does the weather figure in all this?'

'On the night of the robbery it rained heavily and a terrible storm raged. Bad weather is the best thing to keep the villains and coves off the streets of London. This robbery was planned out in advance but not by villains with a long way to travel. Such a gang would have turned back once the storm broke and left the robbery until a night when the weather was better. After all, there was no rush. William Sculthorpe wasn't going anywhere.'

'Unless they deliberately used the noise and disruption of the storm as cover for the attack,' Woods said.

'Yes.' Lavender sighed. 'But my instinct is this is a local job. I think the thieves are members of this community who scurried back to their dry homes afterwards. However, we need to prove this. Tomorrow I want you to travel up and down the roads in and out of Middleton. Knock at the door of every dwelling place you find and ask questions about the night of the storm. Let's establish beyond a doubt that no one saw or heard the gang entering or leaving the area.'

Woods nodded but Lavender felt him hesitate. A slight frown spread across his constable's broad forehead. 'It seems too much for a small county such as this,' Woods said slowly, 'to be plagued with two gangs – both with five members – hell-bent on robbery and mayhem.'

Lavender smiled at Woods' reluctance to let go of the idea that the Panther Gang were involved. 'According to Captain Rushperry, the *Northampton Mercury* has whipped the whole county into a frenzy over this Panther Gang. So when five men are seen running away from the scene of a crime, everyone makes an assumption and imaginations become fevered.'

'So who were it who robbed Sculthorpe?'

'Well, I don't know yet, do I?' Lavender said peevishly. 'Give me some time, Ned. I've only been here a day. We need to learn more about William Sculthorpe, his life – and his enemies. From what we have seen and heard so far Sculthorpe was a secretive man. He's an enigma. I want to know more about him. We shall return to see Billy Sculthorpe tomorrow and ask him about his father, and perhaps my interview with Lady Anne at Rockingham Castle will shed some more light on the past history of this man.'

Woods nodded. 'Yes,' he said. 'I were a bit surprised to find out she supplied him with bottles of the best brandy.'

Lavender nodded. 'Captain Rushperry told us Sculthorpe had been in service with Lady Anne but this generosity towards a former employee goes beyond the kindness usually shown to servants.' A cold breeze had blown up. Lavender pulled down his hat and stepped back from the wall.

Instinctively, Woods followed him. 'So what do you want us to do now?'

Lavender glanced up at the sky. The sun was already sinking in the west. He fished inside his coat pocket, pulled out the ragged money bag Rushperry had given him, and gave it to Woods. 'We've still got a couple of hours of daylight left,' he said. 'You can investigate the origins of this bag and I will make discreet inquiries about the owner of the initials *J.W.* I'll go up to the church and ask the vicar for the registers. The names and the history of most people in both Cottingham and Middleton will be recorded in them.'

'What do you want me to do?'

'Take this bag around every shop and business establishment you can find in the two villages and ask the proprietors if they recognise it. And while you're there, find out who ran up the largest debts this winter. If money was the reason for Sculthorpe's murder, I want to know the names of those with the greatest poverty and, hence, the greatest motive.'

Woods' eyes narrowed and he glanced at Lavender suspiciously. 'You told Sawyer and Clancy this bag and the note weren't important.'

'I may have lied,' Lavender replied. 'We'll meet back at The Woolpack. I need to write a letter to London before I call on Doctor Wallace tonight.' He turned on his heel in the direction of Cottingham.

Suddenly, he stopped and glanced back over his shoulder. 'And while you're at the grocer's, Ned – ask them if they have ever sold ink cap mushrooms to William Sculthorpe.'

Chapter Nine

Lavender trudged up the steep cobbled lane towards St Mary Magdalene's Church and craned back his neck to admire the towering gothic spire which rose up into the cloudy sky above him. *Northamptonshire: the county of spires and squires*, he reminded himself.

Three weathered gargoyles glared down at him with stony eyes as he pushed open the creaking gate and wound his way along the path through the unkempt graveyard. The heavy arched door groaned as he pushed it open and entered the church. It took a moment for his eyes to adjust to the gloom of the lofty interior. Several octagonal limestone pillars held up the dark, vaulted wooden ceiling. Dusty beams of daylight slanted down from the tall, stained-glass windows. The cloying smell of old masonry, musty tapestries and centuries of damp mingled with the beeswax polish used on the wooden pews.

Two men stood talking by the ornate, carved pulpit at the end of the aisle – a carpenter, instantly recognisable by the tools he carried, and a middle-aged man with a full set of bushy whiskers and a well-cut topcoat and hat.

Lavender introduced himself to the two men and enquired about the whereabouts of the vicar.

'I'm afraid the Reverend Allingham is visiting a parishioner at the moment,' said the man with the beard. 'May I be of assistance, Detective? I'm Caleb Liquorish, the churchwarden.' He had barely a hint of the regional accent. Lavender remembered what Sawyer had said about Liquorish being a wealthy local landowner and farmer.

'Thank you,' Lavender said. 'If you don't mind, I'd like to go see the grave of the late William Sculthorpe and afterwards I want to peruse the church registers.'

Liquorish's dull brown eyes widened in surprise beneath their bushy brows but he nodded agreement. 'The registers are locked in the vestry at the moment but I have the key.' He gave a last couple of instructions to the carpenter, then led Lavender outside into the overgrown graveyard that encircled the church. 'Our sexton is ill at the moment,' he said, in apology for the weeds.

Sculthorpe's grave was a simple affair. A single mound of earth in a quiet corner with a plain gravestone propped up against the wall, waiting for the earth to settle so it could be put into position.

William Sculthorpe
Died aged 86
22nd February 1810

'Lady Anne from Rockingham paid for the headstone,' Liquorish said.

The Lady Anne. Again, Lavender thought. 'Why is Mr Sculthorpe not buried with his wife? I understand she died last August.'

Liquorish's mouth set in a thin line of disapproval before he answered. 'She isn't buried here,' he said. 'She had expressed a wish to be taken home to be buried, and that's what Mr Sculthorpe did.'

'What, to Ireland?' Lavender asked, sharply.

'No, Mrs Sculthorpe was from London, and she wanted to be laid to rest there. This was a ridiculous notion if you ask me, but he took her body back to be buried. Reverend Allingham warned Sculthorpe he was too elderly to undertake such a long and distressing journey, but he insisted. I understand his neighbour Miss Bennett took care of his backward son while he was gone. When Mr Sculthorpe was murdered we organised a simple ceremony here after the inquest.'

Lavender nodded. A cold breeze tugged at their hats and flapped their coat-tails.

'How well did you know William Sculthorpe?'

Liquorish stiffened. 'I didn't know him at all. He never attended church and my farm is several miles away in Rockingham. Our paths never crossed but as the local churchwarden I was involved in the arrangements for his funeral.'

'You said your paths never crossed, Mr Liquorish, but I understand you argued with him in the street the week before he died. What was that about?'

'I have already explained this to Constable Clancy.' Liquorish's voice turned to ice and his face darkened with anger. 'I simply tried to persuade him to come to church. A slothful attitude to church attendance is an affront to God. I was concerned that a man of his age should make his peace with God before it was too late, and I was right. Sculthorpe died without God's blessing and forgiveness.'

Lavender's eyes narrowed. Liquorish avoided his gaze. 'I gather you didn't know that William Sculthorpe and his family were Catholics who worshipped quietly at home?'

Liquorish gasped and disapproval followed by anger flashed across his face. 'No, I was not aware of that – and neither to my knowledge were the Reverend Allingham or the Lady Anne. I must inform them immediately.'

Lavender opened his mouth to ask another question, but Liquorish hadn't finished.

'Why, this is the essence of Lucifer! Sculthorpe's lunatic son must be baptised into the Anglican Church. We watchdogs of the fold cannot be silent with the evil of popery in our midst.'

A wave of disgust swept through Lavender but he held back the angry retort that leapt to his own lips. He was suddenly sick of Caleb Liquorish. 'Take me to the vestry,' he snapped. 'I wish to see the church registers.'

Liquorish unlocked the gloomy vestry, gave him a pile of dusty registers and left him alone to read them. Lavender pulled up a chair at the desk and lit a candle. As he flicked through the birth, death and marriage registers of the Parish of St Mary Magdalene the first thing that struck him was how rarely the Reverend Allingham had been called upon to administer to the needs of his flock. There had only been two weddings since Christmas. Lavender's maternal grandfather had been the popular Dean of St Saviour and St Mary Overie in Southwark before his retirement and not a week had gone by without him being called upon to perform marriages and baptisms. Of course, Southwark was a far larger and more overcrowded parish but it didn't look like business had been brisk for the vicar of Cottingham and Middleton over the last year.

As Lavender turned back the pages of the fusty old registers, he saw several names he recognised. Mrs Tilley at the bakehouse had an extensive family within the community – the name Tilley cropped up frequently in the registers. Jed Sawyer had married in the church eight years ago and his two children had been baptised there. The labourer Harry Goode had married at St Mary Magdalene ten years ago and, according to the baptism register, he and his wife already had six children – including a set of twins. Some woman called

Martha Bunning had died a couple of years ago. Was she the wife of Frank Bunning, the landlord of The Woolpack, perhaps? Or maybe the mother of Bunning's nephew Isaac?

Lavender stopped speculating, refocused on his task and looked for names to match the initials *J.W.* A young woman called Jane Webb had borne two illegitimate children in the parish and both bore her surname, but apart from her the only other family whose surname began with a '*W*' were the Wynns – and none of them had a first initial '*J*'.

Disappointed, he sighed and closed the tattered covers of the registers. Pulling on his gloves and hat, he left the vestry. Liquorish and the carpenter were still in the church. Lavender took Liquorish aside and asked him about the whereabouts of the woman called Jane Webb and the Wynn family.

'Jane Webb left the area last summer,' Liquorish informed him with a sneer. 'And she took her bastards along with her. She went to Coventry, I understand. We were glad to see her go. There's no place in Cottingham for women with loose morals and fallen ways. As for the Wynns, well, there's only old Simon and his wife left. They're both elderly and in the poorhouse at the edge of the village.'

Lavender thanked him and took his leave, grateful to be back outside in the fresh air, away from the stench of bigotry that swirled around Caleb Liquorish like flies buzzing over a carcass.

Chapter Ten

Lavender decided to take the path over the top fields along the ridge in order to return to The Woolpack. He estimated it would bring him out onto the steep hill, with the school and the lime kiln, where they had first ridden into Middleton earlier that morning.

The path wound through the meadow and entered a copse of elms. The new foliage on the trees formed a pale green haze that blurred the sharp angles and outlines of the twigs. As the last of the daylight filtered through the tree canopy it created a dappled effect on the carpet of dead leaves covering his path.

To his left, a branch cracked beneath the foot of a heavy animal. *Deer?* He glanced up and glimpsed the shadowy figure of a man disappear behind the tree trunks and into the dense undergrowth. The hair stood up on the back of his neck. He paused for a moment, then scoffed at his own foolishness. *I've spent too much time dodging cut-throats and silk-snatchers in London,* he decided. It was probably just an innocent farm labourer on his way home from the fields.

He didn't see a soul during the rest of his walk and he welcomed the peace and isolation – it gave him time to think. He hoped Woods had experienced better luck with his investigation into the origins of the mysterious cloth bag.

As he had expected, the path brought him to the steep hill at the far side of Middleton near the village school. He knew the pupils would have long since departed but candlelight still glimmered in the window. Suddenly, he had an idea. He leapt up the steps of the schoolhouse and rapped on the door.

A blast of hot air and the smell of tobacco smoke made Lavender blink when the door finally opened. A bald, fat man in his shirt sleeves with a brightly checked waistcoat stretched across his rotund belly clutched a pipe in one ink-stained hand and held the door open with the other.

'Are you the schoolmaster? I'm Detective Stephen Lavender. I'm investigating the murder of William Sculthorpe.'

'Ah, yes, poor old fellow,' said the man. 'I'm Mr Howard, the schoolmaster. How can I help you?'

If Mr Howard was surprised by Lavender's request to see the school register, he didn't show it. He led Lavender into the warm schoolroom, forced his bulk down into his chair and slid the register across the desk to the detective. A pile of papers, covered with childish scrawl, sat on the corner of the desk, a quill abandoned and dripping by their side. Howard puffed on his pipe while Lavender scanned through the names in the book.

It didn't take him long to go through the register. The school only had ten pupils and the only boy with a surname starting with '*W*' was *John Debussy Wallace*, aged twelve.

'Is this Jack Wallace, the son of Doctor Wallace?' he asked.

'That's right,' the schoolmaster confirmed. 'The boy is named John but I understand he's called Jack at home.'

Wallace. Doctor Wallace. Lavender hesitated. What had Mrs Tilley said about the family? That they were lodging with her while their new house was being refurbished in Market Harborough? It sounded like the Wallaces were just passing through the village, but he resolved to find out the first name of the doctor.

'May I ask another favour of you, Mr Howard?' he said. 'I would like to purchase some coloured wax crayons and paper, if I may. Do you have any to spare?' The schoolmaster did and supplied Lavender with a packet of crayons and an artist's sketch pad.

Lavender thanked him and resumed his journey back down the hill to The Woolpack. The purchases in his coat pocket banged against his thigh as he walked.

A fire blazed in the hearth of the taproom when Lavender returned to The Woolpack, but although it took the chill off the cold, it was still a dreary place. Several powerfully built and hard-featured local men were now seated around the low tables, sipping ale, talking quietly and smoking their pipes. They glanced up when Lavender entered but made no attempt to engage him in conversation. Several sheepdogs lay exhausted across the flagstones like matted black and white rugs. The room stank of tobacco, body odour and wet dog. Susie Dicken glided amongst them in her oversized gown, giggling and flirting.

Lavender ordered a tankard of ale, found a quiet table and pulled out his ink and quill. The glassless face of the longcase clock in the corner of the room told him he had half an hour before the London mail coach would pause briefly outside the tavern on its way to the capital. He penned his letter quickly and downed his ale in one gulp when he heard the vehicle pull up outside. Grabbing his letter, he walked out into the cold street and handed it up to the coach drivers.

Frank Bunning stood beside the carriage, with a handful of letters from the mailman on the coach. 'There's a letter for you, Detective Lavender,' he said.

Lavender took it, thanked him and held up the letter to the light of the lantern dangling from the side of the coach. He recognised the handwriting of Captain Rushperry.

'Sir!' Woods strode up the street towards him, his cheeks reddened with the cold. The two men returned to the warmth of the tavern and ordered their supper and another tankard of ale from Susie Dicken.

'Well, that were a waste of time,' Woods said, after the woman left the room. 'No one recognised the money bag – I even went into the undertakers and asked them in there. There's a windmill, some distance out of Cottingham and I didn't make it there today, but I'll take the horse tomorrow and ask the miller if it is his.'

'It won't be worth it,' Lavender said. He had seen the windmill during his walk home from Cottingham. 'There was a westerly wind blowing the night of the storm. I doubt the bag will have blown all the way down into Middleton from the windmill against the force of the gale.' They kept their voices down as they talked. 'I think the bag blew in a westerly direction from this end of the village until it caught itself in the hedge where our sharp-eyed Constable Clancy found it.'

'Mmm,' Woods said. 'So it may have been used by the thieves to carry money out of Sculthorpe's house, after all?'

Lavender nodded and took a deep gulp of his drink. 'I think those coves found the money in that bag at Sculthorpe's. They carried it out and divided up their ill-gotten gains further down the street, before they parted. They didn't know about the note screwed up in the corner of the bag and threw it away into the wind.' He picked up the letter from Captain Rushperry and split open the seal. His eyes widened as he read the contents.

'So what about the note?' Woods asked. 'Did someone send it to Sculthorpe along with a payment of some kind?'

'They may have done,' Lavender said.

'Was he a moneylender, do you think?' Woods asked.

Lavender nodded. 'You may be right. According to Captain Rushperry, Sculthorpe had the means to be a moneylender.' He tapped the letter on the table before him. 'He has heard back from the bankers, Messrs Down, Thornton and Gill. William Sculthorpe had one thousand and fifty-seven pounds, seventeen shillings and sixpence held with them in his London account.'

Woods' tankard stopped midair and his mouth dropped open. 'How much do you suppose he kept in the house?' he asked.

Lavender shook his head. 'Unless we can find some sort of household account book we will never know. But at least young Billy Sculthorpe will be well cared for in the future. I doubt he will have to end his days in an asylum or the poorhouse.'

Woods smiled. 'If I didn't know you better, I'd say you've got a soft place in your heart for that young man – and don't deny it. I've wondered for the last ten minutes why you've got a sketch pad pokin' out of your coat pocket.'

'Nothing escapes you, Constable, does it?' Lavender pulled the crayons and pad out of his coat and slid them across to Woods. 'While I visit Lady Anne at Rockingham tomorrow, you can take this present to Billy Sculthorpe. Gain his trust and try and find out some more about his father. The man is an enigma and his son might have some answers to the mystery. He seemed to respond better to you.'

'Well, as we all know – you frighten the witnesses.'

'I'm supposed to frighten them,' Lavender said. 'I'm a detective.'

Woods grinned and put the crayons and pad in the pocket of his old brown coat. He picked up his tankard and had another drink.

'What about the mushrooms?' Lavender asked. 'Did you find out anything about them?'

Woods belched and wiped the beads of moisture from his mouth with his coat sleeve. 'Nothin',' he said. 'None of the grocers in Middleton or Cottingham sell mushrooms. They said the villagers prefer to go out into the fields and pick their own if they want them.'

'Which may be what William Sculthorpe did,' Lavender said, 'but unlike most of the villagers, he's not country born and bred. He probably didn't recognise the danger of those ink cap mushrooms when he harvested them.'

'I had a bit of luck with the names of bad debtors though,' Woods said. He glanced around to check no one was listening. 'It's Harry Goode – the one who helped out on the night of the murder. He's bushed. He owes money right, left and centre throughout the two villages. There's eleven shillin's at the grocers on his account and another five at the drapers. One pound and eleven shillin's with the butcher in Cottingham.'

'He's over there.' Lavender nodded towards a tall, lanky man in a threadbare coat on the opposite side of the tavern. Long, greasy hair hung either side of a pair of enormous jug ears and framed a face ravaged with the smallpox.

'What? The ugly-lookin' fellah?' Woods asked.

Lavender nodded. 'He came in here about half an hour ago and I heard one of the others calling out his name.'

'His eyes are already shinin' with liquor,' Woods noted. 'So despite his poverty, he's still drinkin' in here every night?'

Lavender nodded. 'I saw in the baptism registry that he's got six children.'

'Huh!' Woods growled. 'And no doubt his hungry nippers are at home in a cold house while he plies himself with brandy.' He glowered his disapproval across the taproom. 'Did you track down anyone with the initials *J.W.*, by the way?'

Lavender sighed. 'Yes. There's a family called Wynn but they're elderly and in the poorhouse. The only other people with a "*W*" surname are the Wallaces, Doctor Wallace's family.'

'He's a *J.W.*,' Woods said. 'I were told by Mrs Tilley at the bake-house. His first name is John. Doctor John Wallace, he's called.'

'You went back to the bakehouse?'

'Well, I had to, didn't I? I had to ask Mrs Tilley about the cloth bag. And his wife too,' Woods added. 'She's also a *J.W.* She's called Judith Wallace.'

'Really?' Lavender said in surprise.

'Mind you,' Woods said thoughtfully, 'the note called someone an *"old bastard"*. That's not very ladylike language for a doctor's wife, is it?'

The corners of Lavender's mouth twitched. 'Exactly how long did you spend with Mrs Tilley and her hot pies?' he asked.

Susie Dicken arrived bearing two small bowls of thin stew and a couple of chunks of dry rye bread. She dumped them down unceremoniously in front of the two officers, then turned on her heel and left. The grey liquid and lumps of congealed fat swirled in the bowls and slopped over the sides. Lavender had seen more wholesome food dredged out of the mud at the bottom of the Thames.

'So how long were you at the bakehouse?' Lavender asked again.

'Not long enough,' his disappointed constable growled beside him.

Chapter Eleven

Mrs Tilley answered the door at Willow Cottage and led Lavender up the stairs to her guests' sitting room. It was a comfortable place with a large fireplace, a thick carpet and several well-upholstered chairs and sofas. A wooden clock ticked quietly on the mantelpiece, surrounded by several china figurines.

Doctor John Wallace was a thin, slightly built man with narrow features and greying hair. He had removed his cravat and undone the buttons on his waistcoat. Mrs Wallace sat with her embroidery in her lap in the fireside chair opposite her husband. Wallace stood up to greet Lavender and held out his hand. The detective thought he saw a flash of pain cross the man's pale face when he moved. Wallace had a limp, moist handshake.

'Please take a seat, Detective Lavender.' Wallace pointed to a vacant chair. He had a soft Scottish accent. 'You won't mind if mah wife stays? Mrs Wallace is familiar with all aspects of Mr Sculthorpe's murder and won't be distressed if we discuss it.' He sat down again beside the fireside, picked up a large lawn handkerchief and coughed quietly into the material.

Lavender bowed to Mrs Wallace. She wore a fetching white lace cap bordered with a broad ruffle over her dark hair. She nodded politely in Lavender's direction and resumed her needlework.

Lavender asked Wallace about the events of the night of the murder.

The doctor frowned. 'I'm nae sure what I can add tae what I've already told the authorities. Have you read the statement I gave tae the inquest?'

Lavender nodded. 'There are just a few issues I would like to clarify,' he said. 'Can either of you remember the exact time when Isaac Bunning came here to seek your assistance?' This was his last hope of clarifying the muddied timescale of the night of the murder.

Doctor Wallace and his wife looked at each other across the hearth, then shook their heads. 'I canna remember the time,' Wallace said. 'I dressed quickly, grabbed mah medical bag and followed young Bunning tae the Sculthorpes'.' He coughed again.

'And what about you, Mrs Wallace?' Lavender asked, disappointed. 'Can you remember the time?'

'I'm afraid not, Detective. We had more pressing things to deal with than checking the clock.' The woman's voice was crystal clear, without a trace of any regional accent but with a slight tone of disapproval. She was a good-looking woman, despite the stiffness of her manner. The couple were in their late forties but Judith Wallace looked younger. Her dark hair had been discreetly dyed and her muslin gown had a high, lacy neck to hide any sagging skin.

'I have seen where William Sculthorpe fell after the attack,' Lavender said. 'You mentioned in your statement there were also lacerations to the back of Sculthorpe's head. Is it possible these were caused when his head hit the kitchen wall as he was knocked backwards into the space between the dresser and the corner of the room?'

Wallace nodded. 'Aye, that's the most likely explanation.' His face dropped into a frown. 'I'll tell you this, Detective,' he said. 'I've been called tae attend the scene of some nasty murders in Glasgow, but it's a long time since I've seen such a brutal attack on a helpless auld man.'

Lavender nodded. 'What about Constable Jed Sawyer?' he asked. 'How bad were his injuries?'

Wallace smiled. 'They're not as bad as the man likes to make out,' he said. 'Yes, he had some nasty lacerations tae his face which had bled profusely when he was attacked – he was covered in blood when I saw him. But his arm's nae broken – badly bruised, but nae broken.'

Lavender nodded. He had suspected this.

'He enjoys being the village hero, I think.' Wallace spoke Lavender's own thoughts.

'Had you ever been called out to attend to William Sculthorpe prior to the night of the attack?' Lavender asked.

This time Wallace shook his head. 'We've only been in Middleton for two months.' A stronger, more violent fit of coughing consumed him and his body shook. Beads of sweat erupted across his forehead as he strained to control the irritation in his lungs.

'We're waiting for our house to be renovated,' Mrs Wallace said. 'My husband's new medical practice is in Market Harborough. We hope to move there soon.'

'Mind you, this hasna stopped the locals in Middleton from takin' full advantage of the fact they now have a doctor in their midst.' Wallace smiled as he spoke. 'Normally they have tae call on Doctor Roberts in Rockingham for medical assistance but there have been several occasions when mah presence has been requested instead.'

'Some people are far too forward,' Mrs Wallace said coldly. 'They take advantage and forget you have a long ride to and from Market Harborough every day.'

Lavender hid his smile. Judith Wallace might be reserved but she was clearly very protective of her husband. 'Did you ever get called out to attend to Billy Sculthorpe?' he asked.

'Aye,' Wallace confirmed. 'The wee fellah had an infection and his father was worried about him.'

Lavender was pleased to hear William Sculthorpe had not baulked at the cost of a doctor for his son. Perhaps the old man had had a softer side to him after all. 'On this occasion, how did William Sculthorpe senior seem to you?' he asked. 'I need a general idea of his health and lifestyle.'

'He seemed in perfect health,' Doctor Wallace said. 'The man was sprightly for his age and walked a good deal.' He turned towards his wife. 'You met him several times on your morning walks, didn't you, hen?'

Mrs Wallace shrugged. 'Yes, but we barely passed the time of day. The man simply grunted and nodded in reply to any greeting.' She bent her head back down over her needlework.

Lavender watched her for a moment, then turned his attention back to her husband. 'I understand young men with Billy Sculthorpe's condition are often prone to infection,' he said, 'and they can have a number of other problems related to their condition: a weak intellect, for example, hearing problems and cloudy eyes caused by cataracts.'

Wallace smiled. 'Well, I've niver found anythin' amiss with Billy Sculthorpe's eyesight or his hearin', if that's what you're asking, Detective. However, his imagination runs wilder than a capercaillie in a pinewood.'

'I've noticed.' Lavender smiled.

'There's a good deal of debate in the medical world about the causes of cretinism,' Doctor Wallace continued. Another coughing fit threatened to erupt but he paused, cleared his throat and it subsided. 'And some professionals are undertakin' research in tae this condition. So far they have discovered there may be several forms of cretinism, each with its own particular symptoms and causes.'

'I once read a medical report that suggested this deformity was connected to stagnant air or bad water,' Lavender said.

Wallace shook his head. 'That's disputed. There are too many cretins, too widespread across the population fer that tae make sense. We're ten years in tae the nineteenth century now and the medical profession is takin' great strides. It's determined tae leave antiquated medieval notions behind. There have been new reports – and evidence – that this malformity is often inflicted on the children of older parents.'

Lavender's eyebrows rose in surprise. 'This is a new development,' he said, genuinely interested. 'And it would make sense regarding Billy Sculthorpe. His father must have been in his sixties when Billy was born.'

Wallace sat forward and shook his head. 'You misunderstand me, Detective. This theory requires the mother to be elderly but the theory is not proven.' He fought back another coughing fit.

'May I ask what prompted your move to Northamptonshire?' Lavender asked, although he thought he already knew why. Glasgow was a notoriously unhealthy and squalid city, rife with cholera and consumption.

Wallace glanced down awkwardly but his wife had no qualms about answering Lavender's question. 'My husband has not been well,' she said. 'The air in Glasgow and the conditions in the city do not agree with him. Lady Anne at Rockingham Castle secured John this position in Market Harborough. We hope this move will help him to regain his health.'

'The coughin' is always worse at night,' Doctor Wallace said simply.

Lavender picked up his hat from the low table at the side of his chair and rose to his feet. 'My apologies,' he said. 'I have detained you both for too long already. You have been most helpful.'

'Our pleasure, Detective,' Wallace said.

As Lavender strode back towards The Woolpack he wished he had questioned the Wallaces further about their connection with Lady Anne Fitzwilliam. Why had she helped the Scottish doctor find a new position? The dowager countess seemed to have a finger in every pie and be involved in the lives of many of the Rockingham Estate's tenants. He shrugged. Hopefully, his trip to Rockingham Castle tomorrow would answer that and several other questions that troubled him about Lady Anne's involvement in the case.

Chapter Twelve

After Lavender left for his appointment with Doctor Wallace, Woods remained in the crowded tavern and enjoyed another tankard of ale beside the fire. A group of men stood in the centre of the room, blocking his vision, but he managed to keep one eye on the labourer Harry Goode, who became increasingly inebriated with ale as the night wore on. A pale young man with thick, curly blond hair and large, wide-set blue eyes joined him at his table. Woods heard Goode refer to this babyface as 'Isaac' and realised this was the final member of the group who had gone to the aid of the Sculthorpes on that fateful night: Isaac Bunning, nephew of The Woolpack's landlord.

He's barely shavin', Woods thought at first, but then he changed his mind. Young Bunning and Constable Clancy were probably about the same age and had similar blue eyes but Bunning lacked the open honesty of Clancy's features. Bunning's eyes drifted sideways and his lips curled cruelly at one side.

Susie Dicken flew to Isaac Bunning's side when he appeared. A lot of raucous laughter ensued and when the woman leant low over Bunning's tankard to pour his ale, she pressed her body into his shoulder in the same provocative way she had served Constable Clancy earlier in the day. Harry Goode made some lewd comment about her exposed cleavage and they all laughed. Woods watched Bunning's hand slide down the woman's back and caress her backside before it slid around her waist. Once his tankard was full, Bunning pulled the woman down into his lap and nuzzled her earlobe through her lank hair.

Woods wondered what her intended, the landlord Frank Bunning, made of his nephew's behaviour. But there was no sign of him.

An elderly white-haired man in a threadbare coat shuffled up to a vacant stool next to the fireside. He clutched a tankard in his arthritic hand and lowered himself painfully onto the stool.

'Mr Jarman?' Woods asked, hopefully.

The old man nodded. 'Who's askin'?'

Woods smiled his friendliest smile. 'I'm Constable Woods from Bow Street in London. We've been called up here to investigate the murder of your friend, Mr William Sculthorpe.'

'Oh, aye? I'd heard yer were comin'. From London, aren't yer?'

'Yes, that's right.' Did the old man's hearing fail him? 'Can I buy you another tankard of ale, Mr Jarman?'

Jarman's rheumy eyes crinkled up in delight as he smiled. 'That'd be most kind of you, Constable,' he said. He placed the tankard on the table in front of Woods. 'That be mine,' he said. 'I've drunk from this tankard since I were a boy.' Woods nodded and gestured across the room to Susie Dicken for service. She scowled and dragged herself up from Isaac Bunning's knee. Once she had served them Woods turned back to Jarman.

'I understand Mr Sculthorpe was an old friend of yours.'

The old man seemed to recoil slightly and frowned. 'I can't say we were friends. We'd just drink together sometimes, that's all.

Mind you,' he added, 'Bill Sculthorpe were old all right, very old. You're right about that. He were the oldest man hereabouts.'

'We're tryin' to find out some more about Mr Sculthorpe . . .'

'He were eighty-six years old,' Jarman said. 'He were the oldest man hereabouts. I'm seventy-one next month. I'm the oldest man in Middleton – now Bill Sculthorpe's passed.' A toothless smile of pride spread across his face.

Woods relaxed and smiled back. This would take longer than he had anticipated. 'Seventy-one years of age?' he said. 'Congratulations, Mr Jarman, that's a considerable achievement.'

'Aye, I'm the oldest man in Middleton now.'

'Do you know about William Sculthorpe's trade?' Woods asked cautiously. 'Did he ever talk about his work with you?'

'Can't say as he did. He hadn't worked for years, hadn't old Bill. He were eighty-six, you know?'

'Why did he move his family here from Brighton?'

'Can't say as I know.' Jarman paused for a moment and stared down at his drink. 'His missus were from Ireland, if it's any help.'

Woods hid his disappointment behind another smile. 'Didn't he tell you anythin' else about his life at all?'

Jarman shook his head. 'Why should he? He only called in here for a glass of brandy when he'd run out of liquor in the house.'

'Did he drink brandy every night?' Woods remembered the poisonous concoction of brandy and ink cap mushrooms Sculthorpe had taken on the night he died.

'Aye, but I hadn't seen him for a week or two,' Jarman added. 'I think he'd got another bottle.'

Woods decided to change tack with his questioning. 'I understand you were in here on the night of the murder.'

'Yes, I were.'

'What did you see?'

'I saw all manner of hell break loose.' The old man sighed. 'I saw Constable Sawyer burst through the door.' He pointed a shaky hand at the entrance. 'He were shoutin' and covered in blood.'

'What happened next?' Woods asked gently. The toothless grin dropped from the old man's face, and he looked a little distressed.

'Frank Bunnin' – and them two,' he waved an arthritic finger in the direction of Harry Goode and Isaac Bunning, 'dashed off with Sawyer to the Sculthorpes'.'

'It must have upset you.'

Jarman nodded. 'I were sorry though to hear what had happened. He didn't have much conversation, didn't William Sculthorpe, but I were sorry he died like that. He preferred to sit quietly, sip his drink and watch folks.'

'Watch folks?'

'Aye, he allus watched folks and listened to their chatter, did William Sculthorpe. He were the oldest man in Middleton, you know? A man shouldn't get to eighty-six and then die like that.'

'I agree.' Another thought struck Woods. 'Were Frank Bunnin' and his nephew in here all night?'

'Frank Bunnin' were here, bobbin' in and out of the room. His nephew came in later with Harry Goode.'

'So Isaac Bunnin' arrived later with Harry Goode?'

'Aye, 'twere just before Frank started to shut up for the night.'

'Was it?' Loud laughter from across the tavern distracted Woods. Susie Dicken sat back down on Isaac Bunning's knee.

'I'm the oldest man in the village now,' Pete Jarman repeated proudly.

Woods nodded, still distracted by the two men and the barmaid. Suddenly, the door opened and Frank Bunning entered the room. Susie Dicken leapt up from his nephew's lap.

'I'll tell you one thing about that night, though,' the old man said and leant forward conspiratorially.

'Yes?'

'He opened up late.'

Woods frowned and gave his full attention back to the old man. 'Who did?'

'Him. Frank.' Jarman's bony, crooked finger jabbed in the direction of the tavern landlord. 'I had to wait outside in the cold for him to open up. His clock were slow. I told him so – but he wouldn't have it.'

Woods frowned and glanced at the glassless clock in the corner of the room with its juddering and exposed hands. 'It was slow on the night of the murder, you say?'

'Aye.'

The loud sound of ripping made Woods glance up. Susie Dicken's earthenware jug smashed onto the wooden floorboards and she screamed. The trailing hem of her oversized dress had caught beneath Isaac Bunning's stool. Broken shards of pottery lay scattered in a dark pool of ale across the floor.

'Yer blitherin' idiot!' she screamed at Isaac.

Every man in the tavern burst out laughing – including young Isaac. The barmaid let out a foul curse and flew at the young lad like a hell-cat. He hunched his shoulders and threw his hands over his head to protect himself from the assault.

'Let the lad be, Susie!' the landlord called out.

She ignored him, grabbed handfuls of Isaac's blond curls and yanked his head backwards. Frank Bunning moved across, grasped the snarling woman around the waist and half lifted, half dragged her out of the door.

'Methinks the lady doth protest too much,' Woods said quietly.

'Aye, you'd be right there, Constable,' Jarman said.

Lavender returned shortly after Pete Jarman left the tavern. Woods told him the information he had gleaned from the old man. 'What do you think it means, sir?' he asked.

Lavender glanced at the battered longcase clock in the corner of the room. He frowned and shook his head wearily. 'I don't know, Ned,' he said. 'If this clock was slow on the night of the murder then Frank Bunning was wrong about the timing of events but the significance of this news eludes me. Perhaps in the morning I'll be able to make more sense of it. Let's retire for the night and make a fresh start tomorrow.'

The landlord led them up the narrow wooden staircase to a cramped bedroom with a low ceiling. It contained two mattresses and little else. Woods had seen more comfortable prison cells in Newgate.

Bunning pointed to the dying embers in the grate. 'We lit a fire a few hours ago to take the chill off the room.'

It hasn't worked, Woods thought.

'I'll be down the corridor if you need anythin',' Bunning added. He pointed to the door at the end of the corridor. 'Isaac is the next room to mine and Susie sleeps upstairs in the attic.'

'I'm sure we'll be fine,' Lavender said.

The landlord nodded and left them in peace.

Lavender held up his candle and looked round the miserable room with distaste. 'No doubt this place has bugs,' he said.

'I don't think I'll notice.' Woods yawned. 'My old bones are that weary even Old Nick wouldn't wake me tonight. I'm sleepin' in my coat though.' He flopped down onto his lumpy mattress and wrinkled his nose in disgust at the unpleasant smell emanating from the mouldy straw beneath him. He knew Lavender would sit for a while longer and even try to make a few notes by the dim light. Woods sighed heavily, thankful that the main responsibility for solving this blasted case didn't sit on his shoulders.

Images floated into Woods' exhausted mind as he struggled to get comfortable. Strange images of stagnant water and coal heaps. It was a river. The river stank. No, it wasn't the river. The mattress stank. He heard the throb of a nearby forge. Woods sighed and rolled over. *It's your heartbeat in your ears*, he told himself. *It's your heartbeat . . .*

Woods shivered in the cold wind from the river. Today the docks were deserted. Massive coal heaps, higher than mountains, stood on the wharf, towering above him. He was a child again and struggled to climb up them. His feet – small feet – sank into the shimmering, slithering black pile as he half walked, half crawled on his belly to the top. The blast furnace roared behind him and scorched his back with its heat. He struggled to his feet, unsteady on the shifting coal. Above his head, towering metal gantries creaked, swayed and groaned in the wind and soot-blackened chimneys belched out filth and grime into the angry red sky.

The sky was angry because of the man. The man who lay at his feet.

He leant down and shook the prostrate man's shoulder with his coal-blackened hand. The throbbing in his head increased. Its rhythm became a loud and terrifying beat.

'Wake up!' he yelled, his voice high-pitched with fear. 'Wake up, will yer? We've got to get out before the wharfinger finds us!'

The body obligingly rolled over. Its bloodied grey brains oozed out from the terrible gash down the side of its head and slithered down the coal like a repulsive reptile.

Woods screamed and lurched forward. He clawed at the empty air as he fell from the top of the coal heap . . . faster, faster.

The image vanished in a flash. Bathed in sweat and confused, Woods sat bolt upright on the mattress and blinked in the poor light.

A dark-haired demon sat across the room eyeing him coldly. A quill poised motionless above his notebook, a guttering candle by his side. 'What the hell are you dreaming about now, Ned?' Lavender asked.

Woods groaned and lowered his head into his hands, waiting for the garish images of his nightmare to fade and sink back into the dark recesses of his mind. 'I were just . . .' he mumbled.

'Shh!'

Woods' ears strained against the unearthly silence of the night.

Outside on the landing, a metal latch clicked open. A door swung on its hinges. Quiet footsteps from stockinged feet padded over the floorboards. Another door opened and shut softly.

'Mmm,' Lavender whispered. 'Someone's abroad tonight.'

Chapter Thirteen

Saturday 3rd March, 1810
Middleton, Northamptonshire

Lavender woke as the first tentative fingers of dawn poked through the ragged drapes of their room. His back ached from the uncomfortable mattress and he still felt weary. At the other side of the chamber, Woods continued to toss and turn and murmur through the bad dreams that had haunted him all night and disturbed his own sleep. Lavender sighed and rose stiffly to his feet. A glance through the dirty window cheered him up. The sun was steady in a cloudless sky. Did it promise spring warmth today?

He suddenly got the urge to walk off his aches and pains. Donning his coat, he descended the twisting wooden stairs of the deserted tavern and went outside, grateful to leave the smell of woodsmoke, tobacco and stale ale behind. He welcomed the fresh air and the warmth of the morning sun. Somewhere in the valley, sheep bleated and cattle lowed hungrily. Crows called to each other from the treetops on the hill. They rose, circling and wheeling, before heading down to their favourite feeding grounds. It promised to be a brilliant day with a sky of white light and ice-blue arched over the world.

Lavender decided to repeat the pleasant walk he had taken the previous day and he set off up the cobbled hill towards the meandering path that led back to St Mary Magdalene in Cottingham. The smell of smoke drifted down from the chimneys of the silent village. He relished the peace and quiet of early morning.

As he retraced his steps, he saw things he had not noticed the first time he walked this way. Red squirrels scampered up the trunks of apple trees in an orchard. Fat wood pigeons cooed above his head in the budding branches of the elms. Primroses sprouted amongst the exposed roots of the trees and muted yellow cowslips peeped out from the swathes of lush grass in the meadow. A row of beehives hummed gently against an ancient stone wall.

He was struck again by the fertility and fruitfulness of this part of England. Dense woodland teeming with game, fat cattle and sheep, fresh garden vegetables and lush agricultural farmland: this was a land of milk, honey and plenty. Yes, some of the residents of Middleton knew poverty. Miss Bennett, for example, eked out a meagre existence for herself and her mother, and the labourer Harry Goode had a mountain of debt. But not one of the inhabitants of Middleton had the skeletal frame or hunger-ravaged features that haunted the faces of those who lived in the filthy and unhealthy slums of the Seven Dials in London. No wonder the residents of this lush valley enjoyed such longevity.

He paused in a meadow at the top of the hill and took in the wonderful view below him where the river cut its course through the soft, marshy clays. The grey rainclouds of yesterday had vanished. Now seen beneath the shimmering clarity of a dazzling sky, the sweeping valley was magnificent.

A woman walked across the field towards him, a wicker basket hung on her arm. The long grass parted silently before her skirts. It took him a moment before he recognised Judith Wallace's face below the black shadows cast by the ruffles of her bonnet.

He bowed. 'Good morning, Mrs Wallace. You're another early riser, I see.'

'Good morning, Detective. Yes, I always think it's a shame to lie abed when there is so much beauty in the world.'

He nodded. 'Indeed, it's the best part of the day.' His eyes lighted on the piles of creamy fungi in her basket. 'You have been picking mushrooms?'

Her eyes followed his own to the basket on her arm. She tapped it lightly with her gloved hand. 'I like to gather a few for John's breakfast.'

'Those are field mushrooms, *Agaricus campestris*, I believe?'

'Yes. You're very knowledgeable, Detective.' She sounded surprised. 'I don't suppose you're able to pick your own mushrooms in London.'

'I have an interest in the flora and fauna of the British Isles,' he said. 'I've read a lot of books on the subject. Tell me, do you ever come across ink cap mushrooms when you're foraging?'

'Oh yes, I've found quite a few recently.'

'Did you ever give any to William Sculthorpe when you met him on your morning walk?'

She took in a sharp intake of breath and seemed to recoil slightly. 'Well, I only met him the once –'

'When was this?'

She shook her head as she struggled to remember. 'A few weeks ago . . .'

'Just before he died?'

'It may have been. I'm afraid I don't remember.'

'And did you give him some ink cap mushrooms?'

'Yes, I think I did. Is there a point to these questions, Detective?'

'There's nothing to worry about,' he said. 'We found some rotten mushrooms in his kitchen and I wondered where they came from.'

She seemed relieved. 'Please excuse me, Detective,' she said. 'I must take these back. The flavour is never good unless they're cooked almost immediately after harvesting.'

He nodded his head in a short bow and she turned on her heel to walk back to Middleton. He watched her as she glided gracefully through the meadow and disappeared beneath the dappled shadows of the trees.

Lavender returned to The Woolpack and joined Woods for breakfast. Susie Dicken served them a meagre plate of ham and greasy eggs.

'Will you gentlemen be stayin' with us another night?' Frank Bunning asked.

'I don't believe we will,' Lavender replied.

'Thank the Lord for that,' Woods muttered as he poked sadly at his greasy egg with his fork.

Lavender retrieved his horse from the forge and set off on the short journey to Rockingham Castle for his appointment with Lady Anne Fitzwilliam.

The road meandered along the base of a steep, wooded escarpment and he soon saw the castle with its creamy, medieval stone walls perched on a rocky outcrop at the end of the ridge. It had a commanding view of the valley. The road twisted upwards towards a pair of castellated drum towers that guarded the arched entrance to the castle grounds. Arrow slits in the shape of a narrow crucifix reminded Lavender of the castle's original military significance.

Inside the grassy enclave of the walls stood a magnificent, three-sided and gabled Elizabethan mansion, complete with mullioned windows and tall round chimneys.

A groom came out of the stables to take his horse and a footman gestured him in through a side doorway. The servant led him through the stone-flagged servants' hall and past the bustling kitchens, where half a dozen white-capped and white-aproned women stirred huge copper saucepans on the range and rolled out pastry on the centre table. His stomach rumbled as the delicious aroma of fresh bread and simmering beef wafted into his nostrils and he remembered the inadequacy of his meagre breakfast.

'You're to wait for Lady Anne in the Panel Room,' the footman told him as he led him through an arched wooden door into the main section of the house.

The Panel Room lived up to its name. A massive medieval stone fireplace dominated one wall but the remainder were covered in deal panelling, now darkened and splitting with age. A fire had been lit in the great hearth, which seemed unnecessary considering the warmth of the day outside. To take his mind off the stuffiness and heat of the room, Lavender examined the armorial bearings carved into several of the wooden panels. He recognised the coat of arms and Latin motto of the Fitzwilliam family immediately; different branches of their family had lived at Rockingham Castle for seven generations. There were other coats of arms and mottos that he didn't recognise. Some of these armorial bearings had small plaques bearing names: Manners, Montague and Debussy.

Debussy. He frowned and pulled out his handkerchief to wipe away the beads of perspiration on his forehead. Where had he heard the name before? Then he remembered the Middleton school register: *John Debussy Wallace*. Debussy was the second name of Doctor Wallace's son. Could Debussy be the maiden name of Judith Wallace? Was she a distant relative of the Fitzwilliams of Rockingham Castle? If so, this would explain the close relationship between her and Lady Anne. He ran his finger around the edge of his cravat to loosen it and let more air near his hot skin. But such a family connection raised more questions than it solved, he realised. If Judith Wallace had been born into the lower echelons of the aristocratic class, why had she married a common doctor and not someone from her own social stratum?

Suddenly, the double doors at the end of the room were flung open by a pair of liveried footmen. A third footman pushed a large, three-wheeled bath chair into the room. Seated back against the black hood was the tiniest and oldest woman Lavender had ever seen. Smothered in blankets, Lady Anne wore a long-sleeved, high-necked black silk dress and had a shawl draped around her thin shoulders. A black lace cap covered her thin, white hair. Richly ornamented with satin ribbon and decorative frills, it was far too large for her old, wrinkled face with its sunken cheeks. Yet despite her obvious frailty, she gripped the long steering handle attached to the front wheel firmly in her arthritic hands and looked him up and down with dark, disdainful eyes.

She manoeuvred the vehicle around the furniture before it came to a halt in front of the huge fireplace. 'Blankets, Erskine!' she commanded, as the footmen bowed and retreated from the room.

Lavender had been so intent on the strange procession wind-ing its way in front of him that he had failed to notice the plain, middle-aged woman who trailed in the wake of the footmen and the bath chair. She now stepped forward and rearranged the plaid blankets around Lady Anne's knees. She straightened up, pushed back a strand of grey hair that had fallen forward over her face and waited patiently by the side of her mistress.

'This is Erskine, my companion,' Lady Anne said. 'You must be Detective Lavender.'

He nodded politely towards Erskine and bowed low to Lady Anne. 'At your service, your ladyship.'

'Humph! Well, we shall see about that!' Lady Anne replied. 'Stop fussing, Erskine, and sit down, will you?' Her companion seated herself in one of the low upholstered chairs in front of the fire. As he had not been granted permission to sit, Lavender remained standing on the other side of the fireplace to the two women.

Lady Anne's bony fingers tapped on the steering rod of the bath chair as she looked him up and down again. She seemed to find what she saw distasteful and turned her head sharply to her servant. 'So, Erskine, Captain Rushperry wrote to Bow Street Police Office to ask for an active and intelligent officer to help investigate the terrible murder of poor William Sculthorpe.' A trail of spittle seeped out of the corner of her thin mouth. She gulped as though she had a problem swallowing. With her head now in profile, Lavender noticed that her chin had virtually disappeared into the wrinkled, lined and sagging skin of her neck.

'Indeed he did, ma'am,' Erskine replied, '– and Bow Street have sent us Detective Lavender.'

Lady Anne nodded. 'This is most unfortunate.'

Her companion nodded her bowed head. 'Yes, it is.'

Lavender's mouth dropped open. He had been unsure about why he had been summoned here today but this was a strange reception.

Lady Anne leant forward in her bath chair. 'We have heard about Detective Lavender, haven't we, Erskine?'

'Yes, ma'am. We have read about him in *The Times*.'

Lavender opened his mouth to speak but Lady Anne hadn't finished. She turned her head and addressed him directly. 'We read about the Portman Square riot which you dealt with, Lavender – and the furore you caused when you sent for the militia to quell the rioters.'

Lavender's mind raced as he desperately tried to remember the incident and how *The Times* had reported it the previous October. He also wondered what offence his handling of the event might have caused the Lady Anne.

Fortunately, she soon enlightened him. 'Despite the fact a magistrate lived only two streets away, you – a mere policeman – took it upon yourself to call out the militia.' Her voice rose with indignation as she spoke.

Ah, yes, *The Times* had made quite a fuss about this. She had an excellent memory if she remembered that.

'I apologise for my presumption on this occasion, Lady Anne,' he said quietly. 'However, it was my strong conviction that urgent action needed to be taken to prevent further injury to both people and the property in Portman Square. There was no time to locate the magistrate. People were being hurt.'

'Huh! You're a nonconformist, Lavender!' and a glob of spittle landed on the blanket as she spat out the words. 'You're a social heretic – with an arrogant disrespect for the natural order of law.'

He bowed his head and hoped she would see the gesture as one of contrition, rather than an attempt to hide the smile in his eyes and the one that itched at the corners of his mouth. 'Again I can only apologise for any offence caused by my actions in Portman Square last October. Please rest assured I will afford the current case my fullest attention and deal with it in line with the law.'

There followed a short pause, which he hoped signified that the dowager countess was mollified. 'Shall we believe him, Erskine?' she asked.

'I don't think so, ma'am,' replied her companion. 'I think he has shifty eyes.'

Lavender glanced up at the dowdy woman in surprise. She sat hunched in her seat with her hands folded neatly on her lap and her own eyes lowered. Her grey head with its plain black cap was bowed towards her knees. He hadn't been conscious of her scrutiny at all. She had kept her eyes averted from him throughout the entire conversation. He wondered just how long the two women had been together as mistress and companion. Erskine's comments suggested she knew exactly what was going through her mistress's mind and they also hinted at a high degree of familiarity between the two women; the ferocious old lady in the bath chair didn't frighten Mistress Erskine.

He knew that Lady Anne's husband, the third Earl Fitzwilliam, had died young and she had never remarried. Their eight-year-old son became the new earl and the heir to Wentworth House, the largest mansion in the country, and to their other substantial estates. Erskine wore a wedding band but he wondered if she might also be a widow.

'Well, Captain Rushperry tells me you're good at your job,' Lady Anne conceded eventually. 'Didn't he, Erskine?'

'Yes, he did, your ladyship.'

'So have you found out who murdered poor Bill Sculthorpe yet?'

'Not yet,' Lavender admitted, grateful the conversation had now turned onto the case rather than his own shortcomings. 'However, we have made several discoveries that may be relevant – and I don't accept this is the work of that notorious Panther Gang from the south of the county.'

She frowned, blinked and stared at him hard. 'What discoveries?'

'Did you know, ma'am, that William Sculthorpe was a practising Catholic?'

'Yes. What of it?' She never flinched or exhibited an ounce of surprise at this news. 'Have you found out anything else? I summoned your help because I feel that there is more to this murder than meets the eye.'

Lavender raised a surprised eyebrow. The years had clearly not dimmed the sharp insight of this cantankerous old lady. 'I agree with you,' Lavender said.

'You do?' She leant forward in her chair.

'Yes, I'm not convinced that it was simply a robbery gone wrong.'

She hesitated for a second and Lavender sensed disappointment in the slight frown that wrinkled her forehead. 'You think they murdered him because he was a Catholic?'

'No,' he said, 'but I don't think this attack was simply motivated by greed.'

'Ah, intriguing, Detective.' She looked relieved and tapped the
steering rod of her bath chair again. The mottled skin on the back of
her hand was paper-thin. 'But pray tell me, are you against the victim because of his faith? Will this affect the dedication with which
you undertake your inquiries?'

'Certainly not,' he replied. 'I'm betrothed to be married and my
future wife is both Spanish and a Catholic. I'm not against Catholics.'

Her beady eyes never left his face. 'And shall you convert to
Catholicism before your nuptials?' she asked.

'No, ma'am. I shall not.'

A wry smile twitched at the corners of her thin lips. 'No,
Lavender, you wouldn't, would you? You're an ambitious man.' Her
smile broadened but it didn't reach her eyes.

'His career means too much to him,' Erskine interrupted. Her
pale face was devoid of emotion as she addressed her mistress. 'He
puts the pursuit of gold before his God. You can't serve God and
Mammon: no man can serve two masters.'

'Isn't that Matthew six, verse twenty-four, ma'am?' Lavender
asked, pleasantly.

'You know your New Testament, Detective,' Lady Anne sighed.
'That is some comfort, I suppose.'

The two women seemed determined to rile him and he wondered why. For their own amusement, perhaps? Their behaviour
and interaction reminded him of a pair of actors he had seen at a
comedy show at a theatre in Covent Garden. The two performers
had worked together to ridicule several members of the audience.
Another thought jumped into his mind. 'Do you follow the old
faith yourself, Lady Anne?' he asked.

She gasped at his perception, then frowned. 'It's not the old
faith, Detective. It's the one true faith,' she retorted, 'and yes, I have

been a Catholic since I was a young woman. Do you know your politics, Lavender?'

'I do.' Where was this interrogation leading?

'Then you will know of my son, William Fitzwilliam, the Whig politician.'

'Indeed I do, ma'am,' Lavender replied, 'and I know he's favoured by the Prince of Wales. There is much talk of a possible Regency this year. If this transpires, Earl Fitzwilliam may follow in your brother's footsteps and become the next prime minister. There can't be many great houses in the country that can boast of two prime ministers in their number.'

She nodded. 'You're well informed, Detective, but what you may not know is that my son intends to reconcile Catholics to British rule in Ireland by delivering Catholic emancipation and ending the Protestant Ascendancy.'

'I would welcome a Catholic emancipation act, Lady Anne,' he said. 'I believe the current system of inequality to be both unjust and unsustainable. The threat to the nation from the Jacobites receded decades ago. To continue to deprive a large section of British citizens of their right to buy land, enter universities or serve in parliament, the military or the magistracies is both unfair and probably detrimental to the country.'

She said nothing but her gaze seemed softer.

'But to return to the case in hand,' he continued. 'I'm curious about William Sculthorpe. I understand he once worked for you, ma'am. Will you tell me in what capacity?'

She waved a thin hand dismissively in the air. 'All you need to know, Detective, is William Sculthorpe once performed a great service for me, for which I rewarded him generously.'

'Will you tell me what that was?'

'I will not. Needless to say, I have retained a great affection for the old curmudgeon ever since. I can't bear to think of him hewn down by cowards. I need you to solve this dreadful case, Detective.'

'Are you familiar with the profession or trade he followed in his youth?'

'I am not.'

'Was part of his reward for this great service he rendered unto you an occasional bottle of expensive brandy?'

Lady Anne smiled broadly and revealed her gums.

'The brandy was a joke, Detective,' Erskine said.

'A joke?' *What joke did a dowager countess share with a common man like William Sculthorpe?*

'Bill Sculthorpe was eighty-six years of age. Next month I will also be eighty-six years old.' Lady Anne bristled with pride.

'Congratulations, ma'am,' he murmured.

'There are not many people who achieve this great age,' Lady Anne continued, 'and Bill Sculthorpe and I were determined to outlive each other. Twice a year – on Sculthorpe's birthday and at Christmas – I would send him a bottle of brandy in the hope he would drink himself to death. Twice a year on the same occasions he would send me the same – with exactly the same wish.'

Lavender's eyebrow rose at the thought that William Sculthorpe sent gifts to the Lady Anne in the hope that they would kill her.

'This joke has gone on for years between us, Detective. You may think we were an eccentric couple of old fools but our longevity was a great source of pride for both of us.'

He didn't know what to think. The way she spoke about William Sculthorpe suggested they had shared an intimacy far beyond that of the normal relationship between mistress and servant. 'Did you ever send him other gifts?' he asked. 'Food baskets, perhaps? Fruit? Vegetables – mushrooms?'

She frowned and looked confused. 'No.'

'How long have you known William Sculthorpe?' he asked.

'Since I was a young woman,' she replied.

So you will know what profession Sculthorpe followed. 'May I ask how you met him?'

A wave of sadness contorted her wrinkled face. Her thin shoulders fell forward. For a moment Lavender thought he had distressed her with his questioning before he realised that she had no intention of answering his last question.

'The thought of outliving the old curmudgeon was one of the few pleasures I had left in life,' she said softly.

Her companion leant forward towards the bath chair. 'But you have won the competition, ma'am. In a couple of months' time you will have lived longer than him.'

'If I live for another couple of months,' the dowager countess replied.

'I feel cheated, Erskine,' Lady Anne complained. 'Bill Sculthorpe didn't die a natural death. Those murdering scoundrels ruined our contest. It's a hollow victory now.' Her voice trailed away in sorrow and Lavender saw for the first time the despondency, exhaustion and frailty of the feisty old woman who had harangued him a few minutes before.

'I will find his murderers,' he said, 'but before I take my leave, is there anything else you can tell me about William Sculthorpe that you feel may help my inquiries?'

She eyed him quietly for a moment. 'Have you seen the coroner's report, Lavender, and the doctor's statement?'

He nodded.

'Erskine and I have seen a lot of illness and death in our lives, haven't we, Erskine?'

'Yes, ma'am. Between us we've buried three husbands.'

Lady Anne's shoulders stiffened beneath her shawl. She sat up straighter and stared unblinking at Lavender. 'In fact, we've probably seen more dead bodies and dying people than that fool of a coroner.'

Lavender frowned. 'What are you saying, ma'am?'

'I saw William Sculthorpe in Middleton on the day he died. I was out in my carriage and he was striding through the village. He waved at me and grinned.'

'He was showing off his fitness,' Erskine said. 'We saw no breathlessness, palpitations or change of colour in his complexion.'

'He was the very picture of health, damn him.'

'Ah,' Lavender said, as realisation dawned. The two women had noted Doctor Wallace's description of Sculthorpe's symptoms just before he died and, like him, they found them incongruous.

'If it is the symptoms described by Doctor Wallace that are bothering you, then I think I can explain,' he said. 'I haven't reported this to the coroner yet but I will do. I found evidence of ink cap mushrooms and brandy in the remains of Mr Sculthorpe's kitchen. I believe he had ham and mushrooms for his supper that night and washed it down with a glass or two of your brandy.'

Lady Anne gasped. 'The stupid fool.'

'Yes, it looks likely that he poisoned himself.'

Lady Anne began to drum her bony fingers on the arm of her bath chair. 'He poisoned himself,' she repeated slowly and turned to her companion. A knowing glance passed between them.

What are you thinking? he wondered.

'Where did he get those poisonous mushrooms?' Lady Anne asked.

He hesitated. 'I'm unsure at the moment but we are trying to find out.'

Lady Anne sank back down against her cushions and sighed. He couldn't read her expression now. 'You are an intelligent man, Lavender,' she said. 'I need you to keep an open mind during this investigation. Something is not right about William Sculthorpe's murder. I can feel it in my old bones – and I think you feel it too. You can take me back to my room now, Erskine – I need to rest.'

Lavender bowed, a little surprised at such an abrupt dismissal. Erskine rose, stepped behind the bath chair and took hold of the handles. But as the two women moved towards the door, Lady Anne held up her hand to stop. She turned back to Lavender.

'I want you to catch those murdering scoundrels who attacked William Sculthorpe, Detective. That is why I am financing the investigation into his death. I don't want you to leave any stone unturned. Not one. Do you take my meaning?'

Lavender bowed again. 'Yes, ma'am.'

'I wish you the best of luck with your investigation – and please don't forget to enlighten me about the outcome.'

Chapter Fourteen

Woods found Billy Sculthorpe sitting in exactly the same place as the day before, still in his voluminous nightgown and surrounded by his beloved drawings. His slanting eyes crinkled with pleasure when Woods walked into the room, the grin stretching across his flat face from ear to ear.

'Ned! You came back!' he said, in his strange, muffled voice.

Due to the warm weather outside, there was no fire in the grate today and the sash window had been raised to allow in some fresh air. The noisy rumble of farm wagons in the street below drifted in through the open window. Woods grinned and sat down on the edge of the bed close to the young man. It wasn't often he got such an enthusiastic welcome.

Billy swivelled around on the floor and rifled through his piles of paper. 'It's good you and Stephen have come back,' he said. 'I have finished the picture of his Magdalene.' He lifted up a drawing, turned and held it out to Woods.

'I'm afraid that sir – Stephen – has to work today,' Woods said, 'but he has sent you this gift.'

Disappointment flashed across Billy's face and he glanced at the closed door, obviously hoping Lavender might still appear. Then his eyes lit up at the sight of the new crayons and pad of paper Woods held out towards him. Billy's excitement in the simple gift was moving. How much kindness and company had the young man known in his life?

'I'll take the picture to him, if you want,' Woods said. 'I'm sure Stephen will like it.'

He took the drawing from Billy and the corners of his mouth twitched in amusement. In true Billy-style, Magdalena had mutated into an evil witch. The biblical beauty with flowing hair and a swirling gown now had vicious red eyes, claws instead of fingers, and a bloated toad sat on her left shoulder.

'I drew Stephen too.' Billy shuffled through the piles, looking for another piece of paper. 'But I only did his eyes and hair. I couldn't remember the rest.' He handed Woods the top half of Lavender's head for inspection.

'Ooh, that's a good likeness.'

Billy had captured the shape and mysterious depths of Lavender's slightly hooded and inscrutable eyes. He had also noticed the gentle wave in the detective's dark hair and the strand poised to fall forward over his forehead. 'Are his eyelashes really as long as that?' Woods asked, surprised. 'They should be on a gal.'

'Ah sure, they are,' Billy said, 'but I need to draw the rest of his face.'

'Well, perhaps I can help you there.' Woods leant forward and felt the corners of his mouth twitch again. 'I shall tell you about the rest of his features.'

Billy picked up his pencil. 'Very well, we shall start with his nose.'

'Oh, that's easy. It's large and curves out and bends like a meat hook.'

Billy blinked and he frowned in confusion. 'I, I . . . don't remember that.'

'Oh, it's right, son,' Woods said. 'He's got a right conk, he has. It walks through the door several paces ahead of him.'

The shoulders of the nightgown shrugged and the pencil flew across the page. Billy sat back on his haunches to examine his work. 'It looks like a Goblin's nose,' he said.

'Yes, but you've forgotten the wart.'

'The wart?'

'Yes.' Woods tapped the left-hand side of his own nose. 'It's a big one, just here. Didn't you see it yesterday? Huge, it is.'

'With hairs stickin' out of it?' The thought seemed to delight Billy.

'Oh, yes,' Woods replied.

Billy returned to his drawing with renewed enthusiasm and the pencil flew across the paper once more. 'I can remember his mouth,' Billy said. 'He had a kind mouth and his face lit up when he smiled.'

'Ah, but don't forget about his missin' teeth,' Woods said.

'Missin' teeth?'

'Yes, he's lost his teeth – here – and here.'

Billy's lips curved up. 'My pa had no teeth left,' he said, and giggled.

Woods saw an opportunity. 'What did your pa do for work, Billy? How did he earn the money to keep you and your ma?'

'Oh, he didn't work,' Billy replied, as he picked up his pencil again. 'He was too old to work.'

'So how could you afford to buy things?'

'I don't buy things.' A wave of sadness flitted over Billy's face. 'I don't go outside.'

'So money is no use to you?' Woods asked.

Billy nodded, then cocked his head on one side and gave Woods a charming smile with his crooked mouth. 'I think that people worry too much about money.'

'Do you know where your father got his money from, Billy-Boy?'

The young man returned his attention to the drawing. 'Yes, Lady Anne sent us the money.'

Woods watched as Billy blacked out two of Lavender's teeth. 'Don't forget to give him a pointy chin,' he said. 'And he has another wart just here on the chin.'

Billy giggled and his face broke out into a broad grin. 'I think you're jestin' with me, Ned. I like your name: Ned. But I like Neddy better, I'm sure. I shall call you Neddy.'

Woods smiled. 'I haven't been called Neddy in a while.'

As Billy sketched out another grotesque wart on Lavender's chin, the sound of conversation drifted in through the open window, along with the delicious smell of freshly baked bread. Two women left the bakery on the street below, talking as they went.

Finally, Billy finished the grotesque caricature of Lavender. Woods winked as he took the paper. 'Why – what a superb likeness! All it needs is a couple of horns to finish it.'

He folded the drawing carefully, along with the one of Magdalena, and tucked them both into the inside pocket of his old brown coat. 'I'm sure, sir – Stephen – will like it.'

'Ah sure, he will – oh, and I drew you the Dark Elves.'

Woods' grin faded. He snapped to attention. 'That were very helpful of you, Billy-Boy. Where is it?'

Billy handed across a smudged and heavily shaded drawing of three black-faced, red-eyed demons with pointed ears and grotesque shadows billowing up the wall behind them.

Disappointment flooded through Woods. The faces and features of the men who had murdered William Sculthorpe were indistinguishable black smudges.

'It were dark,' Billy said. 'Do you like it?'

'I do indeed,' Woods said. 'It will help us track down those coves who murdered your pa and stole his gold.'

Billy glanced up and frowned. 'I've told you before, Neddy,' he chided. 'They didn't get the gold. They got it wrong.'

'What do you mean, son?'

Loud laughter suddenly emanated up from the street below. A group of men had paused just below the window, talking loudly.

Billy froze and Woods saw terror flash across his chubby, flat face.

'When you said that "they got it wrong" . . .'

Woods never got any further with his questioning. The man outside laughed again. Billy shrieked and scrambled across the floor towards Woods. Startled, Woods leapt hastily aside. But Billy threw himself onto his stomach, thrashed his short legs and deformed bare feet and propelled himself beneath the fringed coverlet of the bed. A trail of urine gleamed on the floorboards behind him.

'It's him!' Billy screamed. 'He's come back! The watery veil has breached!' He howled like an animal in pain.

Woods was stunned. He strode over to the open window. Below him in the street, three men stared back up at him, framed in the window: Constable Sawyer, Alby Kilby and a third man he didn't recognise. They had been distracted from their conversation by the terrified wailing emanating from the room behind him. The unknown man turned and dashed back through the door of the bakehouse. Sawyer turned away and walked off down the street.

But Alby Kilby remained rooted to the spot. His hard eyes narrowed and fixed on Woods' face. His brow furrowed and dragged the bushy grey eyebrows across the bridge of his nose to meet in the middle. Something about the big man's anger, his arrogant stance and his glare made Woods start with surprise. Kilby was looking at him as though he hated him.

Chapter Fifteen

'Who was he?' Lavender asked as he swung himself out of the saddle. 'Who was the third man in the group?' Woods held the reins while Lavender dismounted. He had waited at the forge for Lavender to return from his trip to Rockingham Castle.

'It were Doctor Wallace,' Woods said. 'He raced upstairs when he heard Billy wailin'. It took the two of us – and Mrs Tilley – twenty minutes to persuade Billy to come out from under the damned bed.' Woods' face grimaced at the memory. 'He were sobbin' and insensible.'

Having given the sweating horse to the leather-aproned blacksmith, who led it away towards the stables, they walked across the cobbles to a quieter, shadowy corner of the yard. Beside them old axles and a pile of rusting iron hoops leant against the stone wall of the outhouse. Weeds sprouted at their base.

'So it wasn't the voice of Doctor Wallace that upset him,' Lavender said thoughtfully. 'Billy clearly trusts him. It must have been one of the other two.'

'The lad were terrified,' Woods continued. 'He made little sense. He were gabblin' on about the dark elves – I couldn't make head nor tail of what he were sayin'.'

'What was Alby Kilby doing in Middleton?'

'Doctor Wallace said Kilby had ridden over to Middleton to pay his doctor's bill. He'd had some medicine for his wife a while back.'

Lavender nodded and remembered Kilby's sickly wife back in The Angel Inn. Across the yard the blacksmith's apprentice worked the groaning bellows amidst an angry shower of sparks from the glowing furnace. 'What about Jed Sawyer?'

Woods shrugged. 'He were just passin' by, I think. He'd disappeared by the time I got back down to the street – so had Kilby.'

Lavender saw the worried look on Woods' face. 'What's the matter, Ned?'

'It's Kilby.' Woods struggled to find the right words. 'There's somethin' about him – the way he stares. I thought he were a gentle man the other night in The Angel but I'm not so sure now.'

Lavender nodded and remembered how Kilby had stood glowering on the footpath, watching them as they rode out of Market Harborough.

'I know this is daft, sir, but I think we need to find out what he were doin' on the night of Sculthorpe's murder.'

'I know what you mean about Kilby,' Lavender said. 'But I suspect we'll find a dozen or more witnesses in Market Harborough who'll tell us he was working in his tavern all night when Sculthorpe was murdered.'

The two men paused thoughtfully for a moment, then Woods shrugged. 'With respect, sir, I'm not sure we can believe Billy Sculthorpe. Perhaps we shouldn't read too much into this. One minute he were fine, chattin' away to me, and the next he were howlin' like the Devil himself had come after him.'

'The poor fellow is probably still in shock following the attack at his home,' Lavender said.

'Captain Rushperry said he weren't a reliable witness.'

Part of Lavender wanted to agree with Woods – but a part of him resisted. 'That's what we thought about Matthew Carnaby last November in Bellingham,' he said quietly. 'We overlooked him as a potential witness.'

The blacksmith returned from stabling Lavender's horse and resumed his rhythmic hammering of a horseshoe on the anvil.

'The mute fellah?' Woods asked.

'Yes, but it turned out Matthew Carnaby could read and write and that he held the key to the mystery. Ignoring Carnaby was a grave mistake on my part – and the poor gypsy girl paid for it.' The hammer hit the anvil and the high-pitched ring punctuated the silence that followed his words.

Woods nodded sadly. 'You shouldn't blame yourself, sir.'

'I just don't want to make the same mistake again,' Lavender said. 'This case is difficult enough and we can't afford to overlook any clue to the identity of these murderers. This is one of the few leads we have got. Billy Sculthorpe has just heard a voice that frightened him.'

'Well, I don't know what to make of it all,' Woods said. 'We know Constable Sawyer weren't involved in the murder – and the doctor seems like a decent fellah even though he does have the initials *J.W.* I'm not sure he looks like he's capable of assaultin' anyone. It's been a while since I've seen such a scraggy fellah.'

'Yes,' Lavender agreed. 'Doctor Wallace is ill and weak. I doubt he'd have the strength to take part in such a vicious assault – and there is no clear motive.'

'I suppose he could have hired some fellahs to do the work for him,' Woods suggested.

'Oh, well done, Ned.' Lavender's voice rose with fresh hope. He hadn't considered this option before. 'And by the same logic – his wife could have done the same.'

'His wife?' Shock flashed across Woods' face. 'Why would she want to murder Sculthorpe?'

'I don't know but let's keep our minds open.'

Briefly he told Woods about his strange interview with Lady Anne Fitzwilliam. 'She had already worked out from the coroner's report and Doctor Wallace's statement that Sculthorpe had been poisoned – and she clearly suspects that it wasn't accidental.'

'Gawd's teeth! Did you mention that you found Mrs Wallace pickin' mushrooms this mornin'?'

'No, I didn't. We need to know more about her – and let's find out what Alby Kilby was doing on the night of the murder. Our pool of suspects is growing.'

'Oh, and there were somethin' else, sir.'

'Yes?'

'Billy said again how those thievin' coves "had got it wrong" when they were searchin' for his father's gold.'

Lavender stared at him thoughtfully. A loud hiss and a billowing cloud of steam emanated from the forge as the blacksmith immersed the glowing red horseshoe in a pail of water.

'Yes, I remember Billy said that yesterday.' He paused for a moment, then frowned. 'Do you think we've missed something, Ned?'

Woods shrugged, his broad face expressionless.

'Let's go back to the Sculthorpe house,' Lavender said. 'Let's take another look.'

Lavender forced open the creaking unlocked door of Sculthorpe's dilapidated cottage and they stepped inside into the musty gloom of the hallway. Woods ducked his head beneath the low doorframe and followed him up the short flight of wooden stairs to the spot on the landing where he knew Billy Sculthorpe had been attacked. Lavender frowned and tried to picture the scene witnessed by the young man on that fateful night. It was dark. Three shadowy figures with blackened faces moved around his mother's bedchamber, one carrying a piece of furniture. There wouldn't have been much time. Billy would have only had a quick glance before the men moved towards him, blocking out his view.

'"*They got it wrong*",' he said quietly to himself. 'Come on, Billy: what was it they got wrong?'

The narrow bed with its frayed coverlet stood against most of the side wall. The chairs were still piled haphazardly on a chest of drawers in one corner. The faded rug had been pulled back, exposing the gaping hole beneath the floor, the splintered floorboards thrown down beside it. William Sculthorpe had told the thieves his money was hidden in the corner beneath the floorboards of his late wife's bedroom above the kitchen. Lavender's eyes rested on the heap of stacked furniture in the corner behind the door. His eyebrows knitted together across his brow. What if . . . ?

'Help me clear these away, Ned.' He moved to the stack of furniture in the corner, grabbed the upturned legs of a spindly chair and tossed it across the room onto the bed. Together they lifted away the rest of the furniture and dragged the chest of drawers across to the other side of the fireplace. Lavender crouched down and whipped back the fringed edge of the faded rug. A smile of satisfaction spread across his face when he saw what lay beneath.

'Gawd's teeth!' Woods exclaimed. 'So the old fellah had *two* secret hidin' places up here!' An area of the floorboards, about a yard square in size, had been chopped into lengths for easy removal. Years of dust had caked the gaps in between the wooden planks but there was no doubt they had uncovered another secret storage place belonging to William Sculthorpe.

'What do you suppose –?'

'Pass me the poker,' Lavender interrupted. 'The time for speculation is over, Ned. With any luck, this cavity will contain some answers to the mysteries that bedevil us.'

Using the poker and Lavender's pocketknife, the two men levered up the wooden planks. 'No one has moved these for a while,' Woods grunted.

With a loud crack and a shower of dust, the last piece came away from the floor. They peered down into the hole. A heavy wooden box, blackened with age and fastened with a rusty clasp, lay in the void. They hauled it out with difficulty and Lavender attacked the lock with his knife until there was a satisfying click.

'Heaven and hell!' Woods exclaimed when they lifted the creaking wooden lid. 'More popery!'

A large, solid gold crucifix and a string of amber rosary beads lay on top of a pile of battered ledgers and a Bible. The pungent, spicy odour of church incense mingled with the scent of unwashed clothing emanating from the heap of black and white material beneath the ledgers.

Tucked around the edges of the box were bulging leather money bags. Lavender reached out for one, opened it up and poured the contents out into the box. A large mass of golden guineas glinted in the sunlight. Lavender scooped up a handful and let them trickle back down between his fingers, trying to assess how many lay there. Thirty, perhaps? Fifty?

His constable whistled softly and grinned. 'Just look at those yellow boys!' he said. His eyes shone as they flitted between the gleaming coins in Lavender's hand and the other bulging pouches. 'Young Billy-Boy were right when he said those thievin' villains had "got it wrong".' The bloody sapheads pulled up the floorboards in the wrong part of the room and piled the damned furniture on top of a tidy round sum!'

Lavender felt a wave of satisfaction flood through him. He shared Woods' excitement.

'William Sculthorpe obviously kept two hoards of money in here.' He pointed to the other gaping hole in the room. 'Sculthorpe directed the thieves to the hoard beneath the floor by the window, probably hoping they would never find this cache.'

'Judgin' by the difficulty we've just had with those damned floorboards,' Woods said, 'Sculthorpe hadn't touched this particular treasure box in a while. What shall we do now?'

'Let's empty this methodically,' Lavender said. 'You take charge of the coins and I'll deal with the ledgers.'

Carefully they removed the top layer of guineas and stacked them on the floor. Out next came the ledgers, which Lavender stacked beside him. As each layer was removed more money bags were revealed. Woods added another half a dozen to the growing pile.

'There must be a ruddy fortune in here!'

Lavender returned to the box, pulled out the clothing and examined it. The first item was a high-collared, black woollen cloak. He raised an eyebrow at the fine quality of its white silk lining. Beneath the cloak they found an oval-shaped garment of rich purple and ruby brocade. Simply shaped, with a hole in the centre to pull over the head, it was intricately embroidered with gold and silver religious imagery. He ran his finger over the fine golden silk of the embroidered crucifix and smiled. At last they were getting somewhere with this case.

'What is it?' Woods asked.

'It's a chasuble.'

'A what?'

Lavender didn't reply but leant forward to rummage deeper into the pile of clothing. The smell of frankincense and myrrh became stronger with each layer he removed.

Woods wrinkled his nose in disgust. 'What a stench!'

Lavender pulled out several white, long-sleeved linen vestments and a plain black, long-skirted cassock. Below them lay a long golden cord cincture to tie around the waist of the cassock and a richly embroidered, white silk stole. At the bottom of the box were several more rosary beads and a few text books in Latin, which he glanced at curiously before placing them beside the ledgers. They were dull religious tracts. Finally, they found the source of the smell – a silver-gilt box containing the aromatic incense. Beside it lay an ornate, pointed thurible on a long silver chain, which a priest would use to waft the scent of burning incense around the place of worship. The final item Lavender withdrew was an embroidered rectangle of white linen.

'Well, at least now we know the truth about William Sculthorpe's profession,' he said with a sigh of relief.

'We do?' Woods grabbed the last of the leather money bags from the bottom of the box.

'Yes.' Lavender held up the piece of white linen. 'This is an amice worn by a priest during Mass. William Sculthorpe was a Roman Catholic priest.'

Chapter Sixteen

'Gawd's teeth!' Woods dropped the bags of coins to the floor. The clang echoed around the old cottage. 'He were a what?'

'He was a priest, Ned – a Catholic priest. These are the vestments and robes of a Catholic priest and I think it's fair to assume they belonged to William Sculthorpe.'

'Heaven and hell!' Wood's mouth flapped open and shut like the mouth of a fish dragged out of the river. 'How can that be?' He stared hard at Lavender, his grey eyes clouded with confusion. 'Sculthorpe were a married man with a son!'

'I don't know,' Lavender replied. 'Like you, I thought a priest's vow of celibacy was for the duration of their life. I need to seek clarification.'

Lavender picked up the chain of the silver thurible, lifted it above the empty box and let it swing slowly backwards and forwards. 'It has only been legal for priests to take Mass in Britain since 1791,' he said. 'Before this they were hounded by the authorities, arrested and imprisoned. If William Sculthorpe was a priest in his youth, then his would have been a shadowy existence. He would have flitted from one place to another like a ghost hiding in priest holes, attics and cellars – and occasionally finding refuge in the homes of the wealthy Catholic aristocrats. Secrecy would have been second nature to him.'

'You mean wealthy Catholics like Lady Anne Fitzwilliam at Rockingham Castle?' Woods asked.

Lavender nodded. 'At least now I understand the curious relationship between Sculthorpe and Lady Anne. At one point in their lives, Sculthorpe must have been her priest and confessor. They had developed a close relationship over the years, more of a friendship than the relationship we normally see between a mistress and her servant.'

Woods shuddered. 'The thought of that superstitious Latin chantin' – not to mention the confessin' malarkey – it makes me very uneasy,' he admitted.

Lavender smiled. 'Why? Do you have something to hide, Ned? A few sinful thoughts, perhaps?'

'No.' Woods' face crumpled with disappointment. 'Betsy don't allow me to have sinful thoughts.'

Lavender laughed and turned his attention back to the dusty ledgers stacked on the floor beside him. His fingers itched to open them. 'Lady Anne talked about a great service Sculthorpe once rendered unto her for which she had rewarded him generously,' he said. 'She was obviously beholden unto her priest for something – but she wouldn't tell me what or why.' He tapped the ledgers thoughtfully. 'Perhaps the answer is in here.'

'I still don't understand where young Billy and his ma fit into this.'

'Neither do I,' Lavender said. 'I suspect the answer to their mystery lies back in London, where Sculthorpe met his wife and where Miss Bennett told us Billy was born.'

Woods raised his eyebrows. 'You goin' back to London?'

'I may have to.'

'So what shall we do now?'

Lavender roused himself. 'You count up the coins, Woods, and I'll go through the ledgers.'

Woods hesitated and Lavender glanced up. 'I've often found I add up much better on a full stomach,' his constable said. 'That breakfast we had were pathetic.'

'Well, you'd better pay a visit to Mrs Tilley's bakery and purchase some pies,' Lavender said.

Woods didn't hesitate. He disappeared through the door and thundered down the stairs of the cottage. The door slammed, the cottage shook and a tiny shower of plaster fluttered down from the ceiling.

By the time Woods returned, Lavender's own stomach was rumbling. He pushed aside the ledgers, sat back on the late Mrs Sculthorpe's bed and enjoyed the succulent pastry and rich filling of his pie. Warm sunlight continued to pour into the room through the dirty window. He glanced out into the overgrown garden and watched the new foliage on a huge oak tree ripple and gleam like malachite and emeralds.

Woods pulled up a chair and joined him with his own pie. 'I've been thinkin',' he said, in between mouthfuls. 'Perhaps Sculthorpe and his missus weren't married after all. Perhaps she were some sort of housekeeper for him and maybe Billy were her nipper.'

'Perhaps,' Lavender said. 'This would certainly explain why the Sculthorpes had separate bedchambers, although such an arrangement is also common with elderly couples when one becomes ill.'

'Maybe Sculthorpe let her use his name to stop the gossipmongers and their tittle-tattle.'

Lavender nodded and reached for his hip flask to wash down the pie with some brandy. He took out his handkerchief and wiped his mouth. 'I have had a cursory glance at the account ledgers,' he said, 'and it looks like Sculthorpe kept separate accounts for his two caches of money.' He pointed towards the stack of leather money bags on the floor. 'If Sculthorpe's tally is up to date, the coins in those money bags should amount to six hundred and thirty pounds.'

Flakes of pastry flew down the front of Woods' coat as he spluttered. It took him a moment or two to recover from the shock. 'So what with these yellow boys and the other money stashed away at the bank in London – Sculthorpe were flush in the pocket!'

'Yes, his total savings amount to nearly seventeen hundred pounds – a significant amount.'

'I don't know much about priests,' Woods said, 'but this seems like a hell of a lot of plate for a religious man to collect. I always thought most of them were as poor as their cathedral mice.'

Lavender nodded, then frowned. 'You're right, Ned. I've wondered if he came by this money honestly.'

'Do you still think he might have been a moneylender?'

'It's a possibility.'

'What about the stash he kept beneath the floorboards under the window?' Woods asked. 'Were there hundreds of yellow boys in there too?'

'According to the ledgers there were thirty-nine pounds and eleven shillings in that hoard. That seems to have been his money for day-to-day expenses. The larger amount we have uncovered today must have been his savings.'

'Thirty-nine pounds?' Woods gave a hollow laugh. 'There's over six hundred pounds hidden in this part of the room and those thievin' coves only find thirty-nine pounds?'

Lavender nodded.

'The daft sapheads!'

'People have been murdered for a lot less,' Lavender said darkly, 'and don't forget, Ned, the viciousness of the attack suggests the money wasn't the only motive in this crime. I'm convinced if we can establish the real motive – or motives – behind this assault, we shall find our murderers.'

Woods wiped the last flakes of pastry from his mouth with the sleeve of his coat and the two men returned to the items piled on the floor. They worked in companionable silence for the next half an hour. While Lavender frowned over Sculthorpe's account books, Woods carefully stacked, counted and bagged up the hundreds of guineas they had recovered from the chest. Metal chinked softly on metal and dust motes danced playfully in the sunbeams streaming through the window. The piles of gold gleamed and flashed seductively in the sunlight.

'Six hundred and thirty pounds,' Woods said, as he dropped the last coin back into a pouch. He rocked back on his heels and looked across to Lavender, who had a pencil and a notebook in his hand. 'You were right, sir.'

'Good. We can assume Sculthorpe's records were accurate and up to date,' Lavender said. He snapped shut his notebook and replaced it in his pocket. 'We now know exactly how much the thieves stole: thirty-nine pounds and eleven shillings. Captain Rushperry will need this information when the case comes to trial.'

'What else were in those ledgers?' Woods asked. 'Does it give any hint about how the old man came to be so flush in the pocket?'

'Well, there's the bank interest on his savings at Down, Thornton and Gill, of course, and a regular payment from Lady Anne Fitzwilliam.' One corner of Lavender's mouth curled up wryly. 'She has rewarded Sculthorpe well for his mysterious service. These books only go back five years but she has paid him a generous allowance of ten pounds a month for the last five years.'

Woods whistled but Lavender hadn't finished. 'He records her payments each month from "*Lady A*". He has also supplemented his income from various other sources over the years.'

'What were those?'

'He just used initials. But since Sculthorpe moved to Middleton he received regular payments from several other people: *C.L.*, *M.T.T.*, *I.B.*, *J.D.* – and *J.W.*'

'*J.W.*!' Woods exclaimed. 'So the note Clancy found in the money bag were for Sculthorpe after all!'

Lavender smiled. 'So it would seem.'

'But were Sculthorpe a moneylender?'

Lavender frowned. 'It's still not clear. We need to track down some of the owners of these initials and question them about their relationship with Sculthorpe. *J.W.* may have eluded us over the past two days but these others won't. I'm convinced the answer to the mystery of Sculthorpe's murder lies in that innocuous list of initials. I'm sure *C.L.* is the churchwarden Caleb Liquorish, with whom Sculthorpe argued the week before his death – and *I.B.* may be the landlord's nephew, young Isaac Bunning. *I.B.* are unusual initials to own.'

'Heaven and hell!' Woods exclaimed. 'So this is a great discovery, after all!'

'Yes, the ledger says that *C.L.* paid Sculthorpe the greatest amount every month: one guinea.'

Woods let out a spontaneous whistle. 'A guinea every month?'

Lavender nodded. '*C.L.* is rich.'

'Constable Sawyer told us Liquorish had plenty of plate,' Woods said. 'Right, where shall we start, sir? Shall we round up Liquorish and young Bunnin'?'

'Maybe tomorrow,' Lavender said. 'This afternoon we need to return to Market Harborough and report back to Captain Rushperry. We may need his help – and I have to catch the mail coach back to London.'

'You're returnin' to London?'

'Yes, what remains of the Catholic faith in England is centred in London. I should be able to find out more about the Sculthorpe family there, but I will need help from my contacts within the Catholic community. They're notoriously suspicious of any of the establishment authorities and very distrustful of London police officers.'

A cheeky grin lit up Woods' face. 'And would Doña Magdalena be one of these contacts, by any chance?'

Lavender dropped his eyes and smiled. 'Sadly, Magdalena will be no help in this instance at all. I need to find someone who may have known – or heard of – William Sculthorpe when he worked as a priest twenty-five years ago. Magdalena hasn't been in England long enough.'

They split the contents of the box between them. Using an old blanket from the bed, Lavender wrapped up Sculthorpe's ceremonial garments into a parcel. Meanwhile, Woods found an old sack for the money bags. They left the empty box on the floor of Mrs Sculthorpe's bedchamber and carried their haul back to the forge, where they retrieved their horses from the stable. Lavender attached his parcel to the back of his saddle, while Woods attempted to place the money into his saddlebag. It wouldn't fit in, so the two men had to weigh down their coat pockets with the coins.

Woods grinned as he swung himself up into the saddle of his restless horse. 'Remind me to empty my pockets and hand it all over to Captain Rushperry,' he said with a wink. 'You know what a terrible memory I have and I would hate to accidentally walk away with a pocketful of Sculthorpe's yellow boys.'

Lavender grinned and started to reply but the smile fell from his face. Constable Sawyer walked across the cobbles towards them. He had now discarded his dirty sling and his right arm swung by his side. His sharp eyes fell on the parcel behind Lavender's saddle. 'What you got there, Detective?'

Lavender reined in and felt a flash of irritation at the man's impudence. 'A few items pertaining to the case,' he replied coldly.

'What are they?'

'Do you want something, Constable?'

Sawyer's eyes broke away from Lavender's icy glare. 'Are yer leavin' Middleton?'

'For the moment, but we will return soon.'

'Well, I'm glad I've met you before you left, sir.' A broad smile now spread across Sawyer's craggy features and he tapped his arm. 'This old rammer of mine has been much better today and –'

'I'm sure it has,' Lavender said quickly.

Sawyer blinked and the grin dropped from his face. 'I'm thinkin' it were time I returned to work,' he continued. 'I'm sure you need the help of a local man who knows the lay of the land, so to speak. So I'm here to tell you, I'm your man.'

'That's kind of you, Constable,' Lavender said, 'but we're managing quite well on our own.'

Sawyer took in a sharp breath and his bushy eyebrows knitted together as he scowled. 'Well, if you're sure . . .'

Lavender dug his heels into the flank of his horse and urged it forward. Sawyer stepped back hastily as Woods followed Lavender's lead.

When they reached the base of the steep hill at the edge of the village, Lavender reined in and turned round to speak to Woods. 'While I'm gone,' he said, 'trust only Captain Rushperry with details of any discoveries you make.'

Chapter Seventeen

Saturday 3rd March, 1810
Market Harborough, Leicestershire

The pleasant weather had brought the inhabitants of Market Harborough out onto the streets. The marketplace bustled with shoppers and the narrow roads were crammed with farm wagons as the two men wove their way through the town towards the home of Captain Rushperry. Lavender glanced up at the clock face on the towering spire of St Dionysius' as they rode past the church. There were still a couple of hours left before he needed to catch the bone-rattling mail coach back to London. He hated travelling by mail coach but this was the fastest mode of transport to London and speed was imperative in this case.

The Elms, Captain Rushperry's home on the northern edge of town, was a pleasant, stone-built house set in its own grounds. The maid led them into a spacious and comfortable sitting room where Rushperry, now resplendent in a red silk banyan with a matching tas-selled hat, was reading the news-sheet in front of the fire. He rose, extended his podgy hand and greeted them warmly. 'Excuse my attire, Lavender.' He gestured to his voluminous scarlet robe. 'I hadn't thought to see anyone else tonight and have removed my tailcoat. Mrs Rushperry is away and I have enjoyed the life of a bachelor these last two days.' He asked the maid to fetch them refreshments and eyed the parcels they carried curiously. 'Not more Catholic reliquaries, I hope?'

'We found these in Sculthorpe's cottage,' Lavender said. Carefully, he and Woods laid out Sculthorpe's money on the surface of an elegant curved sideboard beneath a large gilt mirror.

'Good grief!' Rushperry exclaimed as the money bags piled higher. His deep-set eyes opened wider when Woods pulled out yet more bulging leather pouches from his coat pockets.

Finally, Woods patted himself down, turned out his empty coat pockets and grinned. 'That's the lot, I think, sir.'

'Sculthorpe had six hundred and thirty pounds in guineas hidden beneath the floorboards in another part of his wife's bedroom,' Lavender said, 'along with these.' They sat down in front of the fire and Lavender showed Rushperry William Sculthorpe's ceremonial garments and account books. He quickly explained what their inquiries had uncovered in Middleton.

'So the old man was a Catholic priest,' Rushperry said thoughtfully. 'A married Catholic priest?'

'We're unsure about that,' Lavender replied. 'I hope to find out more about William Sculthorpe when I arrive in London.'

'Well, let's hope, for the sake of his son, the cretin, that you do,' Rushperry said. 'Billy Sculthorpe is either a very rich young man – or he's an impoverished bastard. The local magistracy would like to know which as soon as possible, especially as we're providing his care. If Billy is not Sculthorpe's legitimate heir, then he will end up in the county asylum.'

Lavender felt Woods shudder beside him. 'I shall return to London on tonight's mail coach and seek information from within the Catholic community about William Sculthorpe,' he said. 'There is still so much we don't know about the man.'

'Well, good luck, Detective.' Rushperry grimaced. 'Catholics are secretive beggars and their society is often closed to outsiders.'

'This is why I thought it better to return to London and make my inquiries in person,' Lavender said. 'I doubt a letter would get much response.'

Rushperry leant forward and prodded Sculthorpe's cassock with distaste. 'I can't stand Catholics,' he said. 'They're nothing but trouble, the lot of them. My grandfather was killed at Culloden, defending King George and our Protestant England.'

Lavender nodded sympathetically. 'Ah, I can understand your dislike, sir. But there will be a lot less trouble now the last of the Stuart claimants to the throne has died and the papacy has recognised the Hanoverian dynasty as lawful rulers of England, Wales, Scotland and Ireland.' He took a sip of black coffee and relished its strong taste.

'You're well informed, Detective,' the magistrate said. He sat back and eyed Lavender sternly. 'However, they still agitate for Catholic emancipation – and continue to stir up trouble in Ireland.'

'Perhaps it's time for emancipation,' Lavender suggested. 'Catholics have been barred from public office and other areas of life for over a century. Lady Anne Fitzwilliam and her son, the earl, seem to think so.'

'Hmmph,' exclaimed Rushperry.

'You did know, didn't you, sir, that Lady Anne is a Catholic?'

Rushperry waved a dismissive hand in the air. 'Of course,' he said. 'I understand she converted to Catholicism when she was an impressionable young woman. She has always been discreet about her religion – and of course one always makes allowances for the eccentricities of her extreme age.'

'Is she a bit of a meddler, sir?' Woods asked. The same question had gone through Lavender's own mind several times over the last few hours.

'No, no, not at all.' Rushperry shuffled his bulk on his seat and changed the subject. 'So what about William Sculthorpe?' he asked. 'Why did he receive payment from others in the village? Do you think he was a moneylender? Had he made himself unpopular by charging usurious levels of interest on his loans?'

'Actually, no,' Lavender replied. 'This was our first theory but I have now discarded it. The ride back to Market Harborough has cleared my mind. There are several things that don't make any sense.'

'Like what?'

'For a start, there is no record in his accounts that he loaned money to other people.'

Woods' cup of tea paused midway from his saucer to his lips. 'So why did those folks give him money?'

'I suspect William Sculthorpe was a blackmailer.'

Woods' cup clattered back down into his saucer. 'A blackmailer? How so?'

'Well, it's the inclusion of Caleb Liquorish's initials on the list and the fact that Harry Goode's initials are not there. We know Goode is in debt to most of the shopkeepers in the area – he would need a loan. But Liquorish is a wealthy farmer who doesn't need money. It seems unlikely he borrowed money from William Sculthorpe – yet Liquorish paid him a regular sum every month. I think Sculthorpe was blackmailing Liquorish. This is why they argued in the street. Sculthorpe found out something about Liquorish which the farmer wanted kept quiet.'

'Pete Jarman, Sculthorpe's drinkin' partner at The Woolpack, told me the old man liked watchin' folks and listenin' to their chatter,' Woods said thoughtfully, 'and of course, he were a priest and used to hearing all sorts of secrets in confession.'

'We don't have any evidence that Sculthorpe worked as a priest while he lived in Middleton,' Lavender reminded him. 'And Liquorish is a zealous Anglican who hates Catholicism.'

Rushperry frowned. 'I feel I need to remind you, Detective, that Caleb Liquorish has been a respected member of the community for as long as I can remember. Yes, the man is overzealous at times but there has never been a whiff of scandal attached to his name as far as I know.'

'Perhaps somethin' happened in his youth?' Woods suggested.

'Good thinking, Constable,' Lavender said. 'Most of us did something foolish and regrettable when we were young.'

'In which case we may never learn the truth,' Rushperry said.

An idea flashed into Lavender's mind. 'Would it be possible for one of your clerks to go through the old court records and see if Caleb Liquorish was convicted of a crime in his youth?' he asked. 'I appreciate this is pure speculation but there are certain things we need to rule out, or to confirm, during our inquiry.'

Rushperry looked surprised but he nodded. 'I'll set a man onto this on Monday,' he said. 'In the meantime, what do you two propose to do?'

'Woods will remain in the area,' Lavender said as he drained the last of his coffee. 'He has a list of leads to follow through and he will also try to identify the other people in Middleton with those initials we found in Sculthorpe's account books. We need to know why they gave money to Sculthorpe. I have never been wholly convinced the motive for this crime was simply theft. I think there is far more to it and that other motives such as revenge and hatred are at play here. Once we have established these motives, then I believe we will find our killers. Meanwhile, I shall return to London as we discussed and try to learn more about our mysterious priest.'

'Well, as I said before, good luck with that, Detective,' Rushperry said. 'I hope it won't be a wild goose chase for you.'

Lavender smiled. 'Never fear, Captain Rushperry. I have some excellent acquaintances amongst the Catholics in London.'

*

Darkness had fallen when Lavender clambered aboard the mail coach and settled back in his seat for the return journey to London. The feeble oil lamp above his head flickered and smoked, causing one of the other passengers to cough frequently into her handkerchief. She and her husband were the only other passengers to board the carriage at Market Harborough.

When the vehicle rolled through the marketplace Lavender saw a familiar figure standing in a pool of light beneath a wall lamp. It was Alby Kilby. For a split second, their eyes met through the glass window of the coach and Kilby's face contorted into a glowering frown. In that split second, a shocking realisation seared into Lavender's mind.

'Good God!' His stomach clenched in horror. Instinctively, he stood up and reached out for the handle of the coach door. His startled brain urged him to leap out of the vehicle and race back to Woods. But the coach jerked and threw him back into his seat as it gathered speed. Beneath the white muslin of his starched cravat, a vein throbbed in his throat. He gasped and tried to make sense of the dread that rose within him.

'Are you all right, sir?' The male passenger leant towards him in concern. 'You look like you've just seen a ghost.'

The image of Kilby's glowering face burned onto the retinas at the back of Lavender's eyes. 'I may have,' he croaked. The man looked shocked, tutted and turned to engage his wife in conversation.

Lavender leant his head back against the wood panelling of the carriage, closed his eyes and tried to calm his heart and shake off the nauseating heaviness that gripped his gut like a vice. The coach plunged down the riverbank, streamed through the ford and picked up speed again as it raced off into the darkness of the Northamptonshire countryside. He glanced back through the window at the glimmering lights of the town as they faded and disappeared.

It was too late. He couldn't turn back. The best he could do was write an urgent note to Ned when they stopped at the next tavern and leave it to be sent back on the mail coach. He just hoped it would reach his constable before Kilby made his move. But for now, Ned would have to manage on his own. *He's an experienced police officer*, he reminded himself. *He's negotiated the most dangerous streets in the capital for the last twenty years.*

Unfortunately, Kilby posed a different kind of a threat to those whom they encountered in the dark lanes of the Seven Dials. Kilby was a menace neither of them could have foreseen.

Chapter Eighteen

Woods enjoyed a hearty supper of rabbit stew and freshly baked bread, washed down with his customary tankard of ale, at The Bell Inn. While he ate, he pulled out the list Lavender had left him and prodded it thoughtfully with a blunt pencil. It would be three days before Lavender returned from London but Woods had plenty to do in his absence. Lavender wanted him to question the owners of the outlying farms and homes around Middleton. They needed to know if anyone had seen or heard Sculthorpe's attackers leave or arrive in Middleton. He also had to track down the owners of the initials in Sculthorpe's account books but Lavender had been adamant Woods wasn't to confront anyone about their relationship with the dead man until he returned. For the moment, a little discreet probing was required.

Woods decided to return to Middleton the next morning but then he remembered it would be Sunday: most of the population would be at church. Fair enough, he would join them. He shrugged his shoulders and his pencil hovered over the final item on Lavender's list: Alby Kilby. They needed to find out if he had an alibi for the night of the murder.

He pushed aside the paper, soaked up the last of the gravy with his bread and wiped his chin with the cuff of his coat. He would make a brief call at The Angel Inn before he retired to bed. One more ale wouldn't hurt and he might find out what he needed to know about Kilby.

The taproom of The Angel was as colourful and cheerful as he remembered, although a thick fog of tobacco smoke hung heavily in the air and dulled the gleam of the brass ornaments and the sheen of the painted water jugs that lined the shelves. Several groups of grimy and hard-featured working men sat around the low tables with their pipes and packs of cards. But there were no polite nods of recognition for him this time. When they glanced in his direction, several of them frowned and stopped what they were doing. An awkward silence descended on the room, broken only by the gentle crackle of the fire in the grate. Woods shrugged and walked over to the bar.

There was no sign of the giant white-haired landlord. Kilby's tall, stooped wife appeared to be alone in the tavern tonight. She glanced at him anxiously through the curtain of lank hair hanging around her sallow and unsmiling face. Doctor Wallace had told him Mrs Kilby had been ill and he felt a stab of sympathy for the woman. Whatever ailed her must be serious for Kilby to call in help from a doctor.

'Evenin', Mistress Kilby,' Woods said pleasantly. His voice rebounded across the quiet room.

'Evenin', officer.' She swallowed nervously.

Officer. So their secret was out, was it? *Well, there is no sense in denying it*, he decided.

'Would you care for a tankard of ale, sir?' she asked.

'That would be most welcome, madam.' He climbed up onto

143

a tall wooden stool, conscious of the eyes boring into his back like daggers. 'I've worked up a real thirst ridin' back from Middleton today – and remembered the good quality of your ale from the other night.'

She blushed at the compliment and busied herself pouring out his drink. Her hair fell forward again and hid her eyes.

Woods raised his voice to make sure the silent men in the tavern heard him. 'We're investigatin' the terrible murder that took place in Middleton. The fearful attack on an old man and his son?'

She nodded and handed him his drink. 'Aye, 'twere a dreadful thing to do to such a frail, old man.'

'Quite,' Woods said. 'It were the night of the great storm. Do you remember it?'

She nodded again. The weather was a safe subject to discuss. 'I do,' she replied. 'The tiles rattled on the roof all night and kept me awake. When we woke the next day one of the stables were flooded.' Woods noted the '*we*' with interest.

'When were that?' asked a voice behind him. Woods turned on his stool. A swarthy man in a collarless shirt and dirty jacket stared back at him. The back of the man's huge hands were covered in tattoos. 'When were the storm?'

''Twere about a fortnight ago,' volunteered another fellow from a nearby table. 'The rain got through my sheetin' and soaked the timber. I thought the damned boat would sink with the extra weight!'

The man with the tattooed hands nodded sympathetically. 'I were down Coventry way two weeks ago with a cargo of coal. I'm glad I missed it.'

'Did you have much business here at the inn that night?' Woods asked the landlady.

She shook her head. 'No, Alby closed up early. Everyone had gone back to their homes. There weren't much point in stayin' open.'

This was a new development. 'What time did you shut?' Woods asked. His mind raced as he tried to work out how long it might have taken a man to ride to Middleton in that atrocious weather.

She shook her head again and moved away from the bar with a jug of ale to top up the tankards of the other men. They had resumed their card games now and relit their pipes, satisfied the London police officer had no interest in them and their affairs. A low hum of conversation filled the smoky taproom. Woods' opportunity to question Rosie Kilby and the other men in the tavern had finished.

Weariness suddenly swamped over him and he yawned. The ale had made him sleepy. He had slept badly ever since his arrival in Market Harborough. *It's an early night for you, my lad*, he decided. Downing the remains of his ale in one last gulp, he climbed off his stool. He and Lavender would interview Kilby about his whereabouts on the night of the murder when Lavender returned.

Woods left the inn to take the short walk back to his lodgings. The cloudless night sky was ablaze with stars and the full moon flooded the marketplace with silvery light. But the temperature had dropped from the earlier warmth of the day. Woods buttoned up his coat, pushed his hands deep into his pockets and set off down the chilly and deserted street. Wisps of straw and litter rustled across the cobbles.

Suddenly, he heard the sound of footsteps behind him. An icy chill ran up the back of his neck. He spun round, pulling his clenched fists out of his pockets.

There was no one behind him but he thought he glimpsed a shadowy figure dart down one of the many alleyways leading off the marketplace. His eyes and ears strained against the darkness and silence of the unfamiliar street. The town stocks and the whipping post made ominous shapes in the gloom. Above his head, a shop sign creaked mournfully in the breeze. He couldn't see anyone. But that didn't mean no one watched him. *Who'd have thought there were so many shades of black in the world?*

Woods expelled a loud breath of frustration, chided himself for his foolishness and continued his journey. He heard no more footsteps but he still had the sensation of eyes boring into his back as he walked. The tension in the tavern had unnerved him, he told himself firmly.

Sighing with relief, he entered the brightly lit taproom of The Bell Inn and made his way up to his bedchamber. He sank wearily into his bed, determined to get a good night's sleep.

His mind, however, had other plans and it refused to shut down. Over and over again, it relived his interview with Billy Sculthorpe which culminated in the terrified man's undignified scuttle beneath the bed. Woods tossed and turned on his pillow as Billy's sobs and screams echoed around his mind. Finally, he fell asleep.

A tiny old woman with a gentle, lined face sat sewing in her rocking chair by the kitchen fireplace in his childhood home. It was his mother. Woods' heart surged with joy. Tilda's white head of hair was bent low over the material, which fell in soft folds onto her lap. Her eyesight was failing, he knew this. He needed to get her some spectacles – and more candles. The silver needle glinted in the firelight as she held it poised above her work in her long, arthritic fingers.

'Ma.' His voice cracked with emotion.

'Neddy.' She lifted up her head and smiled up at him. 'My little Neddy.'

'Not so little now, Ma.' Joy flooded through him in a great wave of relief. She wasn't dead after all.

Suddenly, her smile disappeared and disappointment and pain stretched across her face. 'Why did you kill him, Neddy?' she asked.

'Who?' He gasped with confusion. She nodded her white head towards the prostrate body lying at his feet. He stepped back in alarm. His heart leapt in his chest. It was the dead man from the docks . . . or was it the dead man in another dream? The bloody, grey brains still oozed out from the gash on the corpse's head. This time they slithered down over the striped rag rug on his mother's kitchen floor.

'I'm disappointed in you, Neddy,' she whispered.

Heartbroken, he opened his mouth to scream out his denial – and jerked awake. The dream disappeared in a flash but its vividness left his heart racing and the blood pounding in his ears.

Cursing, he swung his feet over the side onto the cold floor. His fingers trembled as he lit the bedside candle. Then he cradled his head in his hands and tried to pull back the image of his mother's smile before it melted away back into the sleepy recesses of his mind. But all he saw was her heart-wrenching disappointment. He swallowed down his sadness, and the action hurt his throat.

For a few moments he remained still, trying to make sense of this latest nightmare. 'Neddy' was his mother's pet name for him. Billy Sculthorpe had called him 'Neddy' the previous day. Perhaps it had triggered some reaction in his old noddle? 'Damn you, Billy Sculthorpe,' he groaned. 'I'll call you bloody Neddy.'

But who was the dead man with his pate caved in? And why did he haunt Woods' dreams?

Woods steeled himself and tried to remember the faces of the corpses he had come across in his work over the last few years. The last one had been the dead actress whose mysterious death he and Lavender had investigated just before they travelled to Northamptonshire. At the same time they had dragged the bloated body of the pimp out of the Thames. Before that, there had been the soot-blackened body of a child he tenderly carried out of the ruins of a smouldering building. He winced at the memory. He remembered a man gored to death by an escaped bull from Smithfield market. Rows of felons dancing at the end of their ropes on the gibbet at Tyburn, a dead prostitute lying in the gutter of Covent Garden and a man who'd bled to death after being stabbed in a fight. But none of them shared the same head injury as the man in his dreams.

He gave up this gruesome trawl through his memory and shook himself to clear away his melancholy thoughts. *It is no good worrying about it*, he decided as he blew out the candle. He had no memory of the corpse in his nightmare and he was too old to be spooked by his dreams. Sighing, he lay back down, pulled up the blankets and tried to get back to sleep.

Chapter Nineteen

Sunday 4th March, 1810
Market Harborough, Leicestershire

The first light of dawn crept through the gap in the drapes at the window when Woods roused himself, washed, shaved and dressed.

A hot bowl of porridge vanquished his nightmare and soon made him feel more like his old self again. He had just laid down his spoon when he remembered he was about to return to the miserable fare dished up by Susie Dicken in The Woolpack in Middleton. He promptly ordered a second bowl of porridge and a plate of eggs and ham from the landlord as well.

It was still too early to attend church so Woods decided to stretch his legs and take a walk up to the newly built canal basin. It was another beautiful morning full of birdsong and the fresh smell of spring. The grass glistened with dew and the low sun behind the boughs of the trees cast long shadows across his path as he followed the Leicester Road up to the top of the town.

Market Harborough canal basin was far smaller and much quieter than the filthy, crowded docks he had grown up with beside the Thames. It had an unfinished air about it too. There was a single rectangular basin and a solitary, hastily erected wooden warehouse. But it was still a hive of activity. In front of the warehouse, a crane hauled tea chests out of the hull of a barge. Sweating men heaved on the chains and the ropes, their shoulder muscles taut beneath their filthy jackets. Beside them, the wharfinger yelled at them to be careful with their precious cargo.

On the far side of the basin, a group of men shovelled coal into barrows from the hull of another barge and the basin echoed with their shouts and the dull thud and scrape of their shovels. They wheeled the squeaking barrows along a narrow plank off the boat and added the coal to the mountainous piles of glistening fuel on the wharf. As each barrowful shimmered down the side of the coal heap it released a choking cloud of black dust.

Meanwhile, a gang of grubby children raced in and out between the piles of coal. The irritated wharfinger glanced across the water, cursed and yelled out a threat to the youngsters. Woods smiled as he remembered the numerous times when he and his childhood friends had been chased away from the Thames waterfront by furious stevedores.

He walked past several high stacks of timber and headed for the towing path. He had no idea if the path was open to the public or not but he doubted if anyone would try to stop him now most of the town knew he was a police officer. Four lecherous mallards chased an exhausted female duck between two empty and deserted barges moored side by side. Moving gently with the breeze, their mooring lines slowly tightened and then sagged once again.

At the entrance to the basin, another boat waited patiently to unload its cargo of coal. A gaunt, windburnt lad was unshackling the tired horse, ready to lead it to the stable. The lad's silver earring flashed in the sunlight as his deft fingers detached the towing rope from the harness. An older man with a lined and wind-leathered face held the barge steady beside the bank with another rope. He glanced up curiously as Woods walked past, muttering, 'Ar do.'

Woods nodded politely to the fellow but he had no desire to stop and talk.

Weighed down by its cargo, the still boat was low in the water. A fine layer of coal dust covered everything and was etched into the lines on the faces of the men, ground into the palms of their filthy hands. Even the name of the boat on the bow was indecipherable beneath the peeling paintwork. Not that it mattered. Woods knew most of the men and boys who worked the canals couldn't read.

Picking his way carefully between the heaps of horse dung littering the towing path, Woods headed away from the town. The canal meandered like a scar across the rural landscape as it followed the contours of the ridge above Market Harborough. It was more peaceful here. A solitary swan glided seamlessly across the still water with barely a ripple. Beneath the surface he saw the bottom of the canal, where a shoal of tiny fish darted between the swaying strands of weed.

The navvies had cut back the vegetation during the recent construction but already the foliage had crept back towards the edge of the canal, especially on the bank opposite. There, without the trampling hooves of the horses and the scything action of taut tow ropes, the willow weed had grown tall. It now fringed the far bank.

There were other signs that life had washed down this manmade waterway from the pound above. The broad leaves of water lilies bobbed amongst the reeds. Somewhere a bullfrog croaked and a territorial heron eyed him suspiciously from the opposite bank. Woods stopped in his tracks. Herons meant fish. He peered into the water looking for the telltale flash of silver or concentric ripples forming on the surface and for a moment he wished he had his rod and line with him and a few hooks and feathers. It would be a peaceful place to sit awhile and fish.

Suddenly the hairs stood up on the back of his neck and, despite the warm sunshine, he shivered. It was the same uneasy sensation he had felt last night in the deserted town square. Someone was watching him. But when he spun round there was no one there. His ears strained against the gentle lapping of the water on the bank and the birdsong but he heard nothing. He shook his head over his foolishness and continued his walk. Maybe he had been working too hard recently.

Woods rounded a bend and came to an arched brick bridge. The towing path led straight over it and promptly changed to the other side of the canal. He paused on the hump of the bridge, leant on the stone parapet and enjoyed the view of the valley below the ridge. This was the kind of countryside Woods liked best: an open vista with gently rolling hills. He sighed when he thought of Betsy and his children back home in the noisy, overcrowded capital and he wished he was sharing this with them. His little nippers had never seen the countryside. Not real countryside like this. In fact, he couldn't remember the last time Betsy had left the hard, cramped streets of Southwark and walked with grass and soft earth beneath her feet.

He imagined Eddie and Dan careering round the hayfields and little Rachel making daisy chains of wild flowers while dangling her bare toes in the clear water of the canal. Perhaps he should take them out of the city for a day trip when he returned? Although how his diminutive wife would react to such an unusual fancy he had no idea. No doubt Betsy would have an opinion. She usually did. He smiled at the thought.

For the first time today, his mind drifted back to the case and he scowled. Senseless murder, vicious assault, blackmail, poisonous mushrooms and secretive Catholics skulking around the local villages spoiled the image of the rural idyll he had enjoyed only a few moments before. Besides which, it rattled his old noddle when he tried to make sense of it all. Thankfully, he knew he didn't have to – this was Lavender's job. Lavender would eventually solve the mystery. He always did. But for the life of him, Woods couldn't see where this case was heading. Lavender had quickly dismissed the notion that the Panther Gang was responsible for the crime and as far as Woods knew, they still didn't have any credible suspects for the murder.

Now that would have been a feather in their caps, he decided – to have caught those notorious Panthers. They might even have got a mention in the news-sheets – and there would have been a good monetary reward. There always was for villains like them. But no. Lavender had decided Sculthorpe's murder was the handiwork of a local gang. And if there was one thing Woods knew after working with Lavender for twelve years, the detective was rarely wrong.

Woods shrugged. It would all become clear in the end.

A brilliant flash of turquoise distracted Woods from his thoughts. He leant over the stone parapet and watched a tiny kingfisher dart in and out of the glistening water below, fishing for minnows.

'Ar do,' said a gruff voice beside him.

Woods straightened up sharply. Alby Kilby stood beside him with a fishing rod in his hand and a bag of tackle slung over his shoulder. For a large man, Kilby could move quietly.

'Mornin',' Woods replied pleasantly. He stepped aside to let Kilby pass but the landlord wasn't going anywhere. He stopped, leant over the parapet next to Woods and stared moodily at the canal below. The broad shoulders beneath his greatcoat hunched up around his thick neck. His face was now in profile and backlit by the sun. His thick mop of curls gleamed pure white but they did nothing to soften the scowl on his heavily lined face.

'They tell me ye've become a Bow Street Runner,' Kilby growled.

The question was phrased in a strange way, Woods thought, but the answer was simple enough. 'Yes, I'm a horse patrol officer with the Bow Street Police Office in London.'

Kilby shook his head sadly. 'I were never expectin' that.'

'What do you mean?'

The landlord roused himself and straightened up but he avoided eye contact with Woods. 'When I first met you and the other fellah at The Angel, I never thought you were police. I didn't expect that.'

'Why should you? As I told your wife last night, I'm here with Detective Lavender investigatin' the murder of William Sculthorpe in Middleton.'

Kilby nodded his bowed head slowly. 'Yus. That were a bad do. Where's this detective now?'

'Detective Lavender has had to return to London.'

'So yer alone?' Kilby glanced up and Woods saw the excitement flash in his grey eyes. The drooping corners of the landlord's mouth lifted into a half-smile.

Woods hesitated. A warning bell rang in his head. Kilby was a suspect in their investigation and he was behaving strangely. Conscious of the landlord's closeness and powerful build, he assessed his situation carefully. He was alone in an isolated area with a colossus who would have no trouble flicking him over the edge of a bridge like a twig if he felt like it. He had no idea why Kilby might want to harm him but every instinct told him to be careful. To Woods' relief, a plodding horse led by a small boy came around the bend in the canal. A barge soon appeared in its wake.

'Is there somethin' you want to tell me about the night of the great storm, when William Sculthorpe were murdered?' Woods asked sharply.

The gleam in Kilby's eyes was replaced with a flash of confusion. 'No.'

'What did you do that night? Where were you?'

Kilby shrugged. 'We opened the tavern but shut her oop early because of the weather.'

'What time were this?'

The landlord shrugged again and frowned.

'Did you see or hear anythin' unusual that might help us with our investigation?'

'No, I didn't. What you askin' me for?'

'It's my job.'

'Aye, yer job,' Kilby echoed. His throat slowly strangled his words. 'Yer damned, bloody job.'

Woods' mouth dropped open in surprise. Before he could ask what the other man meant, Kilby stepped back from the parapet, lowered his head again and held out a hand towards Woods. It was a second or two before Woods realised the landlord wanted to shake hands with him.

'It's been nice meetin' up with yer, Constable.' Kilby grasped Woods' hand tightly in his great fist and squeezed. The landlord was reluctant to let him go. For a moment, Woods worried Kilby would squeeze the life out of his hand. 'But A've to be on my way now.' Kilby dropped his hand, turned on his heel and headed back down onto the towing path in the direction of Market Harborough, swinging his fishing rod alongside him. He shook his head as he walked.

Gawd's teeth! What were all that about? Woods wondered.

A niggling thought took root in his confused mind. He had the strong impression that Alby Kilby had sought him out to tell him something but had lost his nerve at the last minute.

Woods shrugged. It would keep. In the meantime, he needed to track down some of The Angel Inn's regular customers and try and establish exactly what time Kilby had shut the tavern on the night of the great storm. As yet, the man had no alibi for the time of the murder.

Woods enjoyed the Sunday service at St Dionysius' Church. There were plenty of hymns, the musicians were accomplished and the acoustics in the high-vaulted, stone-arched church were excellent. He liked singing and belted out the words to the hymns in his rich, deep baritone, oblivious to the stares of his neighbours in the congregation who were mesmerised by the singing policeman from London.

After the service, he retrieved his horse from the stables and set out back to Middleton. A thin veil of silvery mist floated above some of the low-lying fields but the sun glimmered hazily in the sky above him.

It took him several hours to travel the seven miles between Market Harborough and Middleton because he called at all the cottages and farmhouses lining the road. The farmers and labourers who answered the door to him were surprised, polite but unhelpful. No one had seen or heard a gang of men riding to or from Middleton on the night of the storm. He knew the gang had disappeared on the Rockingham Road but he reasoned that as he had plenty of time before Lavender's return, he might as well investigate every road in and out of the village.

It was growing dark when he finally handed over the reins of his horse to the blacksmith at the village forge and tramped wearily along the quiet street towards The Woolpack Inn. The tavern was quieter tonight and apart from the Bunnings, Susie Dicken and old Pete Jarman, Woods didn't recognise any of the customers hunched over the low tables.

While he ate the thin stew and soggy dumplings served up by Susie Dicken, Woods watched the interaction between her and the landlord's young nephew. Isaac Bunning didn't miss an opportunity to fondle the woman every time she glided past his table, but then again, neither did half of the men in the room. The jiltish ladybird enjoyed the attention and flirted and giggled her way from table to table, stroking the men's beards and sideburns, touching their hands and sometimes sitting in their laps. As soon as Frank

Bunning appeared, everyone behaved with decorum around Susie and the woman became quieter, more dignified and less tactile.

Woods cursed as he jarred his tooth on a sharp piece of gristle. He spat it out and stared down at the unappetising slop before him. He didn't recognise the meat and wondered if the damned woman had skinned an old cat for his evening meal.

As if on cue, Susie let out a peal of laughter. Frank Bunning was absent from the room and once again she was sitting on Isaac's lap. The young man fondled her left breast. It was obvious to Woods that Isaac's feelings for Susie weren't those a nephew normally held for the woman betrothed to his uncle. But how far had lust led Isaac and Susie? Had they consummated their relationship, and if so, had William Sculthorpe known about this? Did he threaten to tell Isaac's uncle and blackmail the young man for cash? Is that why *I.B.* was amongst the list of initials on Sculthorpe's list?

Woods remembered again how Pete Jarman told him that William Sculthorpe liked to watch folks and listen to their conversations. He also remembered the movement they had heard out in the upstairs corridor during their first night at the inn. Smiling, Woods finally remembered the packet of black powder he had at the bottom of his old carpet bag upstairs. If Lavender wanted evidence, he would get it for him.

He pushed away the remains of his meal, glanced at the uncovered face of the battered old longcase clock in the corner of the drab room and ordered another tankard of ale.

Everything comes to him who waits . . .

Chapter Twenty

Sunday 4th March, 1810
Marylebone, London

Lavender breathed a huge sigh of relief when the hansom cab drew up outside his grey-bricked terrace house in Westcastle Square. He was starving, exhausted and every bone in his body ached, thanks to the twenty-four-hour dash down from Northamptonshire he had endured in the mail coach. Although he didn't as a rule need much sleep, he had pushed himself to the limit with this journey, snatching only a few moments here and there in the uncomfortable carriage. Every time the vehicle had jolted, braked violently or swung into the yard of a coaching inn to change horses he'd been jerked awake.

He climbed out stiffly, paid the driver of his cab and noticed with curiosity another empty cab waiting outside his house. A light still burned behind the drapes of the ground-floor drawing-room window. Magdalena must be entertaining, he realised, and he glanced down at his creased, travel-stained clothing in dismay. His feisty, aristocratic beloved wouldn't appreciate him appearing in her drawing room in this state. Thankfully, a light also still burned in the basement kitchen of the property. His housekeeper Mrs Hobart must still be here. He pushed open the gate in the iron railings that fronted his house and descended the steep flight of stone steps.

Mrs Hobart started with surprise as he entered the well-lit and cheerful kitchen but she recovered quickly. Her plump, friendly face beamed with delight and she bobbed him a respectful curtsey. 'Why, sir, what a surprise! We weren't expectin' you home for several days yet!'

'I didn't expect to return so quickly either, Mrs Hobart.' He peeled off his gloves and undid his coat. 'My current case has unexpectedly brought me back to the capital.' The lingering smell of roast meat and freshly baked bread in the kitchen made his mouth water and reminded him of his empty stomach. He glanced hopefully at the kitchen range.

Mrs Hobart intercepted his glance. 'You must be famished with all that travellin',' she declared. 'I've dampened down the stove for the night but I'll make up a platter of cold meats, bread and cheese, if you like? And I can put on a pot of coffee.'

'That would be excellent, Mrs Hobart,' he said with relief. 'And perhaps a glass of port to go with the cheese?' She nodded, smiled and lifted the black iron kettle back onto the range. His eyes fell on her grey coat and black bonnet thrown over the corner of the well-scrubbed kitchen table. 'I see you were about to depart home, Mrs Hobart. Perhaps Teresa can bring it upstairs?' Normally Magdalena's little Spanish maid spent her evenings down here in the warmth of the kitchen but there was no sign of Teresa tonight.

'The poor gal has a terrible head cold,' Mrs Hobart said, as she sliced a fresh loaf on the breadboard. 'Doña Magdalena sent her to her bed this afternoon. Don't you worry, sir, I'll sort out your supper before I leave.'

Lavender had never had much to do with servants, apart from Mrs Perry, who had laundered his shirts, but he had mysteriously acquired Mrs Hobart along with the property the previous month. After a brief acquaintance, Magdalena had decided they should keep her in their employment. This had proved an excellent decision. Apart from making their comfort her main priority, the kindly old woman hadn't raised an eyebrow when he had moved his foreign bride-to-be and her maid out of their dreadful lodgings in Cheapside and installed them in the house ahead of their nuptials. In fact, she didn't seem unduly concerned that the master of the house had just let himself into her kitchen through the servants' entrance.

Naturally, he had kept up his rooms in Southwark to keep up appearances and protect Magdalena's reputation but he knew theirs was an unusual arrangement, despite being eminently practical. Prior to his departure for Northamptonshire, they had picked out furnishings for their new home and Magdalena's presence in the house meant she was available to oversee their delivery and installation.

'Has Doña Magdalena already eaten?' he asked.

'Oh, yes. She dined earlier.'

'Who is our visitor?' he asked.

Mrs Hobart's face beamed with delight again. 'Why! 'Tis Lady Caroline Clare!' she exclaimed. 'You never told me, sir, that we would be entertainin' aristocracy when you purchased the house. My daughter Joan will be overcome when she hears I've served coffee to a real lady tonight!'

Lavender struggled to keep his face composed in the light of her excitement. He wondered wryly if Mrs Hobart and her daughter Joan would be quite so excited if they knew of Lady Caroline's notorious reputation amongst the Beau Monde of London. Twice widowed, and with a penchant for younger men, Lady Caroline was often impoverished. Baron Clare had left his wife and daughters with very little income and Lady Caroline, a talented artist, was now forced to accept portrait commissions in order to survive.

But her presence in his home tonight was fortuitous – he had intended to call on her the following morning and ask for her assistance. Caroline Clare was also the Catholic daughter of an earl. If anyone could get him the introduction he needed to the British Catholic hierarchy, it was her. Besides which, she owed him a favour or two. A few years ago he had helped extricate her from a delicate situation when a former young lover had threatened to blackmail her, and only last month he had solved the mysterious and tragic death of her stepdaughter Harriet Willoughby.

He now needed to clean himself up and change as quickly as possible. Despite her notoriety, Lady Caroline liked her men clean and fresh. He didn't want her aristocratic nose wrinkling in disgust at the smell of him.

'Please excuse me, Mrs Hobart, while I use your scullery to wash myself and change my shirt,' he said. 'The road from Northamptonshire is very dusty.'

His housekeeper raised her grey eyebrows at such unconventional goings-on but the smile never left her face. Picking up his travelling bag from the tiled floor, he headed for the chilly scullery at the back of the kitchen.

Middleton, Northamptonshire

Back at The Woolpack, Frank Bunning was shutting up his tavern for the night. Woods downed the last of his ale and climbed the narrow wooden staircase up to the miserable bedchamber he had previously shared with Lavender. The room still seemed cramped even though he now occupied it alone. The smell hadn't improved, he noticed. He lowered himself onto one of the lumpy mattresses and waited patiently by the light of his guttering candle, listening.

For half an hour or so, all he heard were the roof tiles shifting above his head in the breeze and tiny showers of soot slithering down the chimney. The last drunk left the tavern below and staggered up the street, singing raucously as he went.

Eventually, Woods heard the soft step of Susie Dicken's heels on the narrow wooden staircase. A faint light flickered briefly in the crack beneath his door as she passed by. He heard the click of the latch as the attic door opened and closed and she went up to her own bedchamber.

Frank and Isaac Bunning came up the stairs together, talking quietly. The two men said 'Goodnight' on the landing and went into their rooms.

As the quiet of the night enveloped the building, Woods opened up his old carpet bag and rummaged through it. At the bottom, he found his old pouch of black powder. He weighed it in his palm and realised he would have to use it sparingly; there wasn't much left.

His ears strained for any sound of movement, Woods took off his boots and quietly let himself out onto the landing. He left his candle in his room but with the door open he still had enough light to find his way to the men's bedchambers at the end of the corridor. Frank Bunning was already snoring but he heard movement within Isaac's room. A candle still burned; its light glimmered beneath the door.

Woods undid the pouch, stooped low and sprinkled the fine black powder along the floorboards. As he backed up the corridor, he silently prayed that neither of the Bunnings would leave their rooms and catch him bent double over the floor of the landing. That might take some explaining.

Only when the last of his precious powder had fluttered out of his pouch onto the floor in front of the door that led up to Susie's attic bedchamber did he beat a silent but hasty retreat back into his own room.

There was nothing to do now except wait until dawn. Woods blew out his candle and settled himself down for an uncomfortable night's sleep on the stinking pile of mouldy straw these people called a mattress.

Just as he drifted off to sleep, he heard the soft click of a door latch and someone move stealthily down the landing. Woods smiled to himself in the darkness. What was that silly expression a toothless old Ethiopian sailor had once told him down at the docks?

Softly, softly, catches the monkey . . .

Chapter Twenty-One

Sunday 4th March, 1810
Marylebone, London

Lavender pushed open the door of the drawing room. Washed, shaved and now wearing a fresh shirt and a burgundy cravat beneath his gold-striped silk waistcoat and a freshly brushed coat, he felt clean and refreshed.

Magdalena and Lady Caroline were draped elegantly across the dark blue velvet sofas in front of the blazing fireplace. They were leaning towards each other, engrossed in conversation like a pair of sisters, and he wondered at the close friendship that had sprung up between his beloved Spanish fiancée and Lady Caroline in such a short time. It was hardly surprising the two women had become such good friends, he realised. They were both widowed young, shared a love of Magdalena's Spain and had their religion in common (although neither of them bothered God much with supplications). In addition to this, they were both impoverished aristocrats with plenty of determination, spirit and resilience in the face of adversity.

'Stephen!' Magdalena rose to greet him. Her beautiful face

glowed with delight and the sound of her soft Castilian accent sent a wave of happiness coursing through his veins.

'How lovely!' she murmured. 'I didn't expect to see you for days.' Her dark, smouldering eyes met his and a spark of mutual understanding and attraction flashed between them again. He wanted to embrace her and press his mouth over her soft lips but he had to be satisfied with kissing the hand she offered to him. *We're not married yet*, she reminded him with her eyes – *and we're not alone.*

'How are you, Magdalena?' he asked.

'Happy to see you.' She gave him a brilliant smile. 'It has been a good day. This morning I also received a letter from Sebastián.'

'Is he well?'

Sebastián, Magdalena's young son, was away at boarding school in Hertfordshire.

'I think so.' She frowned. 'He writes to me in English this time but I can't decipher some of the expressions he uses. We may need your investigative powers to translate the letter.'

'Ah, schoolboy slang.' Lavender shook his head in mock solemnity. 'I'm sorry, Magdalena, but this task may be beyond the skill of a Principal Officer. Even Bow Street's finest can't penetrate the mystery of the language and codes of a British schoolboy.'

Magdalena laughed and led him over to the fireplace, where Lady Caroline remained seated, with her silver-topped walking cane resting against the side of her chair.

Lavender bowed and kissed Lady Caroline's hand. 'Good evening, Lady Caroline. As always, it's a pleasure to see you.' And it was. Caroline Clare had walked with the aid of her cane since the coaching accident that killed her first husband but she was an attractive, witty and intelligent redhead who turned heads in every room she entered. Tonight she wore black ostrich feathers in her pearl-studded turban, reminding him that she was in mourning following the unexpected death of her stepdaughter.

'It's a pleasure to see you again, Detective,' she said.

Lavender appreciated the comfort of the soft upholstery of the cushions on his aching bones as he sank down into his chair next to the fire.

'Have you eaten, Stephen?' Magdalena asked.

'Mrs Hobart is preparing me a cold platter as we speak,' he reassured her. 'I'm afraid this is a brief visit, ladies. The case I'm investigating has brought me home but I must return to Northamptonshire as soon as possible and I have to confess I'm exhausted through lack of sleep. I shall have to return to my rooms in Southwark very soon.'

'What a shame,' Lady Caroline murmured. 'You work too hard, Detective.'

'Would you like a brandy, Stephen?' Magdalena asked.

'That would be very welcome.'

She rose gracefully and glided across to an elegant rosewood console table where she poured him a generous measure. The candlelight caught the gleam of the glossy black curls on the top of her bowed head as she leant over the crystal decanter. The candlelight also revealed the translucent quality of her diaphanous white gown. Lavender caught a tantalising glimpse of her slender waist and curvaceous hips as she moved.

Reluctantly, he tore his eyes away from Magdalena and turned his attention back to their guest. 'I'm relieved to see you here tonight, Lady Caroline,' he said. 'I need to ask for your assistance with my current case.'

The finely arched eyebrows over her sharp, grey eyes rose in astonishment. 'My goodness! How on earth can *I* assist *you*, Detective?'

'I need an introduction,' he said. 'I seek an audience with Bishop John Douglass, the Vicar Apostolic of the London District. I know he won't like police officers but I hope you can persuade him to speak with me.'

'Good grief!' Lady Caroline's eyes widened with surprise. 'Why? What has the old devil done?'

Lavender smiled. 'Nothing criminal that I'm aware of,' he replied. 'I simply hope Bishop Douglass might remember something about an elderly priest called Father William Sculthorpe. It's Sculthorpe's murder I'm investigating in Northamptonshire.'

'What a disappointment! John Douglass is such a dry old stick. For a moment I thought you were going to tell us something interesting and scandalous about the man.'

He smiled again. 'I'm sorry to disappoint you.'

Magdalena returned with his brandy and he took a long drink. The tension eased from his tired body and mind as the amber spirit hit the back of this mouth and warmed his throat and stomach.

'Bishop Douglass is easy to find,' Lady Caroline said. 'The London Catholics use the chapel at the Sardinian Embassy as their base and have done so for the last few decades. No doubt he will be there. He's very old and rarely travels far.'

Lavender nodded. *Old.* This was good. The older the better. He desperately needed to talk to someone who remembered William Sculthorpe's early life.

The brandy, warmth and comfort fired up a devil inside of him. 'Does Bishop Douglass know who you are, Lady Caroline?' he asked.

'Of course he does!' she exclaimed in surprise. 'I've attended Mass several times – at least – well, several times this year. Bishop Douglass is very aware of who I am.'

Magdalena smiled. 'I think Stephen is teasing you, Lady Caroline.'

Lady Caroline's face relaxed into a smile. Lavender had no doubt the bishop would recognise Caroline Clare instantly. Even the most devoted and celibate priest couldn't fail to be affected by the charm, confidence and elegance of her presence. Tonight she wore a black, see-through chiffon overgown above her exquisitely embroidered and decorated silk dress. Lavender had never professed to be an expert on women's fashion but he suspected Lady Caroline was overdressed for taking coffee with Magdalena and wondered if she had another engagement later that evening.

'Well, that's settled, Detective,' Lady Caroline declared. 'I shall take you to meet Bishop Douglass in the morning.'

'Shall I call for you at about nine o'clock?' Lavender asked.

'Good heavens, no! That is a most uncivilised time of the day. No, you may call for me at eleven.'

Lavender's heart sank. He had another call to make after he had met the Vicar Apostolic and he wanted to take the mid-afternoon coach back to Northamptonshire.

'Perhaps we should compromise and meet at ten o'clock?' he asked.

'Oh, very well,' she said. 'Although what my maid will think to such early rising, I can't say.'

'Shall I come too?' Magdalena asked.

'I'm not sure that this would be a good idea, my dear,' Lady Caroline said. 'The moment Bishop Douglass finds out you're betrothed to Stephen, he will want you to arrange a Catholic wedding service. He may become distracted by the peril in which you're placing your soul, which of course we all know will be nonsense.'

Lavender was pleased to see Magdalena nod in agreement. They had decided to marry quietly and simply in the Protestant faith at the Church of St Saviour and St Mary Overie in Southwark, where Lavender's grandfather had been Dean. Out of respect for Lavender's family connection to the church, the current Dean, The Very Reverend George Elton, had overlooked Magdalena's Catholicism and agreed to perform the service. '*It doesn't matter in what building you take your vows, my dears,*' he had said to them. '*God doesn't mind. But he will be watching to see you fulfil them.*'

'In fact, Detective,' Lady Caroline continued, 'Bishop Douglass may try to convert you to Catholicism – with or without Magdalena in the room.'

'I will bear this in mind,' he said wryly.

'Talking about our wedding, Stephen,' Magdalena said. 'They called the banns at St Saviour's for the second time this morning – and no one objected.'

He laughed and smiled at her fondly. 'Did you think someone would?'

'Well, not everyone is happy you're marrying a Catholic,' she said awkwardly. 'Magistrate Read at Bow Street, for example.'

'Magistrate Read wants me to remain married to my job,' he interrupted, more sharply than he intended. He softened his voice when he saw the surprise in her eyes. 'Read will come around to the idea. And as for the rest of our friends and my family . . .' He paused and smiled. 'They're so relieved I have finally found a woman who will have me – that they will object to nothing. They're just so happy to see me settling down in marital bliss.'

The two women smiled. 'We shall marry as soon as I finish this case in Northamptonshire and return to London,' he promised her.

'Ah, the joys of a union across the faiths,' Lady Caroline said. 'You may be interested to know, Magdalena, that Bishop Douglass once had the audacity to inform me that because my first husband was Jewish and we'd eloped, my marriage wasn't a true marriage in the eyes of God.'

Magdalena's dark eyes became troubled. 'What did you reply?'

'I fixed him with my most piercing stare, my dear, and told him if God had opened his eyes and looked into our bedroom he would have been left in no doubt that ours was a true marriage of both body and soul.'

Magdalena's hand fluttered over her mouth and she stifled a laugh. 'What did he say to that?'

The jewels in Lady Caroline's rings flashed in the candlelight as she waved her hand dismissively in the air. 'Oh, he shuffled away and never mentioned it again. But this is why I think you need to keep Bishop Douglass ignorant about your relationship with Detective Lavender and your forthcoming marriage at St Saviour's.'

'I understand,' Magdalena said again.

Lady Caroline reached out for her silver-topped cane and rose stiffly to her feet. 'Anyway, I shall leave you two lovebirds in peace for tonight. I can see you only have eyes for each other and I'm now in the way. Besides which, I agreed to dine with Henry Duddles at Almack's and I'm already half an hour late.'

There was a tap on the sitting-room door. Mrs Hobart had arrived with Lavender's supper tray. She placed it on a side table and went to fetch Lady Caroline's cloak and hand muff. When she returned with the garments, Lavender helped Lady Caroline into her cloak and escorted her outside to her carriage.

Once back in the drawing room, he sank wearily back into his fireside chair and pulled his supper tray towards him. 'Please excuse me, my darling,' he said, 'I'm ravenous.'

'Enjoy your food, Stephen.' She picked up her embroidery basket. While he ate, she sewed with her eyes lowered and her dark eyelashes highlighted against the deep golden skin of her flawless cheeks. They chatted for a while about domestic matters and the arrangements for their wedding.

Contentment flooded through him as he watched her. The soft candlelight made Magdalena look younger than her twenty-nine years. He watched the soft movement of her breasts as they rose and fell with the rhythm of her breathing. His loins stirred and his heart swelled at the prospect of a lifetime of evenings spent by this fireside with this beautiful, vivacious and intelligent woman – and soon he would be able to wake up every morning with her in his bed. He was a tactile and physical man and she was his feminine equal.

He wanted a marriage of deep intimacy with Magdalena. He wanted it to stretch out interminably into their old age. He could see them in twenty, no, thirty years' time, finally exhausted with passionate lovemaking and napping companionably by this fireplace. He would have his arm around her and she would rest her greying head on his shoulder. He still couldn't believe he had persuaded this amazing woman to be his wife. Many years ago he had loved another woman but death had cheated him of his bride and taken Vivienne for its own. 'Not this time,' he murmured softly to himself. 'Not this time.'

She glanced up at him and smiled. 'Did you say something, Stephen?'

He shook his head, sat up straighter and sighed. He knew he would have to leave soon to protect her reputation.

Pushing aside the empty supper tray, he strode across the carpet and joined Magdalena on the sofa. He pulled her towards him, encircled her body in his arms and pressed his lips onto hers. The softness and scent of Magdalena's skin sent a fresh wave of passion coursing through his veins. She moaned softly and writhed in his grasp, exciting him further. Finally she wriggled free and looked up at him, laughing. 'You told Lady Caroline you would soon return to your rooms in Southwark,' she whispered.

'I may have lied,' he replied and winked.

Her smile broadened and the tip of her tongue darted out to wet her lips. 'Mrs Hobart has gone home – but please don't forget that Teresa is still in the house, Stephen.'

What did this mean? Was it an invitation to stay for the night, provided he was careful of her reputation? Would he have to pick up his boots and creep out of the house in his stockinged feet at dawn to avoid scandalising her maid?

He decided to test the water with his caresses. He lowered his head and kissed her neck, her earlobes, her soft cheeks and closed eyelids before planting his mouth onto her lips once more. His arms encircled her waist briefly before his hands took on a life of their own and started to explore the voluptuous curves of her body.

She broke away from his embrace once more. 'Stephen! Let me breathe! Let me rest a moment!' Her eyes smiled up at him and she nestled her head against his shoulder. He held her there, savouring the intimacy, the scent of her hair and her warmth. His exhausted body was torn between his desire for Magdalena and his desperate need for sleep. But his traitorous overactive mind wasn't ready to relax yet.

'Magdalena?'

'Mmm?' She had closed her own eyes now.

'You were born in July, weren't you?'

'Yes.'

'Are you named for your Saint's Day? The Feast of St Mary Magdalene?'

'Mmm.'

'What date is it?'

'July 22nd.' Her eyes flashed open and she smiled again. 'Why do you ask me about my name day, Stephen? Are you already planning my gift?'

He smiled back down at her. 'I met a man who was also born on your Saint's Day.'

'That's nice,' she said, closing her eyes again. 'Is he called Magdalena too?'

Chapter Twenty-Two

Monday 5th March, 1810
Middleton, Northamptonshire

Woods' rumbling stomach woke him well before dawn. He knew that it would. His supper had been so poor the night before it was inevitable he would be famished by early morning. Ignoring his hunger, he pulled on his coat against the cold and relit the candle. He left his bedchamber in his stockinged feet and quietly retraced his steps back out onto the cold landing. Dropping down onto his haunches, he held the candle a few inches above the floorboards.

He could only just see the outline of footsteps in the fine powder against the age-darkened and filthy wood but he saw enough to satisfy himself. A pair of man's footsteps led to the door at the bottom of the attic staircase – and a second pair had returned via the same route. Susie Dicken had received a nocturnal visitor in the night but her visitor was already back in his own bed. Carefully, Woods followed them to the door of Isaac Bunning's bedchamber.

Woods grinned. 'Naughty boy,' he whispered beneath his breath. Gently, he brushed away the powder into the cracks between the floorboards.

It looked likely that William Sculthorpe had been blackmailing young Isaac. And now they knew why.

Isaac Bunning was laying with the woman his uncle intended to marry.

Woods devoured the meagre, greasy breakfast served up at The Woolpack, then beat a hasty path down the main street to Mrs Tilley's bakery for some proper food. Woods also suspected that Mrs Tilley might be able to help him with the next part of his inquiries. Lavender wanted him to identify the owners of the initials in Sculthorpe's account book and he'd suggested Woods use the parish registers in St Mary Magdalene's Church in Cottingham to help him with this process. But Woods knew Mrs Tilley's bakehouse was the pulsating heart of the village. If anyone could tell him who owned the initials *M.T.T.*, *J.D.* and *J.W.*, it would be her.

The doorbell tinkled above his head when Woods entered the bakery. The delicious aroma of freshly baked bread and pastries wafted from her ovens. There were no other customers and Mrs Tilley was kneading dough at the large wooden table in the centre of the warm shop. The sleeves of her striped dimity dress were rolled up, revealing her strong, freckled forearms. She thrust her hands into the soggy dough, raised it in the air, then dropped it back onto the table with a resounding slap. She gave him a welcoming smile. 'Good mornin', Constable. What can I help you with today?'

'I'm hopin' you might be able to help me with our investigation, Mrs Tilley.'

Her eyes widened with surprise. 'Oooh, I'll do what I can.'

'We've uncovered some initials in an old notebook owned by Mr Sculthorpe,' Woods told her, 'and we're tryin' to work out who he were writin' about.'

'What are these initials?' Using a large flat knife she deftly sliced the dough into quarters and shaped each piece into a loaf.

Woods reeled off the list of initials they were investigating.

'*M.T.T.*?' A smile lit up her face. 'Well, that's easy! It's Morgan Turnbull-Thatcher. He owns the haberdashery in Cottingham.' She covered the loaves with cloths, pushed them to one side of the table, then wiped her floury hands on her apron.

'Really?' Woods' face flushed with delight. His quest for information rarely met with such immediate success. He remembered the draper. He had met Morgan Turnbull-Thatcher on Saturday while traipsing around the two villages with Sculthorpe's money bag. Come to think of it, Mr Turnbull-Thatcher had been unusually nervous while Woods was in his shop. The man's hands had trembled when he examined the tatty cloth bag. Woods pulled out his notebook and pencil and made a note of Morgan Turnbull-Thatcher's name.

'Yes, he just calls himself Morgan Thatcher but his full name is painted above the lintel of the shop door,' Mrs Tilley continued. A shadow passed across her face beneath her frilled white cap. 'He hasn't done somethin' wrong, has he?'

'No, no,' Woods reassured her. 'We're just tryin' to work out who Mr Sculthorpe were writin' about in his notebook.'

Satisfied, she nodded. 'Oh, and the *J.W.* will be Doctor Wallace, of course. He attended young Billy a few weeks back when he were ill. That'll be why Mr Sculthorpe wrote about him.'

Woods bit back his disappointment. 'Isn't there anyone else hereabouts with the initials *J.W.*?'

She paused and screwed up her broad face as she tried to remember. 'I don't think so. There were a woman called Jane Webb – but she left the village last year.'

'And what about *J.D.*?' he asked.

'Well!' She laughed. 'I'm not sure where to start there!'

'What do you mean?'

'It's the Dickens,' she said. 'The relatives of that Susie Dicken from The Woolpack. A whole tribe of them lives in those rundown cottages at the other side of Cottingham. Every one of them is as poor as a church mouse – and several of them are right villains!'

She raised her flour-whitened hand and checked off the Dickens using her fingers. 'There's old Josiah Dicken, his son, Jim – and Jim's son, Jim. Then there's Jack Dicken, his brother, Joseph Dicken – oh, and Joan and Jinny Dicken. Jinny has a son called Jerry – and there's a cousin called Jacob too. He's been up before the magistrate for poachin'.'

Woods tried to make notes of these different Dickens but gave up by the time she had reached Joan Dicken. He snapped his pocket book shut and put it back in his pocket with a frown. Investigating *J.D.* would be more complicated than he had imagined.

'It wouldn't surprise me if some of those Dickens had somethin' to do with the robbery at Mr Sculthorpe's.' Mrs Tilley's face darkened and she lowered her voice. 'They're a bad lot, that family. Jack Dicken hurt a man in a tavern brawl and he had another brother, called Simeon, who were transported for theft.'

'You've been very helpful, Mrs Tilley.'

'It's my pleasure, Constable.' She waved her hand over the loaves, pies and tarts stacked high on her well-scrubbed oak table. 'Now is there anythin' else I can help you with?'

Woods grinned and asked her for a small loaf cut into chunks. He had a busy morning ahead of him by the sound of it and he needed to keep up his strength. Smiling, she obliged and cut up the loaf with her bread knife. 'Would you like butter with it?' she asked.

'Oh, that would be most kind of you, Mrs Tilley.'

She reached for her butter dish and spread the creamy yellow butter generously on his freshly baked bread. Woods took it outside to eat. The butter had already melted into the warm, doughy bread and each bite was like manna from heaven.

Woods licked his buttery lips and made a decision. Lavender

didn't want him to alert any of the owners of the initials in Sculthorpe's book that they were of interest to their inquiry, but Woods had come across nervous, sweating types like Morgan Turnbull-Thatcher before and he knew how to handle them. They needed some answers to the mysteries in this case and Thatcher was the man to provide them. Brushing the last breadcrumbs from his coat, Woods turned and strode off towards Cottingham and the draper's shop.

Woods marched up the short flight of stone steps between the two low-fronted, bow windows of Thatcher's shop and pushed open the door. Another tinkling bell announced his arrival. Two pairs of magnified eyes glanced up from behind their wire spectacles as he entered. Miss Bennett was purchasing some reels of thread and a smile flitted across her thin face when she recognised Woods. Morgan Thatcher's eyes also flashed with recognition but he frowned rather than smiled.

Undeterred, Woods walked towards the counter, passing the rolls of gaily coloured silk, woollen tweed and Manchester cotton leaning against the walls of the shop. Thatcher ignored him, pulled out a roll of cheap fabric and bent over the counter to cut a length for Miss Bennett. The hand holding the scissors shook, Woods noted.

'How lovely to see you again, Constable,' said Miss Bennett.

'It's a pleasure to meet you again too, Miss Bennett.'

'This is Constable Woods from Bow Street in London,' she told the draper. 'He's investigatin' the murder of poor Mr Sculthorpe and came to ask Mother and me some questions on Friday.' Thatcher grunted but didn't glance up from his work. 'Have you found out anythin' yet?' Miss Bennett asked. The spectacles magnified the kindness and concern in her soft, brown eyes.

'Our investigation goes very well,' Woods said. 'Fresh information about William Sculthorpe – and those associated with him

– comes to light every day.' Was it his imagination or had the draper's bowed bald head suddenly flushed?

'Oh, that's good news, isn't it, Mr Thatcher?' The draper glanced up at her, unsmiling. There were beads of sweat above his thin lips.

Woods was concerned Miss Bennett might decide to linger and gossip after she had paid for her purchases, so he offered to carry her parcels of shopping to the door of the shop. Once she had left, he dropped the latch and turned round the dangling 'Open' sign so it read 'Closed' from the outside.

Thatcher watched him silently from behind his counter. *Was he trembling?* He was a small-framed man and he had the hint of weasel about him.

'We need to talk, Mr Turnbull-Thatcher,' Woods said sharply. 'Your name has cropped up in our inquiries in connection with William Sculthorpe.' He planted both hands down on the counter and leant forward menacingly towards the draper. 'Now stop bein' a lyin' wrinkler and tell me what you know.'

'I told you on Saturday,' Thatcher stammered. 'I know nothin' about that money bag.'

Woods fixed him with another glare. 'I haven't come here today to talk about the damned money bag. You know why I'm here.'

Thatcher averted his eyes. 'What is it you think I can help you with, Constable?' He took off his spectacles and started to clean them with the edge of his brown apron.

'We've found evidence,' Woods growled. 'About your cash transactions with William Sculthorpe – and I'll say this, Mr Thatcher, it doesn't look good for you.' Thatcher shuddered. 'I'm givin' you the chance to tell me your side of the story.'

'I did nothin' – it were a mistake!'

'What were a mistake?'

'He, he were a nasty old fellah.' Thatcher's voice rose plaintively. 'He watched me – and made accusations. He said I were short-changin' my customers.' The draper glanced up quickly at Woods but dropped his eyes again when he saw the constable frown. 'He said he'd seen it a couple of times and he . . . he . . .'

'Yes?'

'He threatened to tell all my customers if I didn't pay him money.'

'Were you?'

'What?'

'Cheatin' your customers?'

'No! Of course not. It were a mistake – my, my eyesight isn't as good as it used to be.'

'So he were blackmailin' you?'

'Yes – I had to pay him three shillin's a week.' Woods nodded to himself. That was the amount written in Sculthorpe's account book next to the initials *M.T.T.*

'He were an evil old man.' Thatcher's voice rose with anger. 'He made my life a misery – and he enjoyed it. I couldn't afford it – I didn't deserve it! In fact, I had half decided to sell up the shop and move to Grantham to get away from him.' Thatcher pushed his spectacles back on his long, thin nose and glared defiantly at Woods across the counter. 'He didn't care about the misery he were causin' me!'

Woods never flinched. 'And then he died.'

'What?'

'What were you doin' on the night of the 20th February?'

'What?'

'The night of the great storm – when William Sculthorpe were attacked.'

Shock replaced the anger and defiance in the draper's face. 'Good God! Surely you don't think I had anythin' to do with that? I'm an honest, God-fearin' man!'

'Where were you that night?'

'Here!' Thatcher squeaked. 'In our rooms above the shop – all night – with my wife.'

Woods stood back and a wry smile of triumph twitched at the corners of his mouth, desperate to spread across his face. 'Don't make that move to Grantham just yet, Mr Thatcher,' he said. 'I may want to talk with you again.' He turned on his heel and walked out of the shop. Behind him, Thatcher let out a gulping sob.

Chapter Twenty-Three

Monday 5th March, 1810
Marylebone, London

Lavender's hired carriage arrived promptly at ten o'clock at Lady Caroline's home in leafy Lincoln's Inn Fields but she made him wait for another half an hour before she finally appeared at the door of her home. Today she wore a fetching green velvet coat with a matching bonnet and hand muff. Lavender leapt down from the carriage to greet her and saw a lanky young man in a bronze-coloured coat with a pristine white cravat trailing in her wake. It was Henry Duddles, Lady Caroline's latest lover. Duddles reached out to take Lady Caroline's elbow as she descended the stone steps of the house but she shook him off.

'Don't make a fuss, Henry,' she snapped. 'I can manage with my cane.'

'Good morning, Lady Caroline,' Lavender said pleasantly.

'Good morning, Detective. Please excuse Duddles.' She waved her gloved hand dismissively at the young man behind her. 'The silly young fool insists on accompanying us. I have told him that we're embarking on serious police business but – would you believe it? He thinks this is some sort of *rendez-vous amoureux.*'

Lavender bit back his grin and helped her into the carriage. 'Good morning, Duddles.'

The younger man pushed back the thick fringe of blond curls from his face, flushed and nodded sheepishly at Lavender before clambering up behind Lady Caroline. In all the time Lavender had known Duddles, the nervous fellow had barely said a word in his presence. Although by the sound of it, he was saying plenty in private. Duddles seated himself beside the tight-lipped Lady Caroline. Lavender climbed up and shut the door behind him, sat down and waited patiently for the explosion.

The carriage jolted and slid off into the stream of traffic. Lady Caroline smoothed down the gleaming nap of her velvet coat and fiddled with the ebony buttons and black ribbon that trimmed her cuff. Suddenly, she spun round and pointed an accusing gloved finger at Duddles. 'This is preposterous! This boy is jealous, Lavender! He won't believe an eminent detective like yourself needs help from a mere woman!'

Duddles cowered in his corner of the carriage. He looked as though he wanted to disappear into the cracks in the faded leather seat beneath him. Lavender opened his mouth to speak but decided against it. Lady Caroline hadn't finished.

'I had to bring him with me to prove our assignation was genuine! What does he think we will get up to at such a ridiculously early hour? I can't imagine.' She threw up her hands into the air. 'Who on earth plans a romantic tryst for this godforsaken hour of the day? My maid is quite put out at the early start and I'm sure she has done a poor job with my hair.' She raised her hand to the auburn ringlets framing her face beneath her soft, green velvet bonnet and patted them tenderly.

Lavender heard his cue. 'You look perfect, Lady Caroline,' he said. 'As always, you're the picture of elegance and grace.'

'You're so kind, Detective.' She sighed. 'See, Henry? This is how a true gentleman behaves towards his lady. Why didn't you simply compliment me on my bonnet this morning and let me leave with a kiss?'

Duddles opened his mouth to speak but Lady Caroline had already turned back to Lavender. 'Right, now that this is settled, we shall ignore my jealous paramour and you can tell me about this dreadful murder we're investigating.'

Smiling, Lavender told her about William Sculthorpe.

'A priest?' Her eyes widened in surprise. 'No, no – he should never have married. That is most strange. Are you sure the young man is his son?'

'No, I'm not,' Lavender admitted. 'I don't know who he is. William Sculthorpe was a priest in the London area about twenty-five years ago. I don't suppose you remember a Father William Sculthorpe, do you?'

'Good heavens, Detective! How old do you think I am?' Her voice rose with indignation. 'No, no, I was still a carefree child running wild on my father's dilapidated northern estate twenty-five years ago.'

Lavender wasn't entirely convinced but he knew better than to press the matter. Lady Caroline wasn't in good humour that morning. Besides which, he knew she had only lived in London briefly before eloping to the continent with her first husband, Victor Meyer Rothschild. At this time in her history, her mind had clearly been on other things.

'What about Lady Anne Fitzwilliam?' Lavender asked. 'Do you know of her?'

'Lady Anne? The Dowager Countess Fitzwilliam?' A slight frown creased her high forehead as she struggled to remember. 'I have met her once or twice. She's very old, isn't she? I think she lives in the country and rarely comes to London. I know her son, of course, Earl Fitzwilliam. A charming man and very sympathetic to the notion of Catholic emancipation – although I don't believe he's converted to the religion like his mother.'

Lavender nodded and thanked her. 'And what about the name Debussy? I suspect the Debussys may also be Catholic sympathisers, minor relatives of the Fitzwilliams. Does the name mean anything to you?'

'I'm afraid not.' She sighed wearily and turned towards the carriage window. Soft rivulets of rain now ran down the glass, obscuring their view of the pedestrians and shoppers on the crowded pavement outside.

'You know, Lavender,' she said, 'I think there is too much fuss made about religious differences. After all, we all worship the same God, don't we? No matter what we call him, Jehovah, God – or even Allah. I met some charming Arabs while travelling with Victor in Spain.'

'I agree,' Lavender said. 'Men – and women – should be judged on their character and their actions – not on their beliefs. There are good and evil amidst the followers of every faith.'

Her mood lifted and she laughed. 'And there speaks the detective whose job it is to track down the evil ones – which brings us back to your mysterious priest. He certainly sounds like a naughty boy.'

Their carriage drew up outside the cream facade of the elegant chapel behind the Sardinian Embassy. Lavender had not been here before and was surprised at its size. A large white dome rose up at the rear of the church into the cloudy sky and towered above the smoking, red-brick chimneys of the neighbouring buildings. Prior to the Relief Act of 1791, this chapel had been the only place in London where Catholic worship was legal for thousands of people who still followed the faith. It was the chief place of refuge for persecuted Catholic priests – and inevitably the focal point for several anti-Catholic riots. The rioters had set it on fire on several occasions. Bow Street constables, including his own father, were often sent to detain or harass the British citizens who attended Mass at this chapel.

Lavender decided it would probably be best to avoid mentioning this family connection to Bishop Douglass. His Excellency would have lived through those troubled times and the bishop would be very wary once he learnt of Lavender's profession. There was no point in aggravating the man further.

'You can stay in the carriage, Henry,' Lady Caroline told Duddles firmly. 'As you can see, Detective Lavender and I have some serious business to attend to. You'll just get in the way with your chatter if you accompany us any further. Lavender, you may help me down.' Crestfallen, the young man sank back into his seat while Lavender helped Lady Caroline out of the carriage and into the grey drizzle of the street.

They entered the chapel through a pair of great oak doors. Lavender removed his hat and was instantly struck with the brightness of the lofty white aisle and the French and Italian influences on its architecture. The glittering altar with its gold cross, crystal and silver candlesticks, and highly polished silver plate stood directly ahead of them beneath the white dome. The pungent smell of incense hung heavily in the air. There were no seats or pews on the black-and-white tiled floor but cream marble pillars held up overhanging galleries along each side of the chapel. He suspected the wealthier and titled members of the congregation sat up above. How much did a seat cost, he wondered?

They walked down the centre of the chapel towards the altar, passing the rows of wooden confessionals that lined the walls beneath the galleries. Each was embossed with the coat of arms of the Duke of Savoy. Lavender saw the red velvet drapes twitch in one of the confessionals and he heard whispering from within.

A cleric in a plain brown habit with a silver cross around his neck came over to greet them.

'Please tell His Grace that Lady Caroline Clare is here to see him,' Lavender said. The cleric bowed his tonsured head and disappeared into a side door of the chapel.

'What exactly do you want me to do?' Lady Caroline whispered, as they waited beside a large, painted statue of a mournful Madonna.

'Please just be yourself,' Lavender said. 'I will ask the questions – and I will tell him I'm a police officer.'

She nodded.

A wizened old man in flowing white robes and a blue cape hobbled arthritically towards them. A large gold crucifix swayed across his chest as he walked. Bishop Douglass was bald beneath his blue velvet zucchetto and his pale face was criss-crossed with wrinkles. His Excellency was probably in his late sixties, or even early seventies, but the dark eyes that scanned Lavender and Lady Caroline were both sharp and alert.

Beside the detective, Lady Caroline leant on her walking cane and managed to drop the bishop a brief, but elegant curtsey. Bishop Douglass held out his gnarled hand towards her and she raised it to her lips, kissing the glittering amethyst stone on his gold ring.

'Lady Caroline,' Bishop Douglass said softly. 'What a pleasure to see you. You have become quite a stranger to us recently.'

'Oh, I still attend Mass every Sunday, Your Grace,' she replied airily. 'But you know how I hate to create a fuss. I prefer to mingle in with the crowd. You probably just haven't seen me.'

The bishop's thin lips tightened. Lavender knew His Excellency didn't believe this any more than he did but this old man hadn't survived religious persecution and the Gordon Riots without developing a large degree of tact. 'How can I help you, my daughter?' he asked.

'I would like to introduce you to a very, very dear friend of mine, Your Grace.' Lady Caroline waved her gloved hand in Lavender's direction. 'This is Stephen Lavender. He desperately needs your assistance.'

Lavender bowed low but made no attempt to follow Lady Caroline's example and kiss the old man's hand.

Bishop Douglass' white eyebrows rose in surprise. 'Is it a matter of spirituality, my son?'

'No, Your Grace.' Lavender straightened up and cleared his throat. 'It's a secular matter concerning one of your flock. I have just returned from Northamptonshire, where I was called to investigate the brutal murder of an elderly Catholic man. I believe he lived and worshipped in London twenty-five years ago and you may even know of him.'

Bishop Douglass crossed himself and shook his head sadly. 'Ah, the weakness and frailty of mankind,' he murmured. 'Such a terrible loss . . .'

'The murdered man was eighty-six years old,' Lavender added.

'Pray tell me, Mr Lavender, are you a thief-catcher, a constable . . .?'

Lavender took in a deep breath. 'No, I'm a Principal Officer with the Bow Street Police Office in London. I was summoned up to Northamptonshire to investigate this terrible crime by Lady Anne Fitzwilliam of Rockingham Castle.'

'Ah, the Lady Anne Fitzwilliam.' Lavender caught the slight look of alarm in the old man's eyes when he mentioned Bow Street but the bishop's face softened again when he heard Lady Anne's name. 'Well, I'm not sure how I can help you, Detective Lavender, but I will try. Shall we retire to my office and discuss this terrible incident further?'

Lavender bowed his head again. 'I'm most grateful, Your Excellency.'

187

'Don't thank me yet, young man. There may be nothing I can do to assist you.' Bishop Douglass turned back to Lady Caroline. 'Would you care to take my arm, my dear? I can see that you struggle to walk.'

Lady Caroline gave him her most enchanting smile, slipped her arm through his and enquired about his health. As Lavender followed the hobbling old man and limping woman out of the chapel and into the bishop's office he allowed himself a wry smile. It was unclear who was supporting whom. Hopefully, thanks to Lady Caroline's charm and the influence of the Fitzwilliams, those ardent supporters of Catholic emancipation, he would get some answers today.

A thick Turkish carpet covered the floor of Bishop Douglass' office. In front of the window, an oak Chippendale desk gleamed with inlaid brass ornaments and the glossy veneer of rosewood. A small fire burned in the grate and in the alcoves beside it the fireplace was flanked by two tall ebony and gilt baroque cabinets inlaid with pietra dura. It looked to Lavender as though the cabinets had been specially commissioned from their seventeenth-century craftsman; each panel depicted the life of a saint. On the other walls stood floor-to-ceiling bookcases containing hundreds of leatherbound books, most of them religious tracts. Gold crucifixes and paintings of religious scenes from the Bible and the martyrdom of the saints covered the rest of the walls. Dozens of candles in the gold candelabra and chandeliers had been lit to dispel the darkness cast by the miserable day outside.

Bishop Douglass sank painfully into the ornate, high-backed chair behind his desk and gestured for them to sit down opposite, asking his assistant to fetch coffee. Seating herself on one of the chairs facing the bishop, Lady Caroline chattered to him about various aristocratic members of their congregation. Lavender sat beside her, glad that his back was turned against most of the gilt and ornate opulence of the furnishings. He wasn't a particularly religious man but the Protestant in him was far more comfortable in spartan whitewashed churches with a simple wooden cross. There, and only there, did he occasionally feel the shadow of the presence of that simple carpenter from Nazareth. His grandfather had taught him that he didn't need the ancient gold and silver artefacts or precious jewels to evoke the Holy Spirit and find peace, and it was a lesson he couldn't shake off. More than anything this morning, he needed to concentrate and avoid distractions.

'So, how can I help you, Detective?' Bishop Douglass asked.

'Firstly,' Lavender said, 'I need to know about the elderly man who travelled down from Northamptonshire with the body of a woman for burial. I believe the deceased woman was called Bridget and this happened last August.'

Bishop Douglass narrowed his eyes and frowned. 'We're asked to administer the last rites to so many poor souls . . .'

'The woman had already been dead for several days,' Lavender reminded him gently. 'It would have been an unusual situation.'

'Of course, of course. Please understand, Detective, we don't encourage our parishioners to travel great distances with the corpses of their loved ones, but so many of them are desperate for the proper rites and burial . . .' A jolt of recognition flashed across the bishop's lined face. 'Northamptonshire, did you say?'

'Yes.'

Bishop Douglass rose to his feet and padded across the carpet to one of the cabinets by the fireplace. 'Do you know, Detective, I think I might be able to help you after all . . .'

He lifted a key on the chain swinging from his belt and unlocked one of the doors. 'I do remember the incident. The bereaved husband was an extremely frail old man, quite exhausted by the time he arrived here – yet still determined to give his wife a Catholic burial.'

Lavender caught a glimpse of a huge pile of leather-bound

registers. Bishop Douglass removed one of them and hobbled back to his seat.

'Did you meet him yourself, Your Grace?' Lavender asked.

'No, Father James conducted the ceremony but he told me about it afterwards. He was struck by the man's love and piety.' Bishop Douglass continued to turn the pages of the register. Reading upside down, Lavender saw that these were the church records from the previous year. He glanced back at the cabinet with its stacks of leather-bound volumes and he wondered how far those records went back through the years. Maybe this trip to London wouldn't turn out to be futile after all.

Bishop Douglass' amethyst ring flashed as he stabbed at an entry in the register. 'There! See! Mrs Bridget Ahearn, buried on 25th August 1809, aged fifty-three years. God rest her soul.'

'Ahearn?' Lavender echoed, surprised.

'Yes, Ahearn. Is this not the right woman?'

'Is there an address?'

Bishop Douglass glanced down at the register. 'Middleton, Northamptonshire,' he confirmed.

'Then it's the right woman.' Lavender's mind raced, trying to work out what William Sculthorpe had been up to. Why did he bury her as Bridget Ahearn when the woman was known as Bridget Sculthorpe?

There could only be one explanation: she wasn't his wife. She was Bridget Ahearn and she wanted the service that blessed her life and sent her soul to her God to use her proper name. In order to honour her wishes, Sculthorpe had to bury her corpse away from prying eyes in Northamptonshire.

Both Lady Caroline and Bishop Douglass were watching him curiously. 'Do you know if the man called himself Mr Ahearn?' he asked.

Bishop Douglass shrugged. 'I presume so. He certainly told Father James he was her husband. I take it this is the elderly man who has now been murdered back in Northamptonshire? God rest his poor soul.'

Lavender took a deep breath. 'Yes,' he said slowly, 'but his name wasn't William Ahearn. It was William Sculthorpe – and I believe he used to be one of your priests.'

For a moment, Bishop Douglass froze with shock. Time stood still in his opulent office. Lavender heard the fire crackle and the distant rumble of traffic outside in the street.

Bishop Douglass turned red in the face and coughed violently. He leant forward over his desk and gasped for breath. His shoulders heaved as each fresh spasm racked his body. Lady Caroline leapt to her feet and hurried to his side but the hideous seizure afflicting the bishop showed no sign of abating. The dreadful hacking of the old man made Lavender cringe. He went to the crystal decanter on a side table and poured out a generous measure of brandy. By the time he turned round, Lady Caroline was thumping the bishop on his back. With tears streaming down his pale face and his hands flailing in the air, Bishop Douglass signalled for her to stop.

'Are you choking, Your Grace?' she asked frantically. 'Is something caught in your throat?'

He also waved away the glass of brandy offered to him by Lavender. They stepped back and hovered helplessly, unsure what to do next.

The bishop's assistant suddenly appeared with the coffee. The man took in the situation at once, placed the coffee on a small table and hurriedly left the room. He returned immediately with a glass of water. 'It might be best if you wait outside, Your Ladyship,' he said, as he held it up to the lips of the choking bishop. Lavender and Lady Caroline hastily left and returned to the cool interior of the chapel.

'Have we killed him, do you think?' Lady Caroline whispered when they were alone. Her eyes were wide.

'I hope not, for your sake at least,' Lavender replied. 'How many Hail Marys would you have to say in penance before you received absolution for killing a bishop?'

She slapped him on his arm lightly with her gloved hand. 'Naughty boy.' The corners of her mouth twitched with amusement.

Chapter Twenty-Four

Monday 5th March, 1810
Middleton, Northamptonshire

Woods found it hard to disguise his glee as he strode back down the cobbled hill towards Middleton. He beamed from ear to ear across his broad face and he had to shove his clenched fists in his coat pockets to stop himself punching the air in jubilation. The sunshine warmed his face and birds sang joyously in the nearby trees. Part of him wanted to throw back his head and burst into song himself.

This was a significant breakthrough in their investigation and he knew it. Lavender was right. This case was far more complicated than it had initially appeared to be. There were other motives behind the murder of William Sculthorpe besides simple greed for money. Whoever delivered that vicious death blow to Sculthorpe had done it with vengeance in his heart.

William Sculthorpe had been a blackmailer and now Woods had the proof. The sneaky old rogue had extorted money from his neighbours and his crime had come back to bite him. Those he had listed by their initials in his account book were his victims: Isaac Bunning, Caleb Liquorish, Morgan Thatcher, the mysterious *J.W.*

and whichever Dicken it was who owned the initials *J.D.* Each one of these men had a motive to murder and silence the old swindler. The question was: which one of them was it? Or had they joined together? Woods shook his head and stopped worrying about it. Lavender would work it out when he returned from London.

Woods retrieved his horse from the stable in Middleton, swung up into the saddle and set out towards Rockingham, determined to continue his inquiries with the homeowners along the road. In his heart, he knew this was now a fool's errand. The murderers had not disappeared into the stormy night along the Rockingham Road. They were shadowy inhabitants of Middleton and Cottingham and after the murder they had scurried back to their homes like rats. But he relished the exercise of the ride and he knew Lavender would still expect him to carry out these inquiries. The detective didn't like to leave any stone unturned.

As he expected, his questions to the farmers and homeowners along the meandering Rockingham Road met with nothing but blank stares, shaking heads and denials. Finally, he reached the base of the rocky outcrop at the end of the ridge where Rockingham Castle loomed over the gently rolling valley and he decided to finish for the day.

Attracted by the ancient creamy walls of the drum towers guarding the entrance to the castle, Woods turned his horse up the hill to get a closer view. He wondered idly about the mysterious Lady Anne Fitzwilliam who lived within its walls. Did she know she championed a blackmailing scoundrel? Did she care? Was her regular payment to William Sculthorpe also extorted by blackmail? And if so, what did the old rogue know about her that she didn't want to share with the world?

The afternoon sun disappeared behind a cloud and a chilly breeze sprang up out of nowhere. At the top of the hill Woods reined in his horse and asked directions from a man with a cart. The fellow pointed out the Uppingham Road and told Woods it would take him back to Cottingham. Woods thanked him, leant forward and set off at a gallop. The horse's mane lashed across his face and the cold wind bit into his cheeks. His route took him across the top of the escarpment and now and then the trees cleared sufficiently for Woods to enjoy the view of the glistening River Welland meandering through the valley below. It was an exhilarating ride.

By the time he reached the isolated windmill at the top of Cottingham, he was breathless with the exertion and so was his horse. He reined in the animal beneath the creaking sails, dismounted and led the horse to drink at the stream emerging from the nearby woodland. Woods dropped to his haunches, filled his flask and enjoyed a good drink of the fresh, crystal-clear water.

Weariness swept over him and he rubbed his eyes. These disturbed nights were sapping his energy. *Damn those bloody nightmares.* He tied up the horse to a low-slung branch of one of the nearby trees and picked a flat, grassy spot on the soft earth of the glade for a rest. His tired body ached to lie down. It can't hurt to take a nap, he thought, as he stretched out and closed his eyes. There was something soothing about the rhythmical creak of the windmill sails and gentle trickle of spring water, he decided. Even the ground here was more comfortable than that ruddy mattress at The Woolpack. *Just a little nap*, he thought – *and then I'll head back to Market Harborough for a more comfortable night's sleep . . .*

Soon he was swimming in slow motion in the rich gravy of one of Mrs Tilley's pigeon pies. Or rather he was struggling to swim in one of Mrs Tilley's pigeon pies. But he didn't panic. One minute he sank below the surface of the gravy, the next he leisurely kicked his way back up. His arms and legs flailed against the thick gloopiness of the gravy, while his shoulders bumped against gigantic, bobbing chunks of pigeon breast and peas the size of cannonballs. He could taste the salt in the back of his throat. He reached out towards the soft walls of pastry surrounding him but it flaked off in lumps in his hand.

Come on, you daft saphead, he reminded himself, *there must be a way out of here.* But he couldn't see it. Above him the pie crust loomed up into the sky, a sheer, unassailable wall of deliciousness rising up to the bright, white light of heaven. He sighed and swam around the circular wall of his edible prison. Although he kept floundering and the gravy plastered his hair to his head and got into his ears, he wasn't scared. He knew he had to die sometime and there was something satisfying about the thought that he was destined to drown in a lake of warm, salty gravy. Perhaps they would bury him in the pie? It would make a change from the usual wooden surcoat. If they did bury him in this pie, then he would have plenty to eat in the afterlife – just like those old 'Gyptians and pagans who were buried with food and drink. Now that was a good thought.

Suddenly, a huge hand punched its way through the pastry. A shower of flakes floated down onto his gravy-soaked head and the fingers tried to grasp his arm. Alby Kilby's great hand reached out for him, offering him a lifeline.

'Grab my hand, Neddy!' Kilby yelled from the other side of the pie wall. 'I'll save you, Neddy!'

Woods' blood turned to ice. He knew that bloody voice. Agonising memories of the past surged and stabbed at his fevered mind. The warm gravy turned into an icy sludge and the walls of the monster pie crumbled with a roar. The thick liquid surged towards the breach, sweeping Woods along with it. He heard it thunder over the precipitous edge and he braced himself for the fall . . .

Woods jerked awake with a yell and sat up abruptly. He was frozen and darkness had fallen around him. Confused, he blinked and peered into the dusk, trying to make sense of where he was.

His ears heard the movement behind him.

Instinctively, Woods threw himself sideways into a roll – but it was too late. A heavy object landed a stinging blow to the left side of his head. He roared in agony as the crack exploded in his ear and searing pain rebounded around his skull. Lights flashed in front of his eyes and he fought down a wave of nausea. He scrambled to his feet with one fist clenched and the other fumbling for the pistol in his coat pocket. It wasn't loaded but his assailant wouldn't know this.

He glimpsed the back of a large figure in a dark coat and hat disappearing into the shadows of the trees fifty yards away. Ferns swished behind the figure as it vanished into the gloomy undergrowth.

'Come back and fight like a man – you cowardly bastard!' Woods bellowed.

A branch cracked beneath the foot of a heavy animal in the dense undergrowth. He listened. Nothing. Nothing but the mournful creak of the windmill sails as they strained against the cold breeze.

'I said come back here, you bloody coward!' But his curses echoed off the tree trunks and back to mock him. Silence had returned to the glade. The foliage had swallowed up his assailant and Woods knew he was in no condition to go crashing through the trees after him.

Blood dripped down his face and he reached up to inspect the jagged edges of the cut to his head. More warm blood oozed over his fingers as he tenderly examined the wound. The sensitive tissue of his ragged ear stung like hell and bled profusely. It had already begun to swell. His head ached but his ear seemed to have taken the worst of the glancing blow to his old noddle. He needed to wash off the blood before it ran over his eye and obscured his vision but every instinct screamed against turning his back on his attacker and walking to the stream. His feet were rooted to the spot.

A bloodied cudgel, fashioned from a large branch, lay on the trampled grass where he had slept only a few moments before.

Anger surged through him and he cursed himself for his foolishness. He had let down his guard and nearly paid a heavy price for it. There were at least three murderers living in this area. These sneaking curs had heartlessly slain a frail old man. Now one of them had tried to kill – or maim – him so he couldn't do his job. If it hadn't been for that damned dream, the bastard would have succeeded too. If he hadn't jolted awake when he did and sat up, the assailant might have killed him.

The dripping blood became a steady stream and nausea gripped his stomach again. Finally, he tore himself away from the scene of the assault and staggered over to the stream. Each footstep sent a new jolt of pain to his head. He dropped to his knees on the muddy bank, splashed the ice-cold water over his face and scooped up several large mouthfuls to drink.

Somewhere in the woods a nightingale warbled its cheerful song. Woods felt calmer now and more alert. The cold water revived him and it took the sting out of his pain. The sod wouldn't catch him napping again.

His thoughts returned to his strange dream. He heard Alby Kilby's oh-so-familiar voice again and he saw his outstretched hand: *'I'll save you, Neddy.'*

Woods swore as those buried memories jerked back into the forefront of his mind. Raw memories that slashed at his old heart like a knife blade. Memories he had suppressed for years.

Heaven and hell! Why hadn't he recognised Kilby before? It was as if the blow to his head had opened the floodgates and swept away a blockage. The vicious, swirling waters of the past were unleashed like a torrent into his mind. He saw it all again. The dangerous, grimy docks. His mother . . . and Alby Kilby. Alby Kilby stood before him in the docks. Alby Kilby leaning over a dead man. A dead man with his pate caved in . . .

Fuelled with renewed anger, Woods strode across to his horse and hauled himself up into the saddle. He knew he should head for The Woolpack and rest up awhile but he had had enough of this damned village and its murderous inhabitants. Besides which, he had a more pressing matter to deal with now. Wheeling the animal around, he pointed her in the direction of Market Harborough and dug his heels into her flanks. As the animal accelerated to a thundering gallop beneath him and the bitter wind lashed at his injured head, a new and grim realisation dawned on Woods.

He and Lavender had come to Northamptonshire to find a murderer – and now he had found one.

Chapter Twenty-Five

Monday 5th March, 1810
The Sardinian Embassy Chapel, London

Father Colin, the bishop's assistant, invited Lavender and Lady Caroline back into the office.

'Bishop Douglass is very shaken,' he informed them. 'He hasn't been well for some time and must conserve his strength. Please state the rest of your business quickly so he can rest – he has asked me to remain for the rest of your appointment.'

Lavender nodded.

Bishop Douglass was still taking small sips of water from the glass when they re-entered the office. He clutched a lawn handkerchief in his hand but his coughing spasm had abated and some colour had returned to his sunken cheeks. Lady Caroline expressed her sympathy and Bishop Douglass thanked her. Father Colin pulled up a chair at the back of the office and sat down.

'I'm sorry you're unwell, Your Grace,' Lavender said. 'I will now be as brief as I can. I understand you knew William Sculthorpe – and from your reaction, I gather you were shocked to hear his name again.'

Bishop Douglass took another sip of water. When he spoke, his voice was a whispery rasp as if his throat had been ravaged by thistles. 'Yes, William Sculthorpe was a Catholic priest – here in London. But no, I haven't seen nor heard of him for over twenty years. I thought he had retired to Brighton a long time ago.'

'He did spend some years there,' Lavender said, 'but he recently moved to Northamptonshire. Can you tell me what you remember about the man?'

The bishop sighed. There was a short pause while he struggled to find the right words. 'Unfortunately, every organisation has its bad apple, Detective – and Father William Sculthorpe was ours. No one it seems, not even a priest, is immune to the weakness and frailty of mankind.'

'I understand,' Lavender said.

'Can I rely on your discretion?'

Lavender nodded. 'I do not want to cause any embarrassment for your Church, Your Grace. What you tell me will be for my ears alone.'

Lady Caroline leant forward. 'You have my assurance, Your Grace,' she said in serious hushed tones. 'Detective Lavender is an honourable man. He's privy to certain aspects of my life I wouldn't want a soul to know – and he has always been discreet.'

Bishop Douglass eyed her curiously. 'I trust you have also shared these aspects of your life with your confessor, my daughter?'

Lady Caroline hastily sat back in her chair.

'Whatever happened here twenty-five years ago,' Lavender said, 'probably has no bearing on William Sculthorpe's murder but it's important to me to try and understand this man better. I believed his character to have been bad and I think this may be why he was slain so viciously.'

Bishop Douglass nodded and cleared his throat. 'Father William wasn't devout and prayerful in his habits. He was a man of two Gods. He also worshipped the God of Mammon, one of the seven Princes of Hell.'

'How so?' Lavender asked.

'He was a thief, a swindler – and a blackmailer.'

Lavender felt a surge of satisfaction in his chest. He had been right.

'Money disappeared from the church coffers,' Bishop Douglass continued. 'Gold plate and artefacts also vanished. After an investigation we discovered the thief was Father William but we couldn't get them back; he'd sold them.'

'What sort of artefacts?' Lavender asked.

'Valuable artefacts that had been in the possession of the Catholic Church for centuries. These were ancient relics and gold and silver plate we had saved from the chaos of the Reformation and numerous other purges against our Church. It was only small things at first, then our thief grew bolder.'

Lavender thought of the thousands of pounds amassed by Sculthorpe during his lifetime and wondered how much of it, if any, had been acquired honestly. 'Who did he blackmail and why?'

Bishop Douglass shrugged. 'I can't remember their names. All I know was that several members of our congregation went to Bishop James Talbot, my predecessor, and complained about Father William. They said Father William used things they told him in the confessional to try and extort money from them.'

Lady Caroline gasped and threw her hand over her mouth. 'Heaven save us from such a fiend!' The three men in the room glanced at her curiously.

'He was questioned but denied everything,' the bishop continued. 'The man had a compulsion for money – an obsession for gold.'

Lavender nodded. He remembered the bags of gold sovereigns they had unearthed in Sculthorpe's house. 'When was this? When did these incidents occur?'

'I think it was in either 1783 or 1784.'

'Did you bring in the law?' Lavender asked.

The bishop shook his head and let out a small laugh. 'You have to take into consideration the religious hysteria of the times, Detective. Catholic worship – especially taking Mass – was banned. Prejudice against us was rife and attacks on our property and our persons were common. We priests scurried around the countryside like guilty fugitives, seeking refuge where we could. To many of our flock we were a frightening liability and Catholicism in England was dying out. The future of the faith here hung on a knife edge.'

He took a deep breath and a drink of water before continuing. 'To have revealed Father William's crimes would have been the final straw for many of our congregation, who might have abandoned us in disgust. Outside of our circle, such a scandal would have only fuelled the anger and hatred in the country already prevalent against Catholicism. No, Bishop Talbot decided to quietly remove Father William from office and ban him from ever participating in the rites of our religion as a priest again. He was thrown out of the Church and excommunicated by the Pope.'

'And that's when he disappeared to Brighton,' Lavender said thoughtfully. 'Do you know if Lady Anne Fitzwilliam was aware of Sculthorpe's – Father William's – disgrace?'

'I don't know the answer to that question,' the bishop confessed, 'but I suspect not. Lady Anne is a very kind and generous woman. At one time, Father William was her confessor. I'm not surprised to hear she's paying for this inquiry but I doubt she would have done so if she had been aware of Father William's disgrace.'

'Mmm,' Lavender murmured, unconvinced. *You don't know about the mysterious service Sculthorpe once rendered unto the Lady Anne.* Despite Sculthorpe's disgrace, the dowager countess was still fond of the former priest and beholden to him in some way.

'Do you think Father William was murdered because of his religion, Detective?' the bishop asked.

'No, not at all. You may rest at ease on that score. I don't think anyone in Northamptonshire, apart from Lady Anne Fitzwilliam, knew William Sculthorpe was a Catholic.'

'That is a relief.'

'I think William Sculthorpe was murdered because he had started up his old tricks again,' Lavender said. 'I believe he blackmailed several of the other villagers in Middleton.'

'"Can the Ethiopian change his skin, or the leopard his spots?"' asked the bishop. A short pause ensued while everyone pondered this quote from Jeremiah and the bishop coughed again into his handkerchief. Lavender became conscious of the crackling fire once more.

'If there is nothing else, Detective, perhaps I can retire now?'

Lavender roused himself from his thoughts. 'I'm sorry to detain you further, Your Grace, but I have three more questions.'

'Which are?' Father Colin sat down again.

'Have you ever known a family who worshipped here called Debussy? I think they may have been distant relatives of the Fitzwilliams.'

The bishop shook his head and glanced across the room at Father Colin, who also responded with a negative gesture. 'I'm afraid not. We can't help you there.'

'And when William Sculthorpe was banished from the Church, would this have freed him from his oath of celibacy and enabled him to marry?'

A steely glint shone from the bishop's eyes. 'It would not. He made that promise to God; he swore him an oath. Any such act, even after we expelled him from the Church, would have damned him for eternity.'

Lavender's heart sank. Billy Sculthorpe must be Bridget Ahearn's son. He couldn't save Billy now. The strange little man would spend the rest of his days in the county lunatic asylum.

'There is nothing so powerful in drawing the spirit of a man downwards as the caresses of a woman,' Father Colin said. Lady Caroline turned her head and gave the priest her most withering glare. He fell silent and hastily dropped his eyes to examine the pattern in the carpet.

'And your final question?' asked Bishop Douglass, wearily.

'May I be allowed to peruse your church registers for 1783 to 1785? It may help me if I can see the names of the people for whom Father William conducted religious services. Perhaps I can see the baptisms and marriages?'

Bishop Douglass sat back in his chair, shocked. 'That won't be possible,' he said. 'Those records are private and entrusted into our care.'

Lady Caroline smiled and leant forward. 'I can assure you, Your Grace, that Detective Lavender . . .'

'I'm sure the detective is very discreet, Lady Caroline,' the bishop interrupted, 'but the congregation of our church have entrusted me with these records of their lives. Many of them would be disappointed if I let a policeman peruse those records.'

An idea formed in Lavender's mind. There was something he had intended to mention before he left. Now seemed like the ideal moment. 'I may have an artefact in Leicestershire that might interest you, Your Grace,' he said slowly.

'Oh?'

'While searching the premises of William Sculthorpe for clues about his murder, we came across a beautiful reliquary, which I suspect is of immense value.'

Bishop Douglass' eyes became riveted on Lavender's face. 'Go on,' he said.

'The reliquary is in the safe keeping of one of the Leicestershire county magistrates.'

'What does it look like?' asked Father Colin. He too was staring intently at Lavender.

'It's about ten inches high and made of silver and translucent blue enamel. On the carved lid of the box sit a Madonna and child surrounded by two angels. Behind them rise three pointed arches that culminate in elaborate silver finials.'

'It sounds gorgeous,' said Lady Caroline.

'There's more blue enamel on the decorative side panels, which also depict scenes from the life of the Virgin and the Infancy of Christ.'

'And the artefact inside the reliquary?' Bishop Douglass asked sharply. The sick and weary old man had suddenly become quite ferocious.

'Hair,' Lavender told him.

The bishop and his assistant stared at each other in amazement across the room. Lady Caroline arched an eyebrow and smiled in mild amusement at the palpable rise in tension in the room.

'Can it be possible after all this time?' Bishop Douglass whispered. 'Is this the hair of Saint Bernard of Clairvaux?'

'Was this the fourteenth-century reliquary deposited into the safe keeping of the Order of Saint Jerome?' Father Colin asked in equally hushed tones.

'Yes – and it was lost by us,' Bishop Douglass said bitterly.

'Did it disappear around the time William Sculthorpe was stealing from the church?' Lavender asked.

'Yes,' Father Colin replied. 'We thought we would never see it again.'

'Then I will reunite you with your precious reliquary,' Lavender promised.

For a moment, the silence hung heavily in the warm room. Lavender sat still and waited. Lady Caroline glanced from one man to the other, leant across the desk and patted Bishop Douglass on the hand. 'Surely one favour deserves another, Your Grace?' she said.

Bishop Douglass nodded and gestured Father Colin to his feet. 'Fetch Detective Lavender the church records for the years 1783 to 1785. He has proven himself; he can be trusted.'

Father Colin opened another door of one of the great baroque cabinets and pulled out two leather-bound volumes. He carried them over to Lavender and placed them on the desk in front of him. Lavender flicked quickly through the vellum pages of the first register, scanning the entries. 'This shouldn't take long, Your Grace,' he said, 'then we shall leave.'

'I hope you will tell our congregation that the reliquary was returned to you with the help of the Bow Street Police,' Lady Caroline said to the bishop. 'It might help to build a better trust between the Church and the police.'

'I shall do that,' promised the bishop.

Lavender quickly realised he had a chronological list of church activities in front of him and this made his search easier. All the births, deaths and marriages of the London Catholic community were recorded in the same book. Father William Sculthorpe's name appeared frequently in the two registers he perused. Sculthorpe had officiated at many marriages, baptisms and funerals but his name mysteriously disappeared from the records in April 1785. This must have been when Bishop Talbot and the Church had banished him.

Lavender slid his finger back up the page looking for anything he might have missed during his first hasty scan of the records. It stopped suddenly at a short word in faded ink: *Debussy*. In December 1783, William Sculthorpe married a young woman called Judith Anne Debussy to Baron Lionel Ralph Danvers. Lady Anne Fitzwilliam had been a witness at the ceremony. What did it mean? *Judith Debussy – was she Judith Wallace?* The woman in the record was about the same age as the doctor's wife. Had she been widowed and then married Doctor Wallace? And was she the '*J.D.*' in Sculthorpe's book?

'Did you ever know Baron Danvers?' Lavender asked. 'Baron Lionel Ralph Danvers?'

'Of course!' Bishop Douglass smiled. 'I know him well. Baron Danvers is a most devout Christian and a firm supporter of the Catholic Church. A good man. He donates a large proportion of his considerable wealth to the Church and other worthy causes.'

Lavender's stomach jolted. He had not expected to hear that Baron Danvers still lived.

He nearly cried out in shock a second later when Lady Caroline's hand slid onto his leg and lightly pressed his thigh. Fortunately, her intimate gesture was hidden from the view of the other two men. He glanced at her but her features were impassive and she stared straight ahead at the bishop. It was only when she removed her hand that he realised she had something to tell him – in private – about the 'devout' Baron Danvers. Ye gods! He sincerely hoped the baron hadn't been another one of her lovers.

He returned to the fading record in the register. 'This is the record of Baron Danvers' marriage to Judith Anne Debussy here in 1783.'

Bishop Douglass frowned for a moment, then nodded. 'Oh, yes. I remember now. That was his first wife. She died young. Baron Danvers is now married to the Lady Eliza.'

Lavender pressed his lips together and tried to concentrate on the register. The revelations were unfolding so quickly his brain could barely take in each new development and he still had one more record to check: Billy Sculthorpe's baptism. Billy had been born in London. Sculthorpe – or Bridget Ahearn – may have had him baptised here.

Lavender scanned down to July 1785 and narrowed his eyes to search through the baptisms. There wasn't one for Billy. *Think*, he told himself. *Think*. Children are frequently not baptised until several weeks after their birth. He slid his finger down each entry for

July . . . then August, September, October, November . . . Nothing. Nothing at all.

Disappointed, he pulled back his hand upwards and read the ledger entries in reverse order.

Now he saw it. Not the baptism of a young William Sculthorpe, or that of a young William Ahearn, but the burial record of the infant *William Wentworth-Fitzwilliam* on *25th July 1785*.

For a second he was confused – why had his brain jolted and his finger stopped at this particular place? Then the pieces of the jigsaw finally fell into place.

William, Viscount Milton, born and died 22nd July, 1785 at Parkside House, Wandsworth. First son of William, Earl Fitzwilliam, and Lady Charlotte Fitzwilliam.

The truth hit him with the velocity and ferocity of a lightning bolt.

Billy Sculthorpe wasn't Billy Sculthorpe and he wasn't Billy Ahearn either.

Billy was William, Viscount Milton. He was the eldest grandson of Lady Anne Fitzwilliam and the child of her son, one of the greatest landowners in the country.

He was also the rightful heir to two earldoms.

Chapter Twenty-Six

Monday 5th March, 1810
Market Harborough, Leicestershire

It was late and dark when Woods finally clattered into the cobbled yard of the livery stables in the high street and threw the reins of his sweating horse to the ostler. But for once at this time of night, the town square of Market Harborough was a hive of activity. Drovers had arrived with their livestock, ready for the market the next day. Barking dogs steered flocks of sheep into the pens, tethered cattle lowed softly and farmers hailed each other across the street. A couple of drunken, gaudily dressed whores leant on each other for support as they laughed and stumbled across the cobbles. The stench of the livestock and their excrement was stronger than ever.

Woods glanced at the bustling activity, frowned and stomped towards The Angel Inn. He'd forgotten about the ruddy market. The tavern would be full of drunken farmers and drovers tonight.

He leapt up the steps in front of the brightly lit inn and glanced at the sign above his head. 'Albert Kilby – Licensed to sell beers and strong liquors'. Albert Kilby? His arse.

The noise hit him the moment he pushed open the door. As

he had feared, the tavern was packed. Groups of powerfully built, windburnt and animated farmers now competed for space and the attention of the mobcapped barmaids, along with the usual crowd of coal-blackened boatmen and wharf hands. Half a dozen tired sheepdogs sprawled across the wooden floor like a matted black and white carpet. Apart from the usual hum of body odour, tobacco smoke and alcohol, the inn now reeked of wet dog.

No one glanced up at Woods tonight as he hesitated in the entrance. All the glazed eyes in the room were trying to focus on their slurring neighbours. He caught the faint whiff of hot pastry and his stomach rumbled. He picked his way through the crowds, found a small table and a single stool in the corner and sat down. The crowds briefly parted and he caught a glimpse of Alby Kilby smiling and pouring out ale behind the bar. Kilby hadn't seen Woods but his wife had. Rosie Kilby arrived at his table with a jug of ale and a pewter tankard.

She placed the tankard on his table and pointed towards his head. 'My! You look like ye've been in the wars, Constable.'

He tossed a coin onto the table. 'Leave the jug,' he growled, 'and bring me two of your steak pies with gravy.' If he was going to confront Kilby, he might as well do it on a full stomach.

She frowned at his abruptness. 'As you wish, sir.' She turned on her heel and disappeared into the swaying and drunken throng.

Woods poured out his drink and leant back against the wall and glowered in Kilby's direction. It was going to be a long night.

Just before midnight Alby Kilby instructed the last few of his customers to get themselves home to their beds. Kilby's suggestion was greeted by growls of derision from a stubborn table of drunken farmers. Woods leant back on his stool in the shadows and watched. It was darker now. The wicks of the tallow candles that lit the inn guttered in the draught from the door and the fire in the hearth had all but burnt out.

Rosie Kilby sidled across the ale-soaked floor and picked up Woods' empty plate and tankard. 'Did yer enjoy yer supper, Constable?' she asked.

'Yes, thank you, Mrs Kilby,' he replied. 'If Mrs Kilby is actually your real name.'

She started, returned to her husband behind the bar and whispered something to him. Kilby frowned, and glanced in Woods' direction. He turned back to his wife, spoke to her and pointed to the last group of farmers in the bar. Rosie Kilby went over to them and after a bit of cajoling managed to persuade them to their feet. They staggered in the direction of the hallway that led to the front door of the tavern. Rosie followed them out.

Now only Woods and Alby Kilby remained in the room.

He rose to his feet and glared at Kilby. 'We need to talk. Come outside, now.'

Kilby shrugged, put down his cloth and followed Woods towards the rear door of the tavern, which led out into the stable yard. An image of the landlord's huge hairy fists shot through Woods' mind and he realised his mistake immediately. It would be pitch-black outside in the yard. Those cobbles could be slippery and it was unfamiliar territory for him – although not for Kilby. Far better to deal with Kilby inside.

Woods swung round, clenched his fist and thumped the landlord hard in the face. Blood spurted from Kilby's nose and lip but the huge man barely swayed. He raised his left hand to his bleeding face. 'What the . . . ?'

Woods' second punch hammered into Kilby's ribcage. This time the landlord staggered backwards, overturning a table and stool and crashing into the side of the bar. Glass shattered onto the floor.

'Give over, Neddy!' Kilby spluttered. He leant forward and spat out blood.

'Don't you bloody call me that!' Woods launched himself

at Kilby, swung him round by the lapels and slammed him up against the tavern wall. More furniture overturned and Rosie Kilby screamed.

Woods' hands gripped Kilby's thick neck and he squeezed with all his strength.

Now Kilby fought back. He swung an iron fist at Woods' head but Woods leapt back and ducked, catching a glancing blow to his cheekbone. Summoning every last ounce of his strength, and driven by the fury of the Devil himself, Woods lashed out at Kilby's face. He struck home twice – then leapt forward and grabbed Kilby by the throat again.

The landlord struggled to breathe. His hands clawed at Woods' throat, then fluttered back to try and release the pressure on his own windpipe. Their sweating faces were inches apart. Woods saw shock in Kilby's wide eyes. He smelt the stale ale on each rasping breath . . . and he felt the fear in the man.

It was enough. He stepped back, raised his knee and jabbed it as hard as he could into Kilby's testicles. 'And that's for what you did to our mother!'

The landlord wheezed, exhaled a huge grunt of pain, then fell forward onto his knees to nurse his injured balls. A huge surge of satisfaction shot through Woods, who stood back to watch him suffer and regain his breath.

The next second, Rosie Kilby's broom appeared out of nowhere and whacked him on the skull. Its hard edge caught the delicate tissue of Woods' damaged left ear. He swore, staggered and clutched his head as the searing pain exploded in his ear once more and bounced around his skull.

'What the hell do yer think yer doin'?' The furious landlady waved the broom in their faces. 'Are yer bloody Cain and Abel now? Why don't yer just sit down and talk to each other like normal family?'

Woods couldn't respond. He clamped his jaw shut to stop himself from screaming in agony. Blood oozed over his fingers as he grasped what remained of his tattered and swollen ear cartilage. Tears stung his eyes. 'I'll see you thrown in gaol for that, madam!' he spluttered when he finally found his voice. It cracked with pain. 'There's ruddy laws against attackin' police officers.'

'Aye, for them that's on duty, maybes,' she yelled. 'But not for them that's simply thumpin' the hell out of their brothers! And you!' She gave Kilby a hard shove on the shoulder with her broom. 'You great saphead! Why the hell didn't you fight him back?' She slapped him again, then placed her hands on her hips in a gesture of furious defiance.

Woods' gaze shifted between his sister-in-law and the bowed, white head of his grimacing brother, who was still nursing his balls delicately in his cupped hands.

Kilby finally broke the awkward silence. He spoke slowly, and with a slight squeak. 'Actually, Neddy – sorry, Ned. It were Ma who helped me the most. She helped me to escape . . .'

Chapter Twenty-Seven

Monday 5th March, 1810
Lincoln's Inn Fields, London

Lady Caroline sank down onto the carriage seat in a flurry of green velvet and ostrich feathers and turned her sad face in the direction of her young lover and sighed heavily.

'Caro!' Duddles exclaimed in alarm. 'Are you unwell?' He reached out to take her hand in his own.

'No, no, Henry – but I'm so exhausted! Police work is utterly exhausting. I don't believe I have had to concentrate so hard in years. I could barely follow the detective's line of questioning.'

'My poor, poor Caro!' Duddles said. 'You must rest when we return home. I shall dab your temple with a sponge of aromatic vinegar to chase away the megrims.'

'Oh, would you, Henry darling?' She leant towards him affectionately. 'I would be so grateful.'

Lavender grinned, shut the carriage door behind him and sat back on the seat opposite her and Duddles. The coach jolted and slid back into the stream of traffic. 'You were magnificent, Lady Caroline,' he said.

'Was I?'

'Yes. I would never have managed without your help. Your assistance has been invaluable. Thank you.'

'See, Henry?' she said. 'We little women can play an important part in men's business if necessary. Just think – today I may have solved a murder! Have we solved the murder, Lavender?'

He smiled. 'Yes, Lady Caroline, you have solved the murder.' She was so excited it would have been rude to disappoint her with the truth.

'I always knew you would be splendid in everything, Caro.' Henry Duddles beamed from ear to ear.

'But we haven't finished yet!' She raised her hand in the air and pointed at Duddles. 'You must help Detective Lavender too, Henry. You can help. He needs to know the truth about Danvers – Bishop Douglass doesn't understand the man.'

'Danvers?'

'Yes, Lionel Danvers from Southerly Park.'

'Oh, the Middlesex Danvers?'

'Yes, yes. I know you've joined him on the hunt and been to house parties at the manor.'

Duddles flushed as he turned to address Lavender directly. His wide eyes looked sheepish and were half hidden by his thick fringe of blond curls. 'Yes. Lionel Danvers, a swell chap. He serves a damned fine port wine from Portugal and there's plenty of chinks to be won at his card table.'

'No! No!' Lady Caroline rapped Duddles' hand with her fan. 'Never mind the wine and the gambling. Tell the detective what you told me about how he treats his horses and his dogs.'

Duddles nodded. 'Oh, he's a brute on the hunt – I've seen him lame a horse with no shoe rather than miss the kill. He's a bit too ready with his whip too – and not only with animals. He was arrested once for thrashing a footman. Nothing came of the charge, of course.'

Lady Caroline leant forward towards Lavender. 'Bishop Douglass has no notion of the man,' she said crossly. 'He thinks him a saint because he donates to the Church – but he's not.'

A frown creased Lavender's forehead. 'Do either of you know anything about his wives?'

Duddles started. 'He has more than one?'

Lady Caroline laughed and tapped him playfully on the arm. 'No, you silly boy – but he's *had* more than one. His first wife died . . . some years ago, I think.' Duddles sat back in his seat, happy to let Lady Caroline do the rest of the talking. 'Lady Eliza is the current Baroness Danvers but she's very unsociable and I hardly know her. There have been rumours, of course . . . but there always are.'

'What sort of rumours?' Lavender asked.

'That he beats her.' Lady Caroline's voice was quiet now, her tone grim. 'No one ever knows, of course, what really goes on behind the closed doors of any family home, but I've seen her shivering in church on a sweltering August day.'

'Shivering?'

'Yes, shivering – or quivering. One can't always tell the difference. Anyway, she wore a dark blue silk taffeta gown with full-length sleeves and a high neck on that day, which is always significant.'

'It is?'

'Good heavens, Detective, you need a lady assistant. I can see Doña Magdalena will be very busy in future.'

'I normally rely on Constable Woods to provide me with relevant information about the fairer sex and their clothes . . .'

'Well, no wonder British justice is in such a pickle!' Lady Caroline shook her head of auburn ringlets and tutted in frustration. 'Lavender,' she said slowly, as if explaining something to a young child. 'Baroness Danvers wore a high-necked gown with full sleeves on that sweltering day to hide the bruises and lacerations on her skin.'

'Ah.'

'The cad!' Duddles spat out the words in anger, then looked away in embarrassment and anger, fixing his interest on the flower sellers, hawkers and shoppers ambling along the pavement outside. There was a short silence as the two men absorbed the full meaning of her words.

So this was what Lady Caroline wanted to tell him about the 'devout' Baron Danvers when she'd squeezed his leg back in the bishop's office. He felt guilty for assuming she'd had an affair with the brute. Suddenly, he understood her preference for smooth-cheeked young bucks like Duddles who were barely out of the schoolroom. It was easy to instruct these enthusiastic, panting puppies in the niceties of how to treat a lady with love and kindness. Perhaps he should offer to dab Magdalena's temple with aromatic vinegar the next time she had a headache.

'I sincerely hope you're going to tell me there is a warrant out for Baron Danvers' arrest,' Lady Caroline said with feeling.

'Didn't she kill herself?' Duddles asked.

Lady Caroline's black ostrich feathers swished as she swung her head towards him. 'Who?'

'Danvers' first wife. I thought she'd drowned in the River Brent on their estate. Walked into the water naked, or something, didn't she? I remember some of the chaps tittering about it.'

'Good grief!' Lady Caroline's face lit up and she leant forward, forgot herself and gave her consort a pat on his breeched leg. 'Well done, Henry! I'd forgotten all about that!'

A wide grin spread across Duddles' handsome young face.

'This will be the Judith Debussy you asked about.' Lady Caroline swung round to face Lavender. 'I remember it now – it was a terrible scandal.'

'What happened?' Lavender asked.

'They had been married for barely a year. She walked into the river and drowned herself, leaving her clothes on the bank. Danvers tried to hush it up, of course. He told everyone his wife had been ill and died but it was impossible to keep a secret like that in our circle – everyone soon knew about it. It didn't help that Danvers dredged half the River Brent looking for her body. You can't do things like this without attracting comment.'

'Did he beat her too?' Duddles asked.

'I don't know,' Lady Caroline said. 'Once the truth was out, Danvers told the coroner and the rest of the world that his wife had been insane. He said drowning herself had been the act of a madwoman.'

'If he did beat her, I can see why the poor gal threw herself into the river,' Duddles said.

'Danvers was furious rather than grief-stricken after her disappearance, if I remember rightly.'

'Why do you think he was so angry?' Lavender asked.

Lady Caroline threw up her hands and shrugged. 'It was the situation with the heir, of course.'

'The heir?'

'Yes. Danvers didn't have one. Her body was never found and Danvers had to wait seven years before he could marry again in order to produce an heir. I believe Lady Eliza has now borne him two sons.'

Her body was never found . . . Lavender sat back in his seat and allowed himself the luxury of a slight smile. At last the complicated pieces of this puzzle were beginning to fit together.

The carriage drew up outside Lady Caroline's home and he leant forward again. 'Thank you, both of you. Your help has been of immense value. I couldn't have solved this murder case without your assistance.'

The cheeks of both Lady Caroline and Duddles turned pink with pleasure.

Lavender helped Lady Caroline down from the carriage. She held onto Duddles' arm as they mounted the steps to the front door and gave him a brilliant smile when he said something that amused her. She turned back to Lavender when she reached the top. 'I look forward to hearing you have arrested the brute,' she said.

Lavender said nothing and waited beside the carriage until they had disappeared into the house. She would be disappointed, of course. There had been no complaint about Baron Danvers from his current wife or from anyone else but information like this was always useful. One of these days Baron Danvers would get his comeuppance. One of these days . . .

Lavender pulled out his pocket watch and checked the hour. Good. He still had time to make one last call before he had to board the return coach to Market Harborough.

The coachman turned round on his seat on the box. 'Where to now, guv'nor?'

'Tooley Street, Southwark,' Lavender said, as he climbed back into the rocking carriage.

There was just time for a cup of coffee and a chat with the wisest, cleverest and most astute woman Lavender had ever had the pleasure to know.

His mother.

Chapter Twenty-Eight

Monday 5th March, 1810
Market Harborough, Leicestershire

Woods and Alby Kilby sat opposite each other at a table in the deserted tavern. An opened bottle of brandy stood on the table between them. Kilby. Alby Kilby. This wasn't Alby Kilby, he told himself. This was Bert. His brother Bert. His only brother. The brother he hadn't seen since he was nine years old and whom he barely remembered. The brother who had fled from London thirty-six years ago after killing a man.

'Yer a mean scrapper, Ned,' Kilby said. 'Where did you learn to fight like that?'

'In the same streets as you,' Woods snapped.

At the other side of the bar, Rosie Kilby swept up the shattered glass, finally using her ruddy broom for its true purpose. She had extinguished most of the candles and lamps and he and Kilby – Bert – were sitting in half-darkness, sipping their drinks, toying with their glasses and casting sly glances across the table at each other. A strained silence had fallen between them. Slowly, Woods felt his anger ebb away as the brandy warmed his innards.

Perhaps Rosie was right, and they needed to talk. Kilby wanted to talk. He knew this from yesterday morning by the canal but the landlord's words and courage seemed to be failing him again.

Woods sighed. It would be down to him to start the stilted conversation. But that's what he did, wasn't it? Even Lavender said it. Woods had twenty years of experience of interviewing embarrassed and awkward witnesses and they didn't come more embarrassed and awkward than the man in the seat opposite. *Begin with something easy, some common ground . . .* he reminded himself. But no words came.

Every now and then, Kilby raised his hand gingerly to the bruises on his face and his split lip. The dried blood beneath his nose didn't look so vivid in the candlelit gloom but Woods was damned if he would feel guilty about that. Bert deserved a good thrashing after the misery he'd caused his family, and Woods was glad he'd given him one. Besides which, the Kilbys had got their revenge when Rosie had bashed him with that brush. His head still throbbed from the blow and only the liquor kept the pain in his ear at bay.

He had no idea what demon had possessed him today and sent him flying back to Market Harborough like a hothead but he had no regrets. He'd vented his anger and was glad of it, even though part of him knew his gigantic, white-haired brother had made hardly any attempt to fight back. Rosie Kilby was right about that.

'Look here,' Woods said. 'What do I call you? Are you Bert still – or is it Alby?'

'It would be best if you called me Alby,' the landlord said. 'Everyone knows me as Alby Kilby now.'

'You took Ma's family name?'

Kilby nodded. 'I lived and worked with the Kilbys for years on the Coventry canal.'

'Is that where you fled to when you left London? To Ma's folks on the canal?'

Kilby nodded again.

'I'm known as Ned these days,' Woods told him. 'Neddy were just the pet name Ma used for me.'

Kilby smiled sadly. 'You don't remember? I called you it too. You probably don't remember . . .'

Woods had a flashback to his dream, where he was drowning in the salty gravy of Mrs Tilley's pie. Kilby's voice rang in his ears again: *'I'll save you, Neddy!'* Yes, he remembered. He took another hasty drink. It was time to get to the bottom of this mystery once and for all.

But how to get there? It was difficult with one's own kin. For a moment he wished Lavender was here to ask the questions. He would know what to ask and where to start. But Lavender wasn't here and the detective must never know the truth about Alby Kilby. No, Woods had to deal with this on his own.

Common ground . . . he reminded himself. 'Ma died two years ago,' Woods said abruptly. 'She were ill for a while but it were mercifully quick in the end. She never complained.'

Kilby nodded sadly. 'I know. I were there – at her funeral.'

'You were?' Woods didn't remember any strangers at his mother's funeral but then again, had he been looking? All he remembered was the misery of that day, the rain and the oppressive grey clouds. He had wanted to be anywhere in the world but in that damp, windy graveyard burying his mother. If a dark shadow had lurked beneath the dripping yew trees on that grim, miserable and wet day, would he have even noticed?

'Aye, I'd heard she weren't long for this world . . .'

'How so?'

'The Kilbys. Word travels slow on the Thames and the canals but it allus reaches yer ears in the end. I came down to Lunnen on the coach – I thought I might have missed her passin'. I couldn't make meself known to you, of course – I couldn't risk that – but I watched you bury her. Said my own "goodbye", like. I saw you with yer wife, Bertha.'

'Betsy.'

'Aye, that's it, Betsy – and yer three nippers.'

'We've had another child since then,' Woods said. 'Baby Tabitha.'

'Four now, is it?' Kilby raised his glass and the amber liquid glinted in the guttering candlelight. His bust lip curled. A gleam of pride shone out of his eyes. 'Well done, little brother.' He winked at Woods. 'Here's to Baby Tabitha – and yer missus.'

Woods had no choice but to join Kilby in the toast to his daughter and to Betsy. Anything less would have been bad luck. Their glasses clinked and they gulped down another mouthful of the fiery liquor.

It was odd, really odd. His brother had been dead to him for years. Now this stranger claimed the right of a brother and an uncle, to (belatedly) toast the arrival of little Tabby and to congratulate him and Betsy on their fertility. He felt a flash of resentment but it subsided almost immediately.

'We had three who survived,' Kilby told him. 'All lads, and all grown men now. I'd have liked a daughter.'

Woods reached for the bottle and refilled their glasses before raising his own. 'For your sons,' he said. 'And for Rosie.' Their glasses clinked again and more liquor hit the back of Woods' throat. Perhaps this was what other folks did when they met brothers whom they thought were dead. They got drunk.

Kilby cleared his throat. He looked embarrassed. 'About the broom and moy Rosie . . .'

'Don't worry.' Woods sighed. 'Betsy would have done the same.'

Relief flooded across Kilby's face. Murderer or not, the big man loved his wife.

'I'd like to meet Betsy one day,' Rosie called out from the other side of the tavern. 'It sounds like me and her would be well met and well matched.' She was wiping glasses behind the bar by now but her eyes never left the two men. Her broom now leant idly against the wall but Woods had no doubt she wouldn't hesitate to pick it up and lash the two of them if they failed to . . . well, to what? To clear up the past? To talk? To find some sort of kinship?

'So what happened on that day in the docks, Alby?' he said. 'I know some things but not all – and I saw some things too, but it's muddled. Tell me in your own words what happened.'

Kilby's huge shoulders rose and fell with his sigh. 'You were only a nipper. There are ten years between us. You were the only one of Ma's babies to survive after me – and there were a lot who died.'

Woods nodded.

'I were fond of you, Ned,' Kilby said awkwardly. 'You were a good little lad – funny too.' He paused, embarrassed. 'You allus made us laugh with yer daft ways.'

Woods felt affection emanating across the table towards him and memories flooded back of those years when they were a family. He remembered Kilby lifting him up onto his broad shoulders when his little feet were too tired to walk any more. Kilby carrying him everywhere on his shoulders, along the noisy, dirty docks, around the cramped and smoky streets of Rotherhithe and down to the mudflats beside the river, where he liked to play. Kilby taught him how to search for winkles in the rock pools and tease out the flesh from the shell with a pin. He taught him how to hunt for crabs and how to fish.

Woods remembered trying to fight with Kilby when he was mad and his big brother laughing as he parried Woods' tiny fists. He remembered Kilby sitting with his ma beside his bed when he was ill, with concern etched across his broad face. '*Ye'll be fine, Neddy, the pain will soon pass . . .*'

More than anything he remembered his brother's great beaming smile.

I worshipped the ground you walked on, he thought.

'You were my big brother –' Woods said awkwardly and stopped. He didn't want to give Kilby too much hope. It was too early to forgive – he still didn't know what the devil had done.

''Twere difficult for us.' Kilby spoke with more confidence this time. 'You were too young to know the half of it. Pa left Ma soon after you were born and I became the man of the house.'

Woods nodded. 'I don't remember him at all.'

'I were young when he left and it were hard on me,' Kilby said. 'I were unhappy and began to run with a bad crowd. I'd stay out late and cause trouble. I started thievin' with a gang of young 'uns.'

'Oh?'

'We started with small stuff, as boys do. A bit of snafflin' here and there. We took things from shops and dived into the odd pocket or two for moveables.' Kilby's eyes darkened and he reached for the bottle again. The fine white hairs on the back of his huge hand gleamed in the candlelight. 'Ay. Those were dark days. I caused Ma . . . I, I caused her pain.' He threw back his head and downed his drink in one.

Woods tensed at this confession. *Get to the point*, he thought. 'Tell me about the gang you ran with.'

Kilby put down his glass and glanced upwards to the ceiling as if trying to pull down a memory from the rafters of the tavern.

'The leader were a lad called Yabsley. Nasty piece of work he were, a real slyboots. He had pockmarked skin, lanky black hair and eyes right close together, here.' Kilby pointed with two fingers to the bridge of his swollen nose to emphasise his point.

'He also had sommat to prove, did Yabsley. His elder brothers and his father were known as real rogues in Rotherhithe. Yabsley hankered after that fame. He had his eyes set on bigger prizes – and he got more vicious as he got older . . .'

Woods nodded again. He'd seen it all too often before – gangs of young lads roaming the streets, out of work and bored. Stealing for food and stealing for fun until it became the only way of life they knew and the stakes rose along with their daring.

'Anyway, we went to rob a smoker's one night and the owner caught us as we helped ourselves to the tobacco from his shelves. Yabsley beat him bad. The smoker were a right mess, barely alive. I were unhappy about this but one of the other lads in the gang, Tesh, he were mad as hell. He yelled at Yabsley for his cruel ways. He walked out on us and said he'd finished with us. Yabsley threatened Tesh and said he couldn't leave, that nobody walked out on him. But Tesh went anyway. Yabsley said he'd find Tesh and kill him.'

Kilby took another sip of his brandy. 'Two nights later we went to steal timber from a boat in the docks but the lighterman were there and he caught us again. Yabsley cracked him over the pate and pushed the body orf the wharf and into the Thames.'

Woods winced.

'I'd had enough,' Kilby said. 'I didn't want to be part of it no more. I told Yabsley and walked away with his threats ringin' in my ears. I were a soft turncoat and he would do for me if I turned conk on the rest of them.'

'What happened next?'

'About a week later I had a message from Yabsley. He said I were to meet him down on the coal wharf . . .'

The coal wharf. Woods felt the blood begin to pound in his ears. He was there again, a small boy shivering in the shadows of the towering stacks of shimmering black fuel. He smelt the stench of the river and the stagnant pools of water. He heard the roar of the blast furnace and the ominous groan of the swaying metal gantries overhead . . .

'. . . Ma asked me not to go but I weren't afraid of Yabsley. He were no match for me in a fight. That's what I thought he wanted – to fight.'

The pounding in Woods' head got louder. 'What happened?'

Kilby shook his head. The blood had left his face and he looked old and strained. 'Yabsley had culled me like a bird-wit. He weren't there but poor Tesh were – he'd taken a bad blow to his costard.'

Bloodied grey brains oozing out from the gash down the side of his head and slithering down the coal like a reptile . . .

'He'd set me oop for a gull, Ned. They'd killed Tesh and set me oop to take the blame. They wanted me stretched out on the gallows at Tyburn. The wharfinger, coal merchant and other men suddenly appeared. They saw me leanin' over Tesh and began to shout. I looked oop and . . . and I saw you watchin' me. Horror all over yer little face . . .'

'*Run, Neddy! Run!*' Woods felt nauseous as he watched himself stumble and slither over the coal heaps trying to get back to the hole in the fence. Tears streamed from his young eyes. He fell over. His hands and knees oozed blood mingled with coal dust . . .

Kilby had asked him a question. Woods shook himself and snapped back to reality. 'Sorry?'

'I asked you why you were there that day, watchin' me?'

'I'd followed you from the house,' Woods said simply, knowing with complete certainty this was true. 'I'd just rounded the corner and saw you there – leanin' over him. I just followed you.'

Silence.

'You allus were a daft little bugger.' Kilby shook his head sadly and reached over to fill Woods' glass again but Woods held up his hand to stop him. 'No. My head's poundin' enough as it is. Some sneakin' cur tried to kill me this afternoon in Middleton and your missus has just done her best to finish me off with her broom.'

'Someone tried to kill you?'

'Yes. It weren't you, were it?'

Kilby gave a laugh and shook his great head. 'I'd never do that, Ned – no matter what you did to me. I wouldn't ever hurt you.'

'I'm beginnin' to believe you.'

'I realised who you were when you said Ma's name on your first night in here,' Kilby confessed. 'A've tried to speak to you a few times about it all since but I couldn't find the right words – and it didn't help you were police.'

'I didn't know who you were until today – when I got that bash on the head. Were you followin' me through the town the other night when I left here?'

'Yes. What made you become a lawman, Ned?' Kilby's face creased as if the thought pained him. 'The Kilbys never told me about this.'

Woods shrugged. 'The horses, I think. I'm a patrol officer.'

Kilby turned and glanced fondly at the mangy grey horsetail pinned to the wall beside the bar. 'Well, brother, we've got somethin' in common then.'

'Yes,' Woods smiled. 'And there's another thing – fishin'.'

'You like fishin'?' Kilby's eyes lit up with delight.

'I should do,' he said. 'You taught me how to fish, remember?'

Kilby grinned but Woods' smile faded. His mind nagged him again about Kilby's predicament.

'Where is Yabsley now?'

'Dead, twenty years since. I heard about it from the Kilbys. Someone stabbed him through the heart and sent him to the bottom of the Thames.'

'Then he got what he deserved,' Woods growled. 'And the other men in your gang? Those who knew the truth about what happened to Tesh. What happened to them?'

Kilby frowned and fingered his glass as he tried to remember. 'Wilton were hauled up in front of the beak and sent Bayside on a lag ship but I've never heard a word about the others.'

'What about the wharfinger and the coal merchant who saw you with the stiff?'

Kilby shrugged. 'As far as I know, they're still alive and well.'

'So. You're still wanted for murder in London. Anyone who could stand for you as a witness at your trial is either dead, transported or missin' – but those who would speak against you are probably still alive.' It was a statement rather than a question.

There was a short silence before Kilby said, 'Yes, I reckon that's about the run of things.' He was quite cheerful, considering his predicament.

Woods shook his head and sat back in his chair. 'You'd never get a fair trial now,' he said.

Rosie Kilby appeared at her husband's side and placed a protective hand on his shoulder. 'Alby has been more than honest with you, Ned,' she said quietly. 'So what you goin' to do? Will you turn Alby in to the Runners?'

They stared at him, waiting for his reaction, his decision.

He sighed heavily. He'd expected this question. 'I'll tell you what I'm goin' to do, Rosie,' he said firmly. 'I'm goin' to sleep. My old noddle is fair swimmin' with all this. I think my way will be clearer in the mornin'.' He scraped back his chair across the floor and stood up, more abruptly than he had intended. 'Thank you for the brandy. I'll bid you goodnight.'

'Wait!' Rosie grabbed hold of his arm. 'There's a warm room upstairs if you wants to stay the night. It has fresh sheets on the bed and I'll do you a good breakfast in the mornin'. I knows you share yer brother's great appetite.'

'Moy Rosie cooks a damned hearty breakfast,' Kilby said, smiling.

Woods hesitated, as he always did at the prospect of good food. Things had just taken an interesting turn. Kilby might be unconcerned about his fate but his wife was fretting. She didn't want Woods out of her sight in case he went to the magistrate to fetch an arrest warrant for Kilby. Woods had been an officer long enough to recognise a bribe of ham and eggs when he saw one. The desperate woman was tempting him with a warm bed and good food. Would Betsy fight so hard for him? He ruddy well hoped so.

Sleep would have to wait. The decision had to be made now. Kilby's fate spun on the edge of a sixpence and all three of them knew it was Woods' hands that flipped the coin. Woods tried to think rationally about the situation.

In the eyes of the law, he was probably already an accomplice to Kilby's crime. Instead of turning Kilby into the authorities the moment he recognised him, he had raced back here like a hothead, bided his time until they were alone and then thrashed the bugger. If he wasn't an accomplice at the moment, by the time he woke up in The Angel Inn tomorrow morning he definitely would be. Accepting the Kilbys' hospitality would be seen as siding with his brother.

Yet he believed Kilby's version of events. On top of that, he had started to like and respect him. Kilby had led a decent life since he'd fled London. He'd brought up three sons, earned the adoration of his wife and the respect of the local boatmen. It wouldn't have been easy for a fugitive from justice to turn his life around like this.

Woods knew that if Kilby went for trial, his brother would hang for sure. Whatever defence Kilby might have had thirty-six years ago, it was in tatters now. Could he do that to his brother?

He felt his mother's presence at his shoulder. *Don't do it, Neddy*, she was saying. *Let sleepin' dogs lie . . .*

And, after all, who was to know? It had all happened so long ago. Provided Kilby stayed out of Rotherhithe, it was unlikely anyone would ever recognise him and associate him with the unsolved murder.

'*I wouldn't ever hurt you*,' Kilby had said. Woods believed him. Could he hurt Kilby?

No, he couldn't and he wouldn't. His shoulders relaxed and he smiled as everything fell into place. This would be his secret – his and his brother's. No one else would ever find out and there would be no harm done.

'Well, thank you, Rosie. A warm comfy bed is just what my old bones need right now – and I'd welcome a fine breakfast in the mornin'.'

Relief flooded across both of their faces. They knew the significance of his decision to accept their roof over his head for the night. Kilby got up and began to lock up the tavern. Rosie picked up a lamp to lead him upstairs to his bedchamber.

They didn't ask him any more questions and he was glad. He didn't want to talk any more.

As he trailed in the wake of Rosie's flickering candle, another thought lightened his step. He didn't know why, but Woods knew there'd be no more nightmares. It was over.

Chapter Twenty-Nine

Monday 5th March, 1810
Southwark, London

Alice Lavender was sitting by the fireside in the front parlour, her grey head bent over her sewing, when Lavender walked into his parents' house.

Unlike many of their neighbours, who kept their parlours for funerals, Christmas and Easter, Alice had always insisted her family used theirs every evening. They ate their evening meal at the kitchen table but once the dirty crockery and pans were cleared away, they would retire into the parlour. John Lavender would smoke his pipe and read out extracts from the daily news-sheet to the family. Lavender's mother and sisters would sit at their needlework. Sometimes the girls would play cards or one of them would play a tune on the scratched old pianoforte.

When he wasn't up to mischief with little Elizabeth, the young Lavender would curl up in an armchair with a book, pretending to read but secretly listening to his parents' discussion of national events and politics and to the older girls gossiping about their friends and neighbours. He knew he had been a quiet child – and his bookish ways had been a disappointment to his active and boisterous father – but his childhood had been a happy one and many of his favourite memories came from this well-lit room, with its comfortable but worn old furniture and the ancient longcase clock ticking quietly away in the corner.

'Stephen! What a wonderful surprise.' Alice put down her needlework and rose stiffly to her feet. Her patchwork knitted blanket slithered off her lap and formed a brightly coloured pile on the floor. He kissed the soft, lined cheek she offered him. As always, she smelt faintly of violets. He loved her scent.

'I saw Magdalena two days ago,' Alice said. 'She didn't say you were expected home.'

'I wasn't,' he said. 'The case in Northamptonshire has taken an unexpected twist and I've had to return for a brief visit. Unfortunately, I must be on the four o'clock mail coach back to Northamptonshire.' He picked up the fallen blanket, handed it to her and sank wearily into the soft, padded armchair on the other side of the hearth – his father's chair. 'Are you well?' he asked.

'Yes, thank you, Stephen. There are a few pains in my joints and a few more grey hairs on my head but Elizabeth and your father look after me very well.' She lowered her head and regarded him silently over the top of her spectacles. Many people had commented that her wide-set, slightly hooded brown eyes were virtually identical to his own. 'You look tired, Stephen,' she said. 'You work too hard – and you need to visit the barbers.'

'I'm fine, Mother,' he said, smiling.

'Would you like something to eat and drink?'

'Yes, please.' He glanced around. 'Where are father and Elizabeth?' Lavender's older sisters were married but his youngest sister Elizabeth still lived with their parents.

'Your father is out with a friend this afternoon and Elizabeth is shopping.' A wry smile curled up her lips. 'I was enjoying a rare moment of peace.'

'How is your pain?' he asked. Alice suffered from severe arthritis.

She shrugged and smiled. 'I barely feel it.'

'I'll make the coffee,' he said, and rose from his seat.

His mother held up her hand to stop him. 'No, you won't. You shall have a few minutes of rest. I may be a bit slow but I can still make my favourite son a bite to eat when he comes visiting.'

He smiled at their old joke. 'I'm your only son,' he reminded her.

'Well, fancy that!' she said and hobbled out of the room.

He knew better than to try and argue with his mother. He settled back in his father's armchair. For a moment, his eyes rested on the ornaments on the mantelpiece. Alice's collection of porcelain shepherdesses was surrounded by the oval miniature paintings of a young Stephen and his pretty sisters. His proud father had commissioned these miniatures from a local artist. Then he closed his eyes and enjoyed the warmth of the fire. The room smelt of coal smoke and beeswax polish mingled with his mother's violet scent and his father's aromatic tobacco. Smells of his childhood . . .

The next thing he knew, his mother was back in the room, lowering a tray onto the side table. His eyes lit up at the sight of the loaf of fresh bread, the pot of savoury meat paste and the seed cake on the tray. Assorted crockery including a cup and the coffee jug already stood on another table by his elbow. The coffee smelt delicious and strong.

'You should have let me help,' he said guiltily.

'I can manage,' she said, as she handed him a plate. 'Besides which, you need a rest. Didn't you sleep last night?'

'Are we toasting the bread?' Lavender reached for the two brass toasting forks that hung with the rest of the fire irons in the hearth.

'We can if you want. Have you seen Magdalena since you returned?'

'Yes, I called on her briefly last night. She's well.' He stabbed the thick slices of bread with the long metal forks and held them over the flames in the fire. 'We'll probably hold the wedding when Sebastián comes back from school in Hertfordshire at Easter. I think Magdalena wants him to be there.'

While he toasted the bread, Alice poured the coffee and arranged the plates and asked him further questions about their wedding plans. She spread the meat paste onto the toast and told him the latest family news while he washed down his food with several cups of strong coffee. He felt reinvigorated.

'Have you met Magdalena's son yet?' She passed him a generous piece of soft, newly-baked seed cake.

'No, but I'm looking forward to it. He sounds like a lively and interesting young man.'

'He must favour his mother in his temperament.' Alice lowered her head to hide the smile twitching at the edge of her lips. 'I'm sure that you and Sebastián will soon learn to love each other. You will make a good father, Stephen. You're naturally kind and considerate – and a great listener.'

'I think you may be biased in my favour, Mother.'

'No, those are your qualities. They're what make you such a good son, brother and friend and it's those qualities that will ensure you're a good husband and stepfather to young Sebastián.'

The mention of the word 'friend' reminded him why he was here. He put his empty plate to one side and cleared his throat. 'That is an excellent cake,' he said. 'Please pass on my compliments to Elizabeth.' Alice didn't reply. She was watching him through those soft eyes that never seemed to blink. Had he ever seen his mother blink?

'I need to ask you about Tilda Woods.'

'Tilda Woods?'

'Yes, I need to know about her eldest son Bert. The one who vanished.'

'My, that's a long time ago.' Alice put her own plate down on the side table. She looked troubled.

'But she did tell you about him, didn't she?' He paused and waited until his mother nodded a confirmation. 'You knew Tilda Woods for . . . how long?'

'I first met Tilda over twenty years ago but she only had Ned with her by then. Stephen, why do you need to know about Bert? Have you found him?'

Her question caught him by surprise for a moment. 'Yes. I think I may have found him.'

'How?'

'It's staring anyone in the face when they see the two of them together. Bert is a slightly taller but white-haired version of Ned. If you catch them in the right light, as I did, they're very similar in features and expression.'

'Good gracious! Does Ned know about this? Where is Ned?'

'Mother, may I ask the questions, please?'

'But Ned . . .'

'Ned is safe.' *At least, I hope he is.*

She sat back in her chair. 'I'm sorry, Stephen. Please carry on.'

'Can you remember what Tilda told you about Bert? I need to know everything.'

'It's such a long time since we last talked about Bert . . .'

'Please just try.'

She sighed and stared into the dancing flames in the hearth for inspiration. 'Bert had already vanished by the time Tilda moved to Southwark with Ned. The two of us didn't become friendly until Ned started to work at Bow Street with your father. You know how it is with the police families.'

Lavender did know. The Bow Street Police officers weren't popular in London and were regarded with great suspicion by most of the population and often isolated. As a result of this, the families tended to live close to each other for support.

'Please try to remember what you can. It's important.'

Alice sighed again and shifted her unblinking gaze onto the lacy curtains of the window. Lavender sensed she was trying to pluck the old memories from the dark recesses of her mind.

'His full name is James Albert Woods,' she said eventually. 'He was called James for his father but everyone called him Bert to avoid confusion.'

James Albert Woods. James Woods. J.W.

'When he was a young man, he ran with a bad crowd. He got into trouble, a lot of trouble, and broke Tilda's heart. He escaped arrest by the skin of his teeth, she told me. Then one day there was a hue and cry.'

'Why? What had happened?'

'The constables who came to her door said Bert had killed a man down on the coal wharf and he was now a fugitive from justice.'

'Had he? Killed a man, I mean?'

Alice shrugged her narrow shoulders. 'Tilda never believed the accusation. She said Bert had been framed for hanging by some of the others in his crowd.'

'How did he escape?'

Alice smiled. 'Tilda kept him hidden for a while in the cellar, then she smuggled him out of London on a barge belonging to one of her family members. Kilby, I think they were called. Bert told her his version of the events on the wharf and she believed him. She always claimed he was innocent. I'm sorry, Stephen. I can't remember anything more about his story.'

Lavender nodded. 'That's all right. What happened next to Tilda and Ned?'

Her face became serious again. 'Ned was ill.'

'Ned – ill? With what?'

'Well, that's the mystery. It was as if his nerves were upset. He screamed and cried all night with bad dreams –'

'Bad dreams?'

'Yes. He was listless and silent during the day. He stopped eating and Tilda became anxious for him.'

'Ned stopped eating?'

Alice nodded and frowned. 'Yes – it's not amusing, Stephen. Poor Tilda was beside herself with worry. She'd just lost one son and now she thought she was about to lose another. Ned adored Bert and missed him dreadfully after he fled, but the doctor said Ned's listlessness and nightmares were a symptom of something else, something physical. In the end he pronounced that the foul air of Rotherhithe had affected Ned's wits. Tilda moved them both here to Southwark. It worked. Ned recovered.'

Lavender nodded but he'd stopped listening. His mind was with Ned, alone up in Market Harborough, and the fear that first jolted him when he recognised Kilby now returned to gnaw at his guts. Brother or not, Alby Kilby was wanted for murder. He'd successfully covered his tracks and hidden from the authorities for over thirty years. How would Kilby react if Woods made the connection and confronted his brother with the past? Would Kilby turn violent?

Lavender's stomach churned again. He had to get back to Market Harborough as soon as possible. He had sent a note for Woods on the mail coach but he might have been too late. 'Was Bert Woods a dangerous man, do you know?'

Alice shook her head. 'I don't know, Stephen.'

'And as far as you know, Tilda never saw her son Bert again?'

'No.'

He brushed a few crumbs off his lap and stood up. 'I'm sorry, Mother,' he said, 'but I must go now.'

'I know you must.' Leaning heavily on the arms of her chair, she raised herself to her feet. 'It's been lovely sitting and chatting with you, Stephen – just the two of us. Your father and Elizabeth will be sorry they've missed you.' A smile creased across her pale face. 'But I've enjoyed having you all to myself for once.'

He went to kiss her cheek but she drew him into her arms and held him to her breast for a moment. 'Please take care of yourself, Stephen.'

'I will.'

'Take care of Ned.'

'I will.'

'And,' she whispered into his ear, 'when you arrest Bert Woods, remember to tell him that his own mother loved him and thought about him every day until she drew her last breath.'

He kissed her lightly on her cheek. 'I will,' he promised.

Chapter Thirty

Tuesday 6th March, 1810
Market Harborough, Leicestershire

Lavender clambered stiffly out of the mail coach into the dark, cobbled yard of The Bell Inn. He was exhausted after the overnight dash from London. It was raining and a large crowd of people, some of whom stank of liquor, were already at the carriage door, desperate to claim a place on the inside of the vehicle for its onward journey, rather than get drenched by travelling on the outside. Lavender forced his way through the crowd and walked straight into the backside of a fat, wet sheep. 'What the devil . . . ?'

The animal bleated mournfully and shuffled back into the huddled flock tethered outside the tavern entrance. Lavender wrinkled his nose. The strong gamey odour of wet lanolin emanated from the animals. Then he remembered: Tuesday was market day in Market Harborough. Everywhere would be busy.

The inside of the tavern was as crowded as the courtyard outside but thankfully the only four-legged animals were a few exhausted sheepdogs sprawled beneath the tables, while their inebriated owners talked and argued with each other or attempted to play cards or dice. Lavender took his luggage upstairs and noticed that Woods' shaving equipment and carpet bag had gone. Perhaps he was pursuing some lead or clue over in Middleton and had stayed at the village for a few nights? Hopefully he should be back soon.

Lavender returned to the taproom and pushed his way through the drunken farmers until he found an unoccupied table in the corner. He ordered ale and a large plate of meat and potato pie and gravy from the barmaid. He asked the young girl if she had seen or heard from his constable today but she shook her head and looked confused. He glanced around for the landlord with the huge sideburns and saw Fred Newby on the opposite side of the room taking part in a heated debate with several of his customers about the price of corn.

When she brought him his supper, the barmaid also gave him two letters, one of which he recognised instantly as the note he had sent Ned warning him about Alby Kilby. It was unopened. The other was from Captain Rushperry and was addressed to both him and Constable Woods. It was still sealed. The barmaid told him they had both arrived the previous afternoon. Obviously Woods hadn't been here since then. Lavender frowned, pulled out his pocketknife and slit open the letter from Rushperry.

Rushperry wrote that Lavender had been right about Caleb Liquorish. The Cottingham churchwarden had been in trouble with the law in his youth. While perusing the court's records for the name 'Liquorish', Rushperry's clerk had discovered that the churchwarden had been sentenced to thirty days' hard labour back in 1782. Liquorish had wilfully exposed his manhood to a startled group of women returning home from the Kettering horse fair.

Lavender laughed and wondered why he wasn't more surprised to learn Caleb Liquorish was a lewd fellow. A sense of satisfaction welled up in his chest. The complicated strands of the tapestry of this mystery were beginning to untangle and a clearer picture was emerging.

William Sculthorpe had a compulsion about money and when he lived in London he resorted to blackmail to keep his coffers topped up with gold coin. He needed to speak to Caleb Liquorish again to confirm his suspicions, but his theory that Sculthorpe had been blackmailing his Middleton neighbours was becoming more and more credible. For all Lavender knew, he'd probably been blackmailing folks down in Brighton too when he lived there.

Lavender didn't know how Sculthorpe had found out about Liquorish's past crimes, but nothing surprised him any more about the former priest. He had no doubt that the wily old man had approached Liquorish, threatened to reveal his sordid little secret and demanded money in exchange for his silence. One guinea a month was a hefty demand – no wonder the two men were seen arguing – but Liquorish had no choice. If the truth came to light about his youthful perversion, his standing in the community, especially at the church, would be ruined.

Liquorish needed William Sculthorpe to keep quiet but would he have been prepared to murder the old man to ensure his permanent silence? Lavender shook his head. No, Liquorish wasn't the type to get his hands dirty – but he could afford to pay someone to do the deed for him. Would he turn a blind eye if he knew that others planned to rid the village of the blackmailing old rogue? Who amongst Sculthorpe's victims would be prepared to become part of such a conspiracy? He sighed.

'*This is the last payment you old bastard. Leave me alone. J.W.*'

The resentment and anger in that message bothered him. The author of this curt note hated William Sculthorpe with a vengeance. More than any other of Sculthorpe's five blackmail victims, Lavender desperately needed to get to the bottom of the mystery of *J.W.*

Hopefully, Woods would have plenty to report to him by now. He glanced at the door, expecting to see the burly figure of his constable walk through it at any moment. Woods knew Lavender was returning to Market Harborough tonight. They needed to meet and speak as soon as possible.

Lavender took out his pocket watch and saw it was now after ten o'clock. *Where on earth was Woods?* Had some accident befallen him between here and Middleton? Lavender's gut tightened. Had Woods stumbled into the path of one of the dangerous gang of thugs they sought? Had Alby Kilby tried to silence his brother?

Lavender rose to his feet. 'Landlord!'

Fred Newby broke away from his discussion with the noisy farmers and turned his sharp face towards him. He scowled when he recognised Lavender as the one who had hailed him.

'Where's my constable? When did you last see him?'

'I don't know where your man is,' Newby replied, 'but I can make a fair guess.'

'You can? Why?'

'I think you'll find your constable foxed in The Angel Inn along with the dirty bargees and that Alby Kilby.' The farmers around him burst out laughing. 'Your constable has spent most of the last two days in there – drinkin' and fightin'.'

'Well, he shouldn't be hard to find unless he's crawled off into a gutter somewhere,' said one of the farmers.

'Oh, he'll find the tosspot,' replied the landlord, pointing a finger in Lavender's direction. 'He's a detective. That's what they do, those detectives: find folks. Mind you, it's a rum do when they have to spend their time findin' each other.'

The farmers laughed again and made some ribald comments, but Lavender didn't listen. He was on his way out of the door.

It was only a short distance across the market square from The Bell Inn to The Angel, and Lavender strode briskly. But by the time he leapt up the steps beneath the crumbling portico at the entrance of The Angel, his imagination had worked him up to a fevered state. Kilby had done something to Woods. His friend's murdering brother had slit Woods' throat to silence him and then buried the body. Kilby had pickled the body. Kilby had strangled Woods with those great hands of his and thrown his body in the canal . . .

His head pounded as he burst through the door of the tavern and every sinew of his flesh knew Kilby had harmed Woods in some way.

Woods and Kilby were sitting in the nearly deserted taproom, leaning close together over a table. They held tankards of ale and laughed at some shared joke. Relief and anger flooded through Lavender in equal measure.

'Sir!' Woods beamed at him across the taproom. His large, round face was flushed with liquor and his eyes shone. 'You're back! Good to see you. 'Tis well met. Come here to meet . . .'

'I know who he is.' Lavender snapped as he strode across the taproom. His voice cut through the mellow atmosphere like a blade and he knew it. The last two customers glanced across at them.

'You said he were smart,' Kilby said to Woods.

Woods nodded enthusiastically. The drink exaggerated his movements. 'Oh, yes. He's a clever detective. Very clever.'

Seeing them side by side and nodding in agreement, the two brothers were like peas in a pod. One was just a bit riper and larger than the other and both of them were covered in purple and yellow bruises. Woods' left ear was bright red and grotesquely swollen, and Kilby had a magnificent black eye. Had they been fighting? If so, why so close now? What the hell had been going on?

He turned to the two gawping customers at the other table. 'This tavern is now closed for the night. Put down your drinks and leave.'

The two farmers glanced at Kilby for confirmation but Kilby did and said nothing.

'Who the hell are you?' one of the men asked.

'I'm Detective Stephen Lavender with the Bow Street Police Office and I'm shutting down this tavern for the night. If you don't get out this door – now – I'll have you both thrown in the stocks for interfering with a police investigation.'

'Oh, all right, fellah.' The older man of the pair hastily pushed back his chair. 'Don't lose yer shirt. We were just goin' anyhows.' He knocked back the last of his ale, wiped his mouth with the back of his sleeve, stood up and left the room with his companion. They slammed the door behind them. Lavender turned back to Woods and Kilby.

'James Albert Woods,' he said loudly, enunciating each name slowly and deliberately. 'You're wanted for murder back in London.'

'Yes,' Woods slurred. He wagged a finger in the air. 'But he didn't do it.'

Lavender turned to him. 'How do you know this, Ned?'

Surprise flashed across Woods' face. ''Cause he said so, that's why.'

For a moment, Lavender was stunned. He'd known Woods get bowsey with liquor before but he didn't usually lose his wits when in his cups. This nonsense came from more than just inebriation.

'Do you realise his initials are *J. W.*?'

'Ah,' Woods said, 'he were allus known as Bert Woods.'

'For Christ's sake! Kilby is a suspect in the murder inquiry we're conducting in Middleton.'

'Oh, 'tis all right,' Woods beamed up at him. 'He's hardly been out of town for months.'

'How do you know this?'

'He told me.'

Lavender grabbed hold of Woods' shoulders and dragged him to his feet. If Lavender had owned the strength, he would have dragged his drunken constable out of the damned tavern and as far away from Kilby as he could. He thought for a second that Kilby might intervene but the giant man stayed still in his seat and watched the two policemen argue with impassive eyes – one of them blackened and half closed.

'Whoa, sir!' Woods laughed, swayed unsteadily on his feet and shook him off. 'How were your trip back to London . . . ?'

'Damn London.' Lavender pushed his face up close to Woods until he could smell the alcohol on his breath. 'Ned, listen to me – *listen* to me. You're a constable with twenty years of experience of villains. You never take the word of suspects for granted, you know this.'

Woods shook him off and smiled. ''Tis all right, sir – he's my brother.' He screwed up his face in an exaggerated wink. 'I'd know if he were a lyin' wrinkler.'

'He's a suspected murderer, Ned!' Lavender yelled. He was losing control of this situation and he knew it. 'And he hasn't been your brother for over thirty years! He's a stranger who has come back into your life with a load of flannel and he's gulled you into believing his version of events – only a jury can decide if he's innocent or guilty!'

A flicker of doubt glimmered in Woods' eyes for a second. Then it vanished and he beamed again. ''Tis all right, sir. He's a good man, sound.'

Lavender stepped back. This was getting them nowhere. He needed Woods on his own – and sober. He needed him back at The Bell Inn, sleeping off the effects of the ale and brandy. Only then would he be able to reason with him. Either that or he would have to grab Woods' head and bang it against the wall in order to knock some sense into him. 'Pay your bill, Constable,' he said. 'We're going back to The Bell Inn. You're going to sleep off this illusion and sober up.'

Woods opened his mouth to protest but at that moment Kilby pushed back his chair and stood up.

Lavender tensed. Even with the table between them he felt intimidated by the landlord's height and muscular frame. He knew Kilby wasn't as drunk as Woods.

'Wait,' Kilby growled. 'I can see there's trouble between you. I never intended for this to happen. I may be able to help.'

'Hand yourself in to the authorities and make a full confession,' Lavender snapped. 'That would help.'

Kilby shook his white head. 'I can't do that for I weren't the guilty one,' he said. 'A've never killed no one. But I'll give you some news, sommat you'd probably want to hear.'

'Good for you, Alby,' Woods slurred. He fell back into his chair and his head rolled backwards and then jerked forwards again, much to his evident surprise.

'What news?' Lavender asked.

'A've had one boatman tell me he saw five figures lurkin' at Saunt's Bridge this evenin'. Five fellahs who didn't want to be seen.'

'So?'

'And A've had news from a wharf hand that there's a barge not properly laden with timber moored in the basin tonight called *The Swan*. She'll leave at dawn tomorrow. "Leave a gap in the timber," the boatman said to the wharf hands. So they did. They've left a space – a space big enough for men to lie down. Men who don't want to be seen.'

Lavender frowned. 'What the hell are you talking about, Kilby?'

'At dawn, *The Swan* will leave Market Harborough with a light load. By the time she gets to Saunt's Bridge, she'll have a full load. A've heard you're lookin' for a gang of five men. I'm tellin' you they're here – in Market Harborough – at Saunt's Bridge. There's two different fellahs given me two different pieces of news and A've put it together and made one.'

'Are we talking about the Panther Gang? Here? In Market Harborough?'

Kilby nodded.

''Tis time we caught those big cats in a trap,' Woods slurred as he swayed.

Lavender's tired brain raced. He couldn't believe what Kilby was saying. Then again, the Panthers wouldn't be the first fugitives from the law who had chosen to disappear and hide on England's waterways. Kilby knew more about this than any man.

Lavender looked Kilby straight in the eyes. 'Do you swear on your mother's memory this information is true?'

Steady as a rock, Kilby stared back at him out of Ned's soft brown eyes. 'I swear,' he said.

Lavender grabbed Woods by the shoulder again and heaved him back up onto his feet. His eyes never broke away from Kilby's. 'I'm taking Ned back to The Bell Inn,' he said, 'and then I'm going straight to Captain Rushperry. I'll ask him to rouse the militia and we'll go to Saunt's Bridge at dawn to catch these five men.'

Kilby shook his head. 'No. The bank is too open round there. They'll scarper before you get near them. You'd be better to wait for them at the next bridge at Bowden Hall. They'll be on the barge and easier to trap.'

Lavender hesitated, then nodded. 'Very well. I'll take your advice. Bowden Hall Bridge it will be. You can meet us there – just before dawn.'

The landlord started with surprise and scowled. 'What, me? What do you want me for?'

'If you've told me the truth, you've nothing to worry about. If you're lying to me, Kilby, and sending us on a wild goose chase, then, so help me God, I'll have you clapped in irons and transported back to London for trial before you can blink. And if you don't turn up tomorrow, I'll have you arrested anyway. Do I make myself absolutely clear?'

Kilby glanced from Lavender to his brother. Woods was now

half asleep and swaying gently in Lavender's grasp with his eyes closed.

'And if I'm speakin' the truth?'

Lavender lowered his voice. 'Then you and I have an understanding.' He refused to promise anything more.

It was enough. Kilby nodded. 'I'll be there at Bowden Hall Bridge afore dawn.'

Relief flooded through Lavender. Without another word, he headed for the door of the tavern, dragging his inebriated constable in his wake.

Chapter Thirty-One

Wednesday 7th March, 1810
Bowden Hall Bridge, Market Harborough Canal Arm

Lavender shivered and stared eastward along the dark stretch of still water. His eyes strained against the gloom for any movement at the distant bend in the canal. Below him, shadowy figures crept along the towing path on his left before disappearing beneath the dark arch of the bridge. Each of them clutched a musket. On the overgrown right-hand side of the canal, the undergrowth rustled and cracked as more militia men moved into position. There would be no escape for the Panther Gang this time. It was just a question of waiting for *The Swan* to glide into their ambush.

The first red smudges of dawn appeared on the horizon and the smell of coal smoke drifted across from the scattered cottages that made up this small rural community. Out in the fields, sheep began to bleat. Crows called to each other from their nests in the treetops, then rose, circling and wheeling in pairs and groups of three and four before heading off to their favourite feeding grounds.

How long until *The Swan* appeared around the bend, Lavender wondered? How fast did these horse-drawn barges move?

Kilby had been as good as his word and turned up astride a huge horse called Meggie. The gigantic pair made a dramatic sight, silhouetted against the glimmering wall lamps of the market square. *The Swan* would leave the basin at Market Harborough at dawn, Kilby told him and Rushperry. The boatmen never wasted daylight when they had a load. They would have to slow down at Saunt's Bridge so the Panther Gang could leap aboard and hide themselves in the cavity beneath the tarpaulin, but this shouldn't delay them for long.

Lavender's sharp ears picked up the jangle of harnesses and the impatient stamping of restless hooves further along the road to his right. Woods and Kilby stood with the horses. He heard Woods murmuring to the beasts to calm them. Kilby rarely took his eyes from his younger brother's face and seemed happy to let the garrulous Ned do most of the talking. Lavender had seen that look before on the faces of men gazing at their newborn children for the first time. Kilby clearly couldn't believe that his brother was back in his life again.

Lavender had only managed to snatch a couple of hours' sleep last night. He had left Woods snoring in his bed and spent the next few hours rousing Captain Rushperry and the militia. Woods had woken up in a cheerful mood, with no recollection of their argument in The Angel and a far better head than he deserved. Lavender had not been so lucky. His temples pounded with lack of sleep and exhaustion.

The dark-coated bulk of Captain Rushperry joined him on the bridge and followed his gaze towards Woods and Kilby over by the horses. The two brothers had their heads close together again and were deep in conversation. Lavender held his breath and hoped Rushperry wouldn't see the incredible resemblance between the two men. 'Woods and Kilby had better be right about this, Lavender,' he growled.

'They have my confidence.'

'Huh!' Rushperry cast him a sideways glance. 'I'd heard Constable Woods spent a lot of time drinking and fighting in The Angel while you were away in London.'

Lavender smiled. 'This was how he gained Kilby's trust – and that of the canal boatmen. It's what they teach us down in London. We get more information this way.'

'It's a strange way of doing police business, in my opinion,' Rushperry frowned, but he didn't ask any more questions.

Moorhens squabbled in the reeds down in the canal and a solitary swan glided into view, searching for breakfast in the still water. Slowly daylight spread across the countryside. Trees, distant farmhouses and the spire of a church took form as the darkness receded. Dew glistened on the damp ground.

Then, almost imperceptibly at first, Lavender saw movement. A plodding horse rounded the bend in the canal, accompanied by a solitary man. In their wake followed a barge with another man at the tiller. Weighed down with its cargo, the boat floated low in the water.

'Take your positions!' Rushperry hissed at the militia. 'Hide the lights!'

The last of the militia men scurried into their places. Two of them crouched next to Lavender and Rushperry behind the parapet of the bridge, their lanterns still burning at their sides. The bridge arch below echoed with the quiet but chilling sound of men pulling back their musket hammers and ramming their shot down the barrels. Lavender thought of his own pistol in his coat pocket, loaded and ready to use.

Lavender and Rushperry remained on the crest of the bridge, pulled their hats low over their faces and watched the slow-moving procession of man, horse and barge. The man on the bank walked behind the horse, occasionally clipping its flanks with a hazel switch to keep it moving. Only the blackbirds broke the silence that now fell over Bowden Hall Bridge.

'It's Davy George with the horse,' Rushperry whispered to Lavender. 'He's one of the Panther Gang. I'd recognise his insolent face anywhere. I saw him in the dock last summer at the Northampton Assizes when they sentenced him to transportation.'

Lavender nodded and felt a surge of satisfaction. 'Who's the man steering the barge?'

Rushperry shook his head. 'I don't recognise him. He's probably the boat owner. The rest of the gang must be under the hatch or the tarpaulin.'

The barge glided through the water with barely a ripple. They heard the jangle of the great harness and the steady plod of the horse on the stony path. Lavender held his breath. The procession was almost at the bridge when the magistrate yelled, 'This is Captain Rushperry. Hold fast and surrender yourselves to the law!'

Davy George turned and sprinted back down the towing path like a hare. The well-trained horse continued to plod forward but the man at the tiller yelled after George and so did Rushperry. 'Stop! Or we'll open fire!'

Some of the militia must have misheard their captain. On the words 'Open fire!', several of them did. A deafening volley of musket shot followed the fleet-footed George down the path. The man at the tiller lifted the hatch by his feet, dived down into the cabin and slammed the hatch shut above him. Musket fire rained down onto the stern of the boat after him. Jagged splinters of wood flew into the air. The acrid smell of gunpowder floated up on the breeze and the barrage of fire echoed beneath the bridge arch.

When the first shots rang out, the horse reared and neighed in terror, then bolted the last few yards under the bridge. Behind it, the strong rope connecting the frightened animal to the barge snapped taut and yanked it back to the edge of the canal. The horse's hooves jerked out from beneath it and the terrified animal fell into the canal with an almighty splash. Now rudderless and horseless, the boat drifted helplessly towards the bridge with its bow swung out sideways across the entrance.

Davy George was still on his feet and running. One of the soldiers broke cover and raced down the towing path after him.

'Come back, you idiot!' Rushperry yelled. 'Hold your fire!'

There was a sudden flash of blue powder from the drifting barge – and a single shot rang out. The soldier on the towing path screamed, clutched his shoulder and fell to the ground.

'They're firing back!' Rushperry yelled. 'Take cover and reload!' Lavender and Rushperry lowered themselves behind the brick parapet of the bridge. Lavender peered cautiously over the edge at the scene below, his pistol ready in his hand.

'Davy George is escapin'!' one of the soldiers yelled up from the bank.

Lavender heard the clatter of hooves on cobbles. Leaning low over the neck of his horse, Woods thundered over the bridge behind them. He turned her sharply into the field, then ran beside the canal and spurred her forward.

'He'll get himself shot!' Rushperry yelled.

'Give him some cover!' Lavender shouted and fired his pistol at the point where he'd seen the blue flash of powder.

'Fire at the barge!' Rushperry yelled.

Another volley of musket and pistol shot rang out, shattering the wooden boat below them. Splinters flew everywhere. The horse in the canal thrashed against the water and screamed again in fear. The rudderless barge drifted closer to the narrow bridge arch. Through the cloud of musket smoke, Lavender saw Woods, still mounted and bearing down on George. He let himself breathe again.

The barge hit the side of the bridge with a dull thud and a shudder. The bow swung back but drifted forward again and jammed into the narrow arch of the bridge. It wedged tight with a sickening crunch of splintering wood.

Silence fell as everyone listened, watched and waited.

'It's jammed, sir!' shouted up one of the soldiers.

Rushperry raised his head a few inches higher over the parapet. 'Throw your pistols into the canal and come out with your hands held up!'

A single pistol shot whizzed past his ear in reply. Rushperry stepped back hastily, readjusted his hat and swore. 'This is ridiculous!' he snapped. 'They're stuck and they know they're surrounded.'

'How do we get them out, Captain?' asked the young soldier to his left.

Rushperry hesitated, unsure what to do.

'Is this what they call a stand-off, sir?'

Lavender's eyes fell on the glass lantern by the lad's side. It was still alight. 'What do you normally do, son, when you've got rats trapped in a hole?' he asked.

The crouching young soldier looked blank. Rushperry frowned. 'Do you have a plan, Detective?'

'Yes.' Lavender grabbed the lantern, stood up and hurled it hard and fast over the parapet down onto the tarpaulin of the barge. 'Let's burn them out!'

The glass lantern shattered on the taut, oiled cloth stretched over the timber cargo. Blue flames danced across the surface of the tarpaulin, igniting everything they touched.

'For God's sake, Lavender! We want them alive. Stand fast, men! Prepare to take prisoners!'

It didn't take long for the dry timber to burst into flames. Above the crackle of burning wood they heard shouts and frantic movement aboard the barge. Choking grey smoke and flaming embers billowed up out of the mouth of the bridge arch.

Lavender and Rushperry left the bridge and moved to the top of the bank that led down to the towing path, but the smoke made visibility difficult. The burning timber snapped and roared as the blaze spread. They heard loud coughing and panic-stricken voices raised in argument.

'They'll have to come off soon,' Lavender said.

The heat intensified and the vaulted arch of the bridge magnified the roar and crackle of the inferno.

'Look!'

The dirty smoke cleared for a moment. A man balanced precariously on the far gunnels of the boat with the fire at his back. His frantic eyes scanned the far bank.

'He's trying to jump,' Lavender said.

'It's Minards!' Rushperry yelled.

Minards hesitated too long. The flames set fire to his shirt. For a moment he danced on the gunnels, writhing and screaming. Then he hurled himself into the water to douse the flames. They heard him yell, 'Help me!'

'Throw him a rope!' Rushperry shouted across the water.

The fire had burnt through the tarpaulin and the ropes holding the cargo in place. The barge listed as its flaming load shifted. Planks of charred and burning timber slithered into the canal and floated away in the slight breeze.

Suddenly, two of the gang burst out from a corner of the tarpaulin, threw themselves overboard and swam beneath the bridge. Their bid for freedom was short-lived. When they surfaced by the bank on the other side, the muzzles of several muskets pointed down into their faces.

'There's just two left now,' Rushperry said.

Lavender coughed and blinked. The smoke stung his lungs and eyes. 'Look there!'

The hatch of the cabin at the back of the barge slid back. A pair of pistols flew up into the air and landed with a plop in the water.

'Don't shoot!' yelled a gruff and terrified voice. 'We're comin' out!' Two smoke-blackened and choking figures scrambled out onto the towing path – straight into the custody of the militia.

Lavender and Rushperry strode down towards them. Rushperry grabbed the hair of one of the prisoners, yanked up his bowed head and peered into his scowling, blackened face. 'It's Benjamin Panther,' he announced. 'Make sure this fellow has extra weight on his manacles.'

Panther spat at Rushperry's feet and earned a sharp cuff around the back of his head with the butt of a musket for his contempt.

Across the canal, one of the soldiers waded up the bank dragging the semi-drowned Minards behind him. The other two soaking wet gang members were surrounded by militia at the far side of the bridge. Davy George was the only one unaccounted for. Lavender heard the steady clop of hooves behind him on the towing path. He turned. Woods rode towards them, dragging a manacled George on the end of a chain behind his horse. 'We've got all of them now,' he said with a surge of satisfaction.

Woods stopped, leant forward in his saddle and grinned at the chaos before him. 'Decided to give them a pagan funeral, did you, sir?' he asked.

It was another half an hour before they were ready to march the prisoners back to Market Harborough for questioning. The injured soldier had been their first priority and he'd been dispatched to the surgeon in Bowden for treatment. They expected him to recover. Rushperry and the militia were in an ebullient mood. They intended to parade their cowed prisoners through the town before they incarcerated them.

Personally, all Lavender wanted to do was have a good wash and return to bed for a few hours' sleep before he picked up the pieces of the case he had been hired to solve. He was filthy and stank of smoke.

Beneath the smoke-blackened bridge, the burnt-out wreckage of *The Swan* floated aimlessly. Charred wood and debris littered a vast area of the water's surface. The wreck completely blocked the entrance to the bridge and the heat of the fire had cracked many of the bricks.

He leant on the parapet on top of the bridge and watched Woods and Kilby down on the towing path about thirty yards away. The fire had quickly burnt through the strong rope attaching the terrified horse to the barge and it had been able to break free and swim away from the carnage. Unfortunately, it had been unable to climb up the steep banks and was still floundering around in the canal.

Kilby and Woods lassoed it with ropes, pulled it to a section where the bank was less steep and tried to haul it out onto the towing path. They'd taken off their coats and rolled up their sleeves. Their shoulder muscles were taut beneath their filthy shirts and sweat glistened on their faces as they heaved. He heard their deep voices murmuring encouragement to the animal.

For a fleeting second, Lavender felt a pang of jealousy as he watched the two brothers work side by side to save the animal. He and Woods had been like . . . well, like brothers for the last ten years. He had a sudden irrational fear that Kilby would supplant him and his relationship with Woods would never be the same again. There were three of them now, an awkward number.

He shook his head to chase away such a ridiculous thought and chided himself for his meanness. He had no intention of arresting Kilby but the man couldn't set foot in London again. Brother or not, Woods would rarely see him.

Captain Rushperry appeared at his side. 'Well, the canal company won't be pleased about this,' he said. 'It will take days to remove the wreckage of *The Swan* and open up this arm of the canal again for business.'

Lavender managed a grim smile. 'It was the quickest and simplest way to resolve the stand-off, sir, and it involved far less risk for your militia.'

'You're right,' Rushperry conceded. 'But who'd have thought it, eh? We've scoured two counties looking for these devils. Who would have thought we'd find them here, hiding on the English canals?'

Lavender's gaze fell on Alby Kilby and he smiled.

A loud cheer went up along the canal bank when the poor horse finally scrambled up out of the canal. Several of the militia whistled. Woods threw a blanket over the animal's quivering body and turned to shake Kilby's hand for a job well done.

'I'm impressed how this has turned out,' Rushperry said. 'Although I was worried for Constable Woods. He could have been killed.'

'It's his job,' Lavender said simply. 'He's a horse patrol officer – the best we've got. You should see him chase highway men and footpads across Hampstead Heath.'

'Well, there'll be a good reward in this for you. Constable Woods and Alby Kilby will benefit from it too.'

'Thank you.'

'Ted Porter is already talking. He wants to claim King's Evidence and be an informer on the rest.'

'Will you let him?'

A broad smile broke over Rushperry's smoke-smutted face and he shook his head. 'I'll happily let him tell me anything he wants to tell me – and I'll write it down too. But the crimes of these men go back too far. Not one of them will escape the hangman's noose this time.'

Lavender nodded.

'In fact,' Rushperry continued, 'I've no doubt they'll confess to the murder of poor William Sculthorpe before the end of the day.'

'They won't,' Lavender said sharply. 'They didn't do it.'

Rushperry frowned. 'Are you sure about that, Lavender? After all, it turns out they were in this area.'

'I'm sure. I know who murdered Sculthorpe – and it wasn't the Panther Gang.'

Rushperry's mouth dropped open in surprise. 'Good grief, man! You never said. This is excellent news, excellent!'

'I'm waiting for one more piece of information to arrive – a letter in reply to the one I sent to London last week. When I receive it, hopefully all the pieces of the mystery will finally fall into place.'

Rushperry patted down the pockets of his greatcoat. 'A letter, did you say?'

Lavender glanced at him curiously. 'Yes.'

Rushperry took off his glove and pulled a sealed letter out from his left pocket. 'With all the excitement of catching this gang, I almost forgot to give you this,' he said apologetically. 'It arrived for you at the courthouse while you were away in London. Is it the reply you wanted? It has a military seal.'

Lavender nodded, took the letter, pulled out his pocketknife and slit the seal. Despite his exhaustion, he felt the excitement mounting within him. He smiled with satisfaction as he read. His hunch had been correct. He was right about the identity of *J.W.* and now he had the proof he needed.

He pulled out his pocket watch and checked the time. It was just after nine o'clock. 'Your militia have had an early start this morning, Captain Rushperry,' he said, 'but the day is yet young. Once we've returned to Market Harborough and locked up this gang of villains, do you think you and your soldiers would be able to accompany us to Middleton?'

'Of course,' Rushperry said. 'But why?'

'Because I think it's about time we arrested the murderers of William Sculthorpe.'

Chapter Thirty-Two

Wednesday 7th March, 1810
Middleton, Northamptonshire

The drab taproom of The Woolpack tavern was packed with men. Apart from Captain Rushperry's militia and the two constables, Clancy and Sawyer, there were several other 'guests' whom Lavender had invited to call in to the tavern at six o'clock, including Old Pete Jarman and the schoolmaster, Mr Howard. All of them had been promised they might 'learn something of interest about the dreadful murder of William Sculthorpe, late of this parish'. The majority of these 'guests' were now squashed around the low tables in The Woolpack or leaning back against the scuffed walls with a tankard of ale in their hand.

Captain Rushperry raised an eyebrow when he learnt what Lavender planned but he had agreed to humour his desire for a public showdown with the murderers. The magistrate squashed his bulk onto a hard-backed chair next to the fire and struck up a conversation with Old Pete. Mr Howard lit his pipe and tobacco smoke billowed across the room.

Lavender took up position in the central area in front of the unlit fireplace, feeling self-conscious in his burgundy cravat and coat and his gold-striped silk waistcoat. The black coat and waistcoat he preferred to wear for work now stank of smoke and desperately needed the attention of a laundress. To add to his discomfort, Susie Dicken sidled up to him in her trailing gown and whispered lasciviously, 'Now who's a handsome swell?'

The juddering hands of the glassless longcase clock in the corner of the room said five past the hour when Caleb Liquorish walked through the door. His scowl turned into surprise at the size of the crowd in the tavern. The low hum of conversation stopped and everyone turned to look at the churchwarden.

'We don't often see you in here, Mr Liquorish,' Constable Sawyer said.

'No.' Liquorish glanced around the room with distaste as he removed his gloves. 'It's not my custom to frequent places that sell strong liquor. What is this all about, Lavender? I have a church meeting at seven.' He nodded politely at Captain Rushperry.

'Thank you for sparing us the time,' Lavender said. 'As I have explained to everyone else, we have had some momentous news about the murder of poor William Sculthorpe.' This pronouncement was received with a low murmur of approval from most of the Middleton inhabitants. 'As all of you helped us, in one way or another, with our inquiries, I thought it only fair you should all hear about the conclusion of the case together.'

'Very well,' Liquorish said, 'but please get on with it, Lavender.'

'I will – as soon as Constable Woods appears with our last guest.'

Frank Bunning approached him. The bald landlord looked strained, and his pate gleamed with a fine sheen of sweat. 'Shall I get Susie to light us a fire in the grate?' he asked. The woman had been quietly moving around the room filling up the men's flagons. She looked up when she heard them mention her name.

Lavender shook his head. 'No, thank you. I expect it will become quite hot in here soon.'

The schoolmaster laughed. 'Are you speaking literally or metaphorically there, Detective?' he asked.

Suddenly, the door flew open and the lanky, long-haired farm labourer Harry Goode was propelled forcefully into the room by Constable Woods. 'You'll never guess what, Detective Lavender,' Woods said, 'but this here gentleman had a mind to refuse your invitation! I've had a rare time persuadin' him not to be so rude.'

'I ain't done nuthin'!' the pockmarked labourer protested.

'No one said you had,' Lavender said. 'Take a seat, Goode.' The labourer slid onto a vacant stool next to Bunning's baby-faced nephew Isaac.

'Right, before we discuss the murder of William Sculthorpe, Captain Rushperry has an announcement to make.'

Rushperry cleared his throat, stood up and put his podgy thumbs under the lapels of his coat. Everyone turned towards him. 'This morning, thanks to information received from Detective Lavender and Constable Woods of Bow Street Police Office, myself and the militia were able to apprehend all five members of the notorious Panther Gang – plus a canal boatman who had helped them to evade justice.'

'I say, well done!'

'Good work.'

'That's excellent news.'

Everyone started talking at once but Captain Rushperry held up his hand for silence. 'The prisoners have already been transported to Northampton gaol, whence they'll be sent for trial at the Lent Assizes.'

Constable Sawyer banged his fist down hard on the table in delight. 'I always said it were them bastards that did for Old Sculthorpe. Bang up, sir!'

'Well, actually,' said Lavender, 'it wasn't them.'

'What?'

'He's right,' Captain Rushperry continued. 'After extensive questioning of the prisoners this afternoon, I firmly believe they had nothing whatsoever to do with this crime.' He sat back down.

'But I allus thought . . .' Sawyer said.

'So did a lot of people,' Lavender interrupted. 'This was the obvious conclusion to come to in this case, but murderers are often the men – or women – we'd least expect to be the perpetrators of heinous crimes. And the most obvious motives are not always the right ones.'

Lavender paused for a moment to allow his words to sink in. 'Take this vicious assault on William Sculthorpe, for example. Everyone in this community assumed the motive was greed: that Sculthorpe was attacked because the old gentleman was wealthy and kept a large stash of money in his home.'

'But, Detective,' Constable Sawyer interrupted, laughing. 'The villains pulled up the floorboards of the bedroom and took Sculthorpe's money! What else were we supposed to think?' Some of the others laughed with him, nodded and said, 'Aye.'

'There's a lot more to this crime than meets the eye,' Lavender said. 'What Constable Woods and I didn't understand was the viciousness of this attack on the old man. Sculthorpe told the robbers where he hid his money – yet they still assaulted him. Doctor Wallace can verify this. They slammed Sculthorpe's head back against the wall in the kitchen. He was beaten around the head too – by someone who appears to have been a left-handed man.'

'Aye, Lavender is right,' Doctor Wallace confirmed.

The room fell silent now. Lavender had their attention. 'Why did they hurt him so badly when he had already given them what they wanted? We decided there was more to this attack than just greed and suspected that at least one of the attackers who entered Sculthorpe's house was out for revenge.'

'Revenge?' Frank Bunning looked as though he regretted his exclamation immediately.

'Yes, Mr Bunning. Revenge.'

'But what harm had the old fellah ever done to anyone?'

'William Sculthorpe was a blackmailer.'

'A blackmailer!' A murmur of shock and disgust rippled round the room. Some of those present were more surprised than others. Morgan Turnbull-Thatcher, the haberdasher, looked particularly uncomfortable and stared down at the floor. Caleb Liquorish turned grey and a muscle twitched below his left eye.

Lavender held up his hand for silence. 'And in addition to this, William Sculthorpe was also a discredited and disgraced Catholic priest.'

The disgust in the room now turned to anger but no one was more vocal than Old Pete Jarman.

'To think of the nights I sat here drinkin' with the old goat,' he shouted. 'I never knew he were a Creepin' Jesus! Never! Why I'd have spat in his bloody drink!'

Lavender held up his hand again. The grumbling subsided into silence.

'When Constable Woods and I did a thorough search of Sculthorpe's cottage we made several remarkable discoveries. The main one was Sculthorpe's real secret hiding place, which contained amongst other things a large cache of money.'

Sawyer's jaw dropped open. 'How much?'

'Over six hundred pounds in guineas.'

Someone whistled but it was Harry Goode's turn to lead the vocal outrage this time. 'Six hundred guineas?' he yelled. 'Six hundred guineas!'

'Yes, Mr Goode,' Lavender said. 'A small fortune. It would have made a huge difference to a poor man like you, wouldn't it?'

Isaac Bunning placed a restraining hand on Goode's shoulder.

The young cobbler looked pale compared to the vivid redness of Goode's face. Goode scratched behind his huge jug ears and tried to shrug off his outburst. 'Most of us could do with a bit extra,' he said.

'But you need more than just a bit extra, don't you?' Lavender's smile didn't reach his eyes. 'You see, Goode, I happen to know that you're up to your eyeballs in debt with every trader and shopkeeper in the area. You owe a lot of money and this gives you a strong motive to rob and kill William Sculthorpe.'

'Well, I didn't kill him,' the labourer muttered. 'I were in here when those bastards did for Sculthorpe and his son.'

'Yes, he was.' Isaac Bunning nodded his head vigorously. 'I were with him.' The young man had a high-pitched, almost squeaky voice.

'I thought you said the motive for this attack wasn't just greed?' Doctor Wallace interrupted.

Lavender nodded. 'That is right. Apart from the money, we also uncovered a ledger containing the initials of those from whom Sculthorpe was extorting money.'

'The evil old bastard!' Another murmur of anger and disgust swept round the room and Lavender faced a barrage of questions. He held up his hand again and waited for silence to fall.

'This, gentlemen, was one of the reasons I wanted this gathering, so I only had to explain this once. William Sculthorpe was blackmailing five people: four men and a woman.'

'A woman?'

Lavender nodded again. 'Some of his male victims are in this room now.'

There were gasps of surprise and a few short laughs followed by an uneasy silence as the men of Middleton looked with fresh interest at their neighbours. Absolute silence now fell on those gathered, broken only by the sonorous ticking of the old, glassless clock in the corner.

'It's not my intention to embarrass anyone,' Lavender said. 'I do not intend to publicly name Sculthorpe's victims – and victims they were. Blackmail is a crime.' Someone sighed with relief but Lavender couldn't identify who. 'But obviously these people became of great interest to Constable Woods and myself. Nobody hands over their money to a blackmailer happily. Many of Sculthorpe's victims would have been bitterly angry and resentful, maybe even angry enough to want to silence the old man forever.'

'Ah, I see where you're going with this now, Lavender,' said the schoolmaster, Howard.

'It even crossed my mind that several of Sculthorpe's victims might have colluded to exact punishment on the old man.'

'A conspiracy, eh?' Howard asked.

'Yes, and I think this is exactly what happened. Some of Sculthorpe's victims – let's call them "the murderers" from now on, because that is what they are, murderers. The murderers decided to go in the dead of night to deal with the old man. Whether they intended to kill him or simply frighten him at that point, I don't know. But they did kill him in the end so their initial intentions are irrelevant. They robbed the house to throw the constables off the scent of their true motives and make it look like the work of the Panther Gang.'

'Well, they had me fooled, for sure!' Constable Sawyer said, laughing.

'Hold on a minute, Detective,' interrupted Mr Howard. 'You said some of Sculthorpe's blackmail victims are in this room now. Does that mean that his murderers are here also?'

Lavender paused for a moment. 'Yes, they are.'

Chapter Thirty-Three

In the uproar that followed, the militia had to set forward and bar the door. Several people including Caleb Liquorish, Frank Bunning and Harry Goode tried to leave the room.

'Who are these bastards?' Old Pete stood up and glared at his neighbours.

Captain Rushperry rose to his feet and raised his voice above the furore. 'Sit down, everyone, now! Sit down, I said! Put us out of our misery, Lavender,' he added when order was eventually restored to the room.

'I wasn't sure who all Sculthorpe's blackmail victims were at first,' Lavender confessed. 'In his ledger, he only used initials, and it has taken us some time to identify everyone. For example, one of the villains was known by the initials *J.W.*' Lavender fumbled in his coat pocket and pulled out the tatty old bag and the crumpled note Rushperry had given to him on the first night in Market Harborough.

'I recognise that bag,' Constable Clancy said.

'Yes, the sharp-eyed Constable Clancy found this in Middleton the night after the storm. It doesn't belong to any of the shopkeepers in the village and we believe it's the bag used by William Sculthorpe. Within it was a crumpled note. It reads: "*This is the last payment you old bastard. Leave me alone. J.W.*"'

'It sounds like that *J.W.* was one of Sculthorpe's victims,' Mr Howard said.

Doctor Wallace laughed, coughed and looked amused. 'Speakin' as the only *J.W.* in the room, Detective, if you planned tae accuse me of the man's murder, then you will be disappointed. I havna the energy to swat a fly these days, niver mind tae kill a man.'

'Yes,' Lavender agreed. 'But even sickly men can hire assassins – and so can their wives.' Doctor Wallace stopped smiling.

'However, you'll be pleased to know,' Lavender continued, 'that I dismissed the notion that you were *J.W.* less than two hours after I first saw this note.'

'Why's that?'

'I knew you didn't write it when I opened the coroner's report from Sculthorpe's inquest.'

'Ah,' said Doctor Wallace. 'It's mah handwritin', isn't it?'

'Yes, sir, it is. May I congratulate you on owning the most awful handwriting I have ever had the misfortune to read? I followed the doctor's report you penned with great difficulty and knew you didn't write that note – despite sharing the initials *J.W.* with the author.'

Doctor Wallace smiled. 'Thank you.'

'So imagine my surprise when – only a moment later – I turned to a witness statement in the coroner's report and saw the same handwriting staring back up at me.'

In the shocked silence that followed, Lavender turned to the Middleton constable. Sawyer's Adam's apple jerked in his throat as he struggled to swallow. 'May I congratulate *you*, Constable Sawyer, on the clarity and fine penmanship of your handwriting?

You could teach Doctor Wallace a thing or two about the cursive style.'

'You accusin' me of writin' that damned note?'

'Yes.'

'This is bloody daft,' Sawyer snapped, scowling. 'So I write similar, so what?'

'Do you have the coroner's report about your person?' Captain Rushperry asked.

'I do, sir.' Lavender pulled it out of his pocket and handed it over to the magistrate.

'And the note, if you please, Lavender.'

Sawyer slammed his tankard down on the table, rose to his feet and pointed an angry finger in Lavender's direction. 'He's mistaken, sir,' he said. 'I didn't write that note.'

'I shall be the judge of that, Constable Sawyer,' Rushperry said. He pulled Sawyer's statement out of the coroner's report and placed it on his table next to the crumpled scrap of paper Lavender had handed to him. 'There is a similarity, Lavender, I agree. However, this would never be enough to convict a man.'

Sawyer's lips curled into a snarl. 'There, I told you so! You're a bloody idiot, Lavender!'

'Fortunately, gentlemen, there is more.'

'There is?'

'I was even more surprised when I realised Constable Sawyer had written this beautiful statement for the coroner with an injured right arm.'

'Ah well, I'm caudge-pawed,' Sawyer said. 'I write with my left.'

'Left-handed? Yes, I realised this the first time we met. Your right arm was bandaged but you still tossed money around, shifted furniture and grabbed the barmaid with ease.'

Sawyer laughed but there was no humour in his eyes. 'Where does this get you, Detective? I may be left-handed and have pretty letters but there's no crime in that. And I'm not *J.W.*, am I? My name's Sawyer, Jedediah Sawyer – and I've been the respected constable of this village for years!'

'Aye.' Several of the men in the room nodded. Constable Clancy looked pale and worried. His glance swung between Lavender and Sawyer as they exchanged comments.

Lavender walked closer to Sawyer and looked him straight in the eye. 'Your name isn't Sawyer. It's Walton.' Most of the room gasped. 'You're Jedediah Walton – an army deserter, which is why William Sculthorpe was blackmailing you.'

Sawyer leapt towards him. The table overturned between them. 'That's a lie! Damned calumny!' He swung back his left arm to punch Lavender but Woods and one of the militia men grabbed him from behind. Sawyer swore and tried to shake them off but they forced the red-faced and protesting constable back down into his seat.

'Easy, fellah,' said Woods.

'I already had my suspicions about you when we first met,' Lavender said. 'When you told us about your old regiment, the 33rd, and claimed you fought under Lord Cornwallis in the Americas, I decided to write to the 33rd for confirmation of your military service.' He pulled out a letter from his coat pocket. 'I received this reply earlier today from your regiment. The colonel replies that although they have never heard of a Jedediah Sawyer who answers to your description, they did have a Jedediah Walton who took part in the Siege of Charleston.' He folded the letter, replaced it in his coat pocket and stared down at Sawyer. 'Jedediah Walton deserted before the Battle of Yorktown. That's you, isn't it, Sawyer?'

'These are lies, damned lies!' Sawyer tried to stand up again but Woods and the soldier held him. Several others in the room were on their feet now, shouting – mostly they hurled abuse at Sawyer.

'Quiet!' Captain Rushperry was on his feet again but it took several minutes before the melee subsided.

'According to the army records, Jedediah Walton was also a Catholic,' Lavender continued. 'What happened, Sawyer? Did you make your way back from the Americas to London, go to confession – only to find yourself in the clutches of a blackmailing priest called Father William Sculthorpe? Did you confess your desertion to him? Did he try to blackmail you? Was that when you fled north to Middleton to begin a new life with a new name?'

'I'm sayin' nothin' more!'

'You don't have to,' Lavender snapped. 'There are still officers in the 33rd who will recognise you as the deserter. It will be a simple matter to have you identified as Jedediah Walton. And if you aren't a murderer, then I will definitely have you for desertion.'

'I've told you – you bumblin', bloody saphead – I'm Constable Jed Sawyer . . .'

He got no further. Woods gave him a sharp cuff around the back of his head. 'You're no soddin' constable,' he said. 'You're a disgrace to the rank!'

'Aye!' yelled Constable Clancy. 'He is!'

Sawyer swore and rubbed the back of his head.

'But I don't understand, Detective.' Doctor Wallace's voice rose above everyone's and all heads turned in his direction. 'How did Sawyer kill William Sculthorpe? He wasna there. The murderers attacked him when he left Sculthorpe's cottage – I treated his injuries meself.'

Everyone turned towards Lavender. 'Sawyer and his accomplices carried out the robbery and attacked William Sculthorpe. When they left his cottage, the other two men roughed up Sawyer to give him an alibi. Then he staggered in here, claimed he'd been attacked and raised the alarm. After all, who would suspect Middleton's brave police constable of such a heinous crime? The man was a hero for attempting to stop the gang – not a murderer!'

'Good God! Well, he fooled me.' Doctor Wallace looked horrified.

'Like I said, Doctor Wallace, murderers are often the people we least expect. And that wasn't the only trick the gang played.' Lavender strode over to the ancient longcase clock in the corner with its juddering, exposed hands on the glassless dial. 'They intended to carry out the attack late at night when there was hardly anyone about – but they still wanted witnesses to back up their story about an attack on Jed Sawyer by five men.' He reached out and flicked the minute hand of the clock back five minutes. The clock hesitated for a second, then continued with its sonorous ticking. 'So slowly, bit by bit.' He reached up to the minute hand and did it again. 'Someone, here in The Woolpack, put this clock back by half an hour.'

'That's right!' shouted Old Pete. 'I told yer Bunnin' opened up late.'

'You did indeed,' Lavender said. 'And he closed up late as well. When he thought it was nearly ten, it was in fact nearly half past ten.'

'I hope you don't think I had anythin' to do with this,' snapped the landlord indignantly. Sweat gleamed across his bald pate. 'I were here all night with my customers.'

'Aye, that he was,' said Old Pete.

'No, Mr Bunning,' Lavender said calmly. 'It wasn't you – it was your nephew Isaac. He and Harry Goode were Sawyer's accomplices.'

The taproom erupted again. Even Doctor Wallace rose to his feet shouting.

Harry Goode made another futile dash for the door – only to find his way barred by two soldiers. Isaac Bunning trembled when he rose to his feet. 'This is ridiculous! I were in here all night – my uncle will testify. He's my witness – I were here all night!'

'No, you bloody weren't!' Old Pete Jarman waved his cane menacingly in the direction of the young man. 'You came in late – with

Harry Goode. You both arrived just before Sawyer fell through the door with a bloodied nose!'

Lavender pulled three arrest warrants out of his pocket and waved them in the air.

'Jedediah Walton, known as Sawyer,' he shouted above the noise, 'Isaac Bunning and Harry Goode. By the power vested in me by his Royal Highness, the Prince Regent, in the name and on behalf of His Majesty King George III, I arrest you on suspicion of the murder of William Sculthorpe, the robbery at his property and the vicious assault on his son, also known as William Sculthorpe . . .'

It took a while to secure the prisoners. The three murderers were clapped in irons and led out onto the street to wait for the long march back to Market Harborough. All three protested their innocence loudly but their complaints fell on deaf ears. Frank Bunning continued to declare that Lavender must have made a mistake with regard to his nephew. It wasn't until Woods took the landlord quietly aside and explained that Sculthorpe had been blackmailing Isaac – and why – that Bunning blanched and fell silent.

Lavender, Clancy and Woods searched the men's homes for any further evidence pertaining to the case but found nothing.

'The money they stole will have been spent by now,' Woods said.

They returned to The Woolpack, where the prisoners, now subdued, stood shivering in the cold street.

'Shall we get a drink of ale afore we leave?' Woods asked. 'I don't know about you, Constable Clancy, but I find it thirsty work solvin' these crimes.'

The young man grinned. He had been very upset by the arrest of Sawyer but Woods' good humour seemed to lighten his mood.

'I'd have thought you had enough to drink last night to last you a while,' Lavender said.

'Now, now, sir,' Woods said. 'Don't be talkin' like that or the young lad will think I'm a tosspot.'

Apart from Old Pete Jarman, who sat alone with his glass by the fireside, the only other men who remained in the taproom were Captain Rushperry and Mr Howard. Lavender remembered that Caleb Liquorish and Morgan Turnbull-Thatcher had been the first two to scurry out of the door when he arrested the three murderers. The relief that Lavender didn't intend to expose them had been etched across their faces.

Mr Howard reached out and shook Lavender's hand. 'Congratulations on the arrests you've made, sir.'

There was no sign of either the landlord or his barmaid so Woods and Clancy left the room in search of some ale. Lavender sank wearily down into a chair next to Captain Rushperry. The lack of sleep over the last few days had caught up with him again.

'Mr Howard is right,' Captain Rushperry said. 'You and Woods have done well. Like I said earlier today, I'll see you are both rewarded for this. You have rounded up not one, but two dangerous gangs of villains. Northamptonshire owes you a great debt, sir.'

'Thank you.'

'Talking of expenses,' Rushperry said, 'did you find out if Billy Sculthorpe was William Sculthorpe's legitimate son while you were down in London? I'm concerned that now we know Sculthorpe was a priest, the law will assume they weren't related and I will be unable to recoup the expenses I have incurred for his care over the last few weeks.'

Lavender shook his head, sadly. 'I found no evidence of a connection between Sculthorpe and Billy.'

'It's a shame,' Rushperry said. 'Now Billy won't inherit Sculthorpe's money and if no other heirs come forward, it will pass to the crown. There is no money to provide for Billy's care. He can't go into the poorhouse as he's unable to work. No, I'm afraid it will have to be the county asylum.'

Lavender winced. 'Perhaps the Lady Anne . . .' he suggested.

'The Lady Anne?' Rushperry asked sharply. 'Why should she care about a fatherless cretin with no visible means of support?' He shook his head. 'No, I'll send a note to the county asylum tomorrow and ask them to collect him as soon as they can. There's no point in delaying the inevitable.'

Lavender was about to speak when the door opened and Constables Woods and Clancy appeared, clutching tankards and a pitcher of ale. They placed the tankards on the table, pulled up stools and sat down. Woods poured out the ale and Lavender downed his drink in one, his throat parched. Woods immediately refilled his tankard.

'You've done well, sir,' he said. 'That were probably one of the most confusin' cases we've ever had to solve – and I'm just sorry I weren't able to find out who *J.D.* were for you.'

Lavender managed a tired smile. 'Oh, I already know the identity of *J.D.*'

'Constable Clancy?' Captain Rushperry's podgy fingers raised his tankard in the air. 'Will you join me in a toast to these two clever London policemen?'

Clancy happily followed the magistrate's example. 'Detective Lavender and Constable Woods!'

'Well, the villains had me fooled,' Constable Clancy admitted, as he wiped his mouth with the back of his hand. 'I still can't believe they hurt the Sculthorpes so badly and then returned to the cottage as their saviours only a few moments later. The gall of those men!'

'It's often the ones we least expect,' Lavender said. He felt utterly exhausted.

'I'm particularly distressed about Constable Sawyer,' the young man added. 'I'd always admired him as an officer and now I feel, well, foolish.'

'Don't worry about it, son,' Woods said cheerfully. 'The detective here may have marked Sawyer's card early on but I never saw his perfidy. He gulled me too.'

Lavender glanced at Woods' ear, which was still red, sore and swollen. 'It was probably Sawyer who attacked you the other day in Cottingham. As far as I can make out, the other two were still at their work.'

'I hope the bugger hangs!'

'He tried to steer us in the direction of blaming the Panther Gang for Sculthorpe's murder and made several attempts to extract information from us. When we turned down his offer of help and wouldn't let him near the investigation he decided to try and sabotage it instead by crippling you.'

'He damn near killed me!'

'All's well that ends well,' Rushperry said. 'By the way, Constable, why did you bring in the ale?' Rushperry glanced around the miserable, empty taproom. 'Where's Bunning and his barmaid?' In the pause that followed, they heard the sound of banging and raised voices drifting from the rooms upstairs.

Woods leant forward across the table. 'He's a bit busy, sir,' he said in a low voice. 'He's upstairs arguin' with that Susie Dicken and throwin' her out. Unfortunately, Mr Bunnin' wouldn't believe his nephew had anythin' to do with the attack on the Sculthorpes. So I enlightened him on the quiet about why Sculthorpe were blackmailin' his nephew.'

Captain Rushperry laughed. 'Young Isaac was a bit of a lad, was he?'

'Aye,' growled Woods, 'and his uncle is a soft-hearted fool.'

'William Sculthorpe found out about it and blackmailed Isaac Bunning in exchange for his silence,' Lavender said. 'I should imagine the young lad was only too willing to join Sawyer and Goode in the attack.'

'I think most of Middleton knew about Isaac and the girl,' Constable Clancy said. 'It was only a matter of time before his uncle found out. Was Sculthorpe blackmailin' Harry Goode too?'

Lavender shook his head. 'There's no evidence of that. I suspect Goode was motivated by the promise of Sculthorpe's gold. He was penniless and heading for debtors' gaol.'

Captain Rushperry threw back his head and downed the last of his ale with a belch of satisfaction. His fingers reached for the buttons on his coat and he stood up. 'Well, Lavender, thanks to you, for the second time today, I now have to escort a gang of villains to the gaol at Market Harborough. I just hope it's big enough to hold them all. Come along, Constable Clancy.'

Rushperry stopped and turned back before they left the tavern. 'Once we've locked up this gang, the militia intend to hold a little celebration – in The Angel Inn with Alby Kilby. Will you join us?'

Lavender shook his head but he felt Woods sit up straighter beside him. 'I'm afraid I won't, Captain Rushperry – although Constable Woods will probably be there. I'm for an early night in my bed tonight. And tomorrow I must call on Lady Anne at Rockingham Castle – and find a barber.'

There was a nonplussed silence.

Woods leant towards the magistrate and winked. 'You should see him celebrate down in London, sir. When he gets really excited, sometimes he reads a book.'

Rushperry and Clancy laughed.

'Well, if you're sure you won't join us, Lavender?' Rushperry reached for his gloves. 'And on behalf of the magistracies of Northamptonshire and Leicestershire, thank you. Thank you, once again.'

Chapter Thirty-Four

Thursday 8th March, 1810
Middleton, Northamptonshire

Despite the warmth of the spring sun and the prettiness of the prim-roses and lilac hellebores in Mrs Tilley's garden, Lavender felt an icy sense of foreboding as he walked up to the door of Willow Cottage. He intended to seek an interview with Judith Wallace and he knew it would be distressing. He had no idea how she would react when confronted with her past but he suspected it would be painful for her. He wanted to give her a chance to explain herself before he made up his mind about what course of action to follow. His duty was to clap the damned woman in irons and drag her off to the gaol and trial but his conversation with Lady Caroline and Duddles had made him think twice and he wanted to talk to her first.

Lavender had come to Middleton alone. Woods was back in Market Harborough spending some time with his brother before they returned to London later that evening. He'd heard the two men plan to go fishing on the canal. He regretted his decision to leave Woods behind now and he wished Magdalena was here too. Her counsel in this matter would have been welcome.

The weather-beaten sign swung in the breeze above his head. A sudden flash of irritation made him frown and he paused on the doorstep of the guesthouse. *What was the matter with this damned place?* he wondered. Why were there so many criminals and law-breakers in this rural community? Was there something in the spring water they drank that made them into such a large and diverse band of ruffians?

He sighed, shook his head and rapped on the door.

Mrs Tilley led Lavender upstairs to the Wallaces' sitting room, where Judith Wallace was alone with her embroidery. The colour drained from her face when she saw him. *Has she been expecting me?* he wondered. Her husband would have already told her they had uncovered a woman amongst Sculthorpe's blackmail victims.

Once they were alone, she rose unsteadily to her feet. 'How, how can I help you, Detective?'

'I will be brief, Baroness Danvers,' he said. 'I know William Sculthorpe was blackmailing you and I know why.' She gave a little cry and her hand shot over her mouth. She sank back down onto the sofa and covered her face with both her hands as she struggled to hold back her sobs. Her shoulders shook.

He sat down unbidden in the upholstered chair opposite and gave her a few moments to compose herself. When she finally glanced up at him he saw the fear burning in her eyes.

'You know?' she whispered. 'How?'

'You gave your maiden name to your son for his second name and I saw it in the school register. During my investigation into William Sculthorpe, I was given access to the marriage registers at the chapel of the Sardinian Embassy. I have seen a record of your first marriage to Baron Lionel Danvers and I know William Sculthorpe conducted the service. I also know you paid him three shillings a week for his silence. He recorded your payments in his ledger next to the initials *J.D.*'

Her face crumpled and she sobbed into her hands. Her own handkerchief was soaked within moments. Lavender pulled out his handkerchief and passed it across to her. She nodded gratefully between great gulping sobs. 'Please don't tell John! Please don't tell my husband! I don't care what happens to me – but please don't tell John. It will kill him!'

'Doctor Wallace doesn't know about this?'

She shook her bowed head.

'Your affection for Doctor Wallace does you credit,' Lavender said. 'However, I can't see how we can avoid telling him that you are not his legal wife. How long have you been together?'

She blew her nose on his handkerchief and made an effort to pull herself together. 'For over twenty years.' Her voice was croaky. 'We met at an Assembly Room dance in Glasgow.'

'I think you had better tell me what happened, Baroness – from the beginning.'

Still clutching his handkerchief, she folded her hands in her lap and sat up straighter. The previous stiffness in her manner had now vanished. The woman looked vulnerable – and far older than the cold and confident doctor's wife he had first met in this room. 'Yes, yes, I'll tell you – but please don't call me Baroness. I have no right to that title.'

He nodded and waited. The wooden clock ticked quietly on the mantelpiece.

'I made a foolish decision when I was a young woman.'

'How so?'

'I was very close to my father, Detective. My mother died when I was born and I had no older siblings. Although we were related to the Fitzwilliams, we were from a poorer branch of the family and my father was besieged by money worries and hounded by his creditors. When I was seventeen, Lady Anne Fitzwilliam offered me her patronage for a season in London. This was my chance to make a good match that might help my father. His health was precarious and I worried for him constantly. I planned to marry the richest man I could find.'

'You hoped your future husband might help to alleviate your father's debts?'

'Yes. I was naïve, Detective, I know that now. I thought that if I made a good match I might be able to help my father. Danvers was the wealthiest of my suitors and promised to help him. I deliberately pursued a loveless marriage for financial gain.'

She paused and Lavender waited while she struggled to find the words to talk about her marriage. 'I didn't know of Danvers' reputation for brutality at the time. Lady Anne warned me that there were unsavoury rumours attached to his name but I brushed off her concerns. I was determined to have him. It wasn't until after the wedding that I . . .' She stopped and lowered her head in embarrassment. He watched the colour flushing up over the top of her high-necked gown onto the lower part of her face.

'Let me assure you, Detective, I had good cause to flee from my home and my husband.' Her hands began to shake and he heard the catch in her voice. 'I was abused, violently abused. My husband violated and humiliated me in ways a woman should never have to endure.' She swallowed and looked up straight into his eyes. 'My husband treated his dogs better than he treated me – and he thrashed them regularly.'

Lavender looked away, embarrassed. 'I have heard worrying reports about his reputation,' he said.

'As an officer of the law, I'm sure you know that a man can rape and sodomise his wife with impunity . . .'

'What made you decide to leave?' Lavender asked quickly.

'It was Lady Anne's idea,' she said. 'We had become good friends – despite the age difference between us and the opposition from my husband.'

Why doesn't it surprise me that Lady Anne was behind the elaborate plot to extricate Judith Danvers from her marriage? Lavender thought. The dowager countess was probably the most manipulative woman he had ever met. Her devious scheming would have put the legendary Lucrezia Borgia to shame.

'My father had died by then. Lady Anne was my only comfort and ally. We knew Danvers would never let me go and she suggested I pretend to drown myself in the river. Lady Anne organised everything, the change of clothes and the hidden carriage on the lane by the riverbank. I fled up to Glasgow and lived there quietly.' She flinched at a memory and clutched the handkerchief in her lap tighter until her knuckles turned white. 'It . . . it took me some time to recover from what I had been through with Danvers.'

Lavender grimaced and shuffled uncomfortably on the chair. 'I understand why you fled your marriage, Mrs Wallace, but not why you bigamously married Doctor Wallace a few years later. You did know, didn't you, that this is a crime?'

The dark and tearful pools of her eyes looked into his again. 'I saw a chance for happiness, Detective,' she said quietly, 'and I snatched at it.'

He sighed. What else was there to say on the matter? After all, what did they all do in this tenuous and fleeting life, but snatch at happiness?

'The last twenty years have been the happiest of my life, Detective. My marriage to John, our daughter and our son, they have all given me such joy. I know what I did was wrong – and I know it will break their hearts when they find out the truth about me – but if I found myself in the same situation, I would marry John all over again.'

Lavender heard the quiet passion in her voice but he frowned. Whatever the moral rights or wrongs of her initial deception, the woman had broken the law and become a bigamist. Would such a woman have any compulsion about poisoning an old man who threatened her life and blackmailed her?

'What happened with William Sculthorpe?'

She threw up her hands in a gesture of despair. 'Lady Anne forgot to warn me that Father William – Mr Sculthorpe – now lived in the area when John and I moved down here from Glasgow. It slipped her mind that he had married me to Danvers. I bumped into him in the village and he recognised me too. The threats and the blackmailing began almost immediately.'

'Is that why you tried to poison him?'

'I beg your pardon?'

'You gave poisonous ink cap mushrooms to William Sculthorpe.'

Her mouth fell open in surprise, then clamped shut again. Confusion clouded her eyes.

'You knew that ink cap mushrooms are poisonous?'

'Well, yes, but only when taken with alcohol and I didn't give them to him. The mean old man demanded those ink cap mushrooms from me when he saw them in my basket. You should have seen his eyes light up with greed.'

'I only have your word for that, Mrs Wallace. A prosecution lawyer might argue that because you knew your friend Lady Anne kept Sculthorpe supplied with brandy you saw an opportunity to get rid of the old man for once and for all.'

She took in a sharp intake of breath and seemed to recoil. 'Are you accusing me of poisoning William Sculthorpe?'

Lavender shrugged. 'You had a motive and it is obvious from the report your husband wrote after Sculthorpe's death that the poison was already taking effect when Sawyer and his gang assaulted him. If the attack hadn't happened, Sculthorpe would have died from mushroom poisoning.'

She looked horrified. 'But I didn't try to kill him! How was I supposed to know the old sot drank brandy with his breakfast?'

Lavender hesitated. He had the curious sensation he had just been wrong-footed. 'Breakfast? What do you mean "breakfast"?'

'He wanted the mushrooms for his breakfast. I warned him – as I warned you – that the flavour is never good unless they're cooked almost immediately after harvesting. I assumed he would eat them for breakfast. I had no idea he drank brandy in the morning.'

'He drank brandy every evening. Even a gap of several hours between the mushrooms and the brandy would have been enough to make him ill. As it happened, he saved the mushrooms until later and ate them for his supper.'

'It never crossed my mind he was in danger!'

Lavender paused again. Her distress at his accusation seemed genuine and her story plausible enough, based on what he knew of Sculthorpe's character. He could picture the greedy old man forcing her to hand over her mushrooms.

It would be hard to prove her guilt in court, despite her obvious motive to rid herself of the old man. Her lawyer could easily argue that Sculthorpe's poisoning was accidental and self-inflicted. If he pursued this line of inquiry and arrested her, her bigamy would become common knowledge and the charge against her might come to nothing. In addition to this, the three men who later attacked Sculthorpe would face the lesser charges of burglary and assault. Did they deserve that? Common sense told him to let sleeping dogs lie but his innate sense of fairness was bothered by the thought that Judith Wallace should completely escape justice.

'Detective.' She leant forward and stared up at him earnestly. 'I am a bigamist. Yes. I confess to that and I will accept whatever you decide to do with the information – but I am not a murderess!'

An idea formed in Lavender's mind. There was always more than one way to skin a rabbit.

Chapter Thirty-Five

Thursday 8th March, 1810
Rockingham Castle, Northamptonshire

Footmen showed Lavender back to the gloomy Panel Room of the castle. Lady Anne Fitzwilliam sat alone by the crackling fire in the huge medieval stone fireplace. There was no sign of her companion Erskine, and Lavender was grateful for that. He bowed politely to the dowager countess as the footmen left him alone with her.

'Well, Lavender,' said the old lady. 'I understand congratulations are in order. Most of the county's villains now wallow in Northampton gaol thanks to you.'

Lavender smiled. He wasn't surprised that word had already reached Lady Anne about his exploits the day before. Lavender wouldn't be surprised if she didn't have a small network of spies all over the local countryside. He remembered how she had accused him of an arrogant disrespect for the law at their first meeting and his smile broadened as he recognised the irony of her words. Despite her age and fragility, this woman wasn't afraid to interfere in the natural order of the world if she felt it was the right thing to do. She was the one with an arrogant disrespect for the law. He smiled again. Had she recognised in him a kindred soul?

'These men – the army deserter, the labourer and the cobbler – are you convinced they are the ones who attacked William Sculthorpe?'

'They are indeed, ma'am.'

'Then you have done well. Pray, take a seat and tell me how you came to this conclusion and resolved the mystery.' Her arthritic hand waved him towards the chair opposite to hers.

He sat down and briefly explained how he had discovered that Sculthorpe was a Catholic priest and how his inquiries had taken him back to London. Her sharp, dark eyes watched him closely while he spoke but her face registered no surprise when he talked of Sculthorpe's disgrace and his predisposition for blackmailing his neighbours. Of course she wasn't surprised, he realised. *She knew all this already.* The only time she raised her white eyebrows was when he mentioned his appointment with the Vicar Apostolic of London.

'Bishop Douglass agreed to see you?'

'Yes,' Lavender said, 'and he gave me access to some of the Chapel registers too.'

'That was very helpful of him.' No emotion passed over her pale, wrinkled face. No alarm registered in her eyes. 'I have left your payment with my footman. You may collect it on your way out.'

Was this a dismissal? Lavender sat up straighter and returned her unblinking stare.

'In fact, Lady Anne, during the course of my inquiries I have solved several other mysteries besides the murder of William Sculthorpe.'

'You have?' The room was hot. In the silence that followed he was conscious of the ticking of the exquisite ormolu clock on the mantelpiece.

'Yes. For example, I know the truth about young Billy Sculthorpe, the murdered man's son.'

A muscle spasmed in the skin of her sagging neck and she swallowed painfully. 'What is it you think you know, Detective?'

'I know he is William, Viscount Milton, your grandson, and that he is the real heir to the earldoms of Fitzwilliam and Rockingham.'

Lady Anne gave an unladylike snort and pushed herself further back into the cushions of her bath chair. 'Ridiculous!'

'Is it?' Lavender asked. 'Billy Sculthorpe was born on the same day that, according to the records, the infant William, Viscount Milton, was born and died. There is also the matter of the great favour William Sculthorpe once did for you. You told me yourself that you were indebted to the man for some great service. I believe that Sculthorpe, along with Bridget Ahearn – whom I assume was a wet nurse – took care of the unfortunate child virtually from its birth.'

'What nonsense you talk, Lavender!'

'I assume you were at the birth of your first grandson, at Parkside House on that hot July day?' She gave no response. 'Billy's deformities would have been obvious from the moment he first appeared and this would have caused incredible distress to yourself and his parents. After all, he was their firstborn son, their heir. I assume you turned to Father William Sculthorpe for comfort, advice and help, despite his recent disgrace and ejection from the British Catholic priesthood.'

Lavender paused and waited. He expected Lady Anne to rebut his accusation again but she didn't. She sat silently in her bath chair, watching him closely. He sensed that she wanted to find out what else he knew and she watched him for his judgement, his reaction.

'Billy's birth was an absolute disaster for the Fitzwilliam family,' he continued. 'The child would never lead a normal life. If he survived until adulthood he would never be able to run the family estates or take his place in the House of Lords, the Privy Council or in the ruling elite of the country as your son had done. It would have been better for everyone else if Billy had died – but he didn't.

The child was deformed – but otherwise healthy. Someone formed a plan to "remove" Billy from public sight and fake his death.'

'Do you have any proof to support this wild accusation, Detective?'

He didn't, and the elderly, white-haired woman before him knew it. She was now the only living witness to the child's abduction twenty-five years ago.

'Was it your idea to pretend the child had died – or did William Sculthorpe suggest it, I wonder?'

He paused again but Lady Anne remained silent.

'I don't know how this trick was executed – or if the earl and countess are party to the deception . . .'

'They're not.' The words poured out of her mouth in a torrent. 'My son and Lady Charlotte know nothing of Billy Sculthorpe's existence.'

Ah, he had found her weakness: her son.

'Father William – I mean, Sculthorpe – fetched the body of a dead infant from the poorhouse,' she continued. 'We swapped the two babies and smuggled the live one out of the house. No one noticed. No one wanted to look at the cretin in his coffin.'

She paused in order to catch her breath. When she spoke again, her voice was hard as iron. 'There, Detective, you have your confession. Although I will strenuously deny to everyone – so help me God – that this conversation ever took place.'

'Please continue,' Lavender said. 'I want to know what happened next.'

'Everyone was distressed when I announced the child's "death" but they were relieved too. My son and Lady Charlotte had another son the following year, a healthy baby boy. He is now Charles, Viscount Milton. ' She narrowed her eyes and glared at him. 'I don't know what you intend to do with this information, Lavender, or what you think you can do . . . but I have never regretted for one moment the decision I made. God was testing us that night – and I believe I carried out his will. Father William assured me that God would smile kindly on our actions. That this was the best course to take for the child, for my son and for the earldom . . . God would understand.'

'And at the same time, the disgraced priest guaranteed himself a decent income for the rest of his life.' Lavender struggled to keep the cynicism out of his voice. 'You paid Sculthorpe and Bridget Ahearn ten pounds a month for the last twenty-five years to secretly take care of your grandson.'

She frowned. 'You may mock him, Lavender, but Father William was a good man – a special man. He was fallible like the rest of us, yes – but essentially in his heart he was a good Christian. His selfless service to me will have redeemed him in the eyes of God. He will sit at the Lord's right hand again.'

'I doubt his blackmail victims will share your confidence in that,' Lavender said.

Lady Anne turned away and stared into the crackling flames of the fire. *She doesn't want to know about the seedier side of Sculthorpe,* Lavender realised. *She wants to remember Sculthorpe as the charismatic priest she knew in her youth.*

'The child wasn't supposed to live,' she said wistfully. 'They rarely live for so long – that kind.'

'No, they don't – but Billy Sculthorpe did live,' Lavender reminded her, 'and he lives still. Why did you persuade Sculthorpe to move here from Brighton? Was he attracting attention to himself with his blackmailing activities again?'

She shook her head, then dropped her gaze. The frilled lacy cap that covered her thin hair was too large for her, and cast her face into shadow. 'Sculthorpe wrote to me that the Ahearn woman was ill – dying. He had begun to feel the infirmities of old age. He worried he wouldn't be able to cope for much longer with Billy on his own.'

'So you moved the family up to Northamptonshire to keep an eye on them?'

The black bonnet nodded again. 'He wasn't supposed to live . . .'

'But he did live, Lady Anne,' Lavender said, 'and at this moment Billy Sculthorpe shows every sign of outliving you all. Pray tell me, what do you intend to do when you follow William Sculthorpe and Bridget Ahearn to the grave? Will you be able to make provision for Billy without revealing the secret you have kept hidden for almost twenty-five years?'

Her head jerked back in his direction. 'Why do you care, Detective?'

'I have become fond of the young chap. I don't know if you have ever met him but he's entertaining company – and an excellent artist.'

'No, I have never met him. Looking at him on those first few days of his life was enough.' She narrowed her eyes and observed Lavender shrewdly. Then she sighed heavily. 'What is your price, Detective?'

'My price?'

'Yes, your price. The price of your silence? Sculthorpe took ten pounds a month. Every man has his price.'

Lavender leant forward in his chair. 'This is my price, Lady Anne. Provide Billy Sculthorpe with a new and comfortable home, a manservant to dress him in the morning, a tutor to fill in his afternoons – and a drawing master to enhance his talent.'

She gave a hollow laugh. 'You jest, surely?'

'No, ma'am, I don't. It will be seen as a generous act of benevolence by a wealthy lady of quality, nothing more. No one will ever suspect Billy is your grandson for I will keep your secret.'

'Is that all you want?'

'Yes, Your Ladyship – but you need to act soon. Captain Rushperry intends to contact the county asylum today to come and remove Billy into their care.'

She stared at him, her expression a mixture of distrust, disbelief and pity. 'I knew you had an arrogant disrespect for the natural order of law, Lavender, but I had no idea you were such a soft-hearted fool, as well.'

He smiled. 'Then my failings have worked to your advantage, Lady Anne. I shall disregard the laws prohibiting kidnapping and you may take your secret to your grave in exchange for the lifelong comfort and security of Billy Sculthorpe. Do we have an understanding?'

She nodded. 'We do. I shall write a note for you to take back to Captain Rushperry. Billy Sculthorpe shall have a valet and a drawing master and I shall leave ample provision for him in my will. Now, do you have anything else to report to me about this case?'

'William Sculthorpe was blackmailing Mrs Judith Wallace.'

She gasped at the bluntness of his statement. Her mouth fell open, the jaw slack. A trail of spittle appeared at the corner of her mouth.

'William Sculthorpe had married Judith Debussy to Baron Danvers. He recognised her in Middleton and threatened to expose her bigamy.'

Lady Anne's gaping jaw snapped shut. 'You know about that too?'

'Oh, yes.'

He watched her throat jerk as she swallowed painfully. 'My goodness, Detective, you certainly leave no stone unturned during your investigations.'

Her tone was acid but he bowed his head at the compliment nevertheless. The action enabled him to hide his smile. 'Well, that is the instruction you gave me, ma'am.'

'Yes, I did say that, didn't I? It seems I underestimated you, Lavender. Pray tell me what you propose to do with regard to this latest discovery?' He could hear the tightness in her throat as she spoke.

'Nothing about the bigamy,' he said. 'It is not in my remit to catch bigamists. You didn't bring me up here to do that and I fail to see how anyone will benefit from such a disclosure after so much time has passed. Baron Danvers has a new wife and an heir and Mrs Wallace's family are all ignorant of her crime.'

She visibly sighed with relief.

'But I felt you should also know about the mushrooms.'

'The mushrooms?'

'I doubt we could prove it in court but Judith Wallace gave William Sculthorpe those ink cap mushrooms knowing, as I am sure she did, that he was a heavy brandy drinker. It's a little suspicious, don't you think?'

Her eyes never left his face as she paused to consider his implication. 'I'm sure there is nothing to be suspicious about, Detective,' she said eventually. Her voice was lighter now and she waved a dismissive hand in his direction. But he could see that her eyes were troubled.

'I'm sure you're right, Lady Anne.' He bowed low and bit back another smile as he left the room. Lady Anne was no fool and she had been very fond of William Sculthorpe. She wouldn't be pleased with this news. He had planted a seed of doubt in her mind that he suspected would damage her friendship with Judith Wallace. The doctor's wife wouldn't find her patroness quite so obliging in the future.

Justice of a sort had been served.

Chapter Thirty-Six

Thursday 8th March, 1810
Market Harborough, Leicestershire

The sun was low in the sky when Lavender arrived at the deserted canal basin. The trees on the far bank of the canal cast long shadows across the still water. The roosting birds in the trees had fallen silent, although the waterfowl still squabbled in the reeds and called out to their young. The empty barges in the water drifted gently in the breeze, their mooring lines slowly tightening, then sagging once again.

Lavender strode past the high stacks of timber and headed for the towing path, where Woods sat on a low stool, fishing in the canal. The mountains of glistening coal on the wharf across the water stood silent and still.

'Evenin', sir,' Woods said. 'Nice haircut.'

Lavender ran his hand self-consciously through his shorn locks and glanced around. 'It's very quiet here today,' he said.

Woods never took his eyes off his taut line. 'Yes. They've all had to go home early. There's no work on the wharf at the moment. Some daft saphead set fire to a wooden barge further downstream and blocked the cut.'

'Ah.' Lavender grinned, lowered himself onto the vacant stool beside Woods and stretched out his long legs. The sky over the wooded escarpment turned pink as the sun set. He watched a shoal of tiny fish dart between the strands of weed at the edge of the water. 'How's the fishing, Ned?'

'Fair to middlin'.' Woods gently nudged a pair of fat carp lying in the grass with his boot. One of them still gulped for air. He leant down, picked it up and knocked it on its head.

'Where's Kilby?'

'He had to return to the tavern. His missus needed his help.' Woods rummaged around in his coat pocket for a handkerchief to wipe his hands. When he replaced it, he pulled out a small leather pouch and handed it across. 'While I remember, Captain Rushperry sent this for you.'

Lavender smiled when he saw the glint of gold inside. 'Did you get one too?' he asked.

'Oh, yes. There's twenty-five golden boys for me and Alby and fifty for you.'

'Magdalena will be pleased,' Lavender said. 'She's been pestering me to buy a dining table and chairs for some time. She wants to invite Lady Caroline around to eat with us but doesn't think we can ask an aristocrat to join us at the kitchen table with Teresa and Mrs Hobart.'

Woods laughed. 'I told you settin' up home would cost you a fortune.'

'How will you spend yours?'

'I've a mind to come back here at Whitsuntide with Betsy and my nippers. Rosie wants to meet Betsy and I want them all to fill their lungs with fresh air and enjoy the peace of the countryside.'

'Peace?' Lavender said. 'We came up to Northamptonshire to catch a vicious gang of thieves – and ended up catching two. During the course of the investigation we've also uncovered a fugitive from the law, a cheating shopkeeper, an army deserter, a child kidnapper and a bigamist.'

Woods chuckled. 'All in a day's work for you, sir.'

Lavender fingered the bag of coins again. 'They've certainly had their money's worth out of us.'

'So what happened with Judith Wallace and Lady Anne?' Woods asked.

Lavender told him.

'You let them both get away with it?' Woods' mouth opened and snapped shut like the mouth of the dying carp at his feet. 'You didn't make any arrests?' His eyes were as round as the fish's. 'I knew I should never have let you go on your own today. You're ruddy useless with women!'

Lavender smiled. 'Lady Anne tried to bribe me. She called me "a soft-hearted fool" when I refused to take a payment in exchange for my silence.'

'You're soft in the head, more like,' Woods exclaimed. 'One of these women kidnapped her grandson and gave him to a disreputable rogue. The other is a bigamist who faked her own death. They're a right pair of jiltin' jades! Yet you condone their crimes and don't arrest either of them?'

Lavender picked up a flat stone and skimmed it across the surface of the canal. It bounced three times before sinking to the bottom. 'The magistracy invited us here to catch a gang of violent criminals. Well, we've caught them two gangs. Our job is done and they've got their money's worth. They don't need any more arrests. Besides which, it would be hard to prove that either Lady Anne or Judith Wallace harmed anyone.'

Woods jerked the fishing rod. 'No one got hurt? Lady Anne lied to her son and daughter-in-law, stole their nipper and pulled young Billy out of his rightful place in the world!'

'Well, what you don't know doesn't hurt you.'

'Gawd's teeth!'

'Do you honestly think Billy Sculthorpe would be any happier as Viscount Milton?' Lavender asked. 'Can you imagine him coping with the expectations of that role?'

Woods spluttered and yanked his fishing line again.

'And Lady Anne is right,' Lavender continued. 'I have no proof to support my accusation and would probably make a fool of myself if I went public with my claim that Billy Sculthorpe is the rightful heir to the two earldoms. I would also ruin many lives – including Billy's.'

'And what about that bigamist and poisoner, Judith Wallace?'

'There is a very good chance that the poisoning was accidental – and even if it wasn't, it would be virtually impossible to prove in court. I'm reluctant to ruin the lives of Doctor Wallace and his children. He's a good man and innocent of any crime. He's in poor health and appears to be unaware of his wife's deception. I find it hard to judge Judith Wallace too harshly.'

'You'd have a different take on things if it were Doña Magdalena who had done that to you after you were wed!'

'Yes, but she won't run away and fake her own death, will she? I'm not a vicious brute. The law is woefully inadequate when it comes to protecting women from the brutality of men like Danvers. She genuinely believed he was going to kill her.'

'Well, he would now if he ever saw her again!'

'Exactly,' Lavender said. 'Which is why we must keep her secret as well. As you decided yourself with Alby Kilby, sometimes it is better to let sleeping dogs lie.'

Woods bristled with indignation. 'Now don't you try to palm that one off on me! It were you who decided to strike a deal with my brother and offer him immunity from arrest in exchange for information about the Panther Gang!'

'I had no choice,' Lavender said. 'It was the only way I could extract you from a mire of criminal complicity.'

'Oh! So I'm mired in sin and corruption, am I? And you're the Angel of Grace?'

Lavender's smile pulled taut across his face. 'If you like.'

'That's impertinent comin' from a man who tried to roast alive a boatful of suspects. That were the badness comin' out of you, if ever I saw it.'

Lavender stifled his laugh. A swan glided past them in the water and scavenged for titbits in the reeds. 'Judith Danvers saw a chance for happiness,' he said quietly, 'and she snatched at it.'

Woods gave him a sideways glance. 'Lady Anne were right. You're a soft-hearted fool.'

'No, I'm just practical,' Lavender said. 'Northampton gaol isn't actually big enough to hold all of the villains and lawbreakers inhabiting this small part of the county.'

Woods fell silent for a moment, then he nodded thoughtfully. 'I have to confess I never expected to find so many folks with secrets and hidden crimes lurkin' in such a pretty place.'

Lavender glanced at him out of the corner of his eye. 'Are you sure you want to return here at Whitsuntide?'

'Oh, yes.' Woods reeled in his fishing line as the sun finally sank below the horizon. 'And it'll have to be Whit – I'm busy at Easter.'

'Are you?'

'Yes, some soft-hearted fool has asked me to stand as witness at his weddin'. He's snatchin' at happiness, I think, but I've already picked out my new coat for the occasion. I wouldn't want to waste it.' His fishing line swung back towards him. The hook was empty.

Lavender grinned.

Woods stood up and gathered his equipment. 'Oh, by the way, sir, Billy Sculthorpe has drawn you and Magdalena for an early weddin' gift.'

'He has?'

Woods went to his inside coat pocket and pulled out some

folded papers. 'He's done a pretty good impression of your features, if you don't mind me sayin', sir.'

'Yes,' Lavender said wryly. 'He captured my hairy moles in exactly the right light and that's a magnificent toad on Magdalena's shoulder.'

'I thought you'd appreciate them, sir.'

'All I need are a pair of devil's horns.'

'I did suggest that, sir, but young Billy thought this were probably too fantastical. Mind you, he weren't to know that a few days later you'd set fire to a boatful of men.'

Lavender grinned, folded the drawings and put them in his own coat pocket. 'I shall treasure these always. They'll remind me of the successful conclusion of this case.'

'Seems to me we've let a lot of villains go free this time,' Woods said, 'but I'm glad you sorted out Billy-Boy's future with Lady Anne.'

'And that, Ned, is what gives me the greatest satisfaction today.'

The two men paused for a moment to savour the view of the peaceful and gently rolling valley as it sank into evening shadow below the canal embankment.

'We've done well, haven't we, sir?' Woods said quietly.

Lavender nodded. 'Yes, Ned. We have.'

Author's Note

'. . . *The robbery making a great noise in the neighbourhood, an appli-cation was made to this office [Bow Street Police Office] for an active and intelligent officer to go down and investigate the business. Lavender was dispatched and in a short time saw reason to suspect five persons; with extraordinary celerity and resolution, he apprehended the whole of them . . . The county magistrates, in admiration of the zeal, intelligence and courage of Lavender, have resolved to give him a very handsome reward . . .*'

The Times, 27th October, 1818
London

As you can see from the extract above, this novel is loosely based on a real event. In 1818, a gang of robbers burst into the home of an elderly man, William Sculthorpe. They robbed and viciously assaulted Sculthorpe and his son. The real Stephen Lavender was called up to Northamptonshire to investigate the attack.

I first came across my detective's involvement in the case in David J. Cox's excellent book: *A Certain Share of Low Cunning: A History of the Bow Street Runners, 1792–1829*. I was intrigued and decided to follow up Cox's brief mention of the case by research-ing the news-sheet reports of the crime at the National Archives in London.

Both *The Times* and another London news-sheet, *The Morning Chronicle*, reported the vicious assault on the eighty-seven-year-old man in great detail. Unfortunately, they both tended to dwell on the horror poor William Sculthorpe experienced when the men with their 'blackened' faces burst into his house and the salacious and bloodthirsty details of the attack. Do you remember 'the large quantity of clotted blood which had settled in his mouth'? I lifted this unpleasant image straight from *The Times*. Further research revealed that two hundred years ago, thieves generally used soot and charcoal to distort and hide their features during a robbery. The infamous balaclava, now such a popular fashion accessory amongst villains, wasn't invented until the Crimean War in the 1850s.

But neither of the news-sheets explained how the *zealous, intel-ligent and brave* Stephen Lavender had *solved* the crime. Never mind, I thought. I'll make it up. And I did.

I took plenty of artistic licence with this novel. The first thing I did was move the crime back eight years to 1810 so it slotted into the overall time frame I have for the Detective Lavender Mystery Series. My second act was to kill off poor William Sculthorpe. In real life, the elderly man miraculously survived the vicious attack on his person during the robbery. But this wouldn't have worked for a murder mystery novel where someone has to die.

Other significant changes I made were to the names of the char-acters. As I'm sure my readers already know, two-thirds of British men were called John, James, Thomas or William at the start of the nineteenth century, which can be extremely confusing. I kept the names of William and Billy Sculthorpe but nearly everyone else involved in the case has had their name changed.

Next, I turned my attention to the 'five persons' whom

Lavender had arrested and tried to find out who they were. I discovered from the Internet that five men were hanged for burglary on Northampton Racecourse in the March following the attack on William Sculthorpe. Naturally I assumed that they were the five men apprehended by Lavender.

No, they weren't. It transpired that these condemned men were an entirely separate gang of villains operating in the south of the county. It took a lot of help from retired Northamptonshire police officer, fellow writer and County Police Archivist, Dick Cowley, to work this out and I am very grateful to Dick for his assistance. William George, William Minards, John Taffe, Edward Porter and Benjamin Panther (whom I dubbed the 'Panther Gang') had committed all the crimes I described in this novel and were duly hanged for them. But they had absolutely nothing to do with the attack on William Sculthorpe in Middleton. Amused by the coincidence that there were two separate gangs, each with five members, terrorising Nottinghamshire, I decided to include the 'Panther Gang' in the book and use them as a red herring.

With Dick's help, I finally tracked down the names of the villains arrested by Stephen Lavender for the attack on William Sculthorpe. They were Thomas Goode, William Walton (also known as Sawyer), father and son Thomas and William Bunning, and Isaac Goode.

Thomas Goode and William Walton were ultimately sentenced to transportation for the crime but Thomas and William Bunning were found 'not guilty'. The fifth man, Isaac Goode, turned King's Evidence on the others and was released without charge.

Another real-life character who eventually found her way into the pages of this novel is Lady Anne Fitzwilliam of Rockingham Castle. However, please note that the story of Billy Sculthorpe's connection with the Fitzwilliams is entirely fictional and that the real Lady Anne died in 1769.

William Sculthorpe Senior wasn't a discredited Catholic priest, nor a blackmailer. His son didn't have Down's syndrome either. These were all figments of my imagination.

I appreciate that Billy Sculthorpe's story may have been difficult for some people to read but ever since I discovered that one of my husband's Edwardian ancestors had kept a disabled child hidden in the house, I've wanted to explore this issue in fiction. Two hundred years ago, medical science made no distinction between children born with Down's syndrome and other illnesses associated with stunted growth, such as those caused by iodine deficiency, for example. It wasn't until 1866 that a British doctor, John Langdon Down, fully described the syndrome. Prior to that, those with the syndrome were lumped together with everyone else and labelled 'cretins'. It's unpleasant, I know. Unfortunately, many things in the nineteenth century make uncomfortable reading for modern readers but I've tried to handle the issue with sensitivity.

I now had several sub-plots running through my novel and Lavender and Woods had plenty of mysteries to solve besides tracking down Sculthorpe's murderer. But I wasn't finished yet. I like to have a personal sub-plot in these books, involving either Lavender or Woods. This time I decided it would be the story of Woods' long-lost brother, Alby Kilby.

When I discovered that Middleton was only seven miles away from the Market Harborough Arm of the Grand Junction Canal, I ummed and ahhed about whether or not to include some canal scenes in the novel. Canal life is very sedentary but the burgeoning canal network was an important historical development of early-nineteenth-century Britain. I got a lot of pressure from my parents to use the canal in the book. They had owned a canal narrowboat for over thirty years and I still vividly remember my mum's accidental attempt to give us a Viking funeral with burning barbecue coals on the back of the boat one summer. Fortunately, the ensuing fire was quickly extinguished but the experience stayed with me and prompted me to imagine the dramatic events of Chapter Thirty-One.

Mum and Dad were quite shocked when I told them that Lavender was going to burn a boat but they couldn't have been more supportive when it came to writing the scenes. They loaned me all the canal books I've included in the bibliography and spent hours talking with me about the history of the British Waterways and explaining how they operated.

On 10th August, 2015, I drove down to their home in Nottinghamshire to join them for Mum's birthday meal. That evening, very tipsy after several glasses of real ale and a bottle of wine, the three of us retired to their garden patio to plan Chapter Thirty-One. Owls hooted and bats flew over the cloud of smoke billowing from Dad's pipe as we giggled our way through the task. I made notes on scraps of paper as moment by moment we mapped out how the scene would unfold.

'Don't forget to have plenty of wooden splinters flying through the air as the militia shoot at the hatch,' Dad reminded me. Thus revealing in that one sentence the true source of my literary talent.

There can't be many authors whose parents have played such a significant part in the writing of their novel and I feel very blessed to have shared this experience with them. I dedicated *The Heiress of Linn Hagh* to Mum, who fostered my adolescent love of historical fiction. Today, I happily dedicate *The Sculthorpe Murder* to my dad, who edited all the canal scenes for me, checked them for authenticity and virtually wrote Chapter Thirty-One.

I couldn't have done it without you, Dad. Love you loads.

I would also like to thank my friends and fellow authors, the gals in the Hysterical Fictionaires – Jean, Kris, Babs and Claire – without whose daily help and support I would, quite simply, never be able to publish a word. Love you gals too.

Finally I would just like to say to you, the reader, that I sincerely hope you enjoyed this novel, and if you did, please leave me a review on Amazon.

Best wishes,
Karen Charlton,
Marske-by-the-Sea
North Yorkshire
7th January, 2016

Bibliography

Anthony Burton, *The Great Days of the Canals* (David & Charles Publishers, 1989).

David J. Cox, *A Certain Share of Low Cunning: A History of the Bow Street Runners, 1792–1839* (Willan Publishing, 2010).

Charles Hadfield, *The Canals of the East Midlands* (David & Charles Publishers, 1970).

Stephen Hart, *Cant – A Gentleman's Guide: The Language of Rogues in Georgian London* (Improbable Fictions, 2014).

Sheila Stewart, *Ramlin Rose: The Boatwoman's Story* (Oxford University Press, 1993).

Michael E. Ware, *Narrow Boats at Work* (Moorland Publishing Company Ltd, 1980).

Bibliography

About the Author

Karen Charlton writes historical mysteries and is also the author of a non-fiction genealogy book, *Seeking Our Eagle*. She has published short stories and numerous articles and reviews in newspapers and magazines. An English graduate and former teacher, Karen has led writing workshops and has spoken at a number of literary events across the north of England, where she lives. Karen now writes full-time.

A stalwart of the village pub quiz and a member of a winning team on the BBC quiz show *Eggheads*, Karen also enjoys the theatre and won a Yorkshire Tourist Board award for her Murder Mystery Weekends.

Find out more about Karen's work at www.karencharlton.com